SEDUCED

"My family affairs are none of your concern, my lord."

"You are undoubtedly correct. But having been somewhat discourteous at our first meeting . . ."

"Somewhat?"

". . . I am making your present well-being my concern. If this is your first visit to London, Miss St. Claire, we must seduce you."

She turned sharply to look at him. "What?"

He was all innocence. "Seduce you to the pleasures of London, of course."

Her heart steadied a little, but she prickled with an awareness of danger. "I refuse to be seduced, sir." She launched it as a formidable warning. Heavens above, it was unbelievable that such a man have any interest in her, but her instincts were sounding the alarm.

His right hand covered hers on his arm. Warm and strong, it flexed slightly as his lids lowered in a way that raised her pulse rate again. "If you were overeager, there would be no challenge in it, would there? I can never resist a challenge."

They had stopped again and Portia knew she should be concerned about what everyone was thinking, and yet. . . .

In one smooth movement, he raised her chin and brushed his lips across hers like gentle fire.

Books by Jo Beverley

AN ARRANGED MARRIAGE

CHRISTMAS ANGEL

DANGEROUS JOY

THE SHATTERED ROSE

AN UNWILLING BRIDE

FORBIDDEN

TEMPTING FORTUNE

You can also find Jo's stories in this anthology:

AN INVITATION TO SIN

Published by Kensington Publishing Corporation

JO
BEVERLEY

TEMPTING
FORTUNE

ZEBRA BOOKS
KENSINGTON PUBLISHING CORP.
http://www.kensingtonbooks.com

ZEBRA BOOKS are published by

Kensington Publishing Corp.
119 West 40th Street
New York, NY 10018

All Kensington titles, imprints, and distributed lines are available at special quantity discounts for bulk purchases for sales promotion, premiums, fund-raising, educational, or institutional use.

Special book excerpts or customized printings can also be created to fit specific needs. For details, write or phone the office of the Kensington Special Sales Manager: Attn.: Special Sales Department. Kensington Publishing Corp., 119 West 40th Street, New York, NY 10018. Phone: 1-800-221-2647.

Zebra and the Z logo Reg. U.S. Pat. & TM Off.

ISBN-13: 978-1-4201-2055-4
ISBN-10: 1-4201-2055-7

First Printing: March 1995

10 9 8 7 6 5 4

Printed in the United States of America

One

Moonlight shafted into the chilly hall, making mysteries of quite ordinary things.

Surely it was that moonlight, thought Portia St. Claire, that made the intruder look like the Prince of Darkness. White, blade-fine features of eerie beauty; dark leathery wings trailing behind . . .

She jerked her heavy pistol to point at its heart. *"Stop!"*

The figure stopped. Hands appeared. Long-fingered and elegant, they rose slightly in a pacifying gesture, and the movement showed that the black wings were merely a long dark cloak.

Portia sucked in a shuddering breath. That meant the ghostly features must be flesh and blood. It was a common housebreaker, that was all.

Of course, that meant her impulsive action had brought her face to face with a criminal. A wiser woman, hearing breaking glass, would have hidden under the bed. Portia had grabbed her brother's pistol, checked that it was loaded, and crept downstairs to see what was going on.

Her motto was "A fear faced is a fear defeated," but now she wondered if that always held true. This dark intruder did not appear particularly defeated, and having stopped him, she had no idea what to do next.

Beneath his cloak the intruder's clothes must be dark too, for the only places lightened by moonlight were his watchful face, his fine hands, and the froth of white lace around them.

Expensive lace.

He wore a ring on his left hand. The large stone was dark, but something in the way it caught the weak moonlight told her it was a precious jewel. A glint beside his face suggested another expensive ornament, a jeweled earring.

Not a common housebreaker after all.

"I have, if you will notice, stopped." The tone was courteous and his accent spoke of wealth and breeding. His voice carried the drawl of a man of fashion, but was unfashionably deep, and used softly in a way that did not calm her agitated nerves.

"You have stopped," Portia said sharply. "Now you will turn and leave."

"Or?"

"Or I will summon the Watch, sirrah! I heard breaking glass. You are quite patently a housebreaker."

She saw the flicker of movement that was a smile. "I suppose I am. But how do you intend to summon the Watch while guarding me, *mignonne?*"

Portia clenched her teeth. "Leave. Now!"

"Or?" he asked again.

"Or I will shoot you."

"Much better," he approved. "That you could do."

Bryght Malloren was amused.

He had not expected to be amused by this mission but

now, faced by this valiant defender of hearth and home, he was hard pressed not to laugh.

She'd probably shoot him outright if he laughed at her.

She was so tiny, though. Perhaps five foot to his six. Despite full skirts and drowning layers of woolen shawls, he could tell she was lightly built. Certainly the two hands so resolutely gripping the large pistol were small and delicate.

But delicate was not the word that came to mind.

Resolute, perhaps.

Or sizzling.

Energy—part courage, part anger, part fear—crackled from her like sparks from green wood on a fire. He could not tell the color of the hair that flowed loose down her back, but he suspected it would be red. She really would shoot him if he provoked her, and that alone was enough to intrigue him.

It was also inconvenient. He did not have much time in which to complete his mission, and this tiny warrior seemed determined to prevent him. He tried reason first.

"I confess to having broken the kitchen window in order to gain access, madam. But no one answered the door."

"And do you always break into houses when no one answers the door?"

He considered it. "Generally speaking, the houses whose doors I knock upon seem to have servants. You have no servants?"

"That is none of your business!"

But he'd hit a nerve. Who the devil was she? This house in Maidenhead had been rented by the Earl of Walgrave to act as a prison for his daughter, Lady Chastity Ware. Bryght had expected to find it empty now Chastity had escaped.

The young woman raised the pistol a threatening inch. "Leave, sirrah!"

"No."

Bryght heard her hiss of irritation and awaited events with interest. It took a truly callous soul to shoot a stationary person in cold blood, and whatever her qualities he didn't think this pocket Amazon was callous.

He was proved correct. She did not pull the trigger.

"Now," he said. "I have a reasonable purpose in being here."

"What reasonable purpose can excuse housebreaking?"

"I have come to collect a document left by a recent occupant."

She did not waver an inch. "What recent occupant?"

"You are full of questions, aren't you? Let us say, a lady."

"What lady?"

"I prefer not to answer that." Tiring of the game, he stepped forward to disarm her.

He saw her suck in a breath and raise the gun an inch farther. Damn. He threw himself at her legs just as she squeezed the trigger.

Portia was flat on her back, squashed under a giant. Her hands felt numb from the kick of the pistol, and her head was ringing where it had connected with the tiles of the hall floor. Or perhaps it was ringing with the thunder of the pistol shot. She had never fired a gun indoors before. It made a lot of noise.

She stared up dazedly and saw that the house-breaking devil seemed rather concerned.

He raised some of his weight on his arms and she took a deep breath. "How *dare* you!"

"I could hardly let you shoot me."

"Then you should have left!" Portia heaved to try to

throw him off but immediately realized that it was a very bad idea. He was lying between her legs and her simple dress with but the one petticoat was a flimsy barrier.

The way his elegant lips twitched at her predicament made her want to scratch his all-too-handsome face. No one had a right to features which so closely resembled an amused Lucifer, especially a bullying, house-breaking wretch.

"Who *are* you?" she demanded.

"Bryght Malloren, not precisely at your service. And who are you?"

"That, sir, is none of your business." She tried to wriggle from under him, but he had her trapped.

"Then I will call you Hippolyta, Queen of the Amazons." He brushed back a tendril of hair that had fallen over her eyes, and the gentleness of the gesture disconcerted her. The same gentleness was in his voice when he said, "Do you always fight against the odds, Hippolyta?"

His dark hair was disordered, too. It was escaping its ribbon and falling in wavy tendrils about his face. The informality was disarming.

"I had a pistol," she pointed out.

"Even so." And he grinned.

Portia growled. The wretch was *laughing* at her. "Get off me." She made each word clear.

"Not until I claim my forfeit."

"Forfeit?" Portia felt the first touch of real fear. She had been alarmed to hear breaking glass. She had been almost horrified at first sight of the dark creature coming down the corridor toward her. But in some way while bandying words with this man she had not been truly afraid.

Now she realized she was at his mercy. She was not missish by nature, and in her salad days had been a tomboy, but she had never before been unprotected in a strange man's power.

"Forfeit," he said, and the gentleness did not reassure her scurrying heart at all. She found herself staring at his earring—a discreet but expensive-looking jeweled stud. Only the wildest wastrels wore such outrageous ornaments, and only a wealthy one could afford that jewel.

She was in the power of a wealthy, dissolute rake.

He smiled, and it was a devil's smile. "I always claim a forfeit from women who try to kill me."

Portia started to fight in earnest, but her hands were tangled in her three woolen shawls. By the time she'd dragged them free he was ready to capture her wrists.

"Do you ever stop fighting?"

"Would it help?" She twisted against his grip, but it immediately tightened. "You're hurting me!"

"Then stop fighting me."

"I'll cry."

"Can you really do it on demand? I'd be interested to see that."

Portia hissed with exasperation, but her fear was ebbing like the tides. For some reason she simply could not be truly afraid of this man. It was most peculiar.

She became aware that his weight over her—mostly carried by his arms—was almost comforting, and that she was warm when before she'd been chilled. Faint scents came to her, too. Lavender, she thought, from his linen, and a perfume such as men wore, but a subtle one. Not the heavy sort used to cloak dirt and disease . . .

"Can you not force even one tear?" he teased, and Portia snapped her wits back into order. She tested his grip again, but he immediately tightened it just enough to control.

"You don't think I have *reason* to cry?" she spat.

"I don't think you're a weeper, my Amazon, unless you see it as a weapon." And he kissed her.

In all her twenty-five years, Portia had never been kissed like this. Not with a man's hard body pinning her to the ground, and his hands confining her for the assault of his mouth.

But it was a tender assault.

Braced as she was for something much worse, the tenderness almost trapped her. She remembered in time that he was her enemy, and held herself still and unresponsive beneath him.

He drew back, and she heard humor as he said, "What a range of weapons you have, my warrior maid. If I give you the victory in this, will you allow me to collect the document? It can be no concern of yours."

"No."

He laughed and rocked back onto his feet, then helped her up. While she was still finding her balance and gathering her tangled shawls, he sidestepped her and ran lightly up the stairs.

"Stop!"

Portia raced after him, shedding shawls, her shoes clattering on the bare wooden treads. He moved swiftly as if he knew the house, and headed straight for the back bedroom.

That showed he did not know the house at all. That room was empty, stripped of every item of furniture. Perhaps he had the wrong house after all.

She fell into the room after him and grabbed his cloak. "There see! There is nothing here!"

He simply unfastened the cloak and went forward, leaving her with a mass of heavy wool in her hands. She dropped it and plunged after him. He was headed for the fireplace and she ran around him and spread herself in front of it, gasping, "Not another step!"

He stopped mere inches from her. It occurred to her at last that she was being very, very foolish.

This room had two long uncurtained windows and the moonlight was bright, showing him to her clearly at last. Beneath his dark jacket and leather riding breeches was clearly a superb collection of bone and muscle that must out-mass her two to one. Behind the beautiful face was a will that would not be turned from its goal.

His goal just now was the fireplace she guarded with her body.

She swallowed, hoping she did not look as frightened as she felt.

Portia's mother had often bemoaned her daughter's rash nature, blaming it upon the name chosen by her idealistic father. Hannah Upcott did not care for theater at the best of times, and thought Portia's name encouraged an unseemly drive to challenge the world. She had insisted that her second daughter be named Prudence.

Hannah regularly predicted that Portia's reckless nature would land her in trouble, and often quoted the adage: "Those who tempt fortune risk losing all." Portia feared that she was about to prove her mother right, but she still couldn't meekly step aside.

Her opponent made no immediate move to manhandle her. "If there is nothing there, why the heat?"

Despite a racing heart, she looked him in the eye. "You have forced your way into this house, sir. I will not allow this intrusion."

"At another time, Hippolyta, I would be amused to test your ability to allow or disallow, but my business is somewhat urgent. May I point out that the easiest way to have me leave is to allow me to find what I have come for?"

"You will have to prove you have the right to the document. To whom does it belong?"

"I told you. To a lady." There was the warning edge of impatience in his voice.

"And how did it come to be here?"

"Let us say, she was a guest."

She glanced around the stark room. "In here? I doubt it."

"Perhaps she has ascetic tastes. Why, I wonder, are you so fierce in your guarding of this place? Does the Earl of Walgrave deserve such allegiance?"

The name startled Portia. If this Malloren man knew the house was leased by the Earl of Walgrave, then he clearly was not in the wrong house after all.

For the first time Portia wondered if his business here were legitimate. He had, after all, knocked on the door like an honest man. She had heard the sharp raps but ignored them. No one would be knocking at the door looking for her, and being alone in the house she had no mind to open it so late at night.

She said, "The earl, like any householder, has the right to expect that his home be inviolate."

"I doubt the mighty earl would claim this simple place his home. He merely leased it for a purpose. Since it is the earl's property, however, I wonder what *you* are doing here. Housekeeper, perhaps?"

"Certainly not!"

"An intruder, then, like myself? After all, I came upon you skulking in the chilly dark, pistol in hand."

"I was not *skulking!* We are guests, sir. We are well-acquainted with the earl, and he invited us to stay here." Portia would not tell him that she and her brother were impoverished supplicants and that the earl had commanded them to await his pleasure here.

"Us?"

Portia realized she was being trapped into conversation, and conversation was dangerous.

"Us?" he repeated softly.

"Myself, ten hefty brothers, and three servants," she declared, chin high. "They are all out at the moment."

"Only three servants?" he drawled. "How paltry. I require that many to hand me my clothes in the morning."

She was not entirely sure he was joking. "I will not meekly permit you to do what you want here, Mr. Malloren."

"My lord," he corrected amiably, moving a little closer. "Lord Arcenbryght Malloren. An absurd name, but mine own."

Portia was aware of a distressing tendency to both gape and sidle away, but she hit back. "Your rank does not excuse your wickedness, my lord."

"True." He caged her with a hand on the wall on either side of her head. "But it makes it a lot less likely I'll be hauled before the magistrates for my sins, doesn't it?" His height forced her to tilt her head back to meet his eyes, and her neck hurt as she watched his lips lower toward hers. Her heart was pounding and she was beginning to turn dizzy. Damn him, damn him, damn him. . . .

"So, *mignon*," he whispered inches from her lips, "why not just allow me my wicked way?"

Portia admitted at last that she was completely outmatched. He was a lord, a rake, and a large, ruthless man intent on his purpose. She ducked away from him and he let her go, flashing her an all-too-knowing grin.

May the ten curses of Egypt fall on his head!

She gathered what remained of her dignity and gestured disdainfully at the empty hearth and plain wooden surround.

"Proceed, my lord. I cannot wait to see you produce paper out of thin air. Are you perhaps a magician?"

"Perhaps I am." He went forward and instead of looking in the empty grate or up the sooty chimney, he inspected the place where the wood joined the plaster wall. Portia could not resist going closer to see what he was doing.

He was prying at the space between the wood and the wall, but he suddenly cursed and sucked a finger.

"Oh, dear," she said with spurious sympathy. "Have you torn a nail, my lord?"

The look he sent her made her resolve to control her saucy tongue. "Is there truly something behind there, my lord?" she asked more moderately.

"Yes, Mistress Curiosity, there truly is." He dug in his pocket for his pen-knife and used it to work at the problem. "So, you are guests, are you? I would have thought the earl a better host. There seems to be a marked lack of servants, furniture, and heat."

"The other rooms are normally furnished."

"And the heat and servants? Ah, I forgot. The servants are out with your ten hefty brothers."

"Exactly. And I prefer cool temperatures. They are healthier." She crossed her arms, wished for her shawls, and tried not to shiver.

"You must forgive me if I don't believe a word you say, Hippolyta. I doubt it's any concern of mine, however. In fact, if you want to pilfer Walgrave's property, you have my blessing."

Portia felt as if her hair must be standing on end with fury. "How *dare* you suggest . . ."

But he wasn't paying attention. "Ah," he said, and began to slide a folded paper free. He wiggled it carefully out with the tip of the knife until he could grip it, then stood to hold it teasingly before her. "Abracadabra!"

The taunt was the final straw. Portia twitched it out of his loose hold and ran. She was snared by the back of her gown, dragged hard against his body, and the paper was plucked from her hand. "Very foolish," he said.

Portia knew it, for now there was no humor in his voice at all. He had one arm unbreakably around her and the folded paper was in front of her face. It was heavily scented with Otto of Roses and she turned her head away from the smell.

"Do you not care for the perfume?" It was said lightly, but nothing could persuade her that he was in a good humor.

"It is a little cloying, my lord."

"A lady of virtue and discretion, would you say?"

"Hardly."

"But this letter could be to a friend, discussing the latest gowns."

"Is it?"

"I fear not." His tone was almost contemplative.

His arm was a prison as secure as iron bars, but Portia was relaxing. Again, she sensed no direct threat in him, and in fact found this strange embrace almost comforting. It was hard being small, female, and responsible for everything. What would it be like to have a strong man at one's command?

Such foolishness. What point in trusting men when they could lose the very roof over one's head with foolish investments, or on the turn of a card? As her father had done, then shot himself. As her half-brother had done, landing them in this predicament.

She pushed against his hold. "Let me go, my lord. You have what you came for, and I cannot stop you from taking it."

"I'm glad you realize that at last." He relaxed his arm and she pushed free and turned to face him.

She saw she was right. The light humor that had marked him throughout their encounter was shadowed now by something else, and the way he was looking at the papers in his hand was disquieting. Surprisingly, she felt a kind of tenderness, a desire to comfort one who suffered.

Suffered?

"Are those not the papers you came for?" she asked.

His gaze flicked up to hers. "Do you think there is a collection of perfumed love-letters behind the fireplace? What an entrancing thought! I suppose I should check this. . . ." He made no move to do so, however, but turned the papers contemplatively in his long fingers. "It would be a shame to leave with merely a laundry list pushed back there to seal a gap, wouldn't it?"

Portia folded her arms primly. "That, my lord, is no laundry list."

"Recognize the type, do you? Tut, tut, Hippolyta. Yes, I do indeed expect it to be a searing love letter, and one that is part of an illicit, rather than a holy love." He was speaking lightly, but he was not composed of light. He was dark and coiled dangerously tight. Even though she did not feel he posed any direct threat to her, Portia shivered.

They stood there, frozen in the silvered silence for what seemed an age, but then he unfolded the paper and angled it into the moonlight.

She saw his face change.

He could not be otherwise than pale in the moonlight, but now his features tightened as if he read bad news. Portia put aside antagonism and went forward to place a gentle hand on his sleeve. "My lord, what is it?"

He seized her by the front of her gown. "Time for your

secrets, Hippolyta. Who are you, and what are you doing here?"

"I'm the earl's guest!" Her voice came out as a squeak, finally strangled by pure terror.

He pressed her back, back until she was flat against the wall. "No servants. No lights. A pistol, and an unholy interest in these papers. Try again."

"There's a candle in my bedroom!"

"And the pistol?" he queried in caustic disbelief.

"I heard someone break in!"

"And immediately came down to confront the burglar? What well-bred lady would behave that way?" But the terrifying surge of rage was leashed. "Your name, Hippolyta."

She would give anything to be free of him. "Portia St. Claire."

It did not help. He stared at her, new passion blossoming behind his eyes. "St. Claire?" he repeated quietly like a curse. "No wonder you are so anxious to get hold of this letter." His sudden smile was as pleasant as a rank sewer. "What, I wonder, are you willing to trade for it?"

She tried to press back into the solid plaster of the wall, away from his malice. "Nothing. Nothing at all."

"No? But it is very damaging. Do you want proof?" Restraining her with one hand, he flicked open the letter. "It is addressed to Hercules from Desirée. See what she writes. *'I think of your mighty rod in my satin pocket and Weak Tea thinks I moan for him. When we met last week at the theatre, I was wearing your handkerchief between my legs—'* "

She tore at his restraining hand. "Stop it!"

He stopped. "I think Desirée would expect you to try harder to get this back from me, Portia St. Claire."

"I know no Desirée!"

"Come, come. We know it's not her real name."

"Real or not, I do not know her!" She struggled against his grip. "Let me go. Please!" Portia hated the plea in her voice, but she would grovel to get away. She was choking from fear, and her heart was racing fit to burst. She had never before encountered someone so filled with violent anger. "Just take your letter and go," she whispered.

With his back to the long windows, his face was shadowed. "You are willing to let me leave with it without a fight?"

"Yes. Yes!"

"Then why did you try to steal it?"

When she did not answer, he shook her. *"Why?"*

"Just to thwart you!" she gasped.

He abruptly released her. "I'm amazed you've survived to your current advanced age, Miss St. Claire."

Portia sidled away from the madman. "I am only twenty-five."

"I took you for younger, both by your looks and your behavior." The razor's edge of danger had gone, though, and he seemed largely bemused. "Tell Desirée when you report to her that Bryght Malloren has her letter, and will contact her about payment."

She straightened her spine and glared at him. "I tell you, I know no Desirée! You are mad, my lord!"

He just raised a brow and turned to leave, swooping to gather up his cloak as he passed. Portia offered no further protests, but just prayed earnestly that nothing would interfere with his departure.

Something did.

Her young brother Oliver walked in, candle in hand. The wavering golden light was shocking after the time of silver and shadow. "Portia? What are you doing in here in the dark?" He stopped. "Who are you, sir?"

"A housebreaker," said Bryght Malloren curtly. He

glanced back at Portia. "Your other *hefty* brothers and the three servants?"

"Just leave, my lord," Portia replied. Oliver was only half a foot taller than she and no match for this Malloren man.

Oliver, however, did not seem aware of his danger. "Housebreaker?" he queried. "My lord? Servants? What the devil's going on? I'll have an explanation of you, sir!" His free hand reached for his sword.

"Oh, 'struth." And Bryght Malloren plucked the candle from Oliver's hand and knocked him unconscious.

Portia cried out and ran forward. She stopped when the intruder turned on her, his features now demonic in the flaring candlelight.

"When the bantam cock comes round, tell him who I am. As a Malloren I could crush him like a cockroach. As a swordsman, I suspect I could kill him with one hand tied behind my back. And my conscience wouldn't trouble me much over killing a St. Claire."

Her hands became fists. "Get out of here, you arrogant bully!"

He made no move to go, but looked her over coldly. "You improve with lighting, Hippolyta, but you need to learn discretion. Do you really want another battle with me?"

"I wish I still had a pistol. This time I would not hesitate. *Get out!*"

He moved toward her, then halted. "Amazon tears," he said softly. "Now there's a weapon to defeat any man." With an ironic inclination of his head he turned and swept out of the room.

Portia had not been aware until then that she was crying.

Tears of rage, she assured herself, scrubbing the evidence from her cheeks. By heaven, but she meant what she said. If she still had a loaded pistol she would shoot the bully now.

She glanced at her brother, who was stirring, then ran out to the landing to make sure the intruder really did leave. She reached there as the door slammed behind him.

"And good riddance," she muttered. Pray heaven she never set eyes on the man again.

Two

She heard a groan and ran back to Oliver, who was carefully feeling his jaw. "Plague take it. Who was that? And what on earth were you doing entertaining a man here?"

"Entertaining? The devil broke in!"

Oliver scrambled shakily to his feet and straightened his powdered wig. "Broke in? Why? There's nothing of value here. Not for a man like that, at least." Then he reached for his sword again. "By gad, but I'll have satisfaction of him if I can but find out who he is."

"Lord Arcenbryght Malloren is the name he gave."

Oliver's hand dropped from his sword, and he stared at her as if she'd announced the plague was in Maidenhead. "A *Malloren!*"

"You know him?"

"A Malloren? Of course not." He was looking around dazedly, still feeling the effects of that cruel blow.

Portia took his arm and steered him toward the stairs. "He merely came to retrieve a letter that had been left here. Why don't we go down to the kitchen? It's warm there, and I think there's some coffee left on the hob."

When they were on the stairs and he seemed in better order, she said, "Tell me about the Mallorens."

"Rothgar," he stated, as if it were explanation in itself.

"What is Rothgar?"

But they were in the hall now and crumbs of plaster crunched under their feet. Oliver picked up the fallen pistol and looked at the scarred ceiling. "Why the devil was he firing a pistol in here?"

"It was me," said Portia soothingly, steering him on. "I was startled. Unfortunately I didn't hit him."

Oliver looked back at the ceiling. "Unless he was flying, Portia, you never came close."

Portia decided not to enlighten Oliver about the exact circumstances. Though younger than she, he took his position as head of the family seriously. She suspected, however, that if he faced up to Bryght Malloren the results would be disastrous.

There was little danger of it. When he collapsed down at the kitchen table, Oliver sank his head in his hands. "Bryght Malloren. Devil take it. The last thing we need is to be on the wrong side of the Mallorens."

"Who are they?"

Oliver looked up. "The Mallorens? They're one of the great families. Rich and powerful, with connections that run through society like dry rot through timber."

Portia placed two cups on the table. "Then why was such a man breaking into this house?"

"They're known to do their own dirty work at times."

"Dirty work? You make them sound like criminals. Although I must say, that man acted like one."

Oliver grimaced. "People like the Mallorens can damn near do as they please."

The intruder had implied as much. Portia wished she could bring a certain Malloren before the magistrates for his crimes. She'd like to see him in chains. At the thought of him on a gibbet, however, her mind balked. No, she wouldn't want it to go quite so far as that.

She put sugar and a jug of cream on the table. "What did you mean by Rothgar?"

"The Marquess of Rothgar. He's the head of the brood."

Portia returned to the stove for the coffeepot. "I've read the name in the news-sheets. Lord Rothgar takes some interesting positions in the House."

"Doubtless ones which serves his own interests. He's a cold-hearted devil by all accounts. Bryght's a gamester."

Portia froze in the act of lifting the heavy coffeepot.

A gamester.

She had to put the pot down again for a moment.

A gamester. The bane of her existence.

The whole world seemed riddled with an insane addiction to games of chance. Before her time, her father had apparently been a gamester. After marriage he had "reformed," but instead of settling to honest labor, he had turned to investments—risky ones promising astonishing profits.

He had lost all and shot himself.

Only a toddler at the time, Portia had no memory of the event. She had heard of it often enough, however, especially when her mother wished to warn her against any kind of risk-taking.

"Don't you be like your father, Portia—always thinking you are cleverer than the others, that you will win against the odds. Accept what the Good Lord sends."

Portia had a sudden memory of that Malloren man asking if she always fought against the odds. How had he known her so quickly and so well?

It was true that she did not like to "accept what the Good Lord sends" and seemed driven to fight fate. She had often been irritated by her mother and stepfather because they were so accepting, so unwilling to take any kind of chance.

Now she saw she should have been grateful.

Oliver was a risk-taker like her. He loved rough, dangerous sports, and had wanted to join the army. Denied that by his mother's distress, he'd turned to gaming and lost his money and perhaps his home. If he did not raise five thousand guineas within weeks, Overstead Manor would be lost forever.

Bryght Malloren was another of the same type, it would appear, and he was not a young misguided fool like Oliver. He was a mature man, steeped in the vice. Why that should so distress her, she did not know.

Portia looked sharply at her brother. Had Oliver played against Lord Bryght? Had the man not only invaded her home and assaulted her, but filched away her life and home on the roll of a die?

She found the strength to lift the coffeepot and thumped it down on the wooden table. "Do you know Lord Arcenbryght well?" she asked, meaning, "have you gambled against him?"

Oliver gaped at her. "A Malloren? Far above my touch, my dear. I didn't even recognize him in that light. But everyone knows about them."

"What does everyone know?"

"That they're rich, powerful, and let nobody cross them."

Portia sat down opposite. "If they're so rich, why would one be a gamester?"

He sighed with exasperation. "I've tried to explain to you, Portia. *Everyone* plays. The king plays, the queen plays, the ministers of the Crown play. Even the bishops play! And every man who wants to call himself a man, plays."

"But *why?*"

Ever since Oliver had returned to Overstead with the shocking news that he had lost the estate at play, Portia had been asking that question. Why would any reasonable human being risk everything on the turn of a card or the roll of a die?

Oliver poured himself some coffee. "What can I say? A man has to play, Portia, or be thought a demmed strange fellow. It's a sign of courage for a start, of nerve. Not to play is to brand oneself a timid, worthless creature."

"If not to play would be unfashionable and unpopular, then that would take courage, wouldn't it?"

He shook his head. "You don't understand. It's a man's thing, I suppose, though many women play."

"I'd think their husbands would put a stop to it."

"Why, when they play, too?"

"But *why?*" Portia asked again.

"It's exciting," he said simply.

"Exciting? How can it possibly be exciting to lose money?"

"It's exciting to win," he pointed out. "Come on, Portia. It's not like you to be so stuffy. Remember the time you climbed out of your window at night to meet Fort so you could try to catch the Bollard brothers poaching? It was stupid, but I'll go odds it was exciting."

Portia didn't like having her youthful follies thrown up at her. "It was hardly the same sort of thing."

"But it is!" He leaned forward, eyes brightening. "The thrill of that adventure was the risk. The risk of breaking your neck. The risk of a whipping. The risk that the Bollard brothers would catch sight of you and kill the witnesses! It's like that at the gaming tables, Portia. It's exciting to *risk* and to survive. The greater the risk, the greater the thrill! It tests a man's mettle. It makes him come alive. . . ." But then he realized what he was saying and sagged back in his chair. "But I am done with it. Give you my word, my dear."

Portia's hands shook slightly as she poured herself coffee.

Oliver kept promising never to play again, but sometimes she doubted him. He spoke of gaming almost like a man in love, in love with the tainted thrill of chance.

"There are surely other ways of testing your mettle, Oliver."

"I suppose so." He flicked her a look. "The army, for example."

"Oliver, you know it would break mama's heart!"

"Damnation, Portia, it's not surprising I took to the tables. The only thing you let me do is put my clothes on and ride around the countryside."

"You could manage the estate."

"Dull stuff, and you're better at it than I. But I suppose life will be exciting enough now." He gave her a wry smile. "For a start, I'll have to challenge Bryght Malloren."

"No!" Portia exclaimed. "Don't be so foolish."

"He did give me a blow, Portia."

Portia had forgotten that. She'd been thinking of the man's treatment of herself. "It can't be necessary to fight him."

"Maybe not, especially if I never encounter him again. Which seems likely, the way things are. In fact, we had better hope you didn't anger him. We don't need the enmity of the Mallorens to add to our load."

Portia didn't comment on that. She'd opposed Lord Bryght and tried to shoot him, but he hadn't been in a rage until he'd found that letter and she'd told him her name. The more she thought about it, the stranger it seemed.

She pinched some sugar from the cone and stirred it thoughtfully into the dark coffee. "He seemed to recognize the name St. Claire. Can you think why?"

Oliver shook his head. "I suppose your father's family might be known to him. Your uncle is Lord Felsham after all, though he's very minor nobility."

Portia's father had been the third son of Lord Felsham. After his death, Portia's mother had married Sir Edward Upcott, and had more children, two of whom had survived—Oliver and Prudence. Pretty Prudence, who was sixteen and had hopes of a good marriage before her brother made her a pauper. Portia stopped that line of thought.

There *must* be a way to save their home and their future.

"As far as I know, Lord Felsham is a nonentity," she said. "I have an uncle who is Bishop of Nantwich, but he would be of even less interest to these Mallorens." She pulled a face. "But I suppose there could be a blood feud going on with me none the wiser. The St. Claires never approved of father marrying a stocking-maker's daughter. We have no contact with them. I suppose we could see if they are able to help now. . . ."

"I doubt it, Portia. Lord Felsham would have to be a regular Croesus to be able to toss me five thousand guineas without caring about it."

Portia sighed. Five thousand guineas. The price of her life, and the life of her family. It was almost impossible to believe that they were in such straits.

It had started with the death of Oliver's father. Sir Edward had been an honest country squire, but too inclined to indulge in rich foods and port wine. One day he had risen from his bed complaining of indigestion, and fallen down dead.

It had been a terrible shock to the whole family, but none of them had expected the tragedy to have a such a dramatic effect on their lives. Oliver inherited the baronetcy, but being only twenty-one, he was unlikely to unsettle things soon by bringing a bride to Overstead.

However, Oliver had always been restive and unable to settle to country life. He had revived the idea of joining the army. When his family protested—Hannah and Prudence adding tears to their pleas—he had gone off to London "to see a bit of the world."

Portia remembered that they'd all been immensely relieved to have him engaged in such a safe activity. Of course, they'd imagined Oliver in picture galleries, attending Court, and meeting philosophers and writers in the coffee houses.

Instead of intellectual speculations, however, Oliver had been drawn into less lofty ones. He had soon been spending all his time in clubs and gaming hells, both winning and losing. Then had come the disastrous night when he had staked and lost Overstead to a Major Barclay.

Major Barclay now featured in Portia's nightmares—a shallow, shifty individual, with leering eyes and a demonic grimace. And, of course, he must be a trickster and a cheat.

Being a low-minded type, the major had little interest in a small estate in Dorset. He wanted cash and had agreed to let Oliver redeem his home for five thousand guineas. Oliver had failed to persuade the Shaftesbury bank to lend him so much on the estate, however.

Curse the major, and curse the bankers.

Portia wished she had been able to attend the meeting at the bank, but of course it was unthinkable for a woman to take part in such business, even if the woman knew more of the estate than the man.

But she had helped Sir Edward manage the estate and it could bear the loan.

When the bank turned him down, Oliver had been inclined to give up, talking again about joining the army. He was sure he could earn advancement and be able to support his family in modest circumstances.

Portia, however, had not been willing to surrender so easily. As a last resort, she had suggested applying for advice to their neighbor, the great Earl of Walgrave. She had hoped, of course, that he would advance Oliver the money, for he was very rich and was also Oliver's godfather. Unfortunately, the earl had not been at his estate, Walgrave Towers.

Again, Oliver had been inclined to give up and prepare to hand the estate over to Barclay. Portia had fought on. She had discovered that the earl was in Maidenhead and had virtually dragged Oliver here. It was the worst luck that they had arrived at this rented house just as the earl was on the point of leaving. He had ordered them to stay here until he had time to attend to their affairs.

It had sounded promising, but two days had passed with no news, so Oliver had gone out this evening to seek word. Surely he must have discovered something. "Did you find Lord Walgrave?" Portia asked.

He shook his head. "He seems to have left Maidenhead and taken his entourage with him. Face facts, Portia. He's turning his back, too. It's hopeless."

She reached over to grip his hand. "You can't just give up, Oliver. You still have a month to find the money."

He laughed bitterly. "Where?"

"Oh, Oliver, we have to keep trying! Perhaps we can follow the earl. Where did he go?"

"Nobody knows. For heaven's sake, Portia, we can't go chasing after him like hounds on the scent! Do you never know when you're beaten? If Lord Walgrave had been willing to help us, he would have done so."

"He was clearly busy. . . ."

"And always will be."

"There must be *something* we can do."

He drained his cup. "If there is, you must find it then, for I'm at a loss. The only way I can see to raise the wind would be to go to the moneylenders, and the interest they'd charge would break us anyway."

"So, we go home then, do we, and prepare to hand everything over to Major Barclay?"

"What choice do we have?"

Portia fixed him with a look. "We can chase after the earl like hounds on the scent."

"Portia!"

"Oliver, I will not give up until the very end. We will wait a few more days in case Lord Walgrave sends word, but if not I am going up to London to seek news of him. If you don't come, I will go on my own."

Oliver was most unhappy with the plan, and it took Portia nearly a week to get him to agree. Even as they waited in the inn yard for the London Fly to roll in, he was still arguing. "Mother is going to have fits to think of you in the wicked city with only me for escort."

"There won't be much she can do about it, though," said Portia firmly. "And anyway, I hope to be home triumphant before Mama realizes we've left Maidenhead. It will surely only take a moment of the earl's time to settle matters, and with such good news, she'll forgive us."

"If he's there," said Oliver despondently, but he climbed into the coach without further protest.

Portia spent the six hour journey planning how best to approach the earl. He was an old-fashioned Puritan sort of man, and would not take kindly to a woman's voice unless she were pleading prettily for mercy. That wasn't in Portia's style, but if she left it to Oliver she wasn't sure he would carry it off.

By the time they reached the city she had decided she must accompany Oliver to the earl's house. She resolved to do her best to be a quiet, properly behaved lady whilst there. Perhaps she could even squeeze out some tears . . .

That reminded her of Bryght Malloren. How had he known that she did not cry? How had he known that she hated to give up?

In truth, the dratted man had a distressing way of sneaking into her mind, and if she blocked him from her conscious thoughts he invaded her dreams. It was preposterous. He was a gamester and a bully.

But she could still remember lying beneath him, remember his lips on hers. There were wicked moments when she wished she had not held herself impassive and had experienced that kiss to the full.

She was twenty-five and had been wooed, but her suitors had all behaved correctly. She had never been kissed like that. It seemed a large gap in her education, and despite his wickedness, she suspected Bryght Malloren would be an excellent teacher.

Oh but really, her mother was right when she claimed that the St. Claire blood inclined her daughter to wildness. Portia shook her head to throw these thoughts out causing Oliver to ask if she had the headache.

It was as good an excuse as any, but it was her heart which pained her, not her head. That was evidence of acute mental instability. Portia knew it was her fate to be a spinster. She was too short, too thin, too outspoken, and cursed with red hair and freckles.

As the straggling cottages and market gardens became the close-set houses and busy streets of London, Portia fought her insane attraction to a high-born stranger.

By the time she climbed out of the coach in the inn-yard of the Swan, she had won the battle. After all, even if some suitable man were now to make her an offer of marriage, she could not take it. She would be needed at Overstead. She and Oliver were going to have to live quietly and labor hard for many years if they were to pay off the loan the earl was going to give them.

Portia had expected London to be grand and exciting, but this part certainly wasn't. As soon as they ventured from the inn-yard she began to wish herself safe in the country. London was crowded and noisy, and the sewers were clearly inadequate for their purpose, for the place stank.

And it was riddled with vice.

A couple rolled by drunk, and it was not yet dark. She saw a ragged woman leaning against a wall be approached by an equally ragged man. She could not mistake the transaction that was taking place, but the sum involved must be pennies.

How horrible.

She soon discovered that London was expensive for almost anything except whores and gin. It was as well they were not intending to stay beyond a few days for their small purse of guineas would not last long here.

Oliver wanted to look for rooms in the fashionable part of town where he had stayed before. Portia squashed that plan and found them cheap ones on the fringes, in Dresden Street in Clerkenwell. They took two bedchambers and a parlor for two guineas a month, but had to pay an extra ten shillings a week for a daily fire in the parlor, which was a necessity in December.

Portia looked around the simple rooms. "It is a ridiculous amount of money to be paying for such meager accommodations."

"I assure you, Portia, we are living cheap." Her brother couldn't quite keep the sneer out of his voice.

"We cannot afford to waste money, Oliver."

He flushed guiltily. "Oh, I know, I know. I'm sorry. But I don't know how I am to entertain friends in such quarters . . ."

"We're not here to entertain."

He nudged a rickety, scarred table. "I've been thinking that if the earl won't lend the money, I do have friends here. But if I want help from them, I'll have to meet them and entertain them. Thank goodness none of them realize the extent of my losses."

"Do you think they would avoid you if they knew? Then they are not true friends."

"It's not as cut and dried as that, Portia. It's dashed embarrassing being with a man who's all washed up."

And that was true, too. It was why Portia and her mother were keeping the matter quiet in Dorset. If they obtained the loan perhaps no one need ever know the extent of the disaster. If not, they would leave quietly without placing their friends in an embarrassing situation.

She tried to find a compromise. "I understand men in London meet in their clubs and coffee houses. Coffee houses can't be too expensive." And surely don't permit gaming, she thought. "You had best meet your friends there rather than here. But, with luck, there'll be no need. First thing tomorrow, we will go to see if Lord Walgrave is in Town."

Consequently, the next morning they walked the two miles to Abingdon Street, where the earl had his town mansion. As they moved into the grander parts of London, Portia began to see why people thought the capital so fine. The houses here were handsome, and the streets wide and clean. Her spirits began to rise, especially as she was certain that the solution to everything was only minutes away.

She turned onto Abingdon Street in full optimism, only

to come to a shocked halt at the sight of black hatchments on the door of Ware House. She and Oliver mounted the wide steps and knocked at the door. The footman who opened it wore a black ribbon.

"Who has died here, my man?" asked Oliver.

The solemn footman looked them over and decided they warranted a reply. "The great Earl of Walgrave himself, sir. Him they called the Incorruptible."

"Dead?" asked a stunned Oliver. "But I spoke to him not a sennight ago."

"It was very sudden, sir."

"I am the earl's godson. I would like to offer my condolences to the family if any are at home."

"No, sir. But if you would care to leave a message."

They were ushered into the grand but chilly house, and taken to a small room where black-edged paper was available. They both wrote notes of condolence, and left them to be sent to the family. Then a thought struck Portia. This meant that the earl's elder son, Fortitude Ware, was now Lord Walgrave, and Fort was a friend of hers.

She turned to the footman. "The new earl. Is he in town?"

The man looked down his nose, but he had clearly decided to include them in the ranks of the privileged. "No, ma'am. He is at the Towers to attend the earl's obsequies. But he is expected here shortly."

As they emerged, Oliver said, "Zounds, what a coil."

Hope was growing in Portia, however. "But Oliver, it is not all bad. Fort is now the earl!"

Oliver looked at her, brightening. "That's true, and he's always been a good'un. Not high in the instep at all."

"And he's expected in London shortly! You see, it *will* work out."

"There's still no surety he'll lend me such a sum, Portia."

"Oh, I know he will!" Portia was almost dancing with joy.

As they turned the corner, Oliver said, "It's not quite seemly to be so delighted at a death, you know."

Portia bit her lip. "It isn't, is it? But I never cared for the old earl and I truly think we are saved. Just think, we could be back at Overstead with all secure in days!"

Oliver suddenly smiled. "It's good to see you happy again, Portia."

She smiled back. "It's good to have reason to be. Everything is going to work out, Oliver. I told you it would!"

"It *is* all as good as settled, isn't it? Then you must see a bit of London while we wait, Portia. We'll go to the theatre. And if we're to do that, you really should have a new gown—"

"Oliver, stop!" Portia's happiness was fading. "There is no place for this. Think. You are deep in debt. Even if we get the loan, there will be little money for years. We will all have to live very simply to pay it off."

Irrepressible, he replied, "Then let us have one last fling!"

"Oliver!"

"Demme, Portia. It's not like you to be such a dull stick!"

Portia just looked at him, and he flushed. "Oh, I'm sorry. That isn't fair, but it's a dashed shame to be in London, for perhaps the last time for years, and sit in some pokey rooms in Clerkenwell doing nothing."

Portia knew he had a low tolerance for boredom. "There's no need for that," she assured him. "There's no reason you can't visit the coffee houses and meet with your friends. You never know but that you may still need their help in some way."

"That's true enough," he said, brightening. He escorted her home, then set off for the Cocoa Tree.

Portia sighed. She would rather have kept him tied to her side, but knew it was impossible. She put away the rest of their belongings, assuring herself that he couldn't get into serious trouble at a coffee house.

She wasn't entirely convinced. She had not counted on staying in London for long. Even on brief acquaintance, she sensed the power of the city. She was sure it could be a charming and rewarding place; she was equally sure it could be evil. No wonder Oliver had fallen into such trouble here before.

And she had brought him back.

She truly did regret not going back to Dorset, for with Fort down there and now the earl, all could have been settled. How could she have guessed, though, that the earl would die? He'd been elderly, but still a hearty man.

She had to admit, however, that her impetuousness had led her astray again. It seemed she never learned. Her mother would certainly have words to say, and with reason, for she had brought Oliver back into danger.

Even if he kept his word and avoided gaming, there were whores on every street corner, and cheap gin all over the place. She was sure the more elegant variations on the themes were available, too. Portia closed the door of a rickety armoire and told herself firmly that Oliver had never had a weakness for women and drink.

She'd be glad when she saw him safe home, though, and waited anxiously for his return.

But the late afternoon brought only an urchin with a note to say that Oliver was dining with friends. Dining with friends seemed innocent enough, but Portia felt a chill of unease.

The chill deepened when night settled on the city and Oliver neither returned nor sent another message.

Three

Bryght Malloren lounged in a gaming hell called Jeremy's and eyed the young man at the other end of the lansquenet table with a very jaundiced eye. He didn't know his full name, but he was a St. Claire—the pocket Amazon's brother, the one Bryght had knocked out when he'd gone to get that letter.

There were a number of aspects to that encounter he regretted, but knocking out the bantam cock was not one of them. Undoubtedly the wisest course was to ignore him now.

Since when had a Malloren been wise?

Bryght was outside several bottles of excellent claret or he'd probably have noted the young man sooner. On the other hand, the inadequate number and smoky nature of the candles in Jeremy's made vision difficult. The air was marbled by smoke, and full of the smells of tension, excitement, and fear.

Bryght wondered what the devil he was doing in such a low hell. He wasn't in desperate need of funds at the moment.

After an excellent dinner with Andover, Bridgewater, and Barclay at Dolly's Steak House, they'd gone on to the Savoir Faire club. There, they'd consumed a quantity of wine but found the company dull. It was Andover, damn him, who'd suggested checking out the latest hell.

Bridgewater had declined, for he had no taste for this kind of speculation any more, and Barclay had encountered other friends. Bryght had agreed to accompany Andover to Jeremy's in the faint hope that it would prove to be a place where his notorious luck would fail. Not that he would continue to play there if he started to lose, but it would be a pleasantly novel experience.

He hadn't risen a loser in about a year.

Ah well, they said "Lucky in love, unlucky at chance." Clearly the reverse was true. Thanks to Nerissa St. Claire, Bryght had given up on love entirely, and at the tables he could not lose.

Young St. Claire must be in a state of perfect happiness as far as matters of the heart went. He was losing steadily.

The game here was high-stakes lansquenet—a singularly mindless way of risking large amounts of money. There was no skill involved in turning cards unless one cheated. Bryght found it suited him for it took away the guilt of winning.

"Demme!" exclaimed one man, glaring at the two turned up by the banker. "Can the cards never come right?" He stood up and took off his coat, replacing it inside out. "There, perhaps that'll do the trick." He peered through the smoke at Bryght. "Malloren, what's your secret? Demme, man, you never lose!"

"A bitch," drawled Bryght. "Find yourself a bitch, Danforth."

"Any particular breed?" Lord Danforth asked anxiously.

"No, just be sure she'll raise her tail for any cur that sniffs there."

"Do you say so? I'll find one tomorrow. I've tried lucky

heather, and new shoes. Nothing seems to work. Now, let's play."

Danforth himself had lost over a thousand, and a good part of it sat in front of Bryght along with contributions from most of the other men. He played idly with the stack of guineas and vowels. Danforth could probably afford the loss. Others at the table could not. He disliked winning from those who should not be playing, but sometimes it was unavoidable. To refuse to play with a man was to insult him.

At this distance, Bryght couldn't follow how much his pocket Amazon's brother was dropping, but he doubted the young man could afford a penny. What the devil was he doing in a hell like Jeremy's?

It was none of his damned business, he told himself, but guilt over his behavior to that spirited young woman nagged at him. He remembered enjoying the encounter with Portia St. Claire at first, as he had not enjoyed an encounter with a woman for a long time. For a start, he thought, smiling at the memory, there weren't many who tried to shoot him on sight. Or who tried to bar his way with her body.

Her tiny body.

She hadn't been a beauty, but the fire in her angry eyes and the firm line of her mouth had stayed tantalizingly with him. At disconcerting moments he would remember the vibrant energy in her slender body as she fought him, and wonder what it would be like to tussle in a more friendly way with her.

He had no intention of pursuing the question. He'd had a belly full of St. Claires, and his marital attentions—if he had any at all—were firmly directed toward marrying money. His mistreatment of a courageous woman lingered sour in his mind, however, and he would be pleased to pacify his conscience.

With a sigh, he stood.

"I say," said Danforth. "You're not leaving now, Malloren. My luck's about to change!"

"Then I'll play you tomorrow, Danforth." He waved for a club servant to collect his winnings and strolled around the table to where the young man sat. A neat bag-wig, fine satin suit, and clean lace. The family wasn't on its last legs yet.

Did he have a first name for the cub? Hippolyta had addressed him by name, but it had not registered.

"St. Claire," said Bryght. "Care for a private hand or two?"

The young man was so engrossed in the cards being turned up that he didn't respond. Bryght had to tap him on the shoulder. He looked up distractedly, then his eyes widened. "You!"

"I am indeed me. I am inviting you to play with me, sir. In fact, I insist."

The young man's eyes flickered to the game before him, but then he succumbed to the stronger will and rose. Bryght was relieved to see that he had a few guineas to take with him. He settled them both at a table for two and called for wine. "Bézique, Mr. St. Claire?"

"It's not St. Claire. It's Upcott."

Bryght raised his brows. "Half sister? Or is she a widow?"

"Half-sister. And I want to know what happened between you two, my lord. She would never tell me."

Bryght had to give the cub credit for courage. "Then far be it from me to reveal her secrets."

"You can't make me think she enjoyed your attentions!"

"Attentions?" Bryght queried gently.

Upcott glared at him in thwarted silence. He had a handsome, fair-skinned face and looked more intelligent than his behavior suggested. It constantly amazed Bryght that pleasant, sensible creatures could be trapped by the tables.

Perhaps it was not too late for this one. A servant brought the wine and fresh packs of cards. Bryght poured for them both. "My dear Mr. Upcott—"

"Sir Oliver," the young man tersely corrected.

Bryght inclined his head in apology. "My dear Sir Oliver, your sister and I had a small misunderstanding which I regret entirely. I hold her in no disrespect and apologize for any upset I might have caused her. And of course, I also regret our own little misunderstanding."

It was clear that Sir Oliver was daunted by this apology. "Very well, my lord. We'll speak no more of it."

"You are all kindness, sir." Bryght passed over a glass of wine. "Now, please say you will oblige me with a game. Do you play bézique?"

"Of course."

Bryght took it for entire agreement and broke open the two packs of cards, passing them to the younger man for both inspection and shuffling. Then they cut for deal.

When Bryght won he suppressed a sigh. His luck was clearly present in full force. This was not going to be easy.

Bézique was a game involving a great deal of luck, but there was skill involved in keeping track of the cards played, and in the variety of ways to score from the cards in hand. This was just the sort of thing Bryght was good at, and he intended to use his skill to line the lad's pockets. Then he'd send him firmly on his way home and hope never to set eyes on him again.

Bryght had a fine instinct for trouble, and Sir Oliver and his sister were undoubtedly trouble. He played his first card. "You and your sister are now fixed in London, are you?"

Upcott frowned over his play, then took the trick. "Yes, my lord. In Dresden Street."

Bryght placed it on the outer fringes of respectable London, thus confirming that they were not flush with funds. "The death of the Earl of Walgrave must have disordered your plans," he probed.

The young man flushed. "What the devil . . . ? What business is it of yours, sir?"

Bryght made a pacifying gesture. "I am maladroit. Forgive me please." The young man was correct. None of it was any of Bryght's business. He took a trick with the queen of diamonds—a singularly foolish thing to do in bézique, but his opponent didn't appear to notice.

Andover did. He had come to observe the game and he raised an astonished brow at Bryght. Bryght flashed him a message, and his friend wandered off.

In bézique, it was the points scored by combinations in hand that mattered, not tricks won. Sir Oliver knew the rules of the game, but seemed largely unaware of the subtleties. If he didn't avoid the tables, he was undoubtedly headed for debtor's prison, and what would become of his sister then?

By very peculiar play Bryght managed to let Upcott reach the score of one thousand points first. "You win, Sir Oliver. Perhaps we could raise the stakes. Twenty guineas a round?"

Bryght found it easy to raise the stakes, but surprisingly hard to keep losing. Of course his damnable luck kept interfering—he couldn't, for example, neglect to declare four aces when they appeared in his hand—but really the young man had no sense of the game.

By three in the morning, and after the hardest work he'd done in a long time, Bryght had managed to pass over two hundred guineas of his winnings to Sir Oliver Upcott. The young man's eyes were aglow with triumph.

For the past half hour, Bryght had been plying Upcott with wine. Now, when he showed signs of heading back to the lansquenet table, Bryght steered him firmly toward the door and out into the frosty December air.

"I say," said Upcott vaguely. "Night's still young."

"On the contrary. And your sister must be concerned."

The young man frowned over that. "About you and my sister . . ."

"Nothing to it. Absolutely nothing."

"Didn't think so," said Sir Oliver rather morosely. "She's all set to lead apes in hell."

She'd lead the apes a merry dance, thought Bryght dryly. He sent a hovering link boy for a hackney and turned as Andover came up beside him.

"Are we interested in this one?" Andover asked quietly with a nod of his head toward Upcott. He was a loose-limbed blond of very easy-going temperament.

"In a limited way. Having restored his funds, I intend to get him safely home. Then, I hope, my obligations are over."

Andover raised his brows, but made no difficulty. "Right you are."

The one-horse carriage rolled up, and they hoisted the happy baronet into it then followed him inside. He collapsed onto the hard seat and began to sing. Out of key.

As the coach rolled off, Andover winced at Bryght. "What's the interest?"

"Just my noble nature."

"Indeed," said Andover skeptically. "Take to rescuing every unlucky gamester in London and you'll be worn to a frazzle."

"Talking of being worn to a frazzle, do we go on to Mirabelle's after we've delivered this?"

"After last night? I'm exhausted, my dear fellow."

"No stamina. You're a disgrace to your rank."

"Alas, likely true, *mon ami*." They chatted over the rambling songs until the coach halted.

"Sir Oliver," said Bryght, cutting through a chorus, "is this your place? Number twelve, Dresden Street?"

Upcott peered through the window dazedly. "The whole upstairs, my lord, but a sorry accommodation all the same. I'd ask you in, but . . ."

Bryght climbed out and extracted the young man. "You are everything that is kind, but it is late, sir. If I may be so bold, I advise you never to look at cards or dice again. You have no gift for it." He bowed. "My respectful regards to your sister and all that."

Upcott frowned slightly in bewilderment, then nodded. "Excellent, my lord. Excellent. Enjoyed the game. Must play again some day. Let you get your revenge. . . ."

Bryght sighed and left him to find his own way into his lodgings. He commanded the driver to return them to civilization and took his seat again.

"Sister?" queried Andover in interest.

"A chance acquaintance, only."

Now that there were only two of them, Andover stretched out his long legs. "Ah. And I hoped there was a rival for the Findlayson."

"Hoped? How crude of you. How could any woman rival the bounteous Mrs. Findlayson?"

"Certainly none can rival her bounteous fortune, completely under her control."

"Precisely," said Bryght with a beatific smile.

"Why the devil are you so set on a wealthy marriage? With your income from your family and your luck at the tables, you surely have no need of money."

"One always has need of money, it would appear."

Andover frowned at him. "Are you really in straits? I could lend you—"

Bryght laughed. "A penniless Malloren? My dear, it is just that I have sunk a great deal in Bridgewater's scheme."

Andover straightened in surprise. "The canal? You think there's something to it?"

"Don't you?"

"It's madness. Typical of Bridgewater. What's wrong with river transport if roads won't do? It goes against nature, cutting a waterway straight across the countryside."

"Say rather it conquers nature," Bryght responded. "Roads are rutted in frost, become mud soup in rain, and are poorly maintained at the best of times. Rivers turn shallow in summer, and flood in winter. A canal just sits there, always calm and ready to transport goods at a fraction of the cost."

"But the cost of construction!"

"Ten thousand guineas a mile, apparently."

Andover's jaw fell. "How can Bridgewater ever recover those kinds of costs? I heard him say earlier that he's not just going from his coal pits to Manchester. He's going to push to the sea. That's another twenty miles or so. It'll cost a fortune."

"It's already cost his. He's over thirty thousand pounds in debt . . ."

"Zounds."

" . . . and people are very reluctant to lend him any more."

"Hardly surprising. And you've actually lent him money?"

"All I can spare, and nearly all I raise at the tables."

Andover slumped back down again. "I wondered why you'd taken to deep play again." He looked thoughtfully at Bryght. "I've never known you to back a failure. Perhaps I should make him a loan."

"Perhaps you should, but I tell you honestly there's no

guarantee in it. It's a damned risky business. Apart from technical problems—and they're working out how to do things as they go—there are plenty of people who want to see him fail."

"All those with money tied up in river navigation schemes, for a start, never mind those with money in cartage." Andover chewed his thumb. "It'll be a lot cheaper to transport by canal?"

Bryght took out his snuff box and offered his friend a nerve-steadying pinch. "Immensely. By road a horse can pull about a ton. On a canal, it can pull close to fifty."

Andover's hand paused in the act of taking snuff. "Can it indeed? That is quite a saving."

Bryght smiled. "Isn't it? Bridgewater's going to be able to sell coal in Manchester and Liverpool at a fraction of the present price and still make a profit. And he's going to be able to bring imported goods from Liverpool back inland at the same vast savings. We're going to change the face of England and grow very, very rich."

"Or go bankrupt."

Bryght closed his snuff box with a click. "That is a risk. But risk, as you know, is my delight."

Andover chewed over this in silence, but then he asked, "How does Jenny Findlayson fit into this?"

"I'm not willing to let this project fail. If we run out of money, I'll marry the woman and use her money to keep going."

"Zounds, and I thought you were the idealist about women and marriage!"

"That was before I encountered the delightful Nerissa."

"So, she turned out to be a beautiful strumpet. Just give thanks that Lord Trelyn won her hand rather than you."

"Oh, I do," said Bryght.

"And seek a better bride. Jenny Findlayson has all the makings of a shrew."

"But a wealthy shrew. If necessary I'm sure I can find a rundown house and set her to scrubbing floors. . . ."

Andover burst out laughing. "You think to tame her? 'Struth, Bryght, you're a braver man than I."

Bryght leaned back at his ease. "Perhaps I am just well guarded against women now."

Portia twitched awake at a crash in the other bedroom. It was followed by a familiar curse. Thank heavens. Oliver was home! Then she registered that it was the dead of night. Where had he been till such an hour?

Gaming?

No, it couldn't be.

She slipped out of bed, shivering at the icy chill, and wrapped the thin coverlet around herself. When she peeped into the next room the dim moonlight just allowed her to make out Oliver sitting on his bed, rubbing his shin.

"Oliver? Are you all right?"

"Yes. Don't fuss, Portia. Just crashed into the corner of the plaguey bed." She heard the slur of drink in his voice with relief. If brandy was the worst of it, that was not too bad.

He stood and his voice brightened. "Tell you what, Portia. I had the greatest luck tonight!"

"You met someone who would help you raise the money?"

He chuckled. "You could say that. And I won over two hundred guineas from him!"

It was like a blast of icy wind. *Won?*

"Plague take it, Portia. I tell you I won and you sound as if I'd been condemned to hang!"

She gripped her hands tight on the coverlet. "But you *promised* you wouldn't play, Oliver."

"I won't. Or not much," he blustered. "I've told you, a man has to play a bit, Portia, or he'll look demmed fishy. I was with some friends—Twinby has an uncle who's trustee of a bank. Might be a loan there. Couldn't not go with him, could I? And it turned out excellently. See!" He began pulling money out of his pockets and heaping it on the table. Some coins rolled off to spin on the floor.

Portia flung herself after them before they disappeared into some chink in the floorboards. She scrambled to her feet, found the tinderbox, and made a light for the candle. The growing flame reflected merrily off a heap of gold coins.

"See," said Oliver proudly. "Isn't that a pretty sight!"

She couldn't deny it. "Yes. Oh, yes. I don't think it's wise of you to have played, Oliver, but this will be a help. If the worst comes about, this money will allow us to get by for a long time."

"Such dull stuff! With all this, we'll be able to enjoy London!"

"Oliver!"

His smile was brilliant. "Don't turn Puritan on me, Portia. Look at it!" He sank his hands in the pile of gold. "I left the house with only thirty guineas, and I come home with all this!"

Portia swallowed. If he'd left with thirty guineas he'd taken nearly all their small stock of money. He had said he needed a few, and she'd agreed. It had never occurred to her that he would translate a few into thirty.

"You could have lost the thirty," she pointed out, forcing herself to speak mildly.

"But I didn't. My luck's changed!"

Oh lord. It was like the first smell of putrefaction. The

shock of losing so badly had made him swear off gaming, but now he'd had this taste of success, could she stop the rot? Portia's hands shook as she gathered the money into a towel. She had to admit that it made a remarkably heavy bundle.

"Don't I get any of that at all?" he asked plaintively.

"How much do you want?"

"Fifty perhaps. A man has to have money in his pocket."

Portia wanted to remind him that he was deep in debt. No matter how many coins in his pocket, they were not truly his. But she could see there was no point now. She counted out the fifty. "We must keep the rest safe for necessities, Oliver."

"Of course we must." He grinned and flicked one of the golden coins. "After all, there'll be more where this came from."

"Oliver!" Portia protested, seeking the words to turn him from this course.

He shook his head, almost glowing with new hope. "Perhaps we won't need a loan from anyone. People win thousands at the tables every night! Now my luck's changed, we can get Overstead back the way it was lost."

Portia started to argue, but he ignored her and began to struggle out of his clothes. She returned to her own bedroom clutching the bundle of coins. So much gold should be a comfort, but she felt only despair.

She had truly thought that Oliver had learned that gaming was the road to ruin, but this success had changed everything.

Perhaps that was the purpose of it.

For all she knew he had fallen into the hands of a rascal who would tease him on with small winnings until he became over confident and lost all. It was a well-known trap for the unwary, and they called the practitioners of the art "hawks." An appropriately predatory name.

She thumped the bundle down on a chair. Why could Oliver not see what was happening?

On the other hand, what was there left to lose? Clearly Oliver was making such a good pretense of prosperity that the new hawk was not aware that his prey had already lost all.

She wished she could announce it in broadsheets all over London!

Previously Portia had not hidden any of their money, but now she knew she must. She didn't feel comfortable about it, for it was Oliver's, but she wasn't sure she could trust him not to gamble away every last coin.

Oh, but it was a form of madness she dealt with here.

She studied the room with despair. Her simple iron bed and plain armoire offered no cunning place of concealment.

Then she looked at the fireplace.

It had a simple wooden surround much like the one in Maidenhead. When she inspected it, it too had a gap all around between the wood and the wall. A test showed that a guinea would just fit into that gap and not be able to fall farther.

She began to methodically slide the coins in there all the way around, hoping no glint of gold would reveal their situation. That only took care of half the money, but Portia felt better knowing that some of the coins should be safe.

She huddled back into her still-warm bed. They had three weeks left before the New Year, before the evil Barclay claimed Overstead—beautiful Overstead with its fertile fields and glorious gardens. The fields were partly her work, for she had chivvied her stepfather into introducing some of the new methods of agriculture. The gardens were her mother's work, and it would break Hannah's heart to give them to a stranger.

Three weeks left, stuck here in dirty, expensive, wicked London, and it was all her fault. She should have agreed with Oliver and gone home. Having landed them in such a pickle, however, she must keep Oliver away from his vice until Fort came to London.

And what of the rest of his life? taunted a little voice.

Portia ignored it. It was boredom that drove Oliver to the tables. If they could just raise the loan to save Overstead, Oliver would be too hard at work trying to pay it off to be gallivanting to London and falling into evil ways. All she had to do was manage the next few weeks.

But he's gaming again, and he thinks it's the way to solve everything.

If I keep the money I have safe, he can only lose the fifty guineas, and that's fifty we didn't have this morning.

He can run up debts. He didn't have Overstead in his pocket when he lost it, did he? Men sign IOUs—vowels, they call them. Good as gold, they are. What are you going to do if someone turns up with a handful of vowels? Pay up, or see Oliver dragged off to the Fleet?

Presumably in the Fleet he won't be able to lose any more!

Portia was immediately ashamed of that spurt of anger. Of course she didn't want to see Oliver in debtor's prison.

Tomorrow, when he wasn't swayed by brandy and excitement, he would surely see that at best, tonight's win had been a fluke.

Four

Bryght separated from Andover near Bond Street, and let his friend take the hack. He had no particular inclination to find a link-boy even, for the weak moonlight was enough to show his way to nearby Marlborough Square. He knew danger lurked in every shadow, but the only precaution he took was to toss back his cloak and make sure the hilt of his sword was clear. The scavengers of London were generally on the prowl for easier prey.

Marlborough Square was perhaps the finest square in London, with grand houses surrounding a lovely railed garden which even boasted a duck pond. Malloren House stood in the center of one side of the square, set back from the road, and fronted by a paved courtyard. A narrow lane ran down each side, setting it off from lesser houses nearby, but blocked by ornate wrought iron gates. At the back there was a large garden.

As Bryght climbed the shallow stairs to the pillared portico, the night-doorman seated in an alcove leapt to his feet to open one of the heavy double doors.

Bryght recalled a conversation with Portia St. Claire about knocking on doors. He had said he never knocked on doors that lacked servants to open them. The truth was that he rarely had to even exert himself as far as knocking. . . .

Why did that woman keep popping into his head? It

would be foolishness to become embroiled in the affairs of the petty gentry who had to knock at doors, and even— heaven forbid!—answer them, too.

Bryght suppressed a grin as he nodded to the elderly man and passed into the gloomy hall. It would not do to be seen grinning at nothing, or the word would soon be around that he had rolled home drunk. He drank. He did not become seriously drunk, which was yet another reason for his success at gaming.

There was a very soft *woof* and a dark form heaved to its feet by the table holding the candles. Bryght went over to greet Zeno. The Persian Gazelle Hound's head almost reached Bryght's waist, which made it easy to rub his long, silky ears.

This was as well, for neither Bryght nor the dog were inclined to lose their dignity in the relationship. Bryght was not about to crouch down and talk nonsense, and Zeno would never dream of leaping up or employing any of the other fawning tricks common to his species. His greatest sign of devotion was to be at Bryght's side whenever he could.

Bryght's brother, the Marquess of Rothgar, had received a pair of the dogs as a gift. He had intended to keep them both at Rothgar Abbey, but as soon as the male dog had seen Bryght he had firmly attached himself to him. Even as a six-month pup there had been no bouncing enthusiasm, just a resigned recognition of fate. Which is why Bryght had named him Zeno after the founder of the Stoical movement.

He rubbed the dog behind the ears, and Zeno pressed just a little closer—the only sign of approval Bryght was likely to get.

Bryght turned away to light a candle at the night-light. He was the only one of the family in residence at the moment and his standing orders were for the staff to retire early unless he gave other instructions. The house was silent apart from the ticking of clocks and he had to admit that it was pleasant to have Zeno to greet him when he returned to his cavernous home.

'Struth, he was going to turn maudlin!

Well, if he wanted company, he'd go odds there was one person still awake.

Bryght climbed the sweeping stairs, shielding the candle flame from the draft of his movement, and followed by the click of Zeno's claws on the steps. He headed for the room where his guest was doubtless poring over papers to do with his canal.

As Bryght had expected, he found Francis Egerton, Duke of Bridgewater, hunched over a desk. But he was working on accounts, not diagrams.

"Is the news good or bad?" Bryght asked as Zeno flopped lazily in front of the fire.

The duke looked up with a quick, almost shy smile. "Both. There's money for three months, I estimate, barring disasters."

"Such as the canal bursting its banks again."

"Exactly," said the duke with a grimace. "Brindley really does think the trees we're planting along the banks will help."

"And bring profit, too, in time. Genius, Francis."

"Brindley's, not mine."

"You're too modest."

Bridgewater shrugged. He was a slender young man, five years Bryght's junior and an awkward blend of naiveté and shrewdness. As a youth he'd been thought both frail and stupid, but he was proving to be neither. There were many who now thought him mad, but Bryght knew they'd be proved wrong, too.

If the money held out.

Bryght poured brandy for them both. "I won a thousand or so tonight you can have. Less a couple of hundred."

"You lost?" asked Bridgewater with mild surprise.

"On purpose."

"How strange."

"I felt inclined to do a kindly act."

Bridgewater glanced at the window. "And it's not even full moon."

"Christian charity seems amazingly out of favor these days," commented Bryght dryly. "Consider it an investment, then. That'll be more to your mercenary heart."

Bridgewater grinned unrepentantly. "An investment in what, though? Is there profit in it?"

"Only spiritual." Bryght deflected this line of talk. "Do you still intend to return north tomorrow?"

Bridgewater threw down his pen and stretched. "Yes. I've done all I can to push the bill through. I wish to hell Parliament had no say in private enterprise. It would make my life easier."

"What problems are the committee raising now? I'll grant that approving an aqueduct did demand an act of faith since the ill-educated dolts seemed unaware that Roman examples still exist. But it's straight for the sea now, isn't it?"

The duke grimaced. "With a canal, nothing is ever straight except the cut. They're a huddle of nervous fools, though. If no one ever takes a risk, there'll be no progress!"

"Having the aqueduct fail before their eyes doubtless made them cautious," Bryght pointed out.

"A minor flaw, and soon corrected. There's been no problem since."

"Except a couple of expensive floods . . ."

"Whose side are you on? In a new venture there are bound to be problems!"

"Pax," said Bryght with a grin. "I'm teasing you, Francis. But you must admit that for people more cautious than we, it does seem a mad scheme. You ought to have heard Andover on the subject."

"Is it caution, or greed? Behind some of those Doubting Thomases there are people who stand to lose a great deal of money when the canal is working. Brooke practically had an apoplexy speaking against my Bill."

"Be fair, Francis. Brooke isn't thinking of profits. He doesn't care for you cutting a bloody great pathway across his part of the country. Just be grateful you're not trying to do it near Rothgar Abbey or you'd have my brother against you."

"There has to be change if there's to be progress. These conservative old squires will ruin England!"

"I do hope you're not thinking of Rothgar as a conservative old squire."

Bridgewater burst out laughing. "Perish the thought! And I certainly wouldn't care to be up against him." He sobered. "As it is, most of the opposition are venal. Their doubts disappear at the sign of gold. I've given elegant gifts and even naked coin to people I'd rather kick in the ballocks. Gads, but I'd rather see the money going toward construction."

"It's all construction of one sort or another."

"Building fortunes for the greedy? There's honest money to be made everywhere these days, but lazy people here in London look only to bribery and gaming."

Bryght toasted him ironically. "Thank you."

"Lord, not you, Bryght. I know you've no great taste for hells any more."

"And nobody ever offers me a bribe except the beauties hoping for an introduction to Rothgar."

"You could make a fortune that way," Bridgewater remarked with a grin.

"I'm afraid what they offer is not hard currency."

"No. Something very soft. Pity."

"You're turning into a veritable money-grubber, Francis."

"I simply do what I must to reach my goal."

"That goal being profit." Bryght wandered restlessly over to the fire. "Just how virtuous is it to lend money and profit thereby, when others do the sweaty work?"

"We pay the workers a shilling a day or more. It's a fair wage and they're glad of it. Without those willing to provide capital, there would be no work for the laborers and nothing would ever be achieved."

"True enough." Bryght shook off his unusual qualms and returned to the desk to top up their glasses. "So, if you think you've greased enough palms to get your Bill, why not stay a few days and wallow in delicious vice?"

"London bores me, and I want to see how the work progresses."

"You're in danger of becoming a devilishly dull dog, you know. The Deadly Duke."

"Better than 'the Poor Duke,' which is the label I grew up with." He sipped from his brandy. "I'm going to be the richest duke in England, Bryght. What drives you?"

"To be the richest commoner?" Bryght offered lightly.

"There are easier ways to make money."

"At the tables? I lack the ice to strip men of their all."

"On 'Change. I know you enjoy investment more than the tables."

"Ah. But having sunk my funds into your enterprise, I have nothing to venture. I get my speculative pleasures these days with Rothgar's money."

The duke frowned. "I'm sorry. It must gall you to be dependent on him."

"Francis—"

But the duke overrode him. "I seem to have dragged you into a pit, Bryght. I know you invested in me on a whim when . . . well, it was a whim. I'll buy you out as soon as it's possible. It could be soon. Now the aqueduct is working, I actually have people approaching me about loans."

"Without having to be pressured? A change indeed! But I have no wish to abandon the project."

"You've put everything into it, and it's a damnable risky business."

"Francis! Risk is my delight."

The duke grimaced in exasperation. "Bryght, think. What will you do if we fail?"

"What will you do if we fail?"

"I'll still be a duke. That is worth something."

"But a poor duke once again. If we fail—which we won't—I will still be a Malloren. And unlike you, I am not in debt."

"You may end up in debt."

"Devil a bit. I'll just get it at the tables."

"If your luck holds."

"It is not just luck," Bryght pointed out.

"There's nothing but luck when it comes to the devil's bones."

"Which is why I prefer the devil's pictures. Why the gloom, Francis?"

The duke sighed. "If you suffer pangs of conscience at the tables, I suffer them, too. I don't mind risking my all, but you're the only outside shareholder. A shift of power in Parliament, a run of bad luck with the excavations, a mistake by Brindley, and we could be sunk. Even if all those things go right we may still run out of money."

"Which is why I am charming Jenny Findlayson."

Bridgewater frowned at him. "If it comes to the point, will you really marry her just to prop up my shaky dream?"

"Why not?"

"She's a Cit."

"She's a fine-looking woman without any particular vices other than a strong belief in her worth."

"Given her worth, she has reason. But . . ."

"But?"

The duke considered his words. "Forgive me if your feelings run deep, but having met the lady, I do not feel you would suit."

Bryght raised his brows. " 'Struth! Are you trying to tell me Jenny prefers your charms to mine? A duke in the hand and all that? You are welcome to her."

Bridgewater flushed. "Not this duke. I made delicate enquiries. Why get at her money through a broker if I can tap into it direct? She thinks I'm mad and that I'd pour all her money into a failing endeavor whilst expecting her to live on a pittance in a cottage."

Bryght laughed. "I love a shrewd woman. I wonder if she'll be very distressed to find that she's dedicated her fortune to the failing endeavor by marrying me."

The duke put down his glass. "I sometimes think you believe that, Bryght. That I will fail."

Bryght cursed his flippant tongue. "I wouldn't be supporting you if I didn't have faith. But the risk is not a blemish to me." Bryght took the last mouthful of the warm and very fine brandy and let it trickle down his throat. "Achievement without risk is tedious. I have a fondness for inspired insanity, and love a high-stakes game with some point to it. Build the canal, Francis. I'll make sure you have the money."

* * *

Portia awoke the next morning in unusually low spirits. Even under the blows she had recently received, she had always buoyed herself with optimistic plans of action. Now she didn't know what to do.

She had hardly slept after Oliver had come home, and her thoughts had been as bleak as one could expect of that dead time of the night. She had told herself that Oliver had never shown sign of gaming fever before coming to London. Even so, she had been unable to shake off the fear that he was now an incurable gamester, and that even if they obtained a loan, he would somehow lose everything again.

She had even begun to concoct strange schemes of imprisoning Oliver at Overstead so he couldn't play again.

Then she had progressed to considering what would happen if they didn't raise the loan, for now she could hardly blame anyone—even Fort—for seeing Oliver as a bad risk.

On New Year's Day they would have to leave Overstead in the hands of this horrible Major Barclay. And then what?

Their only refuge would be her mother's brother in Manchester, a prospect that pushed her further into gloom. She had visited Uncle Cranford twice and hated it. His house was handsome enough, for he seemed to be prospering. It was in the center of town, however, close to his new manufactories where banks of looms wove worsted and fustian. The house opened straight onto the busy street at the front and had only a tiny garden at the back.

She was a country woman. How could she live without fields and a garden?

All the streets close to her uncle's house were the same, with scarcely a tree or a flower, just lumbering carts bringing raw materials, spun thread, or cloth. The carts stirred up dust and left tufts of wool and cotton to float in the air.

Even if she were to plant a garden, she had to wonder if flowers would thrive in such a place.

But if they lost Overstead, their choice would be Manchester or starvation.

The hours of worrying had so worn Portia down that she could have produced tears, but now that it was a new day she set about turning her mind to optimism.

After all, she thought as she flung back the curtains to let in crisp sunlight, the money hidden behind the fireplace made them safe for a little while. They would not be homeless because they could not afford rent, or starve because they could not afford food.

And Fort was expected in town any day. Even if Oliver continued to gamble, he could not get into deep trouble in a few days. When Fort did arrive, she decided, she would not depend on Oliver. She would go to him herself and put their case. They were of an age and good friends. She knew he would help in some way.

Perhaps he would call out the horrible Major Barclay and kill him! That wouldn't wipe out the debt, but it would be some kind of blow against fate.

As a result of these satisfying thoughts, when Oliver cheerfully insisted that they should go out to celebrate his winnings, Portia didn't make a sour comment. Sitting in these bleak, chilly rooms and worrying about their situation would soon turn her into a shrew. She needed fresh air, and she did want to see something of fashionable London before leaving it forever.

She entered into the spirit of the day by dressing her finest. Portia had only brought a few garments with her and all her wardrobe was country wear, but the quality was excellent so she felt no need to blush for her appearance. She chose an open gown of light brown callimanco, a glossy wool, which showed her best petticoat of embroidered silk.

Since she hadn't lost all sense, she wore a heavy drugget petticoat beneath for warmth. It might be a sunny day, but it was still December.

In view of that fact, it would have been prudent to wear her heavy cloak, but Portia decided to have done with prudence for one day, and put on her short blue silk pelerine. Oliver had bought it for her last Christmas, before his father's death, before their current disasters.

Now, when she fastened it at her neck he smiled proudly. "I chose that blue well, didn't I, Portia? It matches your eyes and lights up your hair." He winked. "You'll catch all the men's eyes today."

Portia glanced in the small mirror. She dismissed the second part of his statement, but she had to admit that the cloak did suit her well. The color did its best for her blue eyes and red hair. It was a shame about the freckles, but she had long since realized that no treatment was going to remove them.

She had tried. She was not vain, but the freckles worked with her small stature and short nose to make her look absurdly young. Perhaps other women wanted to appear younger than they were, but having resigned herself to maturity, Portia wanted all of it.

She remembered someone saying, "By your looks and your behavior, I thought you younger . . ."

Then she remembered who it had been.

"What are you frowning at?" Oliver asked.

"Oh, just follies," she replied and smiled. She fixed a neat flat hat at a jaunty angle on top of her curls, and decided that with the addition of a large fur muff Portia St. Claire, spinster, of Overstead Hall, Dorset, was as fine as possible.

Oliver was equally elegant in a suit of mulberry velvet,

and shoes with a high heel. He did not destroy the effect with a cloak, but he too carried a fashionable muff. With his best powdered wig, he looked a true Town exquisite.

She linked arms with him and gave him a jaunty smile. "Let us venture forth, my dear, and slay London with our magnificence!"

As they strolled toward the more fashionable part of town, Portia deliberately put aside her cares. She simply enjoyed the fresh air and the interesting sights. She was pleased to see that Oliver was not trying to spend money on every gew-gaw they passed, but then he did stop in front of a milliner's. "You don't have a mask with you, do you?"

"Of course not. At this season, there's hardly a need to shield my face from hot sun or dust."

"But it's all the go to carry one. You really should." He was already entering the doorway, and Portia grabbed his coat.

"Oliver! I do not need a mask!"

He smiled at her. "Yes, you do. I just remembered that there's a parade of the foot guards in St. James's Park. I'll go odds all the world will be there. You'll enjoy it—the king will be there, even—but you should carry a mask."

"The king . . . ? But why a mask?"

"Why anything? It's the fashion!"

Portia muttered about fashion, but she allowed herself to be drawn into the store where she chose a very plain, white, full-face mask on a stick. Oliver tried to persuade her to more ornate ones, but she refused all extravagance.

As they left the shop, she said, "I can't think what to do with it."

"Just let it dangle from your wrist by the ribbon. And now—on to St. James's Park, where all the world awaits!"

It was as he said, and all the world—the Polite World,

the Court—seemed to be in the park. The flowers were long gone, and most of the trees were bare, but the gorgeous clothes, the furs, and the jewels served to compensate for nature's lost adornments.

Portia had no great interest in the rich and splendid, but faced by this fairy tale assembly, she could not help but be fascinated. Everyone seemed dressed too finely for a park— the men powdered, and the women in their richest gowns and cloaks. She remarked on this to Oliver.

"That's because the king and queen will be here. This is almost like a Court."

Portia chuckled. "I never thought to be at Court. I must pay attention. I'm sure Prudence will be fascinated to hear about our monarchs."

"Truth to tell," murmured Oliver, "they're an ordinary enough couple, and the queen is positively fusby faced."

"Shush!" she said in mock alarm, and they both laughed.

Portia had a splinter of awareness that this was like the old times when she and Oliver had teased and joked, and that such times were gone. She blocked that thought. For this brief hour she would be happy.

The neat columns of soldiers marched and turned to their officers' commands. Oliver took a genuine interest in it, but he was one of the few to do so. Portia could tell that the lords and ladies were present to see and be seen, not to watch military exercises. She thought their maneuvers as fascinating as the soldiers'. Some were fixed points, whilst others flitted from group to group like iridescent insects dipping nectar from a midsummer bank of flowers.

Among the fixed points Portia noted two clusters centered around women. One was a lively dark-haired woman surrounded by a bevy of flirtatious men; the other was a beautiful blonde dressed in white, whose circle was more sober and mixed.

She poked Oliver to get his attention. "Who are those ladies?"

He looked where she discreetly pointed. "Ah, the rival queens! Rose White and Rose Red, some wags name them. The brunette is Mrs. Findlayson, a very wealthy widow. Her fortune comes from trade, but in view of its size most are willing to overlook that flaw. I wish to heaven she'd smile on me," he said with a grin, "for that would solve our problems nicely. But they say she is determined to marry into the aristocracy."

"And the blonde?"

"The beautiful Lady Trelyn. Society's darling. She is safely married. That's her husband hovering over her so devotedly."

Portia considered the man. He was of medium height and build. With a pale face, gray hair-powder, and dull gray suit he looked almost ghostly in the vivid throng. "Such devotion is very touching."

"Oh, he's certainly devoted. Nerissa Trelyn brought only a small portion to her marriage, they say, and Trelyn is both rich and powerful. He could have married a great deal higher."

"Do people think of nothing but money and station in marriage?"

Oliver shrugged. "Why not marry as well as possible? Perhaps I should consider that route myself. Or you," he said with a smile. "Looking as fine as you do today, perhaps you can save us all through a brilliant marriage."

Portia laughed. "Don't be absurd, dearest."

"No, I'm serious. You are looking your best, Portia, and there is something fetching about you, you know. Men like you."

Portia shook her head with a smile. "Then perhaps liking

has nothing to do with marriage, for my fetching qualities have not fetched me a grand husband."

"I can't think why not."

She gave him a look. "Perhaps my indifferent looks, small portion, and humble origins play a part?"

Oliver, ever the optimist, was not to be dissuaded. "I don't think Nerissa Trelyn came from a station much higher than ours, and she married high indeed."

Portia knew Oliver meant well, but his partiality was embarrassing and she was glad there was no one by to hear it. She looked at Nerissa Trelyn wryly. If one needed that degree of beauty to make a man forget a dowry, she was sunk before she sailed. The lady had pure creamy skin, full pink lips, big dark eyes, and a mass of shimmering golden hair. Add to that a lush figure, graceful movements, and an air of profound *womanliness*.

She was almost the antithesis of Portia.

Portia was saved from further embarrassment by the approach of a trio of Oliver's friends. They were all light hearted gallants, dressed in the height of fashionable absurdity, which meant peacock colors, huge muffs, and high red heels on their shoes. They reminded her rather of ornamental birds.

When the first bunch fluttered on, more arrived, and so it went. As they strolled around the park it became clear that Oliver did have a great many friends. Portia was not surprised. He was charming, and great fun when not gaming.

At one point, Portia noted Oliver give an *en-passant* bow to a tall man in dark green silk and powder, and saw the courtesy returned. The man looked at her rather more closely than she liked, and she felt a twitch of familiarity. "Who was that?"

"Don't you recognize him?" asked Oliver with a teasing look. "That, my dear, was your moonlit marauder."

Five

Portia stopped dead. "Bryght Malloren!"

"Encountered him last night," said Oliver, still in the manner of one who is about to reveal a joke.

Portia resisted the urge to turn and stare after Lord Bryght. He had looked very different in fashionable finery. For some strange reason, the knowledge of who he was had actually speeded her heart. It could not be fear, for it was impossible for him to attack her here.

"What happened?" she asked unsteadily, forcing herself to move on. "Did you fall into an argument with him? Oliver—not a duel!"

Oliver laughed. "Of course not. In fact, my dear, I paid him back for upsetting you and for attacking me. It was from him that I won all that money."

Portia clapped her hands. "Oh, well done!" But that flash of satisfaction immediately faded. Even as she greeted two more of Oliver's friends—one plump, one slender—she was growing uneasy. Oliver had said that he and the Mallorens did not move in the same circles, so how had they come to play?

Was Bryght Malloren a professional gamester—a hawk? He was, after all, just a second son. She knew him to be capable of wickedness. She would not, however, have thought him a cheat. . . .

Oliver was relating his great success to his friends.

"Does Lord Arcenbryght gamble a great deal?" Portia asked.

The plump young man answered. "Bryght Malloren? Plays all the time, dear lady, and has the devil's own luck. I tell you, Upcott, if you won from him last night you're a walking miracle."

Oliver's eyes shone. "Well, I did, and at bézique. That takes some skill. If he's lucky, perhaps the secret to beating him is to stick to games of skill."

His friend shook his head. "I've heard of him winning at piquet, écarté, and whist. Devilish sharp man. But then, all the Mallorens are."

"And quick with their swords," said the slender one, whose long neck and jerky movements reminded Portia of a nervous chicken. "I'd keep out of Lord Bryght's way, if I were you, Upcott. Dangerous men, the Mallorens."

"He insisted on playing with me," said Oliver with an air. "I would have carried on, too, but he called an end to it after losing so much. If he wants his revenge, I'll not refuse."

Portia bit her lips to smother a protest. Bryght Malloren sounded *exactly* like a hawk. She glanced over to where he had paused to converse with a group of men, and promptly had some strange thoughts about birds.

Birds of a feather flock together, or so they said.

In this grand setting Oliver's friends all appeared to be lesser species—nervous chickens, pretty finches, or pigeons who puffed up their chests and strutted about in search of crumbs. Bryght Malloren's friends, however, were predators—strong, self-assured, and sharp of beak and claw. She could imagine their eyes to be like the eyes of the hawk when seeking its next meal.

And hawks preyed upon chickens and pigeons, especially at the gaming table.

The two young men minced off on their high-heeled shoes. Portia was hard put not to giggle at how much they did look like a chicken and a pigeon pecking their way around. She had to tell Oliver, and they ended up stifling laughter.

"But they're good fellows," he said. "Truly."

"They give good advice, at least. I think you should avoid Bryght Malloren."

He flushed. "Don't fuss, Portia. The chances of gaming with him again are small, but if he wants his revenge I can hardly refuse. It would look as if I only played to win."

Portia stared at him. Why on earth would anyone play to *lose?* Before she could frame this question, they were approached by another couple of strutting pigeons. Portia tried to put bird images out of her mind before she embarrassed herself by a fit of the giggles. The thought of hawks quickly sobered her, so that she could attend to the conversation and learn more of gaming lore.

She soon gathered that Oliver was right. In London all men were expected to play, and to seem to care whether one lost or won was the height of bad form. It was also clear that Oliver's friends were not aware that he had lost all.

As the young men talked she saw that they were impressed that Oliver had played against Bryght Malloren—win or lose. Merely speaking to a Malloren would be an event for them.

So why, she wondered, had Lord Bryght played against Oliver?

She made the mistake of glancing over at the man just as he looked across toward her group. He caught her look and raised a brow. Then he bowed farewell to his friends and came over. Though he, too, wore fashionably heeled shoes, he managed not to strut or mince at all.

Portia's heart-rate increased with every smooth step he took. This was ridiculous! He was a bully and a gamester, the type of man she abhorred above all.

He was powdered and wore snowy lace at neck and wrist. His earring was a large pearl. When added to his gold-braided green silk and white stockings it should all have removed the sense of darkness that she had retained from their first meeting. It did not. The gorgeous plumage could not disguise the predator's body, and the artificial paleness of his hair gave his lean face even more dark beauty and strength.

Dangerous, Portia. Dangerous.

He bowed before her. " *'Ill met by moonlight, proud Titania.'*LC0." She had forgotten the power of his resonant voice.

She instinctively raised her mask between them. "You have the wrong play, my lord. My name is Portia."

"Ah yes, the guardian of the door. And also the defender of mercy. *'The quality of mercy is not strained. . . . '* Does that fit better? I hope your brother conveyed my apologies, and that I am forgiven."

Oliver had not mentioned any apology, but Portia did not say so. "I do not wish to speak of it, my lord."

She was very grateful for the protection of the mask, but wished desperately that her unruly body was entirely within her command. Her heart was racing, she knew her cheeks were flushed, and her voice was not as steady as she wished.

He took no offense at her chilly manner, but turned to bow to her brother. "And Sir Oliver. Most enjoyable hand or two we had. We must re-engage one day."

Oliver returned the bow, flushed with pleasure. "Of course, my lord."

As Oliver introduced his friends, Portia forced herself to remain silent, but she hated to see her brother preening to be merely spoken to by Bryght Malloren. His two friends were acting as if a god had come amongst them.

Damn the Mallorens anyway. All this wretch was was a gamester. She breathed deep and slow, commanding herself to icy calm. What she needed to do was find out this man's intent toward her brother.

The wretch turned back to her, not obviously discouraged by the smooth white mask between them. "You are fixed in London at the moment, Miss St. Claire?"

"For a little while, yes, my lord."

"London is greatly favored. I confess I found our last encounter unforgettable."

Portia almost answered that honestly, and told him what she thought of their last encounter, but she forced a neutral answer. "I too have not forgotten, my lord." She added a dart. "I hope your letter proved to be all that you expected."

Something flickered in his eyes. It could be admiration or anger. In the sunlight she realized his eyes were remarkably fine. They were a hazel that could flash green on occasion, or catch the sun with flecks of gold, and they were framed by rich dark brows and lashes. It was hard to ignore eyes like that.

A quizzical widening of those eyes told her that even the mask could not hide the fact that she had been staring. She looked away, grateful that it at least hid her blush.

Then Oliver said, "Bless me, Portia, there's no need to actually *use* the mask."

Reluctantly, she let it fall. "There is a chill wind at the moment." She directed a meaningful look at her unwanted companion.

He did not take the hint. In fact his eyes glinted with knowing amusement. "May I hope you are enjoying London, Miss St. Claire, despite the *chilly* weather?"

"It is very interesting, my lord."

"You may have an opportunity to see the king and queen today."

"That would be a great honor, my lord." Since he would not take the hint and go away, Portia felt obliged to look at him, and was immediately entrapped.

It was not fair that any man be so beautiful. Beautiful as a fine horse, or a hawk on the wing, or lightning searing across a storm-dark sky. She hastily looked away and knew her cheeks were pink.

He was a gamester and a wretch.

"Now what can I have done to offend you, Hippolyta?" he murmured.

She turned to face him. "I will thank you not to use such names to me, my lord."

His eyes laughed at her. "Why not? It is the fashion. Is it not, gentlemen?"

The pigeons adoringly cooed their agreement.

"If you do not care to be the queen of the Amazons," he continued, "or the queen of the fairies, what persona do you want? What quality do you wish me to praise?"

Portia wished he would just go away. "I would wish to be admired for my *inner* qualities, my lord—my wisdom, or my virtue." She put especial emphasis on the last word, for she could not feel at all at ease with his attentions.

"Virtue is so dull," he complained. "I will call you Minerva then, the goddess of wisdom."

"I would much rather you not," she snapped.

"But to go always by your own true name is to be intolerably provincial. Is it not, gentlemen?"

"Oh aye, milord," they agreed in unison.

"Indeed it is, Portia," added Oliver.

Portia gritted her teeth. "Then perhaps I am intolerably provincial, my lord."

"Alas, perhaps you are."

Portia felt a strong desire to hit him over the head with her mask, but suspected that might be his intent. She had the infuriating feeling that he knew exactly what she was thinking.

He smiled. "But fresh country manners are often pleasing to the jaded palate of London, Miss St. Claire. I predict that you will do very well. It must come in the blood."

Portia could not understand what he meant by that wry comment. He must be referring to Oliver, but Oliver was hardly a shining example of success.

"Aye, my lord," said Oliver proudly. "Portia could be a great success if she moved in fashionable circles."

Lord Bryght glanced around. "This environment is not fashionable enough for you, Sir Oliver?"

"No, no, my lord," Oliver stammered. "You mistake me. It is just that Portia is used to the country, and reluctant to mingle with Society."

"Poor Portia." Lord Bryght's tone of mock-commiseration had her hands tight on the stick of her fan. "Then we must encourage you. With your permission, Sir Oliver, your sister could stroll with me for a moment or two."

Oliver looked stunned and rather alarmed, but he stammered out his permission. Portia wanted to object, but was not sure if it would be proper. What harm could there be, anyway, in walking among the crowd with this man?

He extended his arm, and she curled her hand around it. Despite the coolness of the green silk, she sensed the warmth of flesh beneath, and the controlled strength of his body.

A strength she knew only too well.

That reminded her that he had manhandled her and that she disliked him intensely.

As they moved away from her brother, she went straight on the offensive. "I cannot imagine what you are about, my lord, to be singling me out in this way."

"Perhaps I just want to see you by daylight and at close quarters, Miss St. Claire."

She raised her chin, and looked firmly ahead. "If you had any decent shame, my lord, you would not refer to our previous meeting."

"But I don't have any decent shame." Softly, and deep-voiced, he said, "Sunlight becomes you, Hippolyta. It puts golden sparkles in your hair."

Portia's heart trembled, but she refused to be thawed. "If you intend to shower me with flattery, my lord, you should know I pay no attention to false coin."

"False? Do you have not one feature of which you are proud?"

"You twist my words. Pride is a sin."

"Honesty is a virtue, though. How would you describe yourself? In honesty."

She did look at him then. "Small, thin, and past the age of being foolish."

A strangely warm smile flickered. "Are we ever past the age of being foolish, dear lady? At least you must be cheap to feed."

"On the contrary," she lied, temper rising. "I eat like a horse."

"Have you thought of being treated for the worm?"

"My lord! Really!"

"And what of your hair? How would you describe that?"

Portia was about to fall into a full-blown argument with him when she became aware of a number of eyes upon them—some direct, some peeping slyly, or even from behind masks. Pride demanded that she keep her temper. "My hair is the color of rust, I believe, my lord."

"Rust," he said dryly. "And was it metal gray before you went out in the rain?"

"No," she said between her teeth, "but it will doubtless turn to gray in the not too distant future."

"You being so advanced in years?"

"My being so hounded by rascals!"

He raised a brow. "Miss St. Claire, I find you absurd, and suspect you are begging for compliments."

"I am not!" But Portia was aware that she was beginning to enjoy this. She glanced cautiously at him and caught a glint of teasing humor in his eyes.

It was extremely hard not to respond to it.

"Then I won't give you any compliments," he said, eyes still smiling. "I agree. You are short and scrawny and have rust-colored hair. I must warn you as well that some of the rust has flaked onto your nose." He reached out and touched her nose, then looked at his finger. "And does not easily come off."

Portia would not smile, she would not. "I know I have freckles, my lord. You do not have to point them out."

"And your nose is too short," he continued. "I have to admit that your mouth is unfortunately charming, but I suspect you could rectify that by pursing your lips together very tightly. . . . That's it exactly!"

Conquered, Portia burst out laughing. "You are the most infuriating man I have ever met!"

"Excellent. You will not soon forget me, then, will you?"

As Portia struggled for a witty riposte, he added, "We should move on."

Portia became aware that they had stopped for their debate, and thereby become the cynosure of many more eyes. She gladly walked on, face burning. "You are making a spectacle of me, my lord!"

"Do you not want to be famous?"

"Not at all."

"What, then, do you want, Miss St. Claire?"

His tone was so gentle that Portia was strangely tempted to tell him, to pour out all her secret hopes and dreams, but she was—as she had said—past the age of being foolish. She stated firmly, "My desires are none of your concern, my lord." Then she wished she had not used that particular word.

He let it pass, and she knew it was deliberate. "So you make your home in the country, Miss St. Claire."

"Yes, my lord." Portia was both relieved and disappointed to have moved onto such safe ground.

"And do you have family other than your half-brother?"

"A half sister. Prudence is sixteen and very pretty. She would love to be here," she added wistfully.

"I would not recommend it, however, unless you have a formidable protector. Pretty sixteen-year-olds from the country are such tempting morsels."

"Then all London should be ashamed."

"Undoubtedly," he said dryly. "Your sister is with your mother, I assume. And you are the support of them all."

Portia glanced at him in surprise. "I, my lord? Oliver is the head of the family."

"But is he the support?"

He was far too close to the bone. "My family affairs are none of your concern, my lord."

"You are undoubtedly correct. But having been somewhat discourteous at our first meeting . . ."

"Somewhat?"

". . . I am making your present well-being my concern.

If this is your first visit to London, Miss St. Claire, we must seduce you."

She turned sharply to look at him. *"What?"*

He was all innocence. "Seduce you to the pleasures of London, of course."

Her heart steadied a little, but she prickled with an awareness of danger. "I refuse to be seduced, sir." She launched it as a formidable warning. Heavens above, it was unbelievable that such a man have any interest in her, but her instincts were sounding the alarm.

His right hand covered hers on his arm. Warm and strong, it flexed slightly as his lids lowered in a way that raised her pulse rate again. "If you were over-eager, Hippolyta, there would be no challenge in it, would there? I can never resist a challenge."

They had stopped again and Portia knew she should be concerned about what everyone was thinking, and yet . . .

In one smooth movement, he raised her chin and brushed his lips across hers like gentle fire.

She snatched herself away, looking around in alarm. No one was looking at them, however. The king and queen had just arrived.

She glanced back at Lord Bryght. Had he known, or had he been inexcusably daring? His expression provided no answer.

"You—"

His finger touched her lips to silence her. "We must attend the monarch."

The crowd had quieted to attention and were all facing the royal party. The king and queen had come with little ceremony, only accompanied by a half dozen ladies- and gentlemen-in-waiting and a small body of the Guards. They went immediately to inspect and watch the troops on display.

Portia took the time to gather her wits and steady her nerves.

She had to recognize that her reaction to Bryght Malloren was alarming. Even now, without looking at him, she felt his presence beside her in a way she had never experienced with any other person. Whenever he spoke, his mellow voice seemed to stroke her senses and destroy rational thought.

She slid a look sideways. The sight of him fascinated her. He was beautiful—long, lithe, and elegant—but there was something about him that could perhaps be called presence. It was in every small movement of his body, in the lines it assumed, and even the play of sunlight over the planes of his face.

She wished she were an artist. . . .

She called herself to order. He's a bully, a gamester, a hawk, and probably a heartless seducer, Portia. Be on your guard!

He caught her slanting look. "And what do you think of our monarchs, Hippolyta?"

Sensitized to every aspect of him, Portia was turning dizzy. She looked away to study the young king and queen. "They seem rather ordinary. But . . . good. They look like good people."

How inane.

"In many ways they are. They favor fidelity and quiet evenings by the fire. Do you think they will alter the tone of Society?"

Portia looked around. The flock had quieted with the appearance of royalty, but she did not think it was changed. "No."

"You are doubtless correct. What do you think of fidelity and quiet evenings by the fire?"

"They sound delightful." For a moment, Portia regretted the admission, thinking it too revealing, but then she re-

laxed. It should certainly show him she was not a woman
for his amusement. The idea of Bryght Malloren faithful to
one woman and content to stay home toasting his toes at
the fire was ridiculous.

Having done their duty to the troops, the young king and
queen strolled about the park, stopping to chat briefly to
this person or that. Everyone bowed or curtsied as they
passed, as did Bryght and Portia when the royal couple
strolled near by.

At such close quarters, Portia could see that the queen
was indeed very plain, but looked kind. The king was handsome enough but seemed rather anxious.

She wondered what he could have to worry him. He was
not penniless and plagued by a seducer of devastating
charms and no moral fiber whatsoever.

The royal party re-assembled and rolled away. The courtiers
stirred into chattering motion again and Portia took control of
the situation. "I will not allow you to kiss me again, my lord.
It is most improper and could destroy my reputation."

He turned them back toward Oliver, waiting at quite a distance. Portia had not been aware that they had come so far.

"On the contrary. It could make your reputation."

"Not in a way I would like, my lord."

"So, if you have no desire to be famous, and no desire
to be seduced, what do you plan for your stay in London?"

"Nothing. We are merely here whilst my brother attends
to some business."

"Business to do with the Earl of Walgrave, perhaps?"

Portia had briefly forgotten their perilous situation, but
now she stiffened. "That is none of your concern, my lord."

"How excessively private you are, Hippolyta. One might
almost think you had secrets to hide. . . ."

"Doesn't everyone?" But then she remembered wanting

to advertise the fact that Oliver had nothing left to lose. This was an excellent time. "One secret is that Oliver lost his estate at play. He is as good as penniless, my lord."

He accepted the news without surprise. "In that case, if you will take some well-meant advice, Miss St. Claire, you will stop your brother from gaming further."

"How?" she asked bleakly.

His expression was surprisingly understanding. "Ah. As bad as that, is it? Then get him away from London."

"You played with him last night, my lord," she said frostily, "so why the pious sermon?"

"Because I played with him last night."

She glared at him. "At least he won! You lost, but I suspect you will be back at play tonight."

"Almost certainly, but I have not yet lost my all, nor do I have dependents to consider."

Gracious heaven, for all his poise and power this man, too, was helplessly entangled in the vice. Portia wanted to plead with him to abandon gaming, plead just as strongly as she had with Oliver.

Then she reminded herself that Bryght Malloren was no concern of hers. If he lost every penny and shot himself as her father had shot himself—

Her mind balked at the image, and the words escaped. "I wish *you* wouldn't play." When he turned to her, mildly surprised, she hastily added, "I wish no one would!"

His lips turned up. "What then would we do with our long evenings? Ah yes, sit by the fire with our faithful spouses. . . ."

Portia knew she was an awkward red. "You mock, my lord, but it would be better."

"Undoubtedly." The amusement faded. "You frighten me, Miss St. Claire."

"Of course I don't."

"I mean, I am frightened for you. You have something of the Joan of Arc about you."

"I'm no religious zealot, my lord."

He frowned slightly and looked alarmingly serious. "But you are fierce, brave, and have high ideals. That is dangerous in this cynical age. In a just cause you would not hesitate to take appalling risks. I would not want to see you go up in flames."

"There is no danger of that." But his words struck a chord of uneasiness in Portia. She lived these days with a sense of hovering disaster.

"Is there not? You would have shot me that day, wouldn't you?"

She colored at the memory, but said, "Yes."

"Why?"

"I was supposed to allow an intruder to break into the house without objection?"

"A pistol ball in the gut is rather more than an objection, dear Amazon. What would you have done with me writhing to eternity at your feet?"

It was a disturbing picture but Portia would not let him see that. "Called for the Watch," she said crisply.

He laughed out loud. "You would, wouldn't you?" He touched her hot cheek with his knuckle. "You are refreshing."

Portia felt caught in a moment of eternity, and fought it. "Like an ice-cold bath, perhaps?"

His eyes seemed truly warm as he said, "Not quite so harsh, I think. Like a cool fountain on an arid summer's day."

Portia could find nothing flippant to say to this and stared at him like a wooden-headed ninny.

It clearly meant little to him, however, for he continued

lightly, "May I hope that now you will delight Society a little more with your presence, Hippolyta?"

Wooden-headed? More light-headed. Portia felt giddy. Thank heavens it was proper to be supported by his arm, for she needed it. "I . . . I doubt it, my lord," she said unsteadily. "We do not intend to stay long, and we will be living quietly."

"Society is the loser thereby." But he delivered her to her brother without protest, bowed his farewells, and moved on.

Six

Portia watched Bryght Malloren stroll away, wishing there was somewhere nearby to sit down.

"Well, that will have attracted Society's eye," said Oliver. "But I wish you hadn't behaved quite so boldly, Portia. Staring up at him like that . . ."

Heat flooded Portia at the thought of the spectacle she had just made of herself. "I did no such thing!" she declared, fanning herself vigorously with the mask. "Or at least, if I am to look at such a man whilst he talks, I have little choice. He is far too tall. It was all perfectly innocent."

But she lied. There had been nothing innocent about that encounter at all.

Oliver was not impressed by her words, either. "Just bear in mind, Portia, that the aristocracy marry among themselves, and younger sons like Bryght Malloren don't marry at all except for money and land. How could they support a wife?"

At the tables, Portia thought. Except that Bryght Malloren loses. She summoned a light laugh. "Marriage? Who speaks of marriage?"

Oliver ignored her comment. "And sometimes they hunt for sport."

Portia shivered, for she feared Oliver had Bryght Malloren's intent exactly. If only she could understand why he would choose a poor squab such as herself as prey.

"See," said Oliver. "He is now paying court to Mrs. Findlayson."

Portia looked at the vivacious raven-haired beauty, swathed in a cloak of red velvet lined with dark furs. Five handsome specimens hovered around her like gaudy moths at a flame. Or like hawks on the hunt, more like. Bryght Malloren was certainly no fluttering moth.

But then, Mrs. Findlayson did not resemble any common type of prey.

Who, in fact, hunted whom?

"Which gentleman is Mr. Findlayson?" she asked.

"I told you, she's a widow, and looking to use her first husband's money—he was a tea-Nabob—to buy a grand second husband. Bryght Malloren stands high in the bidding."

Now why did that news give Portia a stab of agony?

"And anyway," Oliver continued, "a husband don't hang around his wife in public. It's not done."

Portia glanced around, seeing similar scenes everywhere— ladies preening, and gentlemen flirting, but none presumably with their proper partners.

So much for fidelity and quiet evenings by the fire. He must have thought her ridiculous.

For her part, Portia thought Society's ways disgusting and frightening. If she married, she would not want to shame herself with other men, and she would be devastated to see her husband flirting with other women. Oliver was right. They had no place here except as spectators.

She suddenly remembered Maidenhead, and a letter. A letter, doubtless, from one of these women to one of these men. But not her husband. And that relationship had not been mere flirtation.

Had Bryght Malloren been the lover involved? But why then had he seemed so shocked? And yet he could not be the husband.

Perhaps he was a betrayed lover. A woman who betrayed her husband would not balk at deceiving her lover, too.

Perhaps, Portia thought with a start, Desirée was Mrs. Findlayson, the woman he was courting. The knowledge that his intended wife was so lewd would certainly shock a man, and had there not been mention of tea in that letter?

She glanced back at the scene and saw the widow laughing merrily at Bryght Malloren, her hand placed intimately on his chest. Portia wanted to snatch that intrusive hand away. If Bryght Malloren had been shocked, she thought tartly, it would appear he had made a good recovery.

Portia dragged her eyes away angrily. The man was no concern of hers, and she was no schoolroom miss to run mad over a virtual stranger!

However, now it seemed that everywhere she looked there were men and women behaving in an immodest way. There! She saw a woman allow a man a kiss on the lips whilst others nearby applauded. And only look where that man's hand rested! The scene in the park definitely resembled a flock of predators, and the chatter was beginning to sound just like the shrieking cries of birds of prey.

If she could not return to the simple, decent life at Overstead, then she would welcome Manchester. There were no such immoral goings-on there.

Oliver was saying something else, about money and Mallorens. "I beg your pardon," Portia said. "I did not hear you."

"I said that I'd lay my money on the Findlayson being Lady Bryght before the spring. She'd be a fool not to snap him up. He stands in line to be marquess if his brother dies."

"A somewhat unlikely event, I'd think. And she'd be a fool to trust her money to a man who will throw it all away at the tables." Then Portia realized what she had said and wished she could take the words back. "I'm sorry, Oliver. . . ."

"No matter," he said stiffly. "It's the truth, though at least it was my own money."

But all our lives went with it, she thought bitterly, and all my work on the estate, and mother's beautiful gardens. . . .

The magic of the day shattered. Portia turned her back upon the Findlayson group so that she wouldn't be tempted to so much as glance at Bryght Malloren.

Bryght flirted with Jenny Findlayson, but his mind was on Portia St. Claire.

It had been simple curiosity that had taken him to her. The woman on Upcott's arm had looked so ordinary and yet had to be his sister. He had wondered if his fascinating Amazon was entirely a figment of his imagination.

Seen up close, she had still appeared ordinary, for she was no beauty and her clothes were not in the latest style. It had soon become clear, however, that beneath the prosaic surface she was the woman who had challenged him, fought him, and tried to shoot him.

Today she had no pistol, but she had confronted him with wit and a sharp tongue, and they were as intriguing. Moreover, the glimpse she had given of her home and family had touched him.

London Society would doubtless count him cynical, and

in many ways he was, but he understood family bonds. He
had been born into a happy family and raised with love.
His parents had died when he was thirteen, however, when
the new marquess had only been nineteen and the twins
grubby seven-year-olds.

Relatives had immediately stepped in to take care of the
younger ones, but Rothgar had refused to allow them to be
fostered elsewhere. He had held the family together and
built close ties between them. He had even arranged his
inheritance in such a way that the younger sons found employment and profit in the business of the marquisate. Rothgar had created and nurtured strong bonds among his
family, and Bryght understood without explanation Portia
St. Claire's need to keep her family afloat and happy.

In the Mallorens, however, the load was shared. None
of them was a burden. Bryght feared that Portia gained
little support from her family and was leaned on heavily.
He had been tempted to dig deeper, to find out more
about the individuals, but he could detect a peril as obvious as that.

He was already more interested in Portia St. Claire than
was wise.

By the end of their time together, even her slight build
and unusual looks had appeal, and her fine-skinned face
which showed every emotion had been enchanting him. The
ladies of fashionable London had perfect, creamy complex-
ions; if they were not gifted with them by God, they found
them in a cream pot. Bryght was accustomed to it, though
the fact that Nerissa Trelyn's complexion was her own had
been a significant attraction.

He had not cared before that Jenny wore a discreet layer
of paint. Now he compared her artificial complexion with

a fresh country face sprinkled with freckles, and found it wanting.

He was turning mad.

He was done with romantics, and if he married it would be to money. There was no place in his life for a woman like Portia St. Claire.

He had told the truth, however, when he'd said he was concerned about her. She was too forthright and natural for London, and too inclined to fight against the odds. If her brother was the hopeless gamester it would appear, the perils were terrifying.

Damn it to Hades, but he had no desire to be constantly fretting about the woman!

He looked up from Jenny's teasing face and caught Nerissa Trelyn eyeing him.

He bowed.

She turned away, pretending not to have seen him.

Bryght saw a possible solution to his dilemma. What was the connection between Portia and Nerissa? If Portia was safe beneath the wings of the Trelyns, Bryght need never concern himself with her again.

He removed Jenny's possessive hand and kissed it. "Alas, but I must leave you again, dear lady."

"Indeed?" Her dark eyes cooled. "If you return to that red-haired dab, I will begin to think you insincere, my lord."

Jenny clearly thought that threat would control him, but Bryght merely said, "That would be unfortunate," and left her to interpret it as she wished.

As he crossed to where Portia stood with her brother, he prayed that Bridgewater not require large new sums of money. Before today, he had thought that making a practical marriage with Jenny Findlayson would be easy enough.

Now, for some reason, it was looking like a labor of Hercules.

Portia had blocked Bryght Malloren out of her mind so successfully that she was startled to hear his voice at her shoulder. "Miss St. Claire, a word with you, if you please."

She turned warily.

"What, pray, is your connection to the Gloucestershire St. Claire family?"

Portia was so disordered by his return that she could hardly think. She managed to answer coherently, however. "That was my father's family, my lord. He was a younger son of Lord Felsham." She was pleased enough to let him know that she was not a complete nonentity.

"Then perchance, is Lady Trelyn a connection?"

Distrusting everything about this encounter, Portia frowned at him. "Lady Trelyn?"

"Oh come, Portia," Oliver interrupted. "Nerissa Trelyn! You asked about her earlier."

"She was a St. Claire before she wed," said Bryght.

Oliver stared between them. "You mean Nerissa Trelyn is a connection of yours, Portia? Bless me, why didn't you say so?"

Portia was completely off balance. She flickered a glance at the beautiful Queen of Society. "I don't know. . . . I believe I have a cousin Nerissa. . . . But . . ."

"But have not met," said Lord Bryght. "I thought so. You must permit me to introduce you. Come." He extended his arm.

Portia would not have gone, for she distrusted anything Bryght Malloren did. Oliver, however, urged her on.

Portia was shepherded across the grass to where Nerissa

Trelyn was holding court. In contrast to the Findlayson, Lady Trelyn was cloaked in white satin lined with thick white fur, and was surrounded mostly by ladies. She looked for all the world like a queen with her court.

Portia halted. Though Lady Trelyn was quite young— probably younger than herself—Portia could not think of such a grand lady as her relative. "She will not repulse you, Hippolyta," said Bryght softly. "Not if you are introduced by me."

And what did that mean? Portia wondered as she was propelled forward by a hand on her back—a hand that seemed to be sending hot vibrations down her spine.

Lady Trelyn turned her head and saw them. She froze for a brief revealing moment, but then she smiled and Portia thought she might have been mistaken about that fleeting expression of alarm. Bryght bowed with almost exaggerated reverence.

"Lord Bryght." Nerissa's voice was husky. Portia saw with something like despair that Nerissa's perfect, pearly complexion owed nothing to artifice.

Bryght kissed the bejeweled hand she extended and then straightened to acknowledge the beauty's husband with a much more moderate bow.

No love lost there either, thought Portia.

"I come bearing gifts," said Bryght. "My dear Lady Trelyn, I do believe I have found a cousin for you."

"Cousin?" Nerissa looked between Oliver and Portia.

Bryght urged Portia a step closer. "May I present Miss Portia St. Claire?"

Nerissa looked blankly at Portia for a moment, then laughed with seemingly genuine delight. "Portia! Uncle Fernley's girl? But I have heard of you. How delightful!"

Portia was enveloped in an overwhelming perfumed embrace, and introduced to Lord Trelyn. Introduced in fact to everyone in a dizzying assembly of smiles and names.

"And you, sir?" Nerissa asked at last of Oliver.

He made a profound, adoring bow. "Alas, my lady, I can only claim to be a relative by marriage. I am Sir Oliver Upcott, Portia's half-brother."

He was kissed on the cheek all the same. "But a relative of sorts! This is of all things wonderful. You must come to dine, mustn't they, Trelyn? I want to hear all about your family, and . . . and, oh, everything." Her charming excitement was flattering, and all around beamed upon her. "Let me see. This is Tuesday and . . ." she counted on her pretty fingers and then glanced endearingly at her husband, "Saturday, Trelyn?"

"If you wish, my dear." But he alone was not beaming, and his voice and eyes were cool. He glanced at Bryght Malloren thoughtfully.

Portia, too, wondered what was behind all this. She was delighted to find a relative in London, especially such a powerful and charming one, but could not imagine that Bryght Malloren was motivated by uncontaminated kindness.

"Saturday, then," declared Nerissa. "Do say you will come on Saturday." She made it sound like a humble petition.

"We would be delighted," said Portia honestly. She had been feeling so alone, and now it seemed she had a relative and perhaps a friend. Nerissa was so wonderfully warm-hearted that it was not surprising that everyone seemed to adore her.

Whatever Bryght Malloren's motives, she wanted to thank him for this, but when she turned, she found he was already strolling off.

Back to Mrs. Findlayson, it would appear.

Lord Trelyn's voice jerked her attention away from that

elegant green silk back. "And how do you come to know Lord Bryght, Miss St. Claire?"

She turned to him nervously. "He is merely an acquaintance of my brother's, my lord."

"Ah." Lord Trelyn flicked a strange look at Oliver.

Oh, gracious. Would they interpret that as meaning Oliver was a gamester? What would happen when the Trelyns found out Oliver was ruined?

But Nerissa linked arms with her and drew her away from Lord Trelyn. "I feel as if I have gained a sister. We will be Portia and Nerissa at all times." She chuckled. "Just like in the *Merchant of Venice,* except that there Nerissa was Portia's serving maid. We will have to find you a noble Bassanio!"

For the next fifteen minutes or so, Portia was "my dearest cousin."

Though not much taller than Portia, Nerissa was an overwhelming presence, and Portia could hardly think while drowning in light chatter and rather heavy perfume. When it was time for them to move on she was a little bit relieved.

"Upon my word," said Oliver, once they were out of earshot. "The Trelyns and the Mallorens in one day! We are moving in the highest circles."

"Such high living is more likely to cost money than earn it, Oliver."

"That shows you don't know how the world works. Those great families have patronage at their fingertips. There are government posts worth hundreds, even thousands a year just waiting to be given, and they are given by people like that! Even if Fort lends me the money to redeem Overstead, there will still be a heavy debt to repay. An extra income of a few hundred a year would certainly help."

"It certainly would, but you would not have time for extra

duties, Oliver. If we do get a mortgage on the estate, all our efforts will have to go into paying it off."

He waved a careless hand. "Oh Portia, you know I'm no good at that kind of thing. But anyway, these posts don't actually involve work. One hires someone else to do the job at a fraction of the income."

She stared at him. "But that's *dishonest!* The person doing the work should get the reward."

He shrugged. "That's the way of the world."

In Portia's opinion, the way of the world was wicked.

But she had another problem teasing at her mind. All the time she had been in Nerissa's circle something had tickled her memory. It was an elusive reference, but it was as if she knew Nerissa from elsewhere, and yet she was sure they had never met, not even as children.

Suddenly it came to her.

Nerissa's perfume.

Nerissa's perfume was very like the one on that letter in Maidenhead.

Surely not.

She glanced at Bryght Malloren, who was kissing the hand of Mrs. Findlayson, widow of a tea merchant, and then at the gold and white Queen of Society, who had a taste for heavy rose perfume. . . .

She shook her head. Assuredly not. Neither of them could be Desirée.

She turned to Oliver, and realized that during her abstraction he had arranged to meet some friends in Watkin's Coffee House. Her instinct was to protest, but she could hardly keep him tied to her skirts, much though she wished to.

She feared, however, that good fortune was not turning Oliver's thoughts in the right direction. Quite the contrary.

With a pile of guineas available, and the entrée to the highest circles, he was already full of unrealistic plans.

All the way home he talked of rich sinecures and grand entertainments. He had not only put his debt out of mind, but clearly thought he was on the way to wealth and glory. Portia was so distressed by it that she was glad to wave him on his way. When he had gone, however, she discovered he had taken an extra twenty guineas to go with the fifty she had given him last night.

Seventy guineas! It was a respectable annual income. It was not even safe to be carrying such an amount, and what on earth could he want with so much?

She feared she knew.

He came home late that night, crestfallen and with empty pockets.

Portia leaped up from the chair in which she had been fretting. "Oliver! How could you! You *stole* that money."

"How can I steal what is mine?" he blustered, but without conviction.

Portia bit her lip. It was true that it was his money but he simply couldn't be allowed to throw away seventy guineas a day. And, of course, it had gone on gaming.

"Yes, yes, I played," he admitted, collapsing onto the faded sofa. "And deeper than I meant to. I thought perhaps I could win enough to redeem the estate, then there would be no debt to tie us all. After last night, and our grand success today, I thought my luck had changed. . . ." He looked up despondently. "I won't be so foolish again, I promise, my dear."

He *sounded* sincere.

"I suppose it was Bryght Malloren," Portia said bitterly. How could she have mellowed toward the man? He was setting up Oliver like the hawk he was, intent on taking every last penny.

Oliver's eyes widened with surprise. "Malloren? No, I told you I don't move in those circles. It was a man called Cuthbertson who won most of it. Not a bad sort of fellow. You can't blame him—the luck was just against me. And seventy guineas is nothing. In fact, if I'd had more, I could probably have turned the tide."

Portia just looked at him, a sick feeling in her stomach. In every other respect Oliver was a good and rational man, but in this one matter, he was mad.

She kept her voice calm as she said, "I hope you mean that, Oliver—that you won't play again. What little money we have won't last if you spend it like that." She remembered Bryght Malloren talking of responsibilities, and added, "And you have to think of the whole family."

Oliver flushed. "I know, I know. I was doing it for the family. If we're to have any kind of life at all, we need money."

"Fort will lend you the money, Oliver. We will be able to pay it back if we live simply and work hard."

"It'll be demmed dull for everyone."

"No one will mind if we have Overstead back."

He looked up. "You might not—you love the country and harvests and lambing and such—but Pru won't much like having to turn her dresses and miss the local balls."

He'd brought in their sister, but Portia knew he spoke for himself. He had no interest in country life or economy. "If we're careful perhaps we'll be able to afford some entertainments." She was offering the sop to him as much as to the absent Prudence.

"Going to parties won't do her much good without a dowry."

Portia wanted to snap that he should have thought of such matters before throwing everything away, but she said, "Pru's pretty enough to marry well without. And if she complains, we'll remind her that the alternative is Manchester. She'll learn to count her blessings."

She hoped he was getting the message, too.

Perhaps he was, for he grimaced wryly. "Aye, that'll certainly cool her. Anyway, you'll be pleased to know that when I strolled past the Ware mansion on the way to Watkin's it looked as if they were readying for an arrival. What's the odds that Fort will be in Town soon?"

A weight seemed to slide off Portia's shoulders. "Oh, I do hope so."

She was convinced that Bryght Malloren had offered one truth. The only way to avoid total ruin was to get Oliver away from London—back in Dorset and drowning in hard work.

The next day, trying not to be obvious about it, Portia guarded her room and the money. Oliver tried various sneaky ways to avoid her vigilance, and then faced her.

"Two guineas? You expect me to go out with a mere two guineas in my pocket?"

"You are going out to see if Fort is in Town yet. Why do you even need two?"

"It's a pittance! You will make me appear a pauper!"

Portia's patience snapped. "You *are* a pauper!"

"I'm only a pauper because you are sitting on my money like a miser with a hoard."

"I am sitting on it because you have no sense in these matters!"

"I have more sense than you."

"Then how did you throw everything away at cards?"

"Plague take you, Portia. That isn't fair. I was cheated!"

She planted her hands on her hips. "The more fool you. And the more fool you for playing still."

"Need I remind you that I won two hundred guineas, and from Bryght Malloren, no less?"

"And lost seventy of it last night."

"I was just unlucky!"

"And always will be!"

After a moment of glaring violence, he slammed out of the room leaving Portia badly shaken. She'd never fought with Oliver before because he wasn't of an argumentative nature. He certainly wasn't of a violent disposition, but now she was afraid of him. She feared he was, in truth, mad when it came to gaming.

How was she to avoid disaster?

Her hands were shaking as she took out the small pouch of gold and counted out the rent for three months. She considered carefully, then included money for coals, for bread and ale, and for one meal a day each from the chop house. She took it down to their landlady.

"Why, Miss St. Claire," said the thin woman, sliding the purse into her pocket, "how pleasant it will be to have two such respectable people in my house for so long."

"I may not stay, Mrs. Pinney. I will soon be needed at home."

"Well, you may be sure I will take excellent care of your brother for you. Such a fine young man. There is just one thing . . ."

"Yes?" asked Portia, wondering what new blow was about to fall.

"I think Sir Oliver is a little neglectful about the locks, Miss St. Claire. I rose this morning to find the door unlocked. We could all have been murdered in our beds!"

Portia relaxed with relief. "I'm truly sorry, Mrs. Pinney. In the country . . ."

"This is not the country. Please ask Sir Oliver to be more careful."

"Yes, I will. Thank you."

Portia escaped back to her room, feeling some relief to have matters settled.

She knew she could not stay in London for it was poisoning her, but she wasn't at all sure she could persuade Oliver to leave. If Fort had no help to offer then she would return to Overstead and organize the move to Manchester.

She told herself firmly that even Manchester was a better place than this, and that with courage and hard work a good life could be made anywhere.

She would try to persuade Oliver to go with her. If he would not go, however, she could leave knowing that he would have a roof over his head and a meal a day for a few months.

That left only thirty guineas in the purse, however, and she feared Oliver would notice the lack. She did not want him to even suspect that she had hidden part of the money and so she took out some of the coins from behind the fireplace.

Some of them were jammed and a couple had slipped in too far, and so she had to use a knife to work them free. As she did so, she could not help thinking of Lord Bryght.

Her hands paused in their work. She had been awake half the night puzzling over him, and when she slept he had been in her dreams. He was as alien to her as a hawk in a chicken coop, and just as dangerous, and yet she could not banish him from her mind. She could recall his flickering, subtle smile, the graceful movements of his elegant hands, and the soft magic of his beautiful voice. . . .

She jabbed a coin fiercely with her knife, but instead of loosening it, she pushed it farther back and out of reach.

Damnation!

She rested her head in her hands, fighting tears. Not only was she facing abject poverty, against all reason she was obsessed by a high-born rake of a gamester! No doubt every woman he met fell in love with him and he found it vastly amusing. He probably expected her to be so overwhelmed by the honor of his attentions that she would fall willingly into an illicit affair.

Well, she certainly would not act the fool with a man she hardly knew, especially when most of what she knew about him was bad. He was a rake, and if he had any honorable intentions toward a lady, it was toward a walking fortune called Mrs. Findlayson. Worse still, he was an unrepentant gamester, the one thing above all she detested. And he thought the mere idea of fidelity and evenings by the fire amusing.

What, then, did she see in him?

Sex.

Her cheeks heated at the thought, but it was true. She was twenty-five years old and knew enough of such matters to understand that naked lust could strike the most sensible person. She would like to deny it, but the fact was that she was attracted to Bryght Malloren in a strictly physical way.

But powerfully.

Her body reacted to his body, and in her dreams last night . . .

She hastily returned to prying out some more coins.

If Oliver was mad about gaming, she was running mad in another direction. Her whole family was clearly unbalanced.

But it wasn't just lust, she thought wistfully. He could be charming and had a clever tongue. She did admire a man with an agile mind and a sense of humor. Were he of a station closer to hers and not a gamester . . .

"Devil take you," she muttered to a particularly uncooperative coin, though the words were intended for another target. "You're a man, no more, no less. And not the sort of man for me."

She counted up their money, both the coins still hidden and those in the pouch, and found they had just over a hundred guineas left. It was a great deal of money, but not if Oliver lost seventy a day!

Having done the best she could with their financial affairs, Portia turned to other matters. She settled to writing a letter home in case they had to stay here much longer. Hannah Upcott must assume her son and daughter were still in Maidenhead, but she would expect either their return or news.

Instead of writing, however, Portia's pen began to sketch Bryght Malloren. Portia had some artistic skill and thought she caught part of the lean elegance of his features, but she could not catch the magic.

"There is no magic," she muttered, and put some extra lines in his lashes, trying to convey the drama of his eyes.

It didn't work. She doubted anyone would recognize him. Which was as well.

She crumpled the paper and threw it on the fire.

Let that exorcise him from her mind!

Seven

Portia ate a lonely meal brought in from the chop house by the landlady's son. When Mrs. Pinney invited her downstairs for tea, Portia went because she was bored, but found she had to deflect a series of nosy questions.

Oliver didn't come home until midnight. He said a brusque, "Good night," and disappeared into his room. It was nearly noon when he emerged demanding breakfast.

Portia served him the bread and butter, and made tea with a kettle on the hob, trying to judge what he had been up to the night before. In his current mood he was a stranger. Just for something to say, she passed on Mrs. Pinney's warning about the locks.

"I suppose we should be watchful for thieves," he said and rose from the table. "In fact, I think I should take charge of our money."

Portia stared at him. "Why?"

"It's hardly a task for a woman."

"I don't mind."

He fixed her with an alarming look. "Portia. Give me the money."

Portia had never been afraid of Oliver before, but she knew there was a real risk of violence now. She bit back her arguments and went to get the pouch.

He weighed it with a frown, and spilled the coins to count

them. "Hell and the devil, there's scarce sixty here! Where's the rest?"

Portia met his eyes calmly. "I used it to pay our rent well into the future."

"Till kingdom come, I would think! Plague take you, Portia, what's the point of that when we'll soon be moving somewhere better?"

"Better? Where?"

"Anywhere would be better than this place. You must have been mad to commit us to it."

Portia controlled her own temper, knowing it would be fuel to a dangerous fire. "I thought it safer, Oliver."

"Safer! You think I'll lose it all, but I know better." He scooped the coins back into the bag. "I won again last night. I turned that measly two guineas into twenty. When I come home tonight, everything will be different. You wait and see."

He was leaving. "Oliver, what about Fort? Is he here?"

He paused. "Any day, they said. But now we won't need to grovel to the mighty Earl of Walgrave, or live a life of squalor slaving to pay off an enormous debt." He paused and suddenly smiled, looking a little like Oliver again. "Trust me, Portia. For once, just trust me. I know what I'm doing."

With that he left and Portia sat down with a thump. Was it possible that he knew what he was doing——that he would come home rich? She'd love to trust him, but she didn't. He was going to come home with empty pockets. Thank heavens that she'd paid for their keep and still had some coins behind the fireplace. At least they had their coach fare home.

She laughed without humor. If Oliver had any head for figures he could reckon up their recent expenses and know she had squirrelled away almost fifty guineas. But he hadn't a head for figures. She had to wonder how anyone thought to gain through gambling who couldn't keep track of such minor matters as that.

There must be games that required no skill at all.

But how could someone as cursed with ill-luck as Oliver expect to gain through games of chance?

She shook her head. She would never understand gamesters. A vision of another gamester came into her mind to puzzle her. It was impossible to imagine Bryght Malloren avid-eyed over the turn of a card, throwing good money after bad with insane optimism.

She almost wished she could go to a hell and witness it. Surely that would cure her forever.

"Get out of my head!" she muttered fiercely and made herself think of Oliver.

Was there anything she could do? If she'd been quicker-witted she could have followed him, but what good would that have done? She could not have pursued him into a club or hell. And if she managed that, she could not stop him from playing.

Was she supposed to drag him out by the collar, like an unruly lad?

Portia sighed and rubbed her head. She wished to heaven she could, but Oliver was a man now. Oh, he was still her baby brother but he was beyond her control.

Let the matter play out.

But what if it ended with a pistol to the head like her father?

"I can do nothing to stop it," Portia muttered fiercely and made herself settle once more to writing letters.

She did not attempt a letter to her mother, knowing she would soon be home. Instead, she wrote farewell letters to her friends in Dorset, explaining the sad course of events.

She would not send them until all hope was gone, but they were ready, like winding cloths laid ready near a deathbed.

Having completed that unpleasant task, Portia found she could not just sit and wait for the end. She needed fresh air and exercise and so she walked as far as a nearby bakery to buy some bread. She even indulged in a currant bun, for if Oliver could take so much money out to game with, she could surely pay a penny for a bun. She delayed going home and wandered the streets, distracting her mind with the variety of busy people.

In the end she had to return to her empty rooms to wait. Though it meant using an extra candle, Portia stayed up late, hoping Oliver would come home. She did not feel she would be able to sleep not knowing where he was or what he was doing. By midnight, however, she could not keep her eyes open.

As she climbed into bed, she tried to convince herself that he would have come home if he'd lost all the money, and that he must therefore be winning.

She couldn't believe it. Disaster was hovering like a thundercloud.

Despite her gnawing anxiety, Portia did eventually fall asleep, and when she awoke it was morning. Her first thoughts were panic-stricken and she rushed out, seeking signs of disaster. Snuffling snores from Oliver's room told her that at least he was in his bedroom and alive.

There was no indication of whether he had been lucky or not. There was certainly no pile of gold on the table. She rather thought that if he'd been hugely successful he would have woken her with the news.

A small win, though. Was that too much to hope for?

Even a small loss would be a relief.

Portia was very tempted wake her brother and demand

an accounting, but what was the point? Whatever had happened had happened.

The hours dragged by. Portia tried to settle to needlework or reading, but failed at both. She paced the room restlessly, feeling she must be wearing a hole in the thin faded carpet.

What were they going to do if he had lost all the money?

What if he'd lost more, much more?

Again the image came to her of Oliver raising a loaded pistol to his head. . . .

"No," she said out loud and another faint snore reassured her.

Fort. Fort was their only hope. Not only might he lend them the money, but he might be able to persuade Oliver to give up his madness and return to Dorset. Needing to act, Portia swung on her heavy cloak and went in search of the new Earl of Walgrave.

As she approached the grand house, her heart lifted. A baggage-laden coach was just leaving the door, presumably to go to the mews to unload. Someone had arrived. She ran lightly up the steps and used the shining brass knocker.

Portia knew it was unusual for a woman to call upon a man unescorted, but she hoped to carry it off with a grand air. When the door opened, she informed the footman that Miss St. Claire was here to see the earl.

His expression was not welcoming. "The earl is not at home, ma'am."

Portia stood firm. "I just saw a coach arrive."

"That was his lordship's servants and baggage, ma'am."

He began to close the door, and Portia said quickly, "So he is expected?"

"Yes, ma'am." Then the door was firmly closed.

Portia turned away, deflated but still hopeful. Fort would surely be here today or tomorrow. Despite her prickling concerns, nothing too terrible could happen between today and tomorrow. After all, Oliver already owed five thousand guineas. Any extra sums he had thrown away last night were just raindrops in a barrelful.

Portia didn't know whether to laugh or cry.

She didn't want to go back to their depressing rooms to listen to Oliver snuffle and snore, so she walked around this handsome area of London.

These were wide, well-ordered streets with houses varying from grand to simply elegant. Generally the pavements were flagged with stone, and sturdy metal posts bordered them, offering some protection to pedestrians from the carts and carriages which rolled past. The people she passed were ladies and gentlemen or their servants and children. The gin-alleys and whores could be from another world.

Scattered among the houses were shops filled with goods likely to appeal to the wealthy. Portia peered through small panes of glass at items from around the country and the world, wishing she could take some back to her family. Pru would love that lacy ribbon and it would only cost a shilling a yard.

She squashed the temptation. She was as bad as Oliver, wanting to spend money they did not have.

Retracing her steps to Dresden Street, she suddenly realized she had lost her way. She was not alarmed for she was equipped with Sayer's Map Of London, and she paused to study it. Ah yes, if she went through Marlborough Square she should be back on course, and she would like to see the famous square. It was supposed to be the finest in town.

It was. Bordered by handsome houses of many types, the square included a railed park containing handsome trees, flower beds, and even a duck pond. Even at this bleak time of year it was lovely. In spring and summer it must be delightful.

Portia heard laughter and saw some children and their nurse feeding the ducks.

London had many faces, she mused. Squalid in one aspect, vicious in another, it could also be gracious, and even charming.

She went over to the railings to enjoy the antics of the four young children. One young lad caught sight of her and waved shyly. Portia waved back. The nurse was watchful, but did not interfere and so Portia paused to wistfully enjoy the little ones.

There had been suitors for her hand, but none she had been willing to accept. Her mother thought her unreasonable, but Portia needed to feel absolute trust in a man before she would give her life into his keeping. She had expected Hannah to understand this after her disastrous first marriage, but Portia's mother seemed to think that any man was better than none.

If Portia had accepted one of the offers, however, she might have had children of her own. Now her chances were gone, for she was past her prime and without any kind of dowry.

She had been resigned to her spinster state for years, but she had hoped to be aunt to Oliver's children. She had thought to live on at Overstead, working to make the estate prosper, enjoying nieces and nephews. Her mother expected to be there to enjoy her gardens and her grandchildren. . . .

One of the children looked up and Portia thought the child had noticed her distress. But the girl looked beyond Portia and shouted, "Zeno!"

Portia turned and found herself looking at Bryght Malloren across the width of the street. It took a moment for her to notice the large dog at his side, dark silky coat shining in the sunlight. The dog was still as a statue except for a lazily waving tail, but its bright eyes were fixed on the children.

The children were coming at a run.

The smiling nurse opened the gate, and they spilled out. The children ignored the man and lunged at the dog. It dodged. Portia gasped, thinking it must turn on the innocent tormentors, but she soon saw that this was a familiar game of tag.

The dog weaved and danced, and the children chased after.

"You like children?"

Portia swung back and found Bryght Malloren had crossed to her side.

"Of course I like children!" Her heart was pounding and she was sure her cheeks had turned brick red.

"There's no of course about it. Little monsters, every one."

"Your dog does not seem to feel so."

"He considers these exercises a noble sacrifice in the cause of educating the young." His tone was perfectly serious, but there was a devastating twinkle in his eyes.

Portia could not help but smile back. "He looks to me to be having a wonderful time, my lord."

"Hush! He thinks he has us all fooled."

Portia's smile widened. He echoed it, and she wished he had not done that. It seemed so genuine, as if he, too, were delighted by this chance encounter.

It was all facade, she told herself sternly, but his expression was so warm that it could melt the coolest common sense into soggy idiocy.

He was dressed plainly today in a dark jacket, brown leather breeches, and black top boots. His dark hair was simply tied back and a trifle wind-blown. He carried a tricorn and crop so he must just have returned from riding.

Unlike his satin and powder of the park, there was nothing about these everyday clothes designed to attract or impress. The effect, however, was even more perilous. Such simple clothes made him seem more ordinary, more the sort of man Miss Portia St. Claire of Overstead, Dorset, could be expected to know.

To like.

To love, even.

Good heavens, no. Never that!

"You live here, my lord?" This was to remind herself that no one who lived in Marlborough Square was ordinary.

"Yes, over there." He gestured to the most magnificent house on this side of the square. "Don't be too impressed, though. It belongs to my brother."

"The Marquess of Rothgar?" High aristocracy, Portia. Remember that.

He raised a brow. "Have you been studying my family tree, Miss St. Claire?"

Portia turned away to watch the play—and to hide her reddening cheeks. "Certainly not, my lord. All the world knows such things."

He must have moved closer, for his deep voice came from just behind her ear. "What else does all the world know?"

Portia swallowed, but kept her voice brisk. "Begging for compliments, my lord?"

He laughed, and moved round into her line of sight so she had to look up at him or be pointedly impolite.

Oh dear. If Bryght Malloren was handsome solemn, he was devastating when lit by laughter. He had placed himself so that they were too close, intimately close. . . .

"I doubt," he said softly, "that much the world has to say about my family could be construed as complimentary."

"They say you are rich."

"But what do they say of how we make our money?"

"They say *you* intend to marry it!"

The words were out before she could stop them. Portia wished a convenient hole in the ground would open up for her.

"Don't be uncomfortable," he said. "It's true. What choice do we poor second sons have?" But he took her hand and his thumb rubbed gently against the back of it. They were both gloved, but that did not seem to lessen the power of his touch.

"Hard work?" she queried, far more breathily than she wished.

"Heaven forbid." He pulled slightly on her hand, pulled her toward him.

He wouldn't! Not here, where people could be watching from any of a hundred windows.

"And they say you make it at the tables," she snapped. This was as much to remind herself as to accuse him. *He's a gamester, Portia. The sort of man you most despise.*

"All the world games." He was still drawing her gently into his arms and, alarmingly, she lacked the will to resist.

But just then the swirling group of dog and children swung past, and Zeno performed a sharp turn to circle Bryght and Portia. In following, one child slipped and sprawled onto the ground with a wail.

Portia broke free of Bryght to help the child, but he was ahead of her. He swung the little girl smoothly to her feet, then crouched down at her level to straighten her hat on her short, mousy hair. "No great harm done, I think, little one."

"I'm muddy," the child said with a sniff.

"It'll wash."

"I hurt my hand." The girl held out her right hand, which was scraped a little on the ball of the thumb.

Bryght took it and gave it serious study. "Mainly mud, I think. Shall I kiss it better? Or shall I kiss your hand as a gentleman kisses the hand of a lady?"

The girl, who was about five, looked at him in a surprisingly coquettish manner. She was undoubtedly destined to be a minx. "Properly," she said, extending her hand, palm down in quite the right manner for a lady.

Bryght took the muddy paw and brushed a kiss over the knuckles, then rose to his feet. He gave a sharp whistle, and Zeno evaded a clutching hand and trotted over to his side. The flushed, excited children would have followed, but their nurse controlled them. Bryght sent the girl to join them and they all disappeared into one of the houses.

At the last minute, the children turned to wave and Bryght waved back, grinning.

"Little monsters?" Portia queried, aware that her heart had just suffered a serious blow. He might be an aristocrat, a rake, and a gamester, but he liked children and was kind to them. She didn't think she would ever forget him kissing the hand of a tearful infant.

"I'm waving them on their way," he replied. He fondled his dog's ears. "Miss St. Claire, may I present Zeno, the most stoical of dogs."

The dog had indeed reverted to a stationary pose and an attitude of endless resignation.

Portia extended her hand, and when the dog showed no sign of objecting, stroked his silky head. "He's beautiful." As beautiful as his master, she thought, for in their dark leanness and fine bones there was a similarity. "What is he?"

"A Persian Gazelle Hound. There being no gazelles nearby, he feels no duty to exert himself."

Portia addressed the dog. "Zeno, I think your master slanders you. You do not have the look of a sloth."

"Nor do I," said Bryght, "and yet am I not an idle, purposeless creature?"

Portia glanced up guiltily. It was as if he'd read her mind. He did look too alert, though, too strong, and too healthy for the life he supposedly led. "I do not know you, my lord."

It was supposed to re-create the proper order of things, to remind both him and herself that they were strangers from different orders of society.

But he said, "That can be corrected, Hippolyta." There was something in the tone, something in his eyes, that shivered along her nerves. "I would like to know you better."

Know? As in the biblical sense?

Portia took a step back. "My lord, stop this!" She bumped up against the hard railings, trapped and reminded of Maidenhead. How could she have forgotten that violent encounter?

"Stop what?" He was all innocence, the wretch.

Portia raised her chin. "I do not want your attentions, my lord." Even saying it sounded ridiculous and she thought he might laugh.

Instead, anger flashed in his eyes. "You refuse my *attentions* without even discussing the matter, Miss St. Claire?"

"Yes. There is nothing to discuss!"

"It seems to me that there is a great deal to discuss."

"No!" she protested, thoroughly alarmed by how little she wanted to repulse him. "There is no price you could offer, my lord, that would persuade me to be your mistress!"

He stared at her and now he looked just like her moonlight marauder—capable of attack. Portia earnestly prayed that a hundred eyes *were* watching this encounter.

But then the anger was leashed. "How very insulting," he drawled. His cold eyes studied her, from her neat hat to her sturdy shoes, and all the while his crop tapped against his glossy boots. "What if I were to pay all your brother's debts,

Jo Beverley

Miss St. Claire? Would that weaken the shackles on your virtue?"

Portia felt her eyes widening. "He owes five thousand guineas!"

"Is he worth five thousand guineas?"

"His estate is."

The light had entirely left him and he was darkly sober. "Everyone has his or her price. Would you be willing to give yourself to me body and soul for five thousand guineas?"

He surely could not mean it, but out of fear she hit back. "Are *you* worth five thousand guineas, my lord?"

"Are you doubting my word?" he asked, coldly enough to freeze the pond.

"If I were to enter into such a wicked bargain, I would certainly have to see the money first!"

His breath hissed in. "You are a reckless woman, my Amazon, to insult me so."

"I am not *your* anything, my lord." She tried to push past him, but he blocked her way with his crop.

"What if I make it ten thousand? Your brother clear of debt, your family safe in their home, a dowry for your sister . . ." He smiled, and his voice took on a satirical edge. "Would not *that* be worth your precious, too-long-hoarded virtue?"

The insult stabbed at Portia's heart, but she was frozen. If he were serious, she couldn't refuse. "You would pay all that?"

"Have I not said so?"

Portia gave a great, shuddering sigh and looked down. "Very well, my lord."

He slowly lowered his crop and Portia watched, shivering, as it tapped his glossy boot again.

"Joan of Arc indeed. Your family is not worth it." She could not read his tone at all.

She looked up to meet guarded eyes. "My family is worth any sacrifice, my lord. Is not yours?"

His chin jerked almost as if she had hit him. "I withdraw my offer, Hippolyta. I am no woman's sacrificial pyre." With that he turned and strode away toward the mansion that was his home.

Portia sucked in a deep breath and told herself she was relieved. Of course she was relieved. Her family would never want her to purchase their security with her virtue. She had been raised to believe that death was preferable to dishonor.

But honesty told her there was a touch of regret in her heart. If it hadn't been for that cruel comment about her long-hoarded virtue, the wicked plan might have been attractive. His words had reminded her, however, that she was past her prime. They had made it clear that his proposal had been a heartless joke springing from disdain not attraction.

He had never been serious.

When the door closed behind him, Portia regained some strength in her legs and could go on her way with dignity. She walked out of Marlborough Square, resisting all temptation to look back, or to think of what might have been.

Bryght stalked into the library and slammed the door so hard he only just avoided Zeno's tail. The dog gave a reproachful yelp and settled before the fire with a sigh.

"Now that was a fine piece of work." Bryght splashed some brandy into a glass and downed it. "Such charming behavior would be bound to win the heart of any lady!"

Zeno opened his eyes for a moment, then closed them.

"Quite. What would your mate do if you told her she was stale on the shelf, a dried-up stick, a confirmed ape-leader?"

Bryght went to throw himself in a chair by the fire. Zeno, knowing his duty, rose to rest his head on his master's knee.

"Stop play-acting," said Bryght. "You have no sympathy for me, and you are right. But she made me lose my temper. She seems to have a way of making me lose my temper, the wretched woman. I am normally in control of my emotions and my life."

Zeno made no response to this, so Bryght stroked him gently, being soothed by the silky warmth.

"I express an interest in improving my acquaintance with the lady, and she immediately assumes that I wish to set her up as my mistress!"

Zeno shifted so his big brown eyes looked straight at Bryght. "Of course I didn't," said Bryght. "The thought never crossed my mind!"

He was brought to a halt, however, and forced to review recent comments about mates and winning hearts. "I cannot even consider an honorable offer, and if I did she would doubtless still faint with horror. She approached a liaison with me with all the enthusiasm of someone wading the Shoreditch!"

Zeno closed his eyes and snuffled.

"Be fair, my friend. I cannot possibly consider marrying a penniless woman, never mind one whose brother is like to be a money-drain. She would expect me to constantly tow him out of River Tick. I simply cannot afford it.

"What of Bridgewater?" he demanded of the dog. "I have promised to support his endeavor."

Zeno shifted so Bryght's hand would work on another part of his neck.

"The woman is not even a beauty. She's far too thin, and she *is* rather long in the tooth."

Bryght put down his glass on a tambor table by his elbow and picked up a tortoiseshell snuff box. He took a pinch and inhaled it, hoping the stuff would clear his brain enough to drive Portia St. Claire out.

It didn't work.

What was it about her?

The way she moved, perhaps. It was so light and graceful that other women appeared clumsy by comparison. Even Nerissa.

The way she spoke directly to a point and was not afraid to make her meaning clear. The fluttering, arch uncertainties of fashionable ladies were beginning to grate on him.

The way her clear blue eyes twinkled when she was amused.

The way she tilted her chin when she was angry. The way she fought against the odds. He grinned.

The way she tried to shoot an intruder.

That was where it had first started, this madness. He didn't know another woman who, alone in a house, would have come down to face a housebreaker with a pistol, let alone fire it.

Other women had more sense, he told himself. Portia lacked all reasonable discretion. The thought of what could have happened to her in Maidenhead if he'd truly been a villain was enough to make his hair stand on end. And London was far worse. He didn't dare consider the things that could happen to such a woman in London with only Oliver Upcott for guide and protector.

Why on earth was he interested in a woman who seemed to create trouble as easily as cats create kittens?

Because she had fire in her, and when she smiled, she glowed.

Was she really Nerissa's cousin? He supposed so, but they were very different.

He could only be grateful for that.

Even though Nerissa St. Claire had chosen Trelyn over himself, Bryght had continued to think warmly of her. He didn't despise anyone for bowing to their family's wishes. In fact, Nerissa's acceptance of her duty to her family had gilded her other virtues.

His eyes had been opened in Maidenhead, when he'd read that letter and recognized her distinctive writing and perfume. Shock had turned him mad for a moment, and the name St. Claire had inflamed him further. As a consequence, he had behaved abominably.

It had not taken many minutes in the cool night air that night for him to realize his error. Nerissa did not even know that her letter was missing so Portia St. Claire could not be her tool. She had to be an innocent, her presence in the house a damnable coincidence.

And he had been brutal to her.

He winced. No wonder she was inclined to think the worst of him now.

It had been an excellent lesson, however, on the depths to which a wanton woman could drag a man, and one he had heeded. He had thought his heart and temper well guarded now.

After all, since Maidenhead he'd had his illusions about Nerissa thoroughly shattered. Bryght had even received recent hints that he could have regular enjoyment of Nerissa's charms if he groveled enough.

When whores were free.

Of course, groveling meant giving up that letter, her very

explicit letter to her principal lover. If that came into her husband's hands it would open his eyes.

Bryght grinned and savored more snuff. That's what was behind everything now. Nerissa would do almost anything to get that letter. Bryght was holding it to make sure she did not tamper with his family. He was deriving considerable pleasure from watching her try to get her hands on it.

To torment her, he'd even told her where it was—in a book of sermons which sat by his bed. It had turned out to be an interesting test of loyalty. Four servants had reported attempts to bribe them, and he'd dismissed one footman caught trying to obtain that letter. As far as he knew, the rest of the staff had stood true.

This had all convinced him, however, that though Nerissa had beauty enough to cause riots, she had the soul of a whore, and the instincts of a snake. He stopped sometimes in the midst of perfectly ordinary activities and thanked God that he had not ended up married to her. He pitied poor Trelyn, who did seem to be growing suspicious that his prized possession was not completely unflawed.

Bryght had thought, however, that his experience had taught him to guard both his heart and his temper. Which brought his thoughts back to Nerissa's relative, Portia St. Claire.

Perhaps his interest in Portia was simply that she was Nerissa's opposite in looks, in temperament and—he hoped—in morals. To marry any woman for that reason, however, would be folly.

Marry?

He was not going to marry the likes of Portia St. Claire.

He reached for his brandy glass. If he married at all, it would be a practical business arrangement with plenty of money attached, as it would be with Jenny Findlayson.

His hand paused. He no longer had the slightest desire to marry Jenny Findlayson.

A week ago the prospect had been unexciting but acceptable, and he had been sure he could be a courteous and considerate husband. Now it was different. Now it would be hell.

He could date the change to the moment in St. James's Park when he had gone from Portia to Jenny.

Jenny had seemed coarse. Not in her manners—for though she came from merchant stock she had been raised a lady—but in her style. She really did seem to think that her fortune would buy him—buy whichever man she chose—like a slave.

He sucked in a breath. As he had tauntingly offered to buy Portia. No wonder she had been devastated.

Zeno looked up again.

"Yes, my friend," said Bryght. "I did make a wretched business of it, but it is for the best. She will doubtless never speak to me again, thus saving me from foolishness. Let's hope her brother's affairs can be sorted out and she'll soon be safe back in the country on her five thousand pound estate."

The dog continued to look at him. "You think I should ensure it? Damnation, five thousand is not exactly nothing to me, you know." He sighed. "Oh, very well. It will be a cheap price to guard against doing something a great deal worse. But it will have to be done secretly or I doubt she'll take the money. And the funds will have to come from the tables."

Bryght gently dislodged Zeno's nose and stood up. "Let us hope there are plenty of plump pigeons ready to be relieved of a feather or two."

Eight

After her devastating encounter with Lord Bryght, Portia was consumed by the desire never to set eyes on the man again. That meant she had to have matters settled and leave London as soon as possible.

She hurried back to Fort's house, praying that he would have arrived. Surely he could not be far behind his possessions and servants. The haughty footman was a great deal less friendly this time, and tried to shut the door in her face.

Portia, however, was so forceful in her demand to be allowed to leave a note that he showed her to a reception room. It was a very plain reception room—not the one she and Oliver had used before—but at least she was given pen and paper.

Portia found her hands were shaking almost too much to write. She would be *no* man's whore, not even for ten thousand guineas. Not even Bryght Malloren's . . .

She sucked in a deep breath and settled to write to Fort.

Suspecting that the footman would read the note as soon as she left, Portia was discreet. She merely gave their direction and said that she needed to see Fort as soon as possible.

Pray God he would come soon, and would help them. She had to escape.

Portia gave the note to the servant, then headed directly home, blocking all thought of a certain man from her head.

She entered their rooms to find only silence. Suddenly anxious, for it was the middle of the afternoon, she knocked on Oliver's door.

"Go away. I've the devil of a head!"

Portia almost charged in anyway, but he couldn't skulk there forever. "Would you like something for it, Oliver?"

"No. No thank you, Portia."

Portia sighed and sat to read some Milton, but her mind kept wandering.

It kept returning to the subject of Bryght Malloren. She tried to focus on his brutality in Maidenhead, and on his crude offer and insults today. Instead, her wanton memory threw up Bryght Malloren teasing her in the park, and comforting a grubby child.

He couldn't be all bad. . . .

She was jerked out of her maudlin musings by a knock on the door. Thank heavens. It must be a message from Fort!

She swung the door open to find two strange men there, neither of whom had the look of servants. One was tall and swarthy, the other shorter and wearing an ornate powdered Cadogan wig. They had the appearance of gentlemen except that their clothes were grubby and their eyes were not gentle at all. On instinct alone, Portia began to close the door, but the taller one put out a hand and blocked it.

"We've come to see Sir Oliver Upcott." The accent was that of a well-bred man, but it didn't reassure her.

"He is not at home."

"No? You surprise me."

"Why, pray?"

The man smiled, showing crooked stained teeth. "You had much better let us in, Miss Upcott."

Portia did not move. "My name is not Miss Upcott."

The man's pale eyes sharpened. "You his doxy?"

Portia flushed with anger. "No, sir. I am his half-sister."
She tried again to shut the door. "You will have to come
back later."

He grinned and pushed the other way. Portia could not
hold out against his strength, and in a moment the bullies
were in.

"How dare you!" she protested, but it was hollow. If she
truly believed they had no business here she would be scream-
ing the house down.

Disaster had finally arrived.

The dark man simply said, "Fetch your brother."

Portia moved toward Oliver's room, but the door opened
and he came out in his nightshirt. "What's the commotion . . . ?" Then he saw the intruders and turned pasty as
uncooked dough. "Cuthbertson."

Cuthbertson smiled and bowed. "Sir Oliver, my dear
friend." He walked toward Oliver, his companion strolling
after like a well-trained dog. Despite the fine suit and powdered wig, Portia was sure the second man had no preten-
tions to gentility at all. To confirm her opinion, he leered
at Portia in a way that made her want to empty a chamber
pot over him.

She knew that the worst had happened. Oliver had lost
more than he had started with. How much? If she paid the
debt, would they be left penniless without even coach fare
away from here?

Oliver was trying for his normal manner. "Good day to
you, sirs. But you are here at an awkward time. I'm only
just out of my bed."

"So we see, Sir Oliver. Please, take time to dress if you
wish."

Oliver's eyes flickered uncertainly between the three people. "Not at all. Our business will not take long."

"Excellent. You have the money, then?"

"No," said Oliver, quite boldly. "I'll have to send to the country for it."

"To the country, Sir Oliver? Where in the country?"

"Zounds, man. What is this? A gentleman has time to pay!"

"Convince us you have a chance of paying, Sir Oliver, and we'll gladly give you time."

"Chance? Why, what is a mere three hundred?"

"More than you have, or so I hear."

Portia swayed on her feet. Three hundred? *Three hundred!*

"My estate . . ." said Oliver.

"Was lost to Major Barclay months ago."

Oliver swallowed. "I still have funds."

"Excellent," said Cuthbertson genially. "Then pay us and that'll be the end of it."

"I . . . I don't keep my money here."

The man in the Cadogan wig had been looking around the room as if seeking something of value, but now he turned back to Oliver. "Then we'll stay here while we wait for it to arrive, Sir Oliver." His accent was not that of a well-bred man.

"Stay here?" Oliver asked, his voice squeaking.

Cuthbertson spoke again. "Forgive us for being so distrustful, Sir Oliver, but not everyone is as honorable as you. It has been known for a man to take ship, or to join the army in order to escape his creditors. Some even go knocking on the doors of the Fleet, desperate to get in."

Portia's heart began to pound and her mouth turned paper-dry. What were these men threatening if debtor's prison was a sweet alternative?

Oliver collapsed down on a chair. "I can't pay," he whispered.

Cuthbertson relaxed almost into bonhomie. "Now that's a shame, Sir Oliver. You really shouldn't play where you can't pay, should you?"

"I'll find it somehow, but you'll have to give me time!"

"But time's so tricky, isn't it? Keeping an eye on you for all that *time*. And the money should be mine for all that *time*."

"You heartless devil," Oliver snarled.

"Tut, tut. If you'd won, you'd have pocketed my money and whistled, wouldn't you? Now you have to pay."

"I can't, I tell you! Do your damndest!"

The two men flashed an almost amused look, and Cadogan Wig moved forward to stand close to Oliver. "Well, Sir Oliver, you want us to do our damndest, hey?" He pulled out a wickedly sharp knife. "Shall we take it as fingers, eyes . . . or balls?"

Oliver's eyes bulged and after a moment of frozen horror, Portia started forward. "Stop this! You cannot possibly do such a thing, so stop this foolery!"

Cadogan Wig quite calmly grasped Oliver by the hair and placed the needle-sharp blade by the corner of his right eye. "I assure you, miss, I do it all the time. You'll be astonished at how easy an eye pops out."

A chill of horror trickled from Portia's scalp to her feet. She believed him.

"Oh God," gasped Oliver. "Please don't. Please . . ."

Cuthbertson smiled. "I do believe these dear people are ready to see reason, Mick."

Mick nodded, but didn't move his hand or knife. Oliver appeared frozen with terror.

Cuthbertson turned to Portia. "My dear lady, please sit down. You look a trifle pale."

Portia sat with a thump. This good humor was no reassurance because she knew there was no way they could pay the debt. If she gave them all the money in the house and then sold every last item they had here it would not amount to three hundred guineas.

Cuthbertson sat in a seat opposite, flicking the skirts of his purple coat as he settled. "Now, let me explain this to you, dear lady. Your brother played. No one forced him to. No one even inveigled him to. In fact, he was quite desperate to play. He lost. If I had lost, I would have paid him. It is only fair, therefore, that he should pay me. Yes?"

Portia sat frozen. In a sense he was right, but if ever she'd seen a man who cheated at games of chance, this was one.

He sighed. "We will take your assent as read. Sending him to debtor's prison, however, will do me no good, especially as gaming debts are not legally collectible."

"Well then!" she exclaimed.

"Well then, we have to collect in other ways, don't we?"

"In eyes? What good would that do you?"

He showed his ugly teeth. "It would provide an hour or so's entertainment."

Oliver gurgled with terror and Portia tasted bile. "What then?" she choked out. "What in God's name do you *want?* "

"Three hundred guineas. There is something in this room worth that amount."

"Then take it and begone!"

He laughed, and Mick sniggered. "I fear it is not that simple. If sold, it would be worth the money."

"Then take it and sell it!"

"That was exactly my intent, if you are agreeable."

Portia closed her eyes. "Just take it and go."

"The valuable item, my dear, is a little bit of skin between your legs."

Portia opened her eyes slowly, hearing Oliver squawk a protest. So dulled were her wits by terror that it took a moment to register. "No."

"No?" the man queried. Then he laughed. "Do you think *I* want it? No piece of kitty is worth that much to me. But there are those who think a virgin a treat."

"Dear lord . . ."

"I know a woman who will auction your treasure off to raise the money to pay your brother's debt. By past results you may even make a little profit, for I will not take one penny more than I am owed."

"You *can't*. . . ."

"Or it's fingers, eyes, and balls, sweetheart."

Pounds of flesh. Portia had an interest in the play, *The Merchant of Venice,* since she was named for its heroine. She had never expected to be acting it out.

But here it was not a question of going into court and cleverly outwitting Shylock. Here her role was sacrifice— she was to give up her chastity to save Oliver from torture.

She looked numbly at her brother, frozen in Mick's grip. "Don't do it, Portia. Don't." But he was waxen with terror.

A piece of skin or major parts of Oliver's body.

She stared at Cuthbertson. "You want me to sell myself into prostitution?"

"No, no," he declared in spurious horror. "Not at all. It will be just the once. Unless you get a taste for it."

"Just the once? And someone would pay three hundred guineas?"

"Almost certainly. But I am a fair man and auctions are chancy. If for any reason you don't bring the full amount, I will take what you raise and call it settled."

"Auction!"

"To get the highest price." He looked her over in a surprisingly objective way. "I judge you'll do well. You have that high-bred look, and you're small, especially in the tits. Mirabelle will probably be able to pass you off as quite young. A lot of men like their virgins young."

Portia covered her mouth with her hand. Her brain felt vacuous and she couldn't think clearly at all. She wished she could persuade herself this was a nightmare, but it assuredly was not. She was going to have to do this horrible thing.

"Are we agreed then?" asked Cuthbertson.

Portia stood as calmly and resolutely as she could, praying that her legs would not betray her. "What do I have to do?"

"Come with me. We can probably get it done tonight, and then you can forget all about it."

She gave a shaky laugh at that absurd notion. "Oh God . . ." She looked across at Oliver, still frozen in Mick's threatening grasp.

"Portia—" But his words were cut off as Mick jerked his head hard back.

"Don't worry about him, my dear," said Cuthbertson. "Mick will take good care of him, and I assure you he will not hurt a hair on his head. Unless, of course, you turn coward."

The room was not cold, and yet Portia was chilled through and trembling. Her head and feet did not seem connected at all, and that worried her. It was important—heaven knows why—to act with dignity at this moment.

"Do you have a cloak?" Cuthbertson asked with concern. "It is rather chilly outside today."

Portia forced her reluctant limbs into motion and went to get her heavy cloak.

The woman was called Mirabelle. She was tall, handsome, and very grand in yellow satin over wide hoops.

Apart from an excess of paint, she could pass for any great lady. In fact, Portia had seen great ladies who were painted just as thickly.

Her eyes, though, her eyes were hard.

She had dismissed Cuthbertson with unconcealed disdain and taken Portia to a private room. It was a handsome panelled parlor that could have graced a gentleman's house. Portia didn't know what she had expected of a brothel, but it was not this.

Mirabelle looked her over. "Are you willing?"

"No, of course not! Those men are making me do this to pay my brother's gaming debts!"

If Portia had expected compassion, she was disappointed. "That's generally the way of it." Mirabelle settled on a chaise and waved Portia to a chair. "Let me make the situation clear, my dear. I am a madam, an abbess—call me what you will. I run a house where men, and some women, buy erotic pleasures. I provide almost anything here for a price, but I am not in the business of slavery. There's not an employee in this house held by force. Behind you is a door which leads to a corridor. The corridor leads to the street. You are free to leave at any time."

Portia swivelled to look at the door. She believed Mirabelle, and in a strange way it made everything worse. Every step she took was to be by her own free will. She covered her face with shaking hands. "Have you no pity?"

"I pity you, but not enough to pay your brother's debts. In what other way can I help you? If I were you, I'd let Cuthbertson take it out of your brother's flesh, for if he's a gamester he will always be one. Tomorrow, next week, next month, next year. Someday he will play again, and lose."

Portia feared that Mirabelle was right, but still she couldn't condemn Oliver to torture. A little bit of skin—

that's how she tried to think about it. Just a little bit of skin
as opposed to Oliver's eyes. And how long could it take?
Minutes only. She could do it.

"Will they truly hurt Oliver if I don't do this?"

"Oh yes. But they will hurt him a little then approach
you again. Sooner or later—a finger or eye later—you will
doubtless give in. It's the money they want. Cuthbertson
makes his living this way. Even bankrupts generally have
a young relative somewhere—a toothsome lad, or a female
with a maidenhead still to lose. Which reminds me. Lie
down on the chaise, dear. I must make sure you are not
trying to cheat me."

"I am a virgin!"

"I take nothing on trust. I recommend you do the same."

Portia wanted to refuse, which was ridiculous when she
had consented to much worse. She lay on the long chaise
and closed her eyes as the woman raised her skirts and
examined her. Portia had thought her life had hit its lowest
point weeks ago, but it kept sliding down and down. Could
it go farther than this?

Assuredly.

And soon.

"Excellent," said Mirabelle. "A perfect hymen. Enough
there to prove you are untouched, but not enough to cause
you a lot of trouble. It should go quite easily for you."

Portia sat up and straightened her skirts. It was tempting
to cry, or faint, or even to have a full-blown case of the
vapors, but Mirabelle's very briskness made such reactions
seem ridiculous.

"We may as well do it tonight," said the abbess. "You
won't want to wait. If I send out the word now we should
gather a good crowd and get you a high price."

"You make it sound as if I *want* this!"

Mirabelle's heavily blackened brows rose. "If you're going to sell yourself, do you not want to gain the highest price?"

Portia swallowed. "Oh, by all means. If we are to do it, let us wring every last penny out of my foul ravager."

"Now, now, my girl. None of that. Hate Cuthbertson, if you like. Hate your brother. But they are the only villains in this piece."

"If men were not so vile, there would be no question of selling my body!"

"If men were not so vile, how would you pay your brother's debts?"

And the tears won. Portia collapsed down onto the chaise and sobbed until she was dry, until her chest ached and her head throbbed. Mirabelle did not attend to her in any way and when Portia sat up again, drained and weak, the woman had gone. But she had left a glass of brandy on a nearby table.

Portia took a sip. The burning spirit did help, but not a great deal.

She put down the glass, and on sudden impulse, opened the door to the corridor. She slipped down the passage to a heavy outer door and opened it. It did indeed open onto the street. Or at least, onto a narrow alley that led to the street.

There, not many feet away, people went about their business, and coaches and carts rattled by. She could call for help. In fact, she didn't need help. She could just walk away.

But unless she raised three hundred guineas, Oliver would suffer horribly.

She thought briefly of Nerissa, but could not imagine her chance-met cousin giving her such a sum of money. It was enough for a family to survive on for years.

Then she thought of Bryght Malloren. He'd offered her ten thousand guineas for this little bit of skin.

She stood there, fingers pressed to her head, trying to think. Bryght Malloren had not offered that vast sum for a bit of skin. He'd wanted all of her, body and soul. A slave for as long as he willed it. And it had just been a cruel joke . . .

She still had her map in her pocket and it told her that she was only three streets from Marlborough Square.

Better the devil you know . . .

With a sob, Portia plunged out into the alley. She controlled herself before she reached the street, and merely walked briskly on her way, wishing the light wasn't beginning to go. The people she passed seemed to be servants more concerned with their own business than hers, but she was terrified of attack or pursuit.

Pursuit! She stopped dead so a footman bumped into her and cursed. If she was missed, perhaps they wouldn't pursue, but just start torturing Oliver.

She half turned to go back, frozen in indecision, subject to curious stares from passersby.

But this was her only chance.

She continued, speeding her pace. She was almost running by the time she entered the charming square. It *had* been charming, rather, for now it seemed menacing in the gloom, and the railings around the garden looked like prison bars.

Portia reached the wide steps leading up to the portico and stared up at the great doors of Malloren House. The glossy finish picked up the flames of the two flambeaux that bracketed them, making them seem in truth the gates of hell. To the right of the doors, in an alcove, sat an old man well wrapped in coat and muffler with a brazier nearby. He looked at her curiously.

Portia took a deep breath and ran up the stairs. "I have come to see Lord Arcenbryght Malloren."

The man looked her over and Portia realized for the first time that she had neither cloak nor hat. "He's out."

"Please!" Portia said. "I know I look peculiar, but he will want to see me."

The man's expression softened a little. "Maybe that's true, luv, but he really is out. Come back tomorrow."

"It can't *wait* until tomorrow! Where is he?"

"Now, now, you can't go around London pestering a gentleman, me dear. You go home, and come back tomorrow."

Dear Lord, it was true. Even if she knew where he was— at White's, or the Cocoa Tree, or some great house—she could not gain entry there.

And there was no time.

Time!

She imagined Mick already doing rough surgery on Oliver and fled down the steps to race back through the streets to Mirabelle's. She stopped at one point, wondering whether to try Fort's house, whether he might have arrived.

But there was no time. No time.

She picked up her skirts and ran. Once a man did try to stop her. He grabbed her arm. "Hey, my beauty—"

Portia didn't care if his intent were good or not. She thumped his nose and he let go of her with a curse.

She came to the alley and had to stop to catch her breath. She staggered down it and into the house, then fell into the parlor to find Mirabelle there.

The madam helped her to a chair. "You failed to find help." It was a statement.

"Yes," Portia gasped, sucking in breaths. "Did you tell Cuthbertson I was gone?"

"No, of course not. Until the time comes for the auction, it is no business of his."

"Thank you!"

The woman gave a wry smile. "You have little reason to thank me, but I will help you if I can. I'm sorry you failed to raise the money elsewhere. I know for you gently bred women this is a difficult thing, but it is, in fact, no great matter. If you wish, I can repair you afterward so that you will go to a husband intact again. I wouldn't recommend it, however. Better to trick your husband into thinking he is the first."

"No, thank you."

Mirabelle laughed. "Ah, my dear, do you still have the courage to sneer? Don't try to deal honestly with men. They hold all the cards. The only way to win is to cheat."

Portia refused to answer and just concentrated on steadying her breathing.

"As you will," said Mirabelle. "So, do you wish the whole world to know what you are doing tonight, oh honest one? Or would you prefer discretion?"

Portia stared at the woman. "Oh, mercy," she murmured. "Can it be concealed?"

"Certainly. Your identity has nothing to do with your price. With a wig, a mask, and some paint, your mother wouldn't recognize you."

"I'd like that," said Portia humbly.

"Very well. Come with me."

Mirabelle led the way into an adjoining bedroom and directed Portia to sit at the dressing table. Portia watched in the mirror as the madam transformed her, dressing her red hair tightly and pinning a loose, silky ebony wig on top. It reminded her horribly of Zeno's feathery coat.

Mirabelle gave her plumpers—pads of leather to slide into her cheeks—and then blushed those round cheeks with rouge. She made her lips look fuller with a bright red cream. Then a mask was added. Just a narrow mask over her eyes, but covered with beaten gold.

"You see," said Mirabelle. "The shimmer of the gold distracts from your eyes. No one will even know what color they are. Off with your clothes."

Portia had begun to think of the abbess as almost a friend, now she was shocked back into reality. "What?" Her voice even sounded strange with the plumpers in her mouth.

"You're hardly going to parade before the men in that," said Mirabelle, indicating Portia's plain beige dimity dress. "Anyway, something more suitable will be yet more disguise. Do you have a name you want to use?"

"You haven't asked my real name." With a grimace of distaste, Portia pulled out the plumpers. She'd put them back in at the last moment.

"I don't want to know your name."

Portia swiveled on the bench to face the woman. "You could easily find it out."

"Why would I do that?"

"Blackmail," said Portia coldly.

"I have my standards. Now, I hardly think you want me to announce your real name. What shall I call you?"

Portia sighed and gave the first one that came to mind. "Hippolyta."

"The queen of the Amazons? I wouldn't have thought you had the size for it, dear. Ariel would suit you better. I have some pretty fairy costumes. Would you not care to use one?"

Portia decided she needed the strength of a warrior name. "No, thank you."

"As you wish."

Mirabelle left and a few minutes later a maid came in carrying a gown and some other items. The servant was wearing a striped calico dress, an apron, and a cap. She looked surprisingly proper. She even curtsied. Portia decided she would feel better about all this if she were in a foul stew, surrounded by leering misshapen individuals.

She had stripped down to her shift. Now she saw the shift should go too, for the gown—if such it could be called—was an almost transparent wisp of creamy silk. In view of what she faced, this should not have mattered, and yet it did. She dismissed the maid, and was surprised when she went.

Portia contemplated the silk tunic and then, in a spurt of defiance, put it on over her shift. If Mirabelle wanted more than that, she would at least have to insist on it.

In fact, Portia decided, it did not look too bad. Her cotton shift was plain white and sleeveless, and came down to her knees. The tunic was a fraction longer. Without the shift it would have been transparent, which was doubtless the intent, but over the shift it was not indecent. Portia had never gone about with her legs and arms so exposed, but it could have been much worse.

There was a gilded belt to secure her garments at her waist, and a pair of delicate gold sandals. There was even jewelry of sorts—two cheap, gilt arm bands to go around her upper arms. A bow and quiver completed the costume, though neither were real.

She regarded herself in the mirror. Really, she thought wryly, if she were going to a masqued ball she might be quite proud of her costume. If, that is, she ever dared wear such an outfit in polite company.

She told herself that she'd seen outfits as daring at private balls.

This was not to be a private ball.

This was to be a public auction.

She almost panicked then, but forced herself to be practical. A little bit of skin. That's all it was.

She looked in the mirror again and decided it was as well

that Cuthbertson had agreed to take whatever she raised. She couldn't imagine that she would bring a high price. Men liked a generous bosom and her endowments hardly broke the flow of the cloth over her chest. They liked lush curves and her hips were slim. Normally her stomacher and hoops gave some illusion of shapeliness, but this outfit disguised nothing.

But with the long dark wig, the narrow gold mask, the bold face paint, and the unlikely costume, she did doubt that anyone would know her. Which meant that she could perhaps return home and pick up her life.

It seemed impossible. Was she to go back to Dresden Street and act as if nothing had happened? Go tomorrow to dine with Cousin Nerissa? Return to Dorset and say nothing to anyone?

She started trembling but paced the room angrily, praying that she would stop. Fear and trembling would do no good at all.

Mirabelle returned. She raised her brows slightly at the sight of the shift. "How charmingly modest. How old are you?"

"Twenty-five."

Mirabelle's heavy eyebrows shot up. "If Cuthbertson had known that . . . ! But you look well enough for all your age." Her cold eyes took in every detail. "I would have put you at about nineteen, but with the plumpers and your figure we can go even lower." She walked slowly around Portia. "A nice boyish rump, too. Fourteen. We'll claim you're fourteen."

"Fourteen! That's absurd!"

"No. Put in the plumpers and look at yourself with a stranger's eyes."

Portia turned to look in the mirror again and popped in the plumpers. With Mirabelle standing behind her, and having almost as much height as Bryght, and with the rounded cheeks and full lips, she did look like a pretty child. It was quite eerie, as if she were not herself at all.

"But why fourteen? It's ridiculously young."

"That will raise your price. Some men like young girls."

Cuthbertson had said as much, and now Portia remembered Bryght Malloren saying something about the dangers in London for pretty sixteen-year-olds.

It suddenly struck Portia that it could be Prudence standing here about to be sacrificed. She thanked God it was herself instead.

Taking out the plumpers, Portia turned to face Mirabelle, determined to be practical. "What will I raise, then?"

The madam pursed her lips thoughtfully. "At least the three hundred."

"I can't believe that men would pay so much."

"It amuses them, thanks be to heaven. Where would we all be if it didn't? And, of course, they can show their friends and enemies that a few hundred guineas means nothing to them. Make no mistake, my dear, everything in London is to do with power."

"Power? What power is there in buying a child?"

Mirabelle's mouth turned in a wry smile. "The power of men, that they can buy and sell us? But I buy and sell men, too, sometimes, and sometimes women are the purchasers. Perhaps it is just that they can pay such a ridiculous amount of money for such a trivial thing. You may like to think that."

"It does not seem trivial to me."

Mirabelle shrugged. "As you wish. Since you are ready, come back to the parlor." Once there, Mirabelle said, "I will have a meal sent to you."

"I couldn't possibly eat."

"You may find you can, and it would be wise. You may

also have some wine, or even some opiate. Not too much, though. No man will want you comatose."

"I want nothing."

Mirabelle shrugged and left. Portia paced. It did no good, but she couldn't help it. She repeated to herself all the reasons why this had to be, and tried to convince herself that it was not such a great thing really.

But the man, the monster, who was to invade and abuse her rose up in her mind like a creature of nightmares.

She covered her face with her hands. No matter how terrible her ravishment, it could not be worse than what Oliver faced if she failed. She must go through with it.

She was burningly aware of the door, though, the door to freedom. But it was already dark outside and dressed as she was she couldn't possibly leave. And if she did, Oliver would be horribly maimed. She, who always fought against the odds, had come at last to a battle she could not win.

Determined to hang on to her dignity, Portia tried to read from the surprisingly wide selection of books in the room. She picked up first one, then another, but was unable to settle to anything. She tossed down a book about the animals of Africa. They seemed more civilized than the animals of London.

The maid brought food, and Portia picked at it, but her throat was almost too tight to swallow. She drank some of the wine, though, and that eased her dry throat.

The door was a constant torment. Could anything be crueler than this, to have escape from horror, and not be able to use it?

Nine

Bryght dined at his club with Andover and Barclay, a laconic ex-officer who wore a hook where his right hand had been. As they were leaving for the theatre, they encountered Sir William Hargrove, a wealthy Nabob whose greatest ambition now was to enter the higher reaches of Society. The man had recently acquired a baronetcy, and Bryght expected to hear any day that he had bought himself into the peerage.

Well, there were worse specimens among the aristocracy. Sir William was at least clean and well-mannered.

"Lord Bryght," said the sinewy older man with a deep bow. "I give you good evening."

Bryght returned the bow and introduced his companions. In turn, Sir William introduced the man at his side, Mr. Prestonly, a fat sugar trader from the West Indies.

"Can we interest you in a game, my lords?" asked Sir William eagerly.

Sir William was one of Bryght's favorite victims when Bridgewater needed money. He was wealthy enough to hardly feel the thousands he lost, and clearly thought that associating with the aristocracy was worth every penny. Mr. Prestonly seemed of the same stripe.

Bridgewater was not in great need at the moment, but Portia St. Claire was. After a communicative glance at his friends, Bryght said, "We would be delighted, sirs. . . ."

At that point, however, Mr. Prestonly's shiny red face grew redder. "Hey what, Sir William? I thought we were for this Mirabelle's to see this auction."

Sir William did not look pleased, but he said, "That is true, my lords. My friend here has a wish to attend the affair. One of Cuthbertson's debtors. Perhaps Mr. Prestonly wishes to bid."

Prestonly puffed his cheeks at that, but did not deny it.

Bryght did not conceal his distaste, but having turned his mind to it he had no particular desire to allow these two very plump pigeons out of his orbit. "Why do we not all repair to Mirabelle's? The lady has gaming tables as well as her other attractions."

"Aye," said Sir William with relief. "Excellent notion, my lord. What do you say, Prestonly?"

"By all means!" declared that man and it was settled.

Since Mr. Prestonly did not care to walk any further than he had to, they took a coach to Mirabelle's. Bryght spent the journey gently assuring himself that Mr. Prestonly was as deep in the pockets as he appeared to be.

He was.

He was also a slave-trader who showed not a qualm about the business. After enduring the man's account of slave auctions back home, and some quite revolting stories about female slaves, Bryght decided that relieving him of part of his ill-gotten wealth would be pure pleasure.

There was no clock in the room, but Portia knew by the darkness that the day had gone. When the maid returned with cake and tea, she also lit the candles. Distant noises told Portia that the business of the house was under way. Music played, as if this were a grand house holding an entertainment. Voices could be heard, male voices overlaid by feminine laughter.

Portia was plagued by a sense of unreality. How could this terrible thing be happening to her while nearby, others laughed?

Mirabelle swept in. She had changed into a splendid dress of deep blue silk flounced with black lace and cut very low across the bosom. Her dark hair was dressed high and decorated with an aigrette of blue flowers and jewels. Perhaps real sapphires. Other jewels adorned her neck, fingers, and wrists.

Portia couldn't help but think that her own sacrifice tonight would put a few more baubles on the abbess's over-adorned flesh.

"Still spirited enough to sneer, are we?" asked Mirabelle without offense. "Excellent. The one thing I don't want from you is a state of collapse. Now, we are almost ready and there is an excellent company eagerly awaiting your appearance. Do you want some more wine or some opiate?"

It was tempting, but Portia shook her head. "I prefer to keep my wits intact."

"I'm not sure why, my dear, but as you will. Just remember, once the auction is done, you must fulfill your part of the bargain."

Portia said nothing, and just wished her heart would stop pounding so hard. She was determined to do this with dignity and courage but her treacherous body seemed likely to betray her and plunge her into a dead faint.

"Perhaps I will have something." She picked up the brandy glass and drained it. She choked at the fire of it, but it did steady her head.

"It revives courage, does it not?" said Mirabelle. "And you have courage. What are you going to do about your brother after tonight?"

Portia clutched the glass. "I don't know."

"You would be well advised to cut loose of him. Do you think he would do something like this for you?"

"Yes, of course he would." But Portia wasn't sure. Some people would think preserving virtue was more noble than preserving a life.

"Are you sure you don't want to change your mind?"

Portia realized with surprise that Mirabelle didn't like this situation any better than she did, and wanted her to use the door and walk to freedom. "I can't abandon him," she whispered. "Really, he is a good man but for this one thing." In desperation, she refilled the glass and drained it again.

"No more," said Mirabelle, then shook her head. "You are a veritable Joan of Arc, aren't you?"

Portia started at that, for it stirred a memory.

Mirabelle carried on smoothly, "It is time. There is no need for you to speak or do anything but stand there." She opened the door and gestured Portia to pass through.

Portia wondered if the brandy had been a good idea, for her legs did not seem to want to obey her head. She forced them, however, and left the room.

The passageway was carpeted and soft under Portia's thin sandals. A couple of servants bustled by, giving Portia only a mildly curious glance. The noise of talk and laughter grew louder as she approached an open door. She felt more as if she were watching someone else than doing this herself.

Steered by Mirabelle's hand on her back she walked through the door and stopped dead.

The large room was handsomely furnished and lit by an extravagance of candles. It was full of finely dressed people—mostly men—and Portia was buffeted by a wave of voices, and by air heavy with the smell of perfumes, sweat, and candle smoke.

The babble died. Everyone turned to look at her and Portia was dazzled by the flashes as raised quizzing glasses caught the candlelight. She froze, but Mirabelle pushed her forward, not ungently.

Portia swallowed and walked unsteadily toward a small dais or stage at this end of the room. It stood about four feet off the ground and was lit along the front by more candles backed by reflectors. When Portia mounted to the stage she found herself in bright light and could hardly see past the glare into the room. That was an improvement, but she could still hear the buzz of comment.

"Ladies and gentlemen," said Mirabelle, "your attention please." She came to stand behind Portia, using the contrast in size to emphasize Portia's supposed youth.

The silence became complete.

"My friends," said Mirabelle, "I present to you, Hippolyta."

Bryght was at the rear of the room, concentrating on whist. He heard the change of sound in the room that doubtless meant the star of the evening had arrived, but his attention was on Mr. Prestonly's next card. The man was actually a very shrewd player and was giving Bryght a challenge. He was glad of it. Plucking helpless pigeons, even fat ones, was not at all to his taste.

In a rare burst of unnecessary movement, Mr. Prestonly heaved himself up and craned his neck. "Little thing. Pretty, though. Looks a mere child."

It was clear he did not consider this unattractive. Bryght fingered with satisfaction the two hundred guineas before him. He was starting slow but planned to relieve the merchants of at least two thousand before the night was over.

That would be a comfortable start to getting Portia St. Claire out of London, and out of his life.

Sir William said somewhat testily, "Pay attention to the game, Prestonly."

Mr. Prestonly sat and played low. "Nothing's happening yet." He leered at Bryght. "Don't you ever feel tempted to buy one of these innocents, my lord, and practice for your wedding night?"

"Do you think I need practice?" asked Bryght coolly, considering carefully whether Prestonly was likely to have the last spade. He made his decision and led the five.

Prestonly grimaced and discarded a diamond. "It's different with a nervous virgin though, my lord. I know. Been married twice. And then there's the slave girls . . ."

He stopped because Bryght intended him to stop, and had sent the message with his eyes. Bryght was wondering whether getting Portia safe back in Dorset was worth this.

Prestonly paled and concentrated on his cards.

"My dear Bryght," said Andover mischievously as he took the trick and led a diamond. "I do think you should practice for your wedding night."

Bryght flicked him a look. "What wedding night?"

Sir William played the jack. "What of Jenny Findlayson?" he asked with genuine curiosity. "You've been raising hopes there."

Bryght almost denied the interest, but realized in time that Sir William was a friend of Mrs. Findlayson's brother. He could hardly tell the man that the widow was his contingency plan in case Bridgewater needed more money than they could raise by other means.

Or had been. He doubted it was possible anymore.

It was one thing to marry in cold calculation, meaning

to deal honestly with a wife. It was another to marry completely against his inclinations. Hell for both parties.

He didn't care to look too closely at where his inclinations lay. . . .

Bryght found he'd lost track of the play. When had that last happened to him? "Jenny is a very attractive woman," he said vaguely, searching his memory. Had Prestonly discarded a diamond or a heart?

"Your play, I believe, my lord."

Damnation, that was Prestonly prompting him, and not without a sneer. He pulled his mind back onto the game and banished all women from it.

A diamond. Which meant . . .

"I present to you Hippolyta."

Bryght froze in the act of choosing his card and swiveled, icily certain of what he would see.

At first he thought he was mistaken.

An elfin-slight figure shimmered gold and white on the dais. Long dark curls hung to her waist and her features were much coarser than Portia St. Claire's. He heard Mirabelle describe her as a fourteen-year-old who had come up from the country to learn earthy pleasures from a gentleman. It was possible. Some country girls raised a dowry this way.

She looked a mere child, though.

He should have turned back to the game, but something held him gazing at the girl. She looked young and vulnerable, and much too small to be roughly violated by one of these men.

The bidding started, low as yet, mere foolishness. Suddenly the girl straightened her spine and raised her chin as if defying the bidders to think the less of her.

Bryght cursed under his breath.

It had to be that damn brother.

"Bryght," said Andover, "it's your play."

Bryght tossed his cards on the table. "Your pardon for a moment."

Prestonly looked up with a leer. "I thought you had no interest in these auctions, my lord."

"That has just changed."

Damn it to Hades but that tunic she was wearing scarce reached her knees! At least it wasn't transparent, but without stays, hoops, or petticoats her form was clear to all.

Bryght couldn't help noticing how tiny she was—fine-boned, lightly fleshed, with scarcely more hip and breast on her than a boy. He'd never been attracted to that type of woman before and wasn't sure of his feelings now except that he could not stand idly by while Portia St. Claire was auctioned off for the amusement of this crowd.

He was good at calculating options and odds, and realized almost instantly that he had few. He could not buy Portia and pretend to deflower her, because such events took place in Mirabelle's Rotunda, which had twenty peepholes in the walls for voyeurs. Since Mirabelle sold each place for twenty guineas, she'd fight to the death to preserve that tradition.

He could not snatch Portia away. Even if he paid Mirabelle the money, it could cause a riot. More importantly, it would focus attention on the affair. London would be abuzz with it, and some people were bound to remember the attentions he had paid to a petite woman in the park, a petite woman with a gamester brother. . . .

They might as well post notices all over Town.

Just to go through with it would cause no comment at all. He didn't know, however, if he were capable of raping Portia—or any woman—even to save her from a worse fate.

He looked again at the gold and white figure standing

stiffly in the bright light, chin raised. Was it only his imagination that she was trembling?

She had reason to tremble if she but knew it. Most of the bidders were merely after amusement, but one was Lord Speenholt, who was riddled with the pox and seeking the mythical virgin cure. Another was Gerard D'Ebercall whose tastes ran to the vicious.

He didn't know whom he wanted to murder most—Oliver Upcott or his doting half-sister. Cuthbertson was doomed.

The bidding had crept up to two hundred by the time he saw a way. He turned to Prestonly. "You cast doubts upon my ability to handle nervous virgins, sir. Care to back it with money?"

The man twitched at his tone. "Money, my lord? What do you mean?"

Bryght leant forward on the table. "I'm going to buy that chit, and have her begging for it without even taking her clothes off. If I succeed, you are going to pay me twice what I bid."

The man's eyes flickered nervously, and he swallowed. "I didn't mean to call into doubt. . . ." He smiled weakly. "By all means, my lord. Let us have the little wager."

Bryght straightened, ignoring Andover's raised brows. "Excellent." He turned toward the dais. "Three hundred."

Mirabelle's eyes flicked to his in surprise, for he had never shown interest in such affairs before. But she said, "At last, someone who knows value when he sees it. Three it is. Who will say three-twenty?"

Bryght saw Portia's eyes swivel toward his voice. Standing in the midst of bright candles, she would not be able to see much of the room, and the voices would be disembodied. Had she recognized his? If so, what was she thinking?

Would she know there was no way out of this short of setting the house on fire?

He even considered it, but the chances of getting out alive were small. At this moment Portia might think death in the flames preferable to her fate, but common sense would return in time.

Even with the mask on he could see that she was tracking the betting with apprehensive, jerky movements. He desperately wanted to comfort her.

The bidding had stalled at three hundred and fifty in Steenholt's favor and Bryght would soon have to make his definitive bid. To spite Prestonly, he would have liked to drive the bidding sky-high, but that would create just the kind of notice he was trying to avoid.

He thought it was over, but then a stir at the back of the room announced new arrivals.

"You are late, gentlemen." Mirabelle raised a hand to pause the bidding. "But come and inspect this delicious charmer. Perhaps you would care to purchase the right to her education."

"I don't think so."

It was the new Earl of Walgrave and some friends. Fortitude Ware was in mourning black, but encrusted with silver and jet. From the way he accepted a kiss from an opportunistic whore, Bryght assumed he had not decided to follow in his strait-laced father's footsteps.

Bryght wondered if he could use Fort's arrival to his advantage, but he was damned if he saw how. There was some connection between the Wares and the St. Claires, but it was probably slight. Moreover, the Mallorens and Wares were outright enemies these days, only civil because Chastity Ware had recently married Bryght's young brother, Cyn.

The bidding resumed, but it was dying. Bryght bid four hundred, hoping that would be it.

Speenholt glared across the room. "Four-fifty."

"Four-seventy," said D'Ebercall.

"Five hundred," said Bryght. Damnation, the very figure involved was going to cause talk.

Speenholt pointedly turned his back on the proceedings. D'Ebercall glared at Bryght, but then shrugged. "She's yours."

Bryght waited for a moment, then moved forward, still weighing the possibility of taking his purchase out of here, but having made a wager, he had ruled that out.

The voyeurs were his main problem now. Demand for a spot would be brisk when word got out that there was such an unusual wager on the line. Mirabelle would probably raise her price.

He didn't like the situation one bit, but he told himself he'd avoided the worst of it. By the terms of the wager, Portia would not be violated or stripped naked, but he hated the thought of those avid eyes on her as he drove her to simulated ecstasy.

And what was he going to have to do to make it convincing? He hoped to heaven she was a good actress because he suspected Prestonly would want to watch the wager play out.

"Six hundred," said a new voice.

Bryght turned to stare at the Earl of Walgrave. What the devil . . . ? Fort was no more inclined toward this sort of foolery than Bryght was.

Then Bryght realized that Fort, too, must have recognized Portia. That might be useful, but it indicated a familiarity between them that Bryght did not like. And he certainly didn't like the attention all this was causing.

A buzz of speculation was now running through the room because of the high price and the unusual bidders. Soon everyone would realize that there had to be a personal interest in this.

Bryght took a leisurely pinch of snuff and pitched his voice to carry. "Carrying our *family feud* a little far, aren't you, Walgrave? I have a wager here. I win double the price if I can make this morsel beg for consummation without so much as removing her clothing."

That caused a wave of amused comment. The jaded company was intrigued, but now they would no longer wonder at events. In wagers no one looked for reason.

Fort strolled forward. "A wager, eh? And you worked the bidding high in the security that you would win."

"I only ever play for high stakes, as you know."

"Then overbid me."

Bryght gritted his teeth. Fort had deep pockets and was in the mood for mischief. He would push the bidding into the thousands out of pure malice. Bryght would be happy to squeeze that sort of money out of Prestonly, but the matter would then be the talk of the town for months.

"It would be absurd to pay this chit a fortune, not to mention Mirabelle's twenty percent. I'll play you for her."

Fort was now at Bryght's side. "Play?" he queried.

"Dice. Highest roll." Bryght proffered his snuff box and Fort took a leisurely pinch. Bryght murmured, "You recognize her?"

Fort's eyes sharpened and he studied Hippolyta. Bryght realized then that he'd made a serious miscalculation. Fort had not recognized Portia, but had been motivated solely by a desire to thwart a Malloren. Damn.

Fort's eyes widened. "Hell and the devil, you can't *buy* her."

"What alternative?"

"Get her out of here."

"Please do. I can't see a way to rescue her without raising speculation."

Fort muttered something. "I always knew her bold nature would land her in trouble."

"Gentlemen!" Mirabelle chided. "This is collusion!"

Bryght turned to her. "Indeed it is. But if you and Hippolyta want the money you will have to put up with it. Lord Walgrave and I are establishing a side bet. He claims his amatory skills are at least the equal of mine. We are going to dice for the honor. Highest roll." He turned back to the earl with a challenging look.

Fort's lips tightened. "Better I maul her than you."

"I doubt it." Bryght snared a pair of dice from a nearby table and rolled them. "They seem true. Well, Walgrave? One each. Highest wins."

Or loses, he thought to himself. The winner was not going to endear himself to Portia St. Claire, who wouldn't understand the true situation. She would never want to see her false lover again. That was good, he tried to tell himself. Portia was trouble, and had no place in his life.

Then why not let Fort have her? If he abided by the terms of the wager, she'd be safe enough.

Bryght realized that he didn't want any other man touching Portia St. Claire. He knew then that he was in the mire deeper than he wished, and would be safer out of it. He looked at Fort. "Would you marry her?" he asked quietly.

Fort's brows shot up. "After this? Are you mad?"

Bryght sighed and passed him a die. "One roll each. Highest wins."

"Would you marry her?" Fort asked in seemingly genuine curiosity.

Bryght rolled the smooth die in his fingers. "Yes," he said, and rolled.

A five.

Fort contemplated the white cube and then placed it down, one up. "The whim has passed. By all means pursue your wager, Lord Bryght. And," he added with quiet malice, "I look forward to dancing at your wedding." With that he strolled away, leaving Bryght the victor.

Like a victor who has won the right to be a human sacrifice.

"Congratulations, my lord," called out Mirabelle gaily, "I'll just have your vowel on it, and then you can show your mettle! And who is the other wagerer? We must have it all in the book."

Bryght scrawled the IOU. "A fat sugar-planter called Prestonly. He's doubtless wheezing his way down here. You'd better save him a view." He looked at the madam. "I need a few minutes. Delay things."

Mirabelle's brows shot up, but she nodded.

Bryght swept Portia off the dais into his arms. Cheers resounded. She stared up at him. "No!"

He pushed her head against his shoulder before she said something stupid. "Hush, it won't be too bad."

She was trembling, though.

Bryght was suddenly sickened by the world he inhabited. This tiny woman in his arms could be a frightened child, sold by a broken father, and going to a man blighted by disease. These spectators would still be cheering and scrambling for a pair of peepholes.

Bryght carried Portia into Mirabelle's Rotunda wanting to give her a stern lecture on prudence. Anyone with sense would have abandoned her fool brother to his fate weeks ago. The fact that she could never do that, and that she had the courage to come here today and stand unflinching on the auction block, made him want to wring her neck. It also made her precious to him.

The Rotunda was a perfect circle and the only furniture was a circular bed—a platform, really, padded but covered only with a tight, white sheet. Covers would definitely spoil the fun.

On the ceiling, gods and goddesses lewdly frolicked and the painted walls showed twenty mortals imitating the deities. The difference was that the various pieces of equipment they used—from whips to scented oils—were real and could be appropriated by the users of the room.

The eyes of each abandoned figure were strangely blank, but that was because the observers had not yet taken their places. There was an eerie effect of movement from the figures on the wall, made greater by the flickering candles in colored glass lamps and the faint haze of burning incense. The dimness lent mystery to the scene for the observers, but Bryght could use it to carry off this event.

Had Portia understood anything about the wager? He put her down cautiously and she immediately straightened her garments with a flustered manner that made him want to grin. As if she'd just tumbled on some steps and been helped to her feet.

"Where are we?" she asked, looking around. Then she gaped. "Lud! That's—"

He put a hand to her head to draw her attention to him. "Hush, don't look at the pictures. Listen to me. How good an actress are you?"

Even through the mask he could see her eyes widen. "I've never tried to act in my life!"

"Then tonight is your debut. You have to act the part of

a frightened girl wooed by a skillful lover—myself—into wanting to surrender entirely to his passionate demands."

"Surrender entirely," she echoed, and he could tell that shock and bewilderment had dulled her sharp wits. She might even be drugged. There was no time for subtlety for Mirabelle could only delay the voyeurs a little.

"It's act or do it in reality, Hippolyta."

She jerked under his sharp tone. "You're not going to . . . ?"

"No. I promise I won't harm you. I've made a wager I can make you willing, and without removing a stitch of clothing."

He should have known that the word wager was like a red rag to a bull. "You could always lose your ridiculous wager," she snapped, much more like his Amazon.

"Twelve hundred guineas?"

She gaped again. "What? How could you . . . ?"

"Isn't that sum worth a little acting?" He saw a powerful weapon. "You can have it if we win."

"Twelve hundred guineas?" she whispered.

"A good start on your debts, isn't it? And all from a man who can afford it and deserves to lose more. Agreed?"

She looked around dazedly, her puffed-up face and long dark hair making of her a changeling, but Portia all the same. Then her back stiffened, and her chin went up. "Agreed. But I haven't the slightest idea what to do."

"I'll guide you. But don't be too willing too soon. To begin with, be frightened."

She was frightened, he knew, but she met his eyes. "I'd rather fight!"

"Excellent." He picked her up and threw her on the bed. She landed in a sprawl of skirts then scrambled to her knees in outrage. Before she recovered, he launched himself at her and pinned her down. "Did I tell you we have an audience?" he whispered. "There's twenty peep-holes in the wall and the man I made the wager with is behind one. We'd better do this well."

She went limp with shock. "Watching?"

"And listening if we speak loudly, so be careful. Isn't that terrible? Aren't you angry about it? Now, try to hurt me. Come on. I know you'd like to hurt someone."

Fire flashed in her eyes then and she did fight, not holding back at all. He goaded her so she did her damndest to get her nails at his skin, at his eyes even, spilling out all her fear and rage on him. He lost some skin and gained some bruises, but wasn't in real danger until he grew careless and she almost got his balls with her knee.

He twisted quickly, laughing. "Someone's taught you something, sweetheart."

"Fort! Who would have found a better way than this?"

He hadn't tried to use his strength before, but now he pinned her down ruthlessly. "Such sweet faith you show in him," he hissed. "Your lover is he?"

She bared her teeth, fighting every ounce of his weight. "You . . . you . . . *toad!*"

He almost laughed that all her rage had resulted in such a mild epithet.

"Toad or not, it's me you have to deal with."

"I hate you."

"No you don't. You hate my world." He brought his mouth close to hers as if to kiss. "A side wager, Hippolyta."

Confusion turned her limp and she stared into his eyes. "What? You know I don't gamble. I hate gaming!"

"You dice with the devil all the time, sweet Amazon. What we do here is going to be for show, but if I can truly make you want me, you are not allowed to hate me."

She struggled again. *"Want* you? You must be mad!"

"The whole world seems to think so. Do you agree?"

"How can I not hate you?"

"That's so unchristian," he chided. "And you are a good Christian, aren't you? Pray about it. I'm sure you can overcome the sin."

She was still now—stiff with resentment, but still. "And when I thwart you, what do I win?"

"The freedom to hate?"

"I have that now."

Her words hurt him, but he hoped they were mainly the product of fear. He loosed his hold on her and traced the distorted line of her cheek. "What do you want then, little warrior?"

She twitched away from his hand. "Freedom from you. Forever. Never to see you again. Never to hear your voice. Never to have you touch me in any way."

Despite the hurt, he kept his voice calm. "High stakes indeed. I think I must raise mine. If I win, you must not refuse to see me, or hear me, or to let me touch you as a gentleman may touch a lady. So, on those terms, do we have a wager?"

She stared at him for a moment, weighing it. Then turned her head away. "Why not? Do your worst."

He did not make the obvious comment, but said instead, "A word of advice. The greatest folly in gaming is to be sure you hold the winning cards. Especially when you don't even know the rules of the game."

She struggled then, more furious than afraid.

He laughed just to goad her but he wasn't amused.

He wanted her. In this situation it seemed obscene to desire Portia, but her lithe strength, her flashing eyes behind the gilded mask, her raging *spirit,* had him painfully hard already.

He concentrated on the long dark wig, the plump cheeks,

and the bold face-paint, trying to see her as just a body. She was still Portia through and through. Her eyes shot fury at him, her red mouth was parted by angry gasps, and her small breasts pushed against the soft bodice, begging to be touched.

Gods.

Playing to the audience, he forced a kiss on her. She kept her mouth hard against his but he murmured, "Remember the twelve hundred guineas. Now we've struggled, it's time for me to start seducing you."

She twitched with alarm, fear and doubt in her eyes. He knew she was still not sure of her safety. "Trust me," he said.

It was too much to expect, of course. Her expression told him that she was wishing for a weapon.

With another laugh, he rolled off the bed and began a new play for the audience. They'd be happier to see a bit of skin, and it could have a desirable effect on Portia. He took off his coat, cravat, and shirt. He pulled the ribbon out of his hair to increase the wild effect.

She knelt up on the bed, tense and watchful. "What are you doing?" The plumpers distorted her voice, which was as well, but it was still rather firm for a fourteen-year-old.

"Hoping my beauty can impress you, *child*. Aren't you interested in your first man? Would you like to see more?" He put his hand to the buttons of his flap.

She scrambled backward in genuine alarm. "No!"

He undid one button to tease her, and she swung around to face in the opposite direction. He looked at her stiffly resentful back and suppressed a grin. Only Portia would have such spirit here.

He could see his destiny, and was beginning to accept it with delight, pitfalls and all.

But there were pitfalls. It wasn't going to be easy to woo Portia, and even when he won her as wife there would still be problems. He'd tied up his fortune in Bridgewater's scheme and if he didn't marry wealth he could even end up as his brother's pensioner, which wouldn't suit him at all.

And Portia wasn't just penniless, she was a positive sinkhole for money. If he didn't win this wager, she'd have cost him a small fortune without trying. When they married, she'd expect him to save her home, and then keep towing her brother out of River Tick. Doubtless the rest of her family would prove to be just as expensive.

He accepted it. It was clearly fate. Cupid's arrow. He didn't know how these things happened, but he knew he and Portia were linked now and for evermore. Fort believed he'd trapped Bryght into a commitment, but he'd just pushed him into accepting the inevitable.

Bryght told himself to concentrate on the immediate. He had to get his future bride through this with as little embarrassment as possible, and without revealing her identity. Yet at the same time he had to stir her desire so as to win their wager.

'Struth. He felt a strong inclination to beat his head against the lewdly painted wall!

He fell on the bed and snared her around the waist, rolling her back and under him. At the feel of his half-naked body, she let out a genuine squeal of alarm and struggled.

"Want to bite me, pretty one? I don't mind."

She bared her sharp white teeth and he thought she might actually try to take a lump out of his shoulder, but then she remembered their situation and looked to him for guidance.

"Beg for mercy," he mouthed.

"Oh, my lord, spare me!" she cried. Not an actress to match Peg Woffington, but not bad for a beginner.

"Alas, my pretty, I've paid six hundred for you. But I swear you'll enjoy your initiation." Then he mouthed, "Cry."

She rolled her eyes, but covered her face and started to wail.

He moved off her. She promptly rolled on her front and went into a full-blown paroxysm of grief, beating the bed with her fists, heaving and howling. It was over-acting of the most atrocious sort, but he thought it would have its effect.

Trying to keep a straight face, he patted her back. "Now, now, sweetheart, it won't be so bad. Stop crying."

She wailed louder. *"I want to go home!"*

That should set the stage for act one, he decided. Now he had to at least partly seduce Portia, both to make this convincing and to win their personal wager. The twelve hundred was nothing. He had to win that personal wager.

He had much on his side, much that she was denying. The energy, the magic, that sometimes sparked between two people from first meeting, was alive between them. He had known it from the first and fought it. Now he surrendered to the folly of it and turned his skills to making her surrender, too.

He eased onto the bed then suddenly covered her, head to toe. She stopped wailing and went rigid beneath him. He brushed away the false hair and kissed the back of her neck.

"Don't!" she gasped, and it was genuine.

"But I must," he murmured against her skin. "Isn't it sweet?" He ran his tongue along her shoulder, easing the gown off as he went. "As sweet as you . . ."

She clutched the front of the gown to stop it sliding further. "Please!"

It was right for the frightened child, but it wasn't acting. "Remember," he murmured, "you get to keep all your clothes on. Which is more than I do."

He felt her relax a bit. "That was your own choice," she hissed into the bed.

"Someone had to show the paying customers a bit of skin."

Her hands made fists. "London is foul, and all in it!"

He laughed against her skin and let his teeth graze her. "Considering the king and queen live here, sweeting, that could be seen as treason." He kissed down the top few inches of her spine and she shivered. It wasn't from fear of treason, either.

"Just do it!" she whispered.

"Too soon," he replied and eased off her a little, sliding his hand down to rub at the small of her back. He rubbed firmly there as he teased and tormented her upper back with his mouth.

He heard her breathing alter. Ah, Portia, one day we are going to do this as it should be done, and take it to its beautiful conclusion. Aloud, he whispered, "You are as sensitive as I dreamed, like the finest instrument."

"Or a hair-trigger pistol," she muttered.

He laughed and began to work his hand lower.

With a heave, she turned to avoid that, but his hand ended up in a much more interesting place. For the audience he said, "That's more like it, Hippolyta. I knew you'd come to like it." *Sotto voce* he added, "No, don't fight. Whimper."

Her eyes flashed outraged defiance, but she made a sound like an anxious puppy. It was surprisingly disconcerting and Bryght was strongly tempted to cuddle her. How the devil did men rape these creatures in truth? He'd never concerned himself over it much, and wasn't sure there was anything he could do about it, but now it bothered him.

Getting rid of Cuthbertson would end one foul supply. It wouldn't do anything, however, for other victims, or for frightened brides like Prestonly's poor wives.

He found his hand was stroking her belly in soft, comforting circles, and she was staring at him in wary confusion.

"There's nothing to be frightened of," he said aloud and whispered, "Trust me."

Perhaps there was the slightest trace of trust behind the mask. Daring to be gentle, he kissed her lightly on the lips before leaving the bed to inspect the items on the wall. He relieved one satyric male figure of the oil vial he held and returned to the bed, tipping oil onto his finger and breathing in the aroma.

As he thought. Musky, powerful, and sexy as all Hades if her instincts were attuned to it.

Ten

Portia's mind was all spinning confusion. During the auction she'd been prepared for the worst. Bryght's voice had unbalanced her so she had not known what to think, but when she'd realized Fort was there, she'd been sure of rescue.

But it had been Bryght who'd claimed her, and he had not freed her but brought her to this disgusting room.

Now they seemed to be involved in wagers. If she had it right, she'd get the ridiculous sum of twelve hundred guineas if she could act as if she wanted Bryght Malloren.

And she'd be free of him forever if she could do it by pure acting, without wanting him at all.

She tried to tell herself that would be easy, but she wasn't in the habit of deceiving herself. It was because he could stir desire in her that she needed so badly to escape London. He'd stirred wild desire in her in broad daylight and fully clothed. Now, half naked in the flickering lights he was a creature of her darkest dreams.

And surely more wicked, she reminded herself. After all, he was here in a brothel by choice. He clearly knew all sorts of lewd skills. And he was, of course, a gamester. He was here with her because of a wager!

She watched him warily. He was coming back toward the bed with a vial, tipping it onto his finger. . . .

He smiled, and before she could avoid it, touched his

finger just below her nose so that a tendril of perfume crept into her. She could not identify the smells in it but it was similar to the incense in the air, and it was wicked.

She scrubbed at the tainted spot, but the smell could not be banished.

Pretend, but don't surrender, she reminded herself.

She watched his every move. She was beginning to understand what he meant when he said that she did not even know the rules of this game of chance, but surely she could control her own responses.

Bare-chested, his dark hair loose to his shoulders, his beauty enriched by the wildness of it, he smiled at her. "Don't look so terrified, Hippolyta. You're going to love every moment of this."

She eased away from him. She didn't want to love every moment of this. She wanted to pretend to surrender and have it over with.

As long as he did not accept that surrender.

What if it were a trick? What if when he persuaded her to say she wanted him, he took the permission she gave?

He said to trust him, but she didn't.

Only a fool would trust a rake like Bryght Malloren.

She expected him to cover her again, using his size and heat to melt her senses, but he disconcerted her by sitting cross-legged on the bed by her feet. He grasped one ankle to pull her slightly closer. She let out an involuntary squeak and wriggled her skirts into decency.

He poured oil onto his hands, put down the vial, then began to work the oil into her right foot. He stretched and stroked it, giving each toe special, delicate attention, running his thumbs up her instep so her foot arched to him all by itself. A cloud of the spicy, sultry perfume crept up her body, accompanied by the softening pleasure of his touch.

Oh dear.

She tried to pull her foot away. "What are you doing?"

His grip was too tight. "Exploring you," he said, resting her heel on his thigh, concentrating on her toes, his dark hair falling forward to conceal his face.

By heaven, but he was beautiful. . . .

No, Portia!

He worked meticulously from one toe to the next. "Before we are finished, my Amazon, I intend to know every inch of you, and pleasure most of them."

Portia shivered in earnest. "I don't like this."

He looked up, shadowed and mysterious, magnificent as the ceiling gods, and as powerful. "Liar." His voice was soft and deep as the night sky. "With me you will find the pleasures from your most secret, heated dreams, and you will admit the truth—that you are mad for me."

He wasn't acting. "No!"

He smiled with quiet confidence. "Oh, yes."

Portia again tried to escape but his grip tightened. She flung herself back, her arm over her eyes and sought complete control over her body. His clever fingers were having an effect, though. If he carried on this way he might make his words true.

He raised her leg a little and kissed her toes as he began to massage the oil into her heel, then up the sensitive tendon to her calf. He kissed his way to her instep, and her eyes drifted shut at the sweetness of it . . . but then she forced them open.

She would not give him any reaction. Not a trace.

Then the wetness of his tongue traveled along her foot and his teasing fingers reached the back of her knee.

She squirmed.

No, she wouldn't!

But it was not just her foot and knee. Though he was not touching anywhere else, other parts of her body were heating, vibrating, desiring. . . .

How could her body betray her so?

"How beautiful are thy feet," he said, and it sounded like a quotation. "Delicate, arched, sensitive. Like the rest of you." He was using his deep voice to cast a spell on her. "Sensitive, all of you, arching to my touch . . ."

Portia arched before she knew it. She sucked in a breath and prayed for strength.

He shifted and she was relieved, but it was only to begin the same onslaught on her other foot.

"Your limbs are slender but strong," he murmured. "Your skin is smooth as finest Chinese silk. When I stroke the silk you feel it everywhere, even in your most secret places. Places where you ache to be touched. . . . You are supple as a willow, graceful as a doe as you move in your desire. Fighting with you, little warrior, was pure pleasure. Victory and sweet surrender will be heaven on earth. For both of us . . ."

Touch, perfume, voice, words—they were gradually melting Portia's bones, her muscles, and her resistance. She tried to remind herself that this was all clever tricks and acting, but even so, she ached, she moved.

His hand slid firmly up her calf and down again, and she took a sobbing breath. He rolled her onto her front and stroked the back of her legs, light behind the knees, harder on the calves but always over her skirts, never under.

Portia buried her head in her hands and tried to remember why it was so important to both deny that this was pleasant, and pretend that this was pleasant.

His hands moved up, over her buttocks, and onto the small of her back, to massage there with deep strength.

"You can feel it into the bones and beyond, can't you, little cat? Stretch like a cat. Purr for me. . . ."

And Portia did stretch—she couldn't help it—but she stopped herself from purring. "Enough!" she gasped. "My lord, please . . . !"

"Not yet, not quite yet, but almost, yes?"

He turned her again in a tangle of black hair and skirts and his clever hands brushed her breasts.

Portia wriggled away at that, but even as she did so, her body moved in a way of its own, and he laughed. "Yes, your body wants me, but do you?"

Thinking only of their personal wager, Portia cried, "No!"

He pulled a face at her, and then she didn't know the truth. *Was* he trying to seduce her, or was this all pure acting? If anything, that made it worse. Here she was, wax melting to a puddle in his hands, and he still had his wits about him.

Well, she could keep her wits, too. She draped her arms around his naked shoulders. "Oh, my lord, I lied. I want you. Take me! But if you do," she muttered into his ear, "I swear I will kill you."

"Trust me," he whispered and twisted her for a kiss.

It was a kiss such as she had never imagined—an assault on her senses and her will involving far more than their mouths. His naked arms held her close, and her arms and hands had only his skin to contact—silky skin, warm over muscle and bone. Portia had never before experienced so much body.

The sultry perfume was all over both of them, blending with the smell of his skin and the taste of his mouth so that she couldn't cling on to sanity.

She was on her back now, with him on top—heavy, hot. He was touching her breasts and creating a mad yearning.

She couldn't remember why this was wrong, why they shouldn't . . .

When he released her mouth to trail hot kisses around her cheeks, her ears, her neck, her shoulders, she kissed him back, kissed and tasted every piece of delicious skin that passed her lips.

He nibbled her ear lobe. "Your hips. Move your hips."

Portia was about to say she didn't know how, when he stroked swiftly over her breasts and her hips moved of their own accord. She exaggerated it, telling herself that it was acting, but she knew it wasn't.

She ached inside and her body sought relief of that ache like a flower seeking the sun.

She who had never known a man, knew what could be, what should be. If it hadn't been for the watchers, she would have demanded it here, now, with no regard for virtue or morality.

"Yes, my beautiful one. Dance for me, show me that you want the gift of Venus. . . ."

And Portia danced. Her whole body moved to the rhythm of his touch. Her heart thundered, and she breathed as in the wildest, whirling jig. . . .

"You want me, little one. Yes?"

"Yes!" she gasped. "Oh, yes!"

"Bravo," he murmured, and then was gone.

Portia came suddenly to sanity and watched in despairing astonishment as he paraded around the bed, bowing to the unseen audience. Dimly, she even heard applause.

Her body was still in ferment, stirred almost to madness by his skills, but her emotion was pure rage. She'd be damned if she'd let Bryght Malloren have it all his own way!

She sat up and putting on a girlish voice, cried, "My lord! Please! Do not desert me! Give me all of you!"

He turned, surprised admiration flickering in his eyes. "You're too young, sweeting. Come back in a year or two and I'll give you the next lesson."

"Oh no!" she cried, getting well into her part. "You cannot be so cruel! You have set a fire burning in me and it must be quenched!"

With alarm, she discovered that she did not know what was acting and what was true.

He set one knee on the bed and leaned close to her. "Don't tempt fortune, little one. I will make you burn again, my reckless Hippolyta and quench the flames, too. But not just yet."

It was a promise, and Portia moved back.

Immediately, his hand slid around her neck, restraining her just inches away. "I won my bet, didn't I?"

She wanted to say no, but honesty would not let her. "It will do you no good. I still won't be your mistress."

"Some fates cannot be avoided, *petite*. Remember that." He released her and moved away.

Portia resolved to leave London on the morrow. At crack of dawn. On foot if necessary. With Fort here, the debt would soon be settled.

Fort!

Fort must have recognized her in order to have entered the bidding. How was she ever to face him? But she must face him in order to sort out Oliver's problems and get them both out of the evil entanglements of London before it was too late.

Portia looked quickly at Bryght, who was putting on his clothes again. Had he meant it when he said he'd give her the twelve hundred guineas? It was an enormous sum, but would make all the difference. Even if Fort wouldn't help, the bank would surely take a mortgage for the remainder of the debt. It would be much easier to pay it off, too.

She almost felt she should be grateful. Bryght had rescued her from worse men while leaving her virtue intact. By accident or design he'd solved her family's problems, too.

Accident, for sure.

This whole event was probably part of his plan to seduce her. He'd think after an experience such as this she'd be ready to accept any offer, even a dishonorable one. If so, he had misplayed his hand. Tonight he had shown her that she could not trust her virtue and willpower once he turned his powers and skills against her.

That resolved her to avoid him forever.

She slid off the bed and straightened her twisted garments. She could almost feel again skillful hands roaming over her body with just two layers of cloth between them and her skin.

What would it be like skin to skin?

She shook her head. No.

Bryght was now dressed, though not nearly as neatly as he had been. He looked at her, then suddenly went to the bed and ripped off the sheet. He handed it to her and she gratefully wrapped it around herself.

But she didn't want to be grateful to him.

He opened the door for her with courtly grace and she walked through expecting to have to face those evil, avid eyes again. The entertainment was over, however, and the room had settled to other matters. Drinking and gaming were going on, whilst on the dais, semi-naked women were striking lewd attitudes.

Portia turned quickly away. They, too, were acting sexual abandon just as she had done.

Except that in her case it hadn't been acting, whereas in Bryght's case it had. Portia realized she hated him for that.

A few people looked at her and grinned, but generally nothing was made of their emergence. A very fat, sour-faced man sat nearby. "I give you your victory, my lord," said the man, handing over a slip of paper and eying Portia. "But it was a tame show. Damme if it wasn't."

Portia clutched the sheet closer, feeling fouled by the look in his eye.

Bryght merely said, "I recommend subtlety to you, Mr. Prestonly, next time you attempt a virgin," and steered Portia past the man and into the corridor.

Mirabelle came forward. "Come along, my dear, and we will settle accounts."

Bryght followed and Portia turned on him. "I want nothing more of you."

"You need my help, Hippolyta."

"I do not! If you had the sensitivity of a . . . a *snail*, you'd go away!"

"Toads? Snails?" He grinned lightly. "My dear, you need help with your money. If you take it home your brother will dispose of it almost immediately." He turned to the madam. "I'll handle it all. I'll send you your cut, and pay hers into a bank. I'll take care of Cuthbertson, too."

Mirabelle's brows rose. "You are going to ruin a very profitable little business, my lord."

"I doubt you'll starve. You will see her safely home?"

"Very well."

Bryght took out a gold and enamel snuff box and delicately took a pinch. "And you would not care to spend time in the pillory, would you, Mirabelle, or be whipped at the cart's tail?"

The madam's eyes narrowed dangerously. "Threats, my lord?"

"Promises. You must take great care of her, and no one must even suspect who Hippolyta is."

"I do not know, and have no wish to."

"One day, you will."

Portia looked between them in bewilderment. Why did Mirabelle look maliciously amused? "Far be it from me," said the madam, "to sully such perfect bliss."

"What are you talking about?" Portia demanded.

Bryght replied. "We're talking about keeping your identity concealed."

"No one would recognize me like this," she protested, but then Portia remembered that he obviously had and so had Fort. She clutched the sheet tighter.

"No one will identify you," said Bryght, "unless suspicions are raised."

Portia shivered. "You knew."

"It was the name."

"Fort knew."

"I told him." Before she could demand an explanation of that, he said, "No one will guess the truth if you behave as normal."

She stared at him. "Just go home and act as if this had never happened?"

"What else? Very little did."

"Very little! It doesn't seem that way to me!"

He just smiled in a way that made her want to shoot him. "Mirabelle will make sure you are safe." He bowed to her with elegance. *"A bientot, petite."* With that he returned to the company.

Portia watched him go with a sense of loss, for despite

his words, he would not see her again soon. She was leaving London.

Mirabelle took Portia to her parlor. "Twenty percent to me, and three hundred to Cuthbertson. Your share of Bryght's bid, my dear, is one hundred and eighty guineas. Hardly paltry for such light work."

Portia thought with satisfaction that it was a great deal more, and even from the briefest acquaintance with the fat man, she knew Bryght was correct. She need feel no guilt at taking his money, though her conscience insisted that the wager had been less than honest.

Mirabelle took Portia to the bedroom. "You will want to dress."

As soon as she was alone, Portia looked in a mirror, wondering what she would see. She saw a wild-haired stranger who had panted for Bryght Malloren. She shuddered at the memory, spat out the plumpers, tore off the mask, and unpinned the long, black wig.

There, her hair rather tightly dressed to her head, was Portia St. Claire again. Or was it? Portia St. Claire did not have such reddened lips—and the redness now was passion more than paint. She did not have such knowing, darkened eyes. She did not reek of a sultry perfume.

Portia ran to the wash basin. She scrubbed her face of paint, then stripped off the tawdry silk and adornments. As best she could she washed all trace of perfume from her skin.

Her shift still stank of it and so she left it off, and put her petticoat and stays against her skin, despite the itch they caused. She pulled on her sensible cotton stockings and her dimity gown and returned to the mirror. There at last was Portia St. Claire, spinster, of Overstead Manor, Dorset.

Still, at least, possessed of most of her virtue.

* * *

Bryght wanted to stay with Portia and see her home, but she was stretched to the breaking point. It was hardly surprising. He was feeling fragile himself. Quite apart from an uncomfortable state of arousal, he had been plunged into a depth of emotion he had not thought possible.

Had he ever thought he had been in love with Nerissa? Nothing he'd felt for her had been like this. Nerissa had been desirable for her beauty, her supposed virtue, and her eminent suitability to be a wife. His choice of her had been made on purely logical grounds.

Portia was simply necessary, and his feelings toward her had all the subtlety of a starving man's feelings toward a roast of beef. If it hadn't been for the voyeurs, he might not have found the strength to leave her untouched.

It was better, safer, to let Mirabelle see Portia home, and it would reinforce his disinterest in Hippolyta if he returned to his card game.

As he threaded his way through the noisy room, however, problems swirled in his head. Cuthbertson needed to be handled but any open move against the man might cause questions.

Something had to be done about Oliver Upcott.

Bridgewater would have to be notified that Bryght's ability to support him further was lessened.

Plague take it, but it was a mess, so why was he finding it hard not to grin like a perfect fool?

He casually took his place at the card table, aware of intrigued looks from his friends. Nothing was said, however. Prestonly glowered at him, and though Bryght smiled back, his feelings about the man were similar. Perhaps he could take Prestonly for the rest of Portia's five thousand pound debt.

That would be satisfying.

But at the end of a few hands, Bryght had actually lost a little. He called a halt and ordered wine, taking the opportunity to rise from the table and move a few steps away.

Could he trust Mirabelle to take care of Portia properly? She surely knew the perils of crossing a Malloren. . . .

Andover joined him. "What was all that about?"

Bryght sipped the port. "A wager."

"Indeed?" said Andover skeptically. "Of your own making. It's not like you to take a man like Prestonly seriously."

"I had my reasons."

"I don't doubt it." Andover, too, sipped his wine and mischief glimmered in his eyes. "I think of a hopeless gamester, a sister, and one of Cuthbertson's debtors. . . ."

Bryght flicked him a glance. "Think no more."

Andover blinked. "My dear, my mind is a perfect blank. But a thought does intrude, alas. How are you going to guard against the next time?"

Bryght tapped a finger against his glass. "That had occurred to me." He shrugged and returned to the table. "Let us resume, gentlemen."

Bryght put all thoughts of Portia St. Claire out of his mind, intent on milking Prestonly of a fortune. But then he lost five more hands. He was forced to acknowledge that he couldn't keep his mind on the play at all. Hell, he and Andover had lost the hundreds they'd won earlier and were now down another three hundred.

He threw down his cards. "I'm for home, gentlemen. Do you want my place, Barclay?"

"The night's still young, my lord," said Sir William in surprise.

"You owe me a chance to make up my losses, my lord," said Mr. Prestonly, fingering his winnings.

Bryght rose. "I'll gladly play you another night, Mr. Prestonly." As Bryght passed Andover's seat, his friend murmured, "For home, or Dresden Street?"

Bryght stopped. "You, my friend, are going to become a dead bore."

Barclay overheard, and interjected with surprise, "With the emphasis on *dead?* What's up?"

Bryght laughed. "I am not in the habit of killing my friends."

"Then do you wish a friend's company?" Andover asked.

"No, I really am for home."

Bryght meant it. He was tempted to go and see if Portia was safe, but she wouldn't want such an intrusion now. He could wait until tomorrow.

Back at Malloren House, however, Bryght's mind was still active, circling around financial arrangements. Prestonly had given him a draft on his bank and it should go into the safe. He decided he'd send Mirábelle and Cuthbertson their cut now.

He was aware that this was illogical and even dangerous, but he wanted this affair over with as soon as possible.

He arranged for a suitably heavy escort for the money, then took a corridor that led to the back of the house. It led, in fact, to the suite of offices from which the business of the marquisate was carried out. Most people were unaware that this business was Bryght's major occupation and delight.

When Bryght had finished his schooling and returned from his Grand Tour, he had plunged merrily into the social life of London—in particular into the gaming that went on everywhere. He enjoyed the challenge, particularly of games of skill, and was good at it. For a young man on a modest allowance, the winnings had come in useful, too.

Rothgar had been surprisingly tolerant, perhaps because Bryght generally won. Bryght amused himself sometimes trying to imagine what would have happened if he'd gone to Rothgar one day burdened with a massive gaming debt.

It was not, in fact, a particularly amusing thought.

But after some months, when the thrill was beginning to pall, Rothgar had started to introduce Bryght to a more interesting kind of speculation.

Investments.

And Bryght had fallen in love. He master-minded the Malloren financial affairs from a sense of responsibility, but he would have done it for the sheer excitement. Shipping, cartage, goods from the Orient and Africa, new ventures in England and the Americas. . . . It was the best high-stakes game in the world and England was at the heart of it. Through Bryght's skillful management, the Mallorens were at the heart of it, too, bringing vast profits and substantial power.

Led by Zeno, and shielding the candle from the draft, Bryght entered the outer office where four tidy desks awaited the clerks who labored here during the day. Most people would be surprised at just how businesslike the Mallorens were about their affairs. Ten men worked in these offices by day—clerks, accountants, and a lawyer—but at night the place was deserted.

Not tonight, though. Bryght realized at last how strange it was the Zeno had preceded him instead of keeping his usual place at his heel. Of course he had. The phlegmatic animal had been longing to be in these rooms for hours.

For when Bryght entered the inner sanctum a branch of candles already illuminated his desk and the man working there. He was in shirt-sleeves, but the lace at throat and wrists was of the finest quality. His dark hair was tied neatly back in a bag-wig and he wore a large ruby signet on his right hand.

The Marquess of Rothgar looked up and surveyed his brother. "Trouble?"

Another soft *woof* announced a paler shape uncurling from a spot by Rothgar's feet. Zeno loped over to entwine himself comfortably with his mate, Boudicca.

Bryght could not imagine how he had missed Zeno's enthusiasm for this meeting. He was growing positively muddle-headed, and now he had a problem. Bryght would have given a great deal not to have Rothgar involved in this, but there was no avoiding it now.

"Just a debt to be paid." He went to a safe and unlocked it to take out a bag of money. He counted out four hundred and twenty guineas and put them into two separate pouches. It was, unfortunately, a startlingly large amount of money.

"Saints preserve us," said Rothgar mildly. "Do you mean you are losing?"

"No, actually, I won." Bryght told Zeno to stay, spun on his heel and went to give the pouches to the servants along with directions.

He paused then, tempted to go upstairs. He was in no fit state to handle his brother, but delaying a discussion with Rothgar would just increase the marquess's curiosity.

Though Bryght was the second son, six years separated them. It was not a great age difference now they were men, but it encompassed more than years.

Bryght's early years had been idyllic, but Rothgar's had been marred by his mother's madness and her murder of her second child. Years later, the death of Bryght's parents had brought grief into an otherwise carefree boyhood, but it had been even worse for Rothgar. At nineteen, he had become responsible not only for the marquisate but for five young siblings.

Rothgar had his own reasons for being strongly protective of his family, and Bryght his own reasons for resisting it. Since they were close in age, the paternalism had never been as strong between them, but it was there. Bryght knew that Rothgar let nothing to do with his family escape his notice.

At times it was a damnable nuisance.

There was no choice, however. He headed back to the offices.

Eleven

Portia returned to her rooms in a coach with two of Mirabelle's hefty servants in attendance. They were disconcertingly proper, and even came in with her in case Mick was still there.

There was only Oliver, tied, gagged, and bound.

The men would have untied him, but Portia sent them away, wanting to get rid everything to do with tonight's events. Then she ran to get a knife and free her brother. As soon as his mouth was free he choked out, "Portia, my God! I'm so sorry!"

"It's all right." She sawed at the rope around his wrists. "It's all right. Nothing terrible happened.

He rubbed the rope marks. "But Cuthbertson?"

She was freeing his feet. "Has been paid." She decided impulsively not to tell him the whole. "Bryght Malloren saved me. He bought me."

He grabbed her shoulders. "And nothing happened?"

She smiled through tears. "Nothing happened."

He hugged her close. "Oh, thank God! I've been desperate. I was imagining. . . . Portia, I swear, I swear, I will not play again!"

She pushed back to look at him. "I've heard that before, I think."

He was sober and serious. "This time I mean it. I've

come to my senses. It's not that I love gaming so much any more. But I kept thinking I could find an easy solution to my problem, have everything back just as it was. But I can't. I've made a mess, and we'll all have to live with it, but I won't make it worse again."

Portia kissed him, for at last he did seem resolute. "Then perhaps tonight was worth it. And, Oliver, Fort is here. He . . ." she went hot, ". . . he was there. At Mirabelle's."

"Does he know?" His voice wavered a bit.

Portia grimaced. "I think so. He tried to buy me, too, presumably with the same intent as Bryght."

Oliver sank his head in his hands. "He'll flay me. . . ." But then he stood and stretched his stiffened limbs. "Oh well, another bullet to bite. I deserve it. I think it would be best if I go now."

"Go to Fort? It's midnight."

"Early hours in town, love, and I'd rather get it over with. I doubt I can sleep after all this. If he's not in yet, I'll wait until he comes home. I want this settled so we can get you safe back to Overstead."

She shared that wish. "I'm sure Fort will give you the loan, and then we'll be able to leave tomorrow."

She suddenly remembered the twelve hundred guineas. She couldn't see how to tell Oliver about it without revealing more about tonight than she wished. Well, surely Fort would give Oliver the whole loan, and then later she'd explain the money somehow and pay off part of the debt.

"I'd better dress." Oliver hugged her again. "You are the best and bravest of sisters and I will not fail you in future."

He went purposefully into his bedroom and Portia sat wearily, but with a degree of content. The affair had not gone as badly as it might, and it did seem to have shocked

Oliver into his senses. She hoped Fort did ring a peal over him to complete the job.

And with any luck, they could be on a coach to Dorset tomorrow. She need never see Bryght Malloren again.

She rested her head on her hand and fought tears. They were just tears of weariness. She *didn't* want to see him again. Even if his actions tonight had been to her advantage, he was a rake and a gamester, and the only offer he'd ever made her was an insulting one.

She sent Oliver on his way with a cheerful, confident smile and a teasing reminder to lock the outside door properly, then latched their door after him. She roamed the room restlessly for a while, mind whirling with too many disordered thoughts, then collapsed into a chair to await her brother's return.

She was exhausted, but totally unable to sleep. She tried to discipline her mind, but all she could think of was a man's touch, a man's beauty in flickering candlelight, and a kindled desire that would never come to full flame.

Bryght returned to the office to find Rothgar had poured two glasses of port. "Am I to have an explanation of the mysterious purchase?" Rothgar asked.

Bryght leaned with assumed carelessness against the corner of the desk and sipped the wine. "I see no need. It is not a matter that effects the family." Not yet, at least. He supposed marrying Portia would affect the family, but not unpleasantly. . . . Unless tonight's business became known.

"Over four hundred?"

"Of my own money, Bey." And that wasn't strictly true. Bryght had lent his ready cash to Bridgewater before the duke went north. But he'd soon have more.

Except that it occurred to him that he was deep in debt at the moment. He'd just paid out four-twenty, thinking it was coming from Prestonly's wager, but he'd promised Portia the whole twelve hundred. He didn't begrudge it, but it had been strangely careless of him not to even think of it. With his losses at the table tonight, he was over seven hundred guineas in debt.

Not an alarming amount, but more than he could ever remember owing.

'Struth, if he won Portia St. Claire and it turned out that lucky in love did mean unlucky at cards he was in a pretty pickle. He suppressed a grin. Unless he wanted his brother to guess all, he'd best keep his wits about him.

Rothgar said, "I am as vulnerable to curiosity as any other man, Bryght. Are you going to torment me this way?"

Bryght couldn't help but grin. "Yes."

Rothgar smiled as he shrugged. "So be it."

"And don't employ your busy network to discover what I have been up to."

"So be it," said Rothgar again, but Bryght cursed silently. He knew his brother would keep his word and not pry, but he also knew that he'd made yet another error. He'd told Rothgar that he had something to hide.

Damn.

He'd thought Nerissa had turned his heart and mind to ice, but Portia St. Claire seemed to be thawing it to slush, with all the intelligence one could expect of slush. . . .

Rothgar spoke as if there were nothing amiss. "I have come up to Town for the discussion of the war with Spain and the financing of it. I intend to stay here for some weeks. I note here some trouble in Bridgewater's affairs." He indicated the ledger he had been reading when Bryght came in. "His debt load seems heavy, and there's no certainty he'll get the Bill. I've heard Brooke on the subject and he virtually has a seizure at the mere mention of canals. If the waterway is stopped at Manchester, Bridgewater will be bankrupt. Do you still have faith in that project?"

Bryght snapped his wits into order. "Yes, of course. It's the way of the future."

"It will change England forever."

"Gads, Bey, I never thought you of that stamp. Man must progress. People like Brooke would have us all still living in moated castles."

"There are times," said the marquess contemplatively, "when it would be very comforting to live in a moated castle. Such as when the duke's creditors come howling to the door."

"The family's investment in the canal is moderate."

"Your personal investment is not. You've become a shareholder. You're liable for any and all debts."

Bryght stiffened. How the devil had Rothgar discovered that? "That is my concern."

"In this family, nothing is entirely a personal concern." Rothgar leaned back. "I wonder why you would take such a risk."

"Profit?" asked Bryght lightly.

"Are you trying to do better for yourself than for the family?"

Bryght felt an absurd flash of guilt for perhaps deep within him there was a desire to out-do Rothgar. He didn't know. "I'm more cautious with the funds of others. It would be madness for you to become a shareholder, but you could increase your loans to Bridgewater. He'd welcome it."

"I'm sure he would." Rothgar contemplated Bryght for a moment, but then abruptly switched topic. "How are the cotton manufactories in Manchester progressing? Are they obtaining adequate supplies from India and the Americas?"

So Bryght found himself in a damnably unwelcome inquisition of the financial affairs of the House of Malloren, of the nation, and even of the world. Not that there was anything wrong with his knowledge of those affairs, but he was not in the mood to concentrate.

Had it been wise to trust Mirabelle to see Portia safely home? Would Portia have taken care not to be seen leaving such a place of ill-repute? What would her brother have done and said when she returned? What had she told him . . . ?

"Bryght, do you have concerns about the Northumberland property?"

Bryght realized he'd allowed his thoughts to distract him entirely and failed to answer a question. "No, of course not. The new drainage system is Brand's concern not mine, but the reported yields last year were up to expectations. There's a good chance that coal will be found there, too. It's a sound investment."

Rothgar moved on to some foreign dealings and Bryght forced himself to pay attention. He could plead tiredness, but as he had always been a night-owl Rothgar would be bound to find that peculiar. Rothgar himself seemed to have an inhuman ability to do without sleep entirely at times.

The clocks were striking three when the marquess closed the final ledger. "And your personal affairs?"

"What?" asked Bryght, who felt squeezed dry, and could only think his brother meant Portia.

"You had plans not long ago to buy Candleford Park."

"Oh. No longer."

"You were, as I remember, quite keen."

"Put down the scalpel, Bey. You know damn well that estate was intended for Nerissa."

The marquess studied him with dark, hooded eyes. "And you are no longer interested?"

"Certainly not for Nerissa." Bryght was startled, however, by a clear vision of Portia at Candleford.

He had always seen Candleford as a bower for Nerissa. It was an old, lush estate with ancient spreading trees and a solid house of mellow bricks. He had envisioned Nerissa there, sun-dappled under a tree, just being peacefully beautiful, surrounded in time by peacefully beautiful children.

Now, thinking of the estate, he saw Portia racing across the lawns, fiery hair flying loose of its pins, chasing a laughing scampish child with the same burnished hair. . . .

"I hear talk of a Mrs. Findlayson," said Rothgar.

Bryght was genuinely startled. Jenny Findlayson was far from his thoughts. "You shouldn't listen to gossip, Bey."

"But it is so informative. There will be some other lady one day, and you will want a home for her."

Unspoken between them was the fact that, because of his mother's madness, the marquess had ceded the duty of continuing the line to Bryght.

"As you have doubtless discovered," said Bryght coolly, "at the moment my funds are tied up in Bridgewater's affairs. I doubt Candleford will stay on the market long."

"We could buy it for the family and you could take it over when convenient. It's a fine place, and well situated."

"Perhaps." But Bryght did not want his home at Rothgar's hands. He received a handsome share of the family's profits for his labors, but did not want charity. He realized this damnable inquisition could have waited until tomorrow. It had been designed to wear him down so he would reveal more than he intended, and it might have worked.

He rose to his feet. "Keep your fingers out of my personal affairs, Bey." With that short comment, he left the room.

He only realized a moment later that he had shut the door on Zeno. There was no complaint. Ah well, moral duty could only take any male so far.

Beowulf Malloren, Marquess of Rothgar, leant back thoughtfully in his chair and two dogs sat up to rest their heads on his knees. He played absently with their ears as he considered matters. "Not Nerissa, then," he said to them. "But I didn't expect that after recent events. And not the Findlayson, thank God. But some other woman. Any suggestions, Zeno?"

Zeno had his eyes contentedly closed.

"Such admirable discretion. A problem, whoever she is, for he's guarding the matter from me."

The marquess's siblings had a lamentable tendency to think he would interfere between them and their attachments. Well, perhaps he would if he thought them unadvisable. At least part of his purpose in coming to Town was to look into the matter of the rich widow who was throwing out lures to Bryght.

Last year, Bryght's attachment to Nerissa St. Claire had been a problem, especially as the young woman had made clear advances to Rothgar behind Bryght's back. It was surprising how a clever man could be a fool over a woman.

Rothgar had always handled Bryght with a great deal of care, understanding many of the forces that shaped him. They had an amicable relationship but it was shadowed. It was shadowed mainly by Bryght's mother, which would have distressed her.

Gabrielle, Marchioness of Rothgar, had been a charming, generous, warm-hearted woman who had brought joy and laughter to a house shadowed by murder and madness. All the world, including her children, had adored her, but perhaps Bryght—her oldest child—had been closest to her heart.

Rothgar had appreciated his stepmother's qualities, though he knew he had never treated her with the warmth she wanted. Perhaps, even when too young to understand, he had been responding to her own ambivalent feelings.

He was a child, and Gabrielle reached out to all children, especially sad ones. But he was also the quiet moody son of the madwoman who had murdered a newborn and caused such grief to her husband, and he carried that woman's blood.

Gabrielle had treated her stepson with as much love and care as her own children, but she had never concealed the fact that she did not think his blood should be passed on. She had raised Bryght to provide the next generation of Mallorens.

That was perfectly reasonable, but it had gone further.

She had wished her stepson dead.

It had only been the once, as far as anyone knew. Rothgar—Lord Grafton then—had been brought home to the Abbey deathly ill of a fever picked up during a rash adventure on the seamy side of London. Gabrielle, his father, and Bryght had been by his bed, and he had known he was dying.

Gabrielle said, "Perhaps it is for the best."

His father said, "No," but without great conviction.

Bryght exclaimed, "No! I don't want Bey to die. Don't wish him dead." He had flung himself on the bed as if to protect his older brother from harm.

Perhaps it was duty, but Rothgar thought it was guilt over that death-wish that had driven his stepmother to drag him back from death by will alone. She had nursed him, but more importantly she had berated him, refusing to allow him to slip away. At times he had wanted to beg her to let him go, but he was too weak even for that.

By the time he was strong enough to speak, she was ill herself, for she caught his illness. No one was able to drag her back from death, though the marquess tried. Then he, too, succumbed. Rothgar had risen from his sickbed responsible for his parents' deaths, and responsible for holding his family together.

He had never let anyone know that he had been aware of that crucial conversation.

However, he suspected that Bryght carried a little of his mother's guilt, for though he hadn't wished his brother dead at that moment, he must have wished later that Rothgar had died rather than his parents. Certainly Gabrielle's clear desire that Bryght marry and produce a future marquess now had the power of a sacred duty.

Rothgar approved, for he knew Bryght was well-suited to marry. He liked women and children, and was generally patient and willing to compromise. There had always been a danger, however, that in his desire to fulfill his mother's dreams to the letter, he would choose with his head rather than his heart.

At least the Findlayson seemed safely out of the running, and Nerissa was both married and unmasked.

But the new, mysterious candidate for Bryght's hand was a powerful one.

For as they had gone through the ledgers of accounts and investments, Rothgar had deliberately made several mistakes, and Bryght—sharp-brained Bryght to whom figures and facts were life-blood—had not even noticed.

Rothgar extinguished the candles thoughtfully and left the offices. Despite Bryght's warning, he would have to investigate matters.

When they entered the hall Zeno gave a *woof* that was much sharper than usual, particularly for night-time when he knew he was not allowed to make noise other than to sound an alarm.

Rothgar looked around, but there was nothing amiss.

The dog loped over to the front door and waited there.

Rothgar followed. "He's gone out, has he?" He opened the door and looked at the chilly rain. "Are you sure?"

Zeno gave what seemed suspiciously like a sigh and slid out into the chilly dark.

Rothgar closed the heavy door thoughtfully. He'd give a great deal if Zeno could submit a written report tomorrow.

Bryght was on his way to Dresden Street.

He had intended to go to bed. In fact, he was exhausted which was unusual for him, but even as he climbed the stairs, thoughts of Portia had jangled in his mind and he had known he could not sleep until he was sure of her safety. He had gone to his room to get a heavy cloak and to put on boots, and had then returned downstairs and left the house.

The streets were mostly quiet at this dead hour, for there was an icy rain and even the skulking predators had burrowed into their hovels. A stinking night-soil cart rattled by, hauling off excrement to dump into the river. Once Bryght passed a watchman, patrolling with his bell and lantern. The man peered at him suspiciously, clearly wondering why any honest body would be out in such weather at such a time.

Bryght ignored him, but was perfectly aware that he was acting the lovesick fool. If Rothgar found out he'd die laughing, or clap him in an asylum. Even under Nerissa's thrall Bryght had not behaved like this.

But his feelings for Nerissa had not been like this.

There was only the slightest click of claws to warn him before Zeno appeared dark, wet, and silent at his side.

"Damnation," said Bryght. "I suppose you announced to all that I had gone out again."

Zeno just snuffled, head down against the rain.

"If you don't care for the weather, you could have stayed at home with your lovely mate. But I suppose she's not in heat yet. It must be convenient to have times when you are not pulled toward her."

The dog ignored him.

"A taste of the fruit can be fatal, though," Bryght mused. "Having experienced Portia's passion, I am addicted as madly, as insanely, as an opium eater. Will it kill me, do you think?"

Bryght laughed and abandoned the unproductive conversation, abandoned, too, unproductive speculation about the state of his heart. He was bewitched by something that could neither be explained nor controlled and he was happy to surrender.

He arrived at the house and saw candlelight in an upper room. He had rather hoped to find the place peaceful and dark, for then he would have no excuse to intrude.

Why would there be a light so many hours after Portia should have gone to bed?

He tried the door.

He expected to find it locked, but it opened, increasing

his concern. He entered the dark, narrow hallway, all senses alert for trouble. Finding none, he gave Zeno a quiet command to stay by the door and moved further into the chilly house. This reminded him a little of his visit to Maidenhead. He hadn't sensed trouble then, and had found a great deal— Nerissa's letter, and a dangerous Amazon.

If he'd not met Portia there, his life would still be orderly. But if he'd not met Portia there, tonight she would have been raped by Steenholt or D'Ebercall in front of twenty salivating voyeurs.

He climbed the stairs as quietly as his boots allowed. He could not hear even a trace of conversation from the upper floor, which was strange for this house was not particularly sturdily built. He could hear the scrabbling of mice, and the ticking of a clock in a downstairs room.

He came to the door that must lead into the lighted room and hesitated. It was more than likely that opening this door would change his life forever.

He shrugged and tried the knob. The door was latched from the inside. That was as it should be, but his nerves told him all was not well. He took out a pen-knife and inserted it through the crack where the door met the jamb. The latch flipped up easily. 'Struth, but she should have more security than this.

He pushed the door carefully in case of squeaks, but it opened silently and a guttering candle showed him Portia slumped in a chair. For a heart-stopping moment he thought she was dead. Then he saw that she was asleep there in her clothes.

Where was her damned brother?

He closed the door gently, and walked over to her.

Small, light, and with a face relaxed by exhaustion, she looked like the child Mirabelle had claimed her to be, but his body was not responding to a child. Her full-skirted dress and stiff stomacher disguised her figure, but he was burningly aware of the reality he had known earlier.

He moved his eyes, and found himself studying one slender hand where it lay relaxed in her lap. Delicate but strong it matched the vision in his head of her writhing under him, tiny but ferocious.

With a shake of his head, he repelled the memory. Was he a raw youth to invade a woman with such thoughts?

But why was she alone? He doubted Cuthbertson would have harmed her brother, or that she would be quietly here if he had.

The poltroon must have run off and abandoned her.

Bryght trimmed the smoky candle, then sat in a nearby chair to think. He'd like to apply his usual cool logic to the situation, but it seemed beyond him. What he really wanted was to gather Portia into his arms and carry her through the rain-swept streets to the safety of Malloren House. It was a foolish plan, but appealing all the same.

He shook his head. Presumably his brain still existed somewhere within the mass of sensation and emotion which ruled him. It was his brain that was needed if he were to help Portia.

She could not live here alone until her brother returned. It was neither proper nor safe and there was no guarantee that Upcott would return.

Especially if Bryght found him first.

She had money now, but she still needed protection. In case there was any trace of suspicion about last night, she needed a solid aura of respectability. . . .

With relief, Bryght felt his brain click into operation like a fine chronometer, following many calculations at once—

her family, her brother's estate, Fort, Nerissa, Mirabelle, Cuthbertson. . . .

He began to see the way.

The first thing, though, was to get his weary Amazon to bed.

Soft-footed, he explored the lodgings and found her bedroom. He turned back the sheets and wished he had a warming pan for them, for the air and the bed were chilly. She would be warmer, though, beneath the covers.

Then he went back to the parlor and gathered her into his arms smiling at how little she weighed. He half hoped she would wake, for that could prove interesting, but though she stirred, she slept on. In fact, she turned her head slightly against his coat and laid her hand on his chest in a trusting movement.

He halted to savor the moment.

He wished it were a greater distance to her bed, a longer time before he must put her down. With a wry smile at his own foolishness he moved on, but halted beside the bed. His agile brain came up with a number of plausible reasons why he should lie down with her—to warm her, to protect her. . . .

He shook his head. He wanted, with alarming intensity, to make love to her—completely, fully—and it wasn't the lust that could sometimes take a man, but something deeper. He wanted to explore her even more than he had done, and in much better circumstances. He wanted to enter her. He wanted to be the first, the only. He wanted to mark her as his for all time.

This was madness. There was no practical or material advantage in marrying this woman.

He smiled.

So be it.

He laid her carefully in the center of the sheet and eased off her shoes. He placed them neatly beside the bed then drew up the covers and tucked them around her. Unable to resist, he leaned down and kissed her brow. She stirred and he froze, half-hoping, half-fearing that she would wake.

After a moment, however, she turned and snuggled under the blankets.

Her hair was gathered up in a tight knot and he wanted to loosen it so it spilled long around her, but he had been foolish enough for one night.

But the vision returned, the vision of Portia running across the lawns of Castleford, red hair flying, laughing as she chased a laughing, mad-cap child.

He had never seen her laugh.

He had never seen her run in the sun.

But the vision was true.

Bridgewater's needs would have to take second place to Portia's. In fact, Bryght might not be able to help the duke much in future, for Portia had such a deep aversion to gaming that she would nag him to death.

He could understand that, after the ruin such matters had made of her life.

If Bridgewater failed, however, as a shareholder Bryght would fail too. Even if that did not occur, he'd sunk so much money into the canal that his income now was the modest one from the estate plus a little from other investments. It would be adequate, but would not cover the purchase of an estate like Candleford.

Yet that vision had the power of truth.

He shrugged, returned to the parlor, and extinguished the candle. Then he left, closing doors softly behind him. He had no way to re-latch Portia's door, or to lock the door onto the street. He could only pray that his beloved would stay safe for the remainder of the night.

On his return to Malloren House, Bryght found no sign of his brother and was glad of it. He ignored tiredness and settled to constructing meticulous plans for his Amazon's welfare. Mirabelle would not talk, nor would Cuthbertson once Bryght dealt with him.

That left two entwined problems—Portia's scurvy brother, and her home. He would find out who had won the estate. With luck it would be a gentleman willing to extend the period of grace; more likely it was another such as Cuthbertson. In either case, Bryght would need plump pigeons in order to gather the money to pay the debt.

Before redeeming the estate, however, something had to be done to prevent Oliver Upcott from losing it again.

Bryght formulated a plan and considered how many people were needed to carry it out. The Malloren properties—particularly the London mansion and the Abbey—were heavily staffed with footmen, maids, grounds-staff, and grooms. This was not just because the Mallorens insisted upon good service, but because the service required could sometimes be out-of-the-ordinary.

As soon as the sun was up, Bryght summoned some of these excess servants and sent them out, eyes and ears open, to attend to certain tasks. Most were to operate in London, but two went to Dorset to act in the matter of Sir Oliver Upcott.

Next, Bryght sent a note to his brother-in-law, the Earl of Walgrave.

In the matter of business recently discussed between us, it would appear that the property is not well-secured. It would oblige me if you could find new storage until the full acquisition can be arranged.

Bryght knew that using Fort carried risks, for he'd rather harm a Malloren than help one, but if Portia was under the aegis of the Earl of Walgrave the gossips would hesitate to speculate. Bryght suspected Fort would play along, pushing his plan to force Bryght to marry a woman without status or fortune to recommend her. Bryght would be delighted and amused to watch Fort striving to bring about the match, thinking he was tying a millstone around a Malloren's neck.

It occurred to Bryght that another source of protection for Portia was the Trelyns. It was not one Bryght favored. He'd introduced Portia to Nerissa in an attempt to get her out of his life. Now he was committed to her, he had no desire for his beloved to be entangled with people who wished him ill.

"Behold, thou art fair my beloved, yea pleasant. As the lily among thorns, so is my love among the daughters . . ."

With a laugh, Bryght sank his head in his hands. He was a wretched case indeed when he was driven to quoting the Bible!

Twelve

Portia awoke in her bed, fully dressed and with no clear notion of how she arrived there. She struggled from under the covers feeling rumpled and poorly rested, aware of strange dreams flickering at the edge of her mind.

After such an experience she would have expected nightmares. All she could remember, however, were dreams of heated passion, and a strange one of a man carrying her gently and pressing a kiss to her brow.

She rather thought she had dreamed of Fort. She smiled. It was a sweet dream, but no more than a dream. She was no wife for the Earl of Walgrave especially after her adventure in the brothel. Damn Bryght Malloren for telling Fort who she was. Why would he do such a thing?

With a sigh, Portia went out in search of Oliver, hoping he had good news. There was no sign of him, but then she noticed a letter propped on the table.

Dearest Portia,

You are deep asleep so I will not wake you.

Things are well on the way to being solved. Fort ripped me apart as I deserved, but he has agreed to the mortgage. He has insisted, however, that I take a commission in the army.

Portia stared at the letter in disbelief. After all the work she and her mother had done to dissuade . . . ! How could Fort do such a thing?

And that is not entirely true, Oliver continued. *Fort has long known I want the life, and now says it would be best. That boredom would lead me back into trouble. I think he may be right. I'm not needed at Overstead, for you take care of the place better than I. Perhaps I'll make my fortune through war and return home covered in loot and glory.*

Anyway, I'm off to Overstead to reassure Mama and Pru and talk to the colonel of the 5th. By the time I'm back, Fort says the mortgage will be arranged. He seemed to want you to stay here to discuss this business with him. I didn't argue since I want to make speed and you know more of the estate's affairs than I. He's promised to keep an eye on your welfare.

Your loving, contrite brother, Oliver.

Stay here! Portia stared at the scribbled letter in disbelief. How on earth could Oliver think she could stay here?

Then she realized she had said little about the events at Mirabelle's. Certainly she had given her brother no inkling of the effect Bryght Malloren had on her, or of a dangerous wager. Oliver thought Bryght had merely bought her out of there and sent her home, and clearly Fort had not enlightened him.

In fact, Portia recognized Fort's hand in this. Fort could persuade Oliver of almost anything, and knowing Portia would not approve of Oliver buying a commission, he'd neatly made sure she could not interfere.

Devil take the wretch. She paced the room angrily. He had no right to send Oliver into such danger!

She stopped suddenly, however, recalling all the recent disasters and dangers. What other solution was there? Oliver *was* bored, and showed little interest in the land. He'd been mad to join the army since boyhood.

She sighed. Perhaps it was for the best, though it would cast their mother into the vapors.

Then it dawned on her at last that Overstead was safe.

Overstead was safe!

A smile broke on her face, and tears escaped. Tears of joy. Thank God, thank God, the worst was over and Overstead was safe! A few more days and she could return home. She would continue her improvements and pay off the debt. Doubtless Oliver would love the army and cover himself with glory.

The battle was won!

It was as if a leaden, clinging blanket slid from Portia and she could stand straight and breathe freely for the first time in weeks.

Still smiling, she became aware of discomfort from her tightly dressed hair and began to remove the pins. It was a relief to let it down and work her fingers through it. She rubbed at her tender scalp, and finger-combed the hair loose around her shoulders.

Then she realized she was still in yesterday's crumpled clothes and began to change. As she unlaced her stays, however, she saw she wore no shift and began to remember.

She pushed the memories away. That was over. She didn't need to think of Mirabelle's. She didn't need to think of Bryght. She would stay quietly in her rooms until Oliver returned, and need never see Bryght Malloren again.

As she took off her creased petticoat, however, she wished she could remember going to bed last night. It was strange that she would go to bed in her clothes, no matter how tired.

She tried to think back. Oliver had gone out, and she had

sat up to await him. . . . She couldn't remember anything more until she woke up this morning. She must have put herself to bed in her sleep.

How peculiar.

Then, as she hung up her dimity gown, she saw her shoes placed neatly by the bed.

She had put herself to bed in an extraordinarily orderly manner, for she had the bad habit of stepping out of her shoes and leaving them in the middle of the room. This summoned a bewildered laugh. How strange to be tidier asleep than awake.

She wanted a bath, but that was not possible so she poured cold water into the basin and began a thorough wash. When she washed her face, however, she found a quantity of paint on the towel and scrubbed until every last trace was removed. If only she could scrub away all memory of the previous night as easily.

She doubted she would ever forget the desire Bryght Malloren had stirred in her.

She was fastening a fresh gown when there was a knock on the door. She rose to answer it then hesitated, thinking of Cuthbertson. But no. That must be over.

She swung it open ready to take on whatever trouble awaited, but it was only the landlady's boy, Simon, come with some coals to make up her fire. He had also brought her breakfast of bread and butter and small beer.

It seemed bizarre to Portia that these daily routines were going ahead as if nothing had changed.

In a sense, nothing had.

Yet it felt as if everything were different.

The first touches of warmth from the fire were welcome, and Portia thanked the young man then sat to nibble the bread.

Every time she let herself think, however, her wayward mind turned straight to Bryght Malloren. She was going to run mad here alone for a week with nothing to do.

Her thoughts were interrupted by another knock at the door. Portia went warily to open it, but it was merely Mrs. Pinney in a belligerent mood.

"Miss St. Claire," she said, tiny mouth pinched into a little bud. "Where is your brother? If, indeed, brother he is."

Portia was taken aback by this unexpected attack. "Half-brother," she said. "He has had to leave for a few days, though I wonder how you know."

"I know because he was seen to leave, sneaking away like a thief in the night!"

Portia stiffened. "Our rent is paid well in advance, Mrs. Pinney. If my brother wishes to leave, he is free to do so."

The woman backed away a little, her mouth softening in surprise at this attack. "Surely, miss. But he left the door unlocked again. We could all have been murdered in our beds!"

Portia's outrage lessened. "I'm sorry. . . ."

"And gentlemen!" continued Mrs. Pinney, mouth pursing again. "My good neighbor across the street says you were brought home late at night by gentlemen, and that a strange *gentleman* left here at nearly dawn! What do you say to that, then?"

"It is nonsense!" Portia saw that her firm denial had impressed the woman, and added, "I was escorted home by the servants of . . . of a friend. My brother left to catch the early coach. There was nobody else here. Your neighbor must have been mistaken."

"Um, perhaps," muttered the woman, eyes shifting. "She did speak of a monstrous creature, which seems unlikely."

"A creature?" Portia wondered if she were still asleep and dreaming.

"A huge black hound," the woman whispered, "that crept after the Prince of Darkness like a foul specter."

"Really, Mrs. Pinney!" But the words stirred a memory for Portia. Then it struck her that when she had first seen Bryght Malloren she had thought of the Prince of Darkness, of Lucifer himself. And Bryght had a large dog. Could he have *been* here. Been *in* here?

Mrs. Pinney flushed under Portia's exclamation, and nodded. "Yes, it is as you think, Miss St. Claire. Gin. So sad. . . . But," she added, with a return to her former belligerence, "there will be no more neglecting of the locks, or out you go! And your brother had best be back soon. I don't hold with young women living alone, particularly those who like to be abroad at night!"

Portia bit back another protest. "Sir Oliver has gone to Dorset, Mrs. Pinney. He will be back within the week."

"A week!" declared Mrs. Pinney. "That is a great time to leave a single lady unattended."

Portia could have delivered a lecture on the question of who had been attending whom, but merely said, "Since I have nowhere else to go, and know of no one who would come here to attend me, there is nothing to be done about it."

"I could put you on the street," the woman said. "This is a decent house, and I'll not have it otherwise!"

"Nor would I!" Portia protested, "And you cannot evict me when the rent is paid."

The woman was about to speak when her son raced up the stairs. "Ma! There's a grand coach at the door!"

Portia's first thought was that it was Bryght Malloren

come to seize her. But when she followed the landlady into the hall to look down the stairs, she saw Fort.

He was dressed quite casually in dull blue and top boots, and his brown hair was simply tied, but it was certain this house had never seen his like. The two powdered footmen added splendidly to his ambience. He left the men at the door and mounted the stairs with eloquent disdain. Mrs. Pinney and her son melted out of his way and he ignored them.

"Cousin Portia," he said with a friendly smile and extended hands. "How wonderful to find you in London!"

When she put her hands in his, he carried them to his lips and kissed each. "You look a little tired, which is hardly surprising given this dismal place. We must see what we can do."

He shut the door on the gawking Pinneys and released her hands. Portia remembered then that Fort had been at Mirabelle's, had bid on her, diced for her, and according to Bryght, would not have been able to get her completely free.

She had absolutely no idea what to say to him.

He was as tall as Bryght and a little heavier in build. He made the small room shrink even further, but he was Fort with whom she'd run wild in Dorset years ago and his slanted smile was familiar. "I thought you'd given up madcap adventures, Portia."

"I thought so too. Oh, Fort, thank you for helping us!"

"It was nothing," he said and eyed her warily. "I rather thought you'd ring a peal over me about the military."

"I might have done, but I see now it may be for the best. But I do hope Oliver doesn't see much action."

"Portia, don't be foolish. The only way to keep him out of trouble is to keep him in the thick of things. It's a damned shame the war's about over. You have almost mothered him to disaster."

"Are you going to put it all at my door, then? That seems unfair."

"Not all of it. Your mother and pouting Pru have done their part. Let him go."

She pulled a face. "It seems I have no choice. At least I am able to manage Overstead while he is gone. I assure you you will be repaid in full in not too many years."

"It is nothing," he said again, and Portia found it rather irritating. It was doubtless true that five thousand guineas was nothing to the Earl of Walgrave. It had nearly ruined her.

"In fact," she said, "we can pay off a good part of it immediately, for Bryght Malloren gave me the proceeds of his wager last night." There. She was rather proud of the cool way she had referred to it.

"Did he, by gad? Twelve hundred? I suppose he owed you something since you must have helped him win." His lip curled. "Rather a dishonorable bet, if one thinks about it."

"No more dishonorable than auctioning children!"

He shrugged carelessly. "The main thing is to see what can be done with you until Oliver returns."

"I can stay here now your visit has covered me with glittering respectability." But then she remembered that Bryght Malloren might have been here and shuddered.

"You see it is not proper," Fort said. "I could offer you refuge at my house, but it is a bachelor establishment at the moment and you are not even a relative. . . ."

"I don't expect you to house me, Fort."

"Do you not have any acquaintance or connection in Town?"

"No, we have only been here for a few days. Oliver has friends, but . . ."

"But, no," he completed with a raised brow.

"There's Nerissa, I suppose."

He looked a question.

"Nerissa Trelyn. She is apparently my cousin." Portia laughed. "I was supposed to dine there tonight."

A strange flash of humor touched his eyes. "But that is the perfect solution. Explain your plight—say Oliver was called out of town on urgent business. Lady Trelyn will be bound to take you in."

"Oh, I couldn't. . . ."

"She will insist. Trelyn—dull dog that he is—is a stickler for family responsibilities. You will be secure there in the highest levels of Society."

Secure. It was a delicious word. Portia remembered how charming Nerissa had been and the decorum that had surrounded the Trelyns in the park. In that circle there would be no risk of being importuned by a rakish gamester. "Do you really think it the thing to do?"

"Assuredly." And yet something in his tone made Portia's instinct twitch a warning.

"I don't like to impose."

"It will not be an imposition. Now, do you have ready funds? You should travel by chair."

"I have been used to walking about the town."

"I do not recommend it. I would take you, but Trelyn looks askance at any sort of wild living and I've done my share. My escort wouldn't add to your consequence. If we truly were cousins, it would be different." He smiled with genuine affection. "I do feel a family connection, Portia, and I will look out for your welfare."

"Thank you, Fort." She went into his arms. "It means so much to have someone to help me."

He hugged her. "Everything is going to work out well

for you, I promise. But please stop fighting every battle, Portia. I know you too well for my sanity. The thought of you loose on London will turn me gray."

She laughed. "You weren't used to be so cautious! I'll try to act a decorous lady, but I do hate to give in without a struggle."

"I know it. Give in on this little thing, though. Promise you will take a chair wherever you go."

She smiled up at him. "Very well."

"And send word to me when you're settled. If Lady Trelyn fails you, I'll arrange something else. We really can't have you here like this."

She impulsively rose on tiptoe to kiss his cheek. "Thank you."

He kissed her back, lightly on the lips. "I did think you were past the age of being so foolish, though."

"So did I," she said wistfully, her thoughts all of Bryght Malloren.

Portia admitted then that it was not just her rooms that were insecure, but her heart. Bryght had invaded, and with very little effort could conquer. She needed stronger defenses.

So, as soon as Fort had left, Portia put on her hat and prepared to set out to visit the Trelyns. She found Mrs. Pinney hovering.

"A fine gentleman, your cousin," the woman said in a blend of awe and suspicion.

"The Earl of Walgrave?" Portia queried, smoothing her leather gloves.

The woman's eyes went wide. "The one they call the Incorruptible?"

"No, his son," said Portia crisply. "I am about to visit a relative to see if I can stay with her during my brother's absence. Please call me a chair."

"Very wise." Mrs. Pinney was almost groveling now. "A young woman can never be too careful of her reputation, my dear."

This struck Portia as funny, but she managed not to laugh.

She waited while Simon ran to a nearby stand for a chair, and fretted about Bryght. Why on earth would such a man be creeping about Clerkenwell in the middle of the night? Perhaps the gin-sodden neighbor had imagined the whole.

She pressed her hands to her head, fighting to remember something of last night after she had drifted off to sleep.

Nothing. There was nothing, except that dream of a tall man carrying her, and kissing her brow. Fort. She had dreamed of Fort.

But Portia suspected that when Bryght Malloren took off his shoes, he put them neatly side by side beneath the bed.

She shivered at the thought, but held onto sanity. Clearly nothing terrible had happened. Whatever Bryght had been up to—if his presence wasn't all a construct of gin and fear—nothing too terrible had happened.

But she couldn't stay here. She'd never sleep in peace again. She needed refuge, and surely Nerissa Trelyn would offer it.

Two men trotted up the street between the poles of a sedan chair, and put it down so Portia could enter. In moments, she was swaying on her way to Trelyn House.

Thirteen

The Trelyn mansion boasted a massive pillared portico and was separated from the street by a railed courtyard. Portia suffered some qualms for it seemed the height of presumption to ask to live in such an imposing residence. The chairmen trotted up to the gate in the railings without hesitation, however, and the gatekeeper let them in without so much as asking Portia's business. Her nervousness abated a little. For all its grandeur, this wasn't a royal palace. The men carried her across the neatly swept flagstones and up the wide steps to the massive double doors.

There they lowered the chair and opened the door so she could alight. There was a box here, rather like a sentry box, and a man in it, guarding the portal.

Portia, keeper of the door . . .

Portia shivered. She must keep Bryght Malloren out of her mind.

This doorkeeper did demand her name and business, but upon hearing it immediately passed her on to a footman inside the house. Portia hesitated long enough to pay her chairmen then entered Trelyn House.

She paused, arrested by the grandeur of the tiled circular entrance hall lined with niches each containing a classical statue. Before her, a pale marble staircase curved gracefully up between white iron banisters, bathed with cold light from a circular window high above. It was perfection but it was hardly welcoming. One nearby anteroom appeared to be full of marble statues of writhing serpents with people in their toils.

In fact, this was more like a classic temple than a home, and it was both silent and very cold. Portia was rapidly losing her nerve at the idea of throwing herself on Nerissa's charity.

She gave the footman her name, quite expecting to be told that Nerissa was not at home. Instead she was taken to a small but perfect reception room. She supposed the name St. Claire must command some respect here.

The reception room had a fire in the grate and the air was not cold, but the effect of the decor was still cool. The walls were covered in silver-gray paper painted with tiny bluebirds. Pale blue silk brocade curtains hung at the narrow window, and the four white chairs were covered in blue and gray striped silk.

Portia did not sit, but paced anxiously. If Nerissa refused her she wasn't sure what to do next. Mrs. Pinney would have to allow her to stay since the rent was paid, but she would not feel safe. What if Bryght Malloren returned?

She reminded herself that she was under the protection of the Earl of Walgrave, hard though it was to think of Fort by that mighty title.

The footman returned. Instead of showing Portia the door into sunlight he led her up the pristine stairs, along an elegant, pale-carpeted corridor, to milady's intimate boudoir.

This room was in complete contrast to the rest of the house. It was an ornate confection of silk draperies and hand-painted wallpaper in shades of pink and cream, all over-heated by a huge fire. Portia did not have time to take it in, for she was immediately engulfed in a perfumed embrace.

"My dearest cousin! I have been scolding myself for not

appointing a sooner meeting, and here you are, hours before expected."

Despite this effusive greeting, Portia gained an impression of guardedness from Nerissa. It was not surprising, but did not augur well. She took the seat indicated on a chaise, and was poured chocolate from a silver pot by Nerissa's own plump, pale hands.

Her hostess was as lushly beautiful as her boudoir. Her shimmering golden hair hung in waves down her back. Her loose undress gown was of cream silk embroidered with roses, and trimmed with deep borders of the finest lace. It rested at the very edge of her shoulders and dipped to expose the swell of her full breasts.

"Now tell me, Portia, why are you calling so early?"

Portia realized with a start that it *was* abnormally early to pay a social call. There was no point in dissembling. "I am in a predicament."

"I guessed it. You must tell me, dearest cousin. I will help if I can." But again, the expression in Nerissa's big brown eyes was at odds with her warm tone. Portia feared that Nerissa would not care to have anyone else's troubles thrust upon her.

"My brother has been called away . . ," she started.

"And left you here alone?" asked Nerissa in astonishment.

"Yes. It was a matter of some urgency."

"Even so, he should not have left you unprotected. What will you do now?"

It clearly was not leaping to Nerissa's mind that she invite Portia to visit her.

"I don't know."

Nerissa was sipping chocolate, considering Portia with surprising shrewdness. "Do you know many people here in London?"

"No. I'm afraid not."

"But what of Bryght Malloren?"

Portia almost spilled her chocolate. "What do you mean?" Did the whole world know the truth?

"In the park," said Nerissa. "You seemed to know each other so well, then. Many people noted it."

Portia could have wept with relief. She steadied her hands and hoped she could lie convincingly. "He is an acquaintance of my brother's only."

"That surprises me. What could they have in common?"

Portia tired of deception. "Gaming."

"Ah." Nerissa leaned back, but her eyes were sharp. "I think you do not approve."

If Nerissa wanted assurance that Portia was not afflicted with gaming-fever, she could have it. "I loathe gaming. And now, thank heaven, Oliver has seen the error of his ways."

"How fortunate. Many are not so wise. I fear Lord Bryght is a notorious gamester."

"So I understand."

Nerissa picked up a small biscuit and nibbled at it. "But handsome, you must admit."

Portia was assailed by a vision of a naked torso and wild hair. "I suppose he is," she admitted, for to deny it would be ludicrous. "But handsome is as handsome does."

"You must not be so harsh about a man who is a mere acquaintance." But the words were not a reproach. "Why do you dislike him so?"

Portia could not mention her recent grievances, so she turned to older ones. "Lord Bryght encouraged Oliver to play. I'm not sure he didn't tease him on with small winnings so that he would lose more."

Nerissa's brows rose sharply. "But, my dear, you are accusing him of being a hawk!"

"Yes, I suppose I am." But Portia was suddenly puzzled by the fact that it was *Cuthbertson* who had won in the end, not Bryght. Could there be a connection between Bryght and Cuthbertson? It seemed unlikely.

Nerissa was gurgling with laughter. "Please do not call Bryght a hawk to his face. Trelyn hates disturbances."

"Do you not think Lord Bryght capable of such deeds?"

Nerissa's expression cooled almost to petulance. "I think Bryght Malloren capable of anything, but if he is a hawk, I cannot imagine him hunting field mice." She eyed Portia thoughtfully. "If you think he tried to injure your brother, however, perhaps you want revenge."

The mood in the room had suddenly changed, and Portia did not know how to take Nerissa anymore. "I could not get revenge against such a man," Portia said, "nor do I wish to. I just want to avoid him."

Nerissa's expression reminded Portia of a stalking cat. Not a wild animal, but a sleek house cat out after mice for sport. "Women generally find Lord Bryght very attractive," she purred.

"I do not deny that he is handsome."

"Attractive for more than his appearance. Rumor says he is a skillful lover."

Portia felt her face flame. "I know nothing of such things, Nerissa."

"My dear! I speak only of flirtation in your case. Has he not flirted with you? In the park, for example?"

Portia looked down at the unsteady cup in her hands. What was behind all this? "Yes, I suppose he has flirted with me," she muttered.

You are supple as a willow, graceful as a doe as you move in your desire.

"And you did not care for it?"

"Yes, my beautiful one. Dance for me, show me that you want the gift of Venus. . . ."

"It made me most uncomfortable," Portia snapped.

She looked up and thought she saw a trace of pitying amusement in Nerissa's dark eyes. "Perhaps we should teach you to flirt, my dear," said her cousin. "Then you would not be uncomfortable. You could even turn the tables and upset *his* comfort."

Portia jerked so that some of her chocolate spilled. "Really, Nerissa. I want nothing further to do with the man!"

"Lud, how heated you are. I thought when he introduced you to me that he admired you. Do you not think he admires you?"

Portia felt exactly like a mouse being toyed with by a cat. How had she ever thought Nerissa charming? "No," she said firmly, putting down her cup and mopping at the spill with a serviette.

"He took you about the park on his arm and appeared very taken by your charms."

"It was merely a game to him."

"But games are serious business to Bryght Malloren, and he always wins. . . ."

Portia lost control and leaped to her feet. "Please, Nerissa, do not tease me in this way! Lord Bryght was merely making fun of me, and I would much rather never see him again."

"Are you really such a coward?"

"No!"

"Well, then?" purred Nerissa. "*I* sense he is attracted and I never mistake such matters. If you were to play your cards aright, Portia, you could have him on his knees begging for your favors. And then, you could spurn him. Would that not be the most satisfying revenge?"

Portia felt almost sick at the thought. "No."

"Are you *afraid* of him? No harm will come to you under our protection. All I am suggesting is that if—when—he pays you attentions, you encourage him. Then, when he is entranced beyond reason, you show him you do not care at all."

"No!"

They stared at each other in a battle of wills, and then Nerissa shrugged and laughed. "Alas. It seems you have not the spirit for revenge. Many do not." In a dazzling switch she became the charmer again. "But you must come and stay with me, dearest cousin, until your brother returns. It will be such fun to introduce you to Society."

Portia was thrown off balance. She was no longer sure she wanted to live here, but having come how could she refuse? "You are kind, Nerissa, but I will be happy to live very quietly. . . ."

Nerissa ignored her. "Perhaps we can find you a husband." She looked Portia over with a calculating eye, "In fact, you could do surprisingly well despite your lack of curves."

Portia was horribly reminded of Mirabelle. "I don't pretend to any beauty, Nerissa, and I am twenty-five years old and portionless."

"But you have attracted Bryght Malloren."

"I have *not!* I tell you, Nerissa, it was just some *game* he played in the park. Heaven alone knows why."

Nerissa hummed thoughtfully, her eyes stripping Portia down to her separate parts. "You look younger, being small. There is a lightness to your movements which is attractive. With a softer hairstyle and clever dressing, we need not despair."

Portia was close to despair. "I do not want to marry."

"Marriage is every woman's duty," said Nerissa piously. "Think of the benefits to your family."

Portia supposed that was true, but even if she could attract a suitable offer she had promised to take care of Overstead. "I am resigned to spinsterdom, Nerissa."

"Oh, do not give up hope quite yet! If you come to stay with me, you will meet many eligible gentlemen who will see the value of a connection to Trelyn. And you will be doing me a kindness." Suddenly, she was a gentle petitioner. "I am with child, you see, and Trelyn hovers over me so. The dear man speaks of finding me a companion, but how much better to have one like you."

Portia was congratulating her cousin on her fertility when Nerissa rang a silver bell by her hand, and a footman appeared. "Is my lord at home?"

"Yes, milady."

"Then ask if he would visit me."

Portia rose and smoothed her skirts. "Nerissa . . ."

Nerissa laughed, a rather throaty gurgle. "Oh do not fret so, my dear. Trelyn is your cousin by marriage. He will adore you as I do."

When Lord Trelyn entered, he showed no sign of adoring Portia, though the look he gave his wife came close. Did he always wear gray? He was dressed rather plainly today in gray cloth trimmed with silver. He suited his cool, classical house rather better than he suited this ornate room.

What a strange match this was.

"Trelyn," cooed Nerissa. "Dearest Portia has come to call."

Lord Trelyn took Portia's hand and raised it to within inches of his lips, as was proper. *"Enchanté.* But were we not to see you this evening, Cousin?"

Portia dropped a curtsy and looked to Nerissa for help.

"Poor Portia is in a plight, Trelyn. Her brother has been called suddenly out of Town. Would it not be delightful if she were to come and be my companion for a while? We could show her London."

Lord Trelyn waved Portia to her seat, and sat in a chair close by his wife. "I do not care to see you tire yourself at this time, my dear."

It was as good as a refusal and Portia was almost relieved.

Nerissa pouted and laid a plump hand on his gray sleeve. "It will not tire me to take Portia to a place or two, Trelyn, and I declare I am like to expire of tedium here alone. You are so engaged in government business, and you do not like me to go out with only servants in attendance. Please, dearest one."

The look Lord Trelyn gave Portia was not particularly friendly, and he followed it with an interrogation. Oh, he disguised it as conversation, but Portia felt as if both her family and herself were being turned inside out. He certainly was very protective of his wife.

She was forced to admit that Oliver's business had been the purchase of a commission, but managed to conceal all matters of debts.

"We must approve of those so keen to serve the king," said Lord Trelyn, though Portia suspected that he considered Oliver a rash fool.

He went on to question her association with Bryght Malloren. "You were seen to walk about the park on his arm, seemingly on terms of great familiarity, Cousin Portia."

"I did not know how to refuse, my lord," she confessed. "As for familiarity, he paid me some attentions. I made it clear, I hope, that I did not welcome them."

What a bare-faced liar she was becoming.

"He would be a match far beyond your expectations, Cousin."

Portia met his colorless eyes. "Precisely."

He nodded with a touch of approval. "You seem to be a sensible woman and of an age to be past foolishness."

Portia wished that were true.

Lord Trelyn turned to Nerissa. "Very well, my dear. If it would please you to have your cousin here to keep you company, I am willing to have it so. I still do not wish you to indulge in too many social affairs, but those we do attend, Cousin Portia may attend with us."

To Portia, it seemed a grudging agreement, but Nerissa smiled ecstatically and held up her hands. "Trelyn, you are the *dearest* of husbands!"

He took both hands and kissed them, and this time his lips did touch the skin. A suppressed passion in the gesture sent a shiver down Portia's spine. It was clear that Lord Trelyn adored his wife, and yet she would not care to be adored like that.

He was cool again when he turned to look over Portia. "If Cousin Portia is to share in our life, my dear, we must order her some new gowns."

"Oh, but I have enough clothes," Portia protested.

Lord Trelyn smiled coolly. "I doubt it. You must permit me this small indulgence, Cousin. You are to be Nerissa's companion, and we would want to repay you in some way."

So it would be a form of salary, would it? He was neatly putting her in the position of servant rather than family, and perhaps was anxious that Portia not disgrace him.

So be it.

Portia curtsied a gratified acceptance, and he left.

Nerissa immediately sent a command that her favorite mantua maker attend her. "Dear Trelyn to think of such a diversion. I adore clothes, but in my present condition there is little point to it. I tell you truly, this wifely business is quite tedious."

"When is the baby due, Nerissa?"

"In May. Can you imagine how huge I will be? Already I have no waist at all!" She discontentedly smoothed her gown at the front, though under the layers of silk Portia could see no bulge. "I do not like it," Nerissa said, almost to herself, but then shrugged. "But at least I can dress you." She considered Portia once more. "You are rather thin. You should eat more. Gentlemen prefer curves, my dear."

Your limbs are slender but strong, your body supple as willow.

The invasion of those traitorous memories loosed Portia's temper. "But a little while ago, Nerissa, you were claiming I would have gentlemen swooning at my feet!"

It bounced off her cousin. "Oh, dearest, your thinness is not a *fatal* flaw. I am merely thinking that it will do no harm to use frilling at the bodice to disguise your flatness there. And we must certainly not expose your shoulders. We will let Madame Baudelle decide. She can perform miracles. As for your hair, it is perilously close to red, you know, and despite the many nostrums advertised, I have never found anything that takes away freckles. . . ."

Portia sighed and let her cousin chatter. She did not understand Nerissa at all. To talk of Portia attracting swarms of men was ridiculous, but she had never felt a freak. Nerissa's artless comments were making her feel lacking in all departments.

She could only be grateful when Nerissa lost interest in critical evaluation and moved on to gossip. Her cousin wiled away the half hour before Madame Baudelle arrived with a monologue on Society. Portia found it boring, for she did not know the people, but she listened carefully. After all, this was how she was to earn her keep, by listening to Nerissa prattle, and she would be wise to find out all about the world she was planning to enter.

Even though Nerissa chattered of entertainments and scandals, Portia grew interested despite herself. She sensed that Mirabelle had been correct—the underpinnings of this round of pleasure was politics and power. Whigs and Tories, Crown and Parliament, City money and Society rank: all these power struggles were being played out in ballrooms and boudoirs.

"You mentioned Rothgar," Portia said at one point. "He is Lord Bryght's brother, is he not?"

Nerissa raised a brow. "I thought you had no interest in the man."

Portia damned her ready color. "I did not say that. I have no desire to be entangled with him, but I think it wise to know one's enemies. Rothgar seems to have a great deal of influence."

Nerissa's face turned almost bitter. "The man has a lust for power and an uncanny way of getting it. He is dangerous."

"Yet you wanted me to play tricks on Lord Bryght."

"Bryght deserves to suffer for what he has done. It needn't involve Rothgar. He is out of town."

Portia had at last found a discussion that interested her, but at that moment the mantua maker arrived.

Madame Baudelle proved to be young and sharp-eyed. She was delighted at the thought of a profitable order of gowns, particularly at this dead part of the year. Soon she and her two assistants were fluttering around Portia, measuring and assessing. Drawings and fashion dolls were produced and considered, though Portia noted that madame consulted Nerissa far more than she consulted her.

An acute nose for where the true power lay.

Portia began to feel like one of the exquisite mannequin dolls herself, a mere frame for lovely fabrics.

"My cousin will require at least one gown quickly," said Nerissa.

With a somewhat sly look, Madame Baudelle produced a swatch of beautiful material, a cream silk embroidered with multicolored birds. "With this," she said, "a gown could be made quickly, for it would need little trimming."

Portia gasped at the beauty of the fabric. It must cost a fortune.

Nerissa was staring at the fabric greedily, and Portia was sure she would demand that it be made into a gown for herself, but then she suddenly relaxed. "Why not? How soon?"

"Three days, milady."

Nerissa nodded and waved her on her way.

Portia was unbalanced again, for to order such a gown was truly generous. She thanked Nerissa warmly. "I have never seen material half as fine. I'm afraid it will cost a great deal."

Nerissa shrugged. "It is just money. Money is nothing."

Portia was tempted to burst into hysterical giggles. She managed to control the urge. "For the immediate, I will have to make do with my old gowns, Nerissa. I must return to my rooms to collect my possessions."

Nerissa agreed, but insisted that Portia go in the Trelyn carriage with footmen to attend her. So Portia returned to Clerkenwell in state. Half the street came out to gawk at the grand equipage and liveried servants, and Mrs. Pinney almost had palpitations. Portia instructed the woman to keep the rooms in readiness and to tell Oliver, as soon as he returned, where his sister was.

That done, she quickly packed her boxes. Then, while the men were carrying them down, she retrieved the coins from behind the fireplace. They would provide some security and independence.

And what of the money Bryght Malloren had said he would put in a bank for her? She wanted that money, but she did not want to deal with Bryght to get it. She certainly couldn't ask Lord Trelyn's help, for then she would have to explain where it had come from.

When her box was carried out, Portia looked around the dismal rooms and sighed with relief. Dresden Street had contained little but worry and pain, but in well-guarded Trelyn House she would be safe. As she traveled back to the Trelyn mansion, however, seated on satin, and with an embroidered footstool for her feet, Portia was fretted by anxieties.

On the surface matters seemed excellent. She would be companion to Nerissa. She would listen to her chatter, share her needlework and other pastimes, and go with her to the quieter kind of social event. It would only be for a few days, anyway.

Oliver would soon return, a member of the King's Army. Fort would pay the odious Major Barclay. Portia would return to Dorset and her former life.

Everything was arranging itself at last.

So why was she sitting upright with her hands clasped, instead of lounging back, at ease?

And why, when the coach rolled into the railed courtyard in front of the Trelyn's house, and the great gilded gates clanged shut behind her, did Portia feel as if she were being delivered to a prison instead of to a place of refuge?

If it was a prison, it was a luxurious one. Portia was given a charming bedroom, though in typical cool shades, and a small boudoir. The rooms were scattered with valuable *objets d'artes,* and the handsome white-draped bed was decorated with knots and bandings of rich silver cord.

Two maids busied themselves in putting away Portia's clothes and other possessions.

Nerissa, dressed now in her usual public wear of elegant white, came to observe. "I hope you can bear these rooms, Cousin. I'm afraid the whole house is quite plain. I am trying to persuade Trelyn to indulge a little more in color, but thus far I have only been successful with my own rooms."

"It is very elegant."

Nerissa pouted. "But so dull."

Portia wanted to ask her cousin why she had married Lord Trelyn when they had so little in common, but it would be impertinent. Since the aristocracy seemed to marry for advantage, doubtless personal tastes did not enter into it.

"Now," said Nerissa, "if you are settled, we will go out. I am sure there are any number of items you need, and I have been pining for such a trip. A man is a tedious shopping companion."

"Lord Trelyn likes to accompany you to the shops?" Portia asked in surprise as she took her light cloak out of an armoire.

"The dear creature will hardly let me out of his sight! But he has agreed that we shall go today without his escort, for he must be at the House. Something very dull to do with the country's debt."

"Dear Lord. Is the whole country in debt?"

Nerissa laughed. "Oh, my dear, if you wish to discuss such matters, you must ask Trelyn. But I gather war is expensive. There is something called a sinking fund which sounds most alarming, though I am told it is a good thing. Now, are you ready? Why, what a pretty pelerine. It suits your hair and eyes quite marvelously."

Portia followed Nerissa down to the coach thinking wistfully that Oliver would have been pleased to hear that.

The shopping trip was unlike anything Portia had experienced in her life. It seemed that Nerissa bought everything that caught her eye and that she must do so frequently, for she was well-known everywhere. She was trailed through a succession of establishments by adoring sales clerks and groveling proprietors.

It was as much a social occasion as a mercantile one. Nerissa was constantly encountering people and stopping to embrace, introduce, and share scraps of gossip—some of it quite scandalous. Portia uneasily remembered her visit to the park, and her sense of corruption in Society. She could not like it, but since most of the people they mingled with now were ladies, at least there was no impropriety.

There were some men around, however.

As they were leaving a silk warehouse, a very tall man bowed and Nerissa stopped rather abruptly. "Lord Heatherington." Her voice turned husky. "What a surprise to see you here. You have need of silks and satins? Pockets, perhaps?"

The handsome, dark-haired gentleman bowed low over her hand. "Who could have need of anything when you are by, dear lady?"

Nerissa gave her distinctive gurgling laugh. "What flattery, my lord. Come, let me present you to my cousin, Miss Portia St. Claire. She is to stay with us for a while and accompany me. Is that not delightful?"

Lord Heatherington bowed over Portia's gloved hand. "A pleasure, Miss St. Claire." He was already turning back to Nerissa. "A charming child. I'm sure she will prove useful."

"Portia is a little older than me, my lord," Nerissa chided with a laugh. "Her apparent youth is but her delicate size and her naiveté. She is fresh from the country."

Lord Heatherington turned to study Portia with a raised brow. "That makes a difference, dear lady. I adore anything or anyone fresh from the country. . . ."

Portia shuddered, reminded of the night before.

Nerissa tapped his arm with her finger. "But being fresh and unspoiled, she has no taste for your flirtation, sirrah!"

Lord Heatherington captured Portia's hand. "That is cruel of you, Miss St. Claire. If we do not flirt, we die."

Portia tried to tug her hand free. "That is to be absurd, my lord!"

"But so is not to flirt." His grip on her hand was unbreakable, and he raised it to his lips, watching her closely, almost scrutinizing her. Then, he seemed to dismiss her from his mind entirely as he turned back to flirt with Nerissa.

Portia was distressed by the incident, but even more distressed to realize that now she might as well not be there. She suspected that Lord Trelyn would not approve of this encounter. There was nothing unseemly about the conversation—it was all gossip and badinage—but the atmosphere was wicked.

Was this just flirtation, or something worse?

Portia was no guard, however, to object to Nerissa's choice of companion, so she just stood by until Lord Heatherington moved on.

As they proceeded down the street, Nerissa said pettishly, "I do hope you will learn to play the game a little, Portia. You will be a figure of fun if you stiffen up every time a gentleman pays you a compliment."

"I'm sorry. I just cannot find it comfortable."

"What a prude you are. You will have to practice. How else will you find a husband?"

"I do not want a husband, Nerissa, but if I ever have one, I would prefer a man who does not flirt."

"He would have to be a dull dog."

Then, catching Portia unawares, they encountered Bryght Malloren. He was in casual dress again, but without his dog. Portia half expected some dramatic change in him, some open acknowledgement of what had occurred between them, but he bowed as if they were the most casual of acquaintances and introduced his companion, Lord Andover.

Lord Andover, a loose-limbed, handsome blond, seemed far too pleasant to be friend to such a man.

Portia was so absorbed in her thoughts that her wits were wandering. She was caught off-guard when Nerissa said, "Lord Bryght! We have just been saying that Portia must learn to flirt. You are such a master of the art, why do you not teach her a little as we go?"

Portia stared at her cousin, but Nerissa merely smiled, captured Lord Andover's arm, and turned to walk ahead. Portia had no choice but to follow with the man she most wished to avoid.

Fourteen

"Relax, Hippolyta," he said softly. "You are surely safe in my company here."

She turned sharply, intending to reproach him, but found herself silenced by something almost gentle in his expression.

"So," he said, easily covering the moment, "Nerissa has taken you up. You are very fortunate."

Portia hastily walked after her cousin. "After my shame, you mean."

"No, I do not mean that," he said with an edge. "I mean that her standing and respectability are just what you need."

"If you want thanks for having introduced me to my cousin, you may have them, my lord."

"Your happiness is thanks enough, I assure you." He was keeping pace with her without difficulty.

Portia knew good manners dictated that she make light conversation, but her mind was blank. How could she talk of the weather to a man with whom she had been so outrageously intimate?

"I hope you are not too much distressed by your adventure," he said.

The gall of the man! "We will forget it, if you please, my lord."

"You are always telling me to forget our encounters," he

said somewhat plaintively. "I find myself quite unable to do so."

"Please, my lord . . . !"

"As you wish," he said lightly. "Then perhaps I should admit that I have skipped some important lessons during our encounters, and should now teach you how to flirt."

Portia was dreadfully off-balance, teetering between the attraction she always felt for this man and her fear of its power. She speeded her pace, wanting to be closer to the others. "I do not think so, my lord."

"Nerissa commands, and we should obey the Queen of Society."

"I do not think it is your habit to obey."

He captured her hand and slowed her pace. "You cannot totally repulse me, you know. Remember the terms of our wager."

Portia knew her cheeks were scarlet. "My lord, I wish you would not speak of it!"

"Then humor me, and let us flirt and become acquainted."

She looked at him then. "There is no purpose in it!"

"Why not?"

"Our tastes differ too far."

"Do they?" He tucked her hand into the crook of his arm. "I'm not well acquainted with your tastes, Miss St. Claire. Do you like roast lamb?" She snapped an exasperated look at him, and was trapped by a beguiling smile. "I wish you nothing but good, you know."

"No." It was rejection of both him and his statement. And a rejection of the effect he could still have on her.

He frowned slightly. "Then do you like chicken?"

Portia found herself alarmingly tempted to laugh. "My lord, cease this!"

"You do not care for food at all?"

"Of course I do."

"I thought so. I remember that you eat like a horse."

Portia spoke between her teeth. "I simply do not care to discuss food with you."

"Then let us talk sex."

Portia came to a frozen halt, staring at him, her mouth half open.

"Food or sex," he said pleasantly. "Which shall it be?"

"Is that a threat?"

He appeared genuinely startled. " 'Struth, no. You can trust my discretion. It is, however, a topic of mutual interest, you will agree."

Portia dragged her hand from his arm. "You are disgusting."

"Devil a bit. I am just seeking a topic of conversation in which we both have an interest."

"The Bible," said Portia icily and swung on her heel to catch up to Nerissa and Lord Andover.

She thought that would be the end of it, but he kept pace with her. " *'How beautiful are thy feet with shoes, O prince's daughter,'* " he quoted. Then added, *sotto voce*, "Or without."

Portia refused to rise to his tormenting. "Is that from the Bible, my lord? I don't recognize it."

"Perhaps your Bible was carefully edited."

"What nonsense. All I know is that my feet are not particularly beautiful, and I am not a prince's daughter."

"But you are wearing shoes."

She shook her head in exasperation. "That, my lord, I must admit."

"Shall I go on?" In his deep, beautiful voice he said, " *'The joints of thy thighs are like jewels, the work of the hands of a cunning workman. Thy navel is like a round goblet—'* "

"Stop it!" Portia swung to face him. "That is *not* from

the Bible, my lord, and I am appalled that you would link such lewdness with the Holy Book!"

Unfortunately, her raised voice attracted Nerissa's attention, and the other couple turned back to join them.

"Are you fighting, Portia?" asked Nerissa playfully. "I thought you were taking lessons in flirtation." Her eyes flickered avidly between them, seeking secrets.

Portia kept her gaze fixed on the green-flecked eyes of her tormentor. "I do not care for lies."

There was a silence and then Nerissa said, "It is not wise, Portia, to accuse a gentleman of lying."

Portia knew she had gone farther than she should, but she raised her chin. "If I am wrong, I will apologize."

Perhaps there was anger in him, but he smiled. "If you are wrong, Miss St. Claire, you will have to do more than apologize. You will have to pay a forfeit, won't she, Lady Trelyn?"

"That does seem fair, my lord," said Nerissa, dimpling at him, and enjoying every minute of this.

Portia wished she could tell them both to go to Hades. "That would not be proper, my lord."

"It is not proper to accuse a gentleman of lying," he pointed out. "Do you withdraw your accusation?"

Portia felt cornered. She had once again allowed her impulsive nature to throw her into an awkward situation. She had studied her Bible long and well, however, and was confident that there was no such lewdness in the Holy Book.

She called his bluff. "I do not withdraw, my lord. So, what forfeit will *you* pay when you admit your wickedness?"

His eyes sparkled and she suddenly remembered their last wager. He had warned her then of the folly of believing she bet on a certainty. On the other hand, though she knew little about sexual intimacy, she knew her Bible very well.

"What forfeit do you require, dear lady?" he asked. "A kiss, perhaps."

Portia hissed in a breath. "I require freedom from you, my lord. Forever. Never to see you again. Never to hear your voice. Never to have you touch me in any way."

Nerissa gasped, and Bryght's eyes widened in recognition. The amusement drained out of his features. "How rash you are," he murmured. "So be it. You will be hearing from me, Miss St. Claire, about our challenge, and about the settling of debts." His bow was somewhat abrupt, then he and Lord Andover moved away.

Nerissa stared at Portia. "Whatever are you up to, you foolish creature? To avoid a Malloren is perhaps wise. To challenge one in public . . ."

"He lied," said Portia, frowning after Bryght Malloren. Lud, but even angry he had a grace and style that made other men look clumsy.

"I do rather doubt it. What did he lie about?"

Portia dragged her wanton mind away from the wretch and concentrated on deflecting Nerissa's curiosity. She did not even want to recall the words he had quoted, or the memories they stirred of the previous night. They could not possibly be in the Bible. "A foolish matter," she said briskly. "One thing is sure. Lord Bryght will not now be able to pester me."

Nerissa just shook her head and led the way back to the carriage.

As soon as Portia was home, she flicked through her well-worn copy of the Bible, paying particular attention to the sections she read less often. After a while she relaxed. The shocking words were not there.

She had won at last, and was safe from Bryght Malloren forever.

* * *

That evening the Trelyns dined at home. Though Portia's best blue silk gown could not possibly compete with Nerissa's confection of cream brocade and lace, it seemed adequate for the occasion. Nerissa's maid had dressed Portia's hair in an elaborately attractive style and set some white roses in it. Portia felt she had no need to blush.

In fact, she was feeling in good spirits. Her encounter with Bryght Malloren had settled matters once and for all. In addition, even if he were wicked enough to break the terms of their wager, she was as safe at Trelyn House as if in the Tower.

After dinner, however, as they drank tea in the drawing room, Nerissa pleaded prettily that they attend the Willoughby soirée.

"My dear," said Lord Trelyn, "I do not wish you to exhaust yourself."

"Trelyn, I am likely to exhaust myself with tedium!"

"That is not very polite to your guest."

Nerissa flushed, but said prettily, "But it is Portia I am thinking of, Trelyn. You know I want to introduce her to Society. How are we to do that if we stay at home?"

Portia protested that she was happy to live quietly, but Nerissa over-rode her with pouting pleas. A flutter of panic began in Portia's stomach. She did not want to go anywhere where she might meet a certain man, and she was terrified that someone might recognize Hippolyta.

She pinned her hopes on Lord Trelyn, but in the end he said, "As you wish, my dear."

Portia wished he had more resolution.

"And if we are to go out," Nerissa said happily, "we really should pass through the Debenhams' rout."

"Perhaps I should stay at home," Portia said. "My gown—"

"Is charming." Nerissa's tone allowed no argument. "I will lend you my pearls."

"I would not mind remaining at home," Portia said desperately.

Nerissa's smile was sweetly implacable. "But you are my companion, Cousin."

And so Portia allowed the maid to arrange glowing pearls around her neck and wrist, in a brooch, and in an aigrette for her hair. The mirror assured her that the jewelry raised the quality of her gown a good few notches. Nerissa even lent her a fan—a precious item of mother-of-pearl and gold.

Portia rippled it open and shielded her worried face. If she had to do this, she was pleased to be doing it in style.

When the maid suggested paint and plumpers, however, Portia refused with a shudder.

"You are rather pale," said Nerissa doubtfully.

"I am as I am."

Nerissa laughed. "How strange you are!"

As they turned to leave the room, Portia said, "Nerissa, what sort of events are these? Whom shall we meet there?"

Nerissa waved a beringed hand. "Everyone who is anyone! Well no. Perhaps not. The Willoughbys' affair will be extremely proper, with music of the highest order. That means," she said with a rueful smile, "that the more lively members of London Society will disport themselves elsewhere."

Portia relaxed a little. She should have realized that Lord Trelyn would not attend a wild affair. And Bryght Malloren would surely not waste an evening on proper behavior and excellent music.

That being the case, Portia determined to enjoy herself. Tonight would be her first grand London entertainment, and probably also one of her last. In years to come she would have one brilliant night to remember.

Or two, she thought wistfully, thinking of brilliance of an entirely different order.

Soon they were in a carriage in a queue of carriages and sedan-chairs waiting to disgorge their glittering occupants at the door to the Debenham mansion. As this house was on the next street to the Trelyn's house, it all seemed absurd to Portia, but Nerissa assured her that it was unthinkable to attend these affairs on foot.

Portia looked out of the window at the queue ahead, and the queue behind. "Goodness. The whole world must be trying to get in!"

"Only the elite," said Lord Trelyn, and Portia could tell he enjoyed counting himself of that number. She suspected he even enjoyed the people lining the streets to watch the carriages go past. Some of the gawkers seemed to recognize Nerissa for they called out her name. She inclined her head just a fraction in gracious acknowledgement and the famous Trelyn diamonds shot fire. The Queen of Society indeed.

Was this why Nerissa had married Lord Trelyn?

Portia decided it was mean-spirited to be dissecting her hosts' intimate affairs, and put it out of her mind. Instead, she pressed to one side to look down the queue. "People seem to be leaving as enthusiastically as they are entering. I fear the event must be a disappointment."

"You dear ninny!" laughed Nerissa. "It would be the worst of bad taste to stay long, for then how would other people get in? Everyone is on his way elsewhere, as we are. We will just greet our hosts and move through the rooms, commenting to our friends what a terrible crush it is."

"And then what?"

"And then we will leave. It is just that extracting ourselves will take even longer than getting in." She gave a twinkling smile. "It is all quite ridiculous, but one must."

Why? Portia wanted to ask, but she knew the answer. It was the way of the world.

It proved to be just as Nerissa said. They arrived at the double-fronted house to find every window lit, with the blinds drawn back. They joined a queue of gorgeously dressed men and women waiting to mount the central staircase to greet their hosts. Portia's eyes began to hurt from the glare of gold lace and jewelry.

The heat from bodies and candles was appalling. She saw a few women and one man faint and be carried away, and prayed she would not similarly disgrace herself.

Eventually they had the opportunity to greet Lord and Lady Debenham and move into the rooms. No question here of sitting to talk, for all the furniture had been removed.

Despite the crush, Nerissa was in her element, greeting and being greeted by all. She charted a course through the crowded rooms like the expert captain of a vessel—always heading forward, but tacking from one group to another. Portia and Lord Trelyn floated behind like bum-boats.

Portia was introduced to so many people her head was swimming. Lord Trelyn stood by his wife like someone showing off a prize possession. Or guarding one.

Then a tall man in black velvet and rubies approached and made a bow. Nerissa extended her hand and the man's lips passed the correct distance over it, but the sudden coolness could be felt.

"Lord Rothgar," said Nerissa, and Portia snapped to attention.

There was not a great resemblance between the marquess

and his brother except in height and aura. Lord Rothgar's hair
was powdered, but she fancied it was pure black underneath.
His features could be called handsome, but they would make
no one think of an angel, not even a devilish one.

Upon introduction, he bowed over Portia's hand with exquisite grace. "Another St. Claire. London is blessed."

She dropped a curtsy. "I cannot compare to Lady Trelyn
in beauty, my lord."

"One such beauty is enough for any world, Miss St. Claire.
Perhaps you should seek instead to rival her in virtue."

He contrived to make it seem an insult. Apparently all
Mallorens were alike in that at least.

She met his eyes. "Surely everyone should aspire to virtue, my lord."

His lips twitched in a dismissive smile. "What an extraordinary notion." With a bow to Lord Trelyn, he moved on.

Portia hissed in annoyance and would very much have
liked to continue the debate.

Nerissa gave a nervous laugh and fanned herself rather
rapidly. "So you are willing to take on Rothgar, too! I confess, you are bolder than I. The marquess disturbs me."

"He cannot hurt you, my dear," said Lord Trelyn, but he
gave Portia a curious look. She feared she would have to
endure another inquisition later.

Nerissa smiled at her husband. "Of course he cannot hurt
me, Trelyn. He would not dare. He is so strange, though,
and they do say his mother was mad."

"Mad?" Portia asked in surprise.

" 'Tis said she killed her child—a younger one than the
marquess, of course—and then herself. There is bad blood
in the Mallorens."

"If it is that bad blood you refer to," said Lord Trelyn,
"then only Rothgar has it. The others of the brood had a

different mother—a charming woman. I remember her slightly."

"How fair you are, Trelyn," said Nerissa rather sourly. "You must admit that they are all wild."

"That, I admit, my love. Alas, there is another of that wild brood here tonight."

Portia followed his gaze and saw Bryght in full dress of russet velvet and powder. Her heart began to pound and she had to suppress a desire to edge away, to try to melt back into the crowd.

She reminded herself that he could not in honor approach her.

Portia glanced at Nerissa's husband and was reassured by the intense dislike in his expression. She wondered why Lord Trelyn felt so strongly, though. He was looking at Bryght as if he were a rival. . . .

Portia suppressed her lewd imaginings. First Lord Heatherington, now Lord Bryght. There were doubtless a host of reasons for Lord Trelyn to dislike the Mallorens.

She kept a wary eye on Lord Bryght, though, and thus saw him heading towards her. Suddenly hot, she fanned herself vigorously, still watching him over the fan.

He did not approach them directly, for he had to stop and greet a number of people, including that of Mrs. Findlayson, whose grip on his arm at one point seemed almost clawlike. If Portia needed more evidence of his wickedness, there it was. The whole world knew he was wooing Mrs. Findlayson and her fortune. He had absolutely no business flirting with another woman, making wagers with her, overwhelming her senses on a brothel bed, and pursuing her thereafter!

He could not approach her.

He could not!

He did.

When he finally bowed before them, Portia was almost breathless.

"You look somewhat heated, Miss St. Claire." He neatly appropriated her fan to ply it for her. "Perhaps you are not accustomed to such crowds."

Portia wanted to cut him for breaking their pact, but did not dare do that here. "That is true, my lord."

"Or have you been reading your Bible?"

Portia froze, staring into his eyes. They seemed more gold than green now, but they were the eyes that had watched her from inches away as he kissed her, stroked her. . . .

"I read it daily, my lord," she said icily.

He fanned her, undisturbed. "Perhaps I should send you a new one, then—if Lady Trelyn will permit."

Nerissa laughed rather nervously. "A Bible, my lord? That would be a novel gift from you. Have you turned to religion?"

"Religion can be surprisingly rewarding, Lady Trelyn." With that shot, he let Portia's fan ripple closed, and replaced it in her numb hands.

As they watched him stroll away, Lord Trelyn asked, "What was that about?"

"Nothing of importance, my lord," said Portia quickly. But truly, she was feeling dizzy. Was it the heat, or his confidence? He seemed so sure of himself.

She told herself that bluff was part of a gamester's stock-in-trade.

Nerissa studied Portia. "Lord Bryght is correct, though, Cousin. The heat does not agree with you. Your cheeks are clashing with your hair." She charted a straight course for the stairs, saying, "You were generally admired, though. Your delicate build does serve to make you look younger than your years, and you are graceful in movement and manner."

"Thank you," said Portia, feeling rather like a schoolroom miss being told that her French exercise had passed muster.

Soon they were at the outer doors. The Trelyn carriage rolled up and they entered to go on to the Willoughby soirée.

A few minutes later, Bryght strolled down the stairs arms linked with Andover.

"Where now?" asked Andover lazily. "I have no idea why we are being so fine and sociable tonight, my friend. These affairs are demmed dull."

"Lady Willoughby's soirée, of course."

Andover stopped to look at his friend. "Screeching sopranos and fervent harpists? My dear, I begin to doubt you."

Bryght smiled. "How foolish."

"Ah so. What then is the attraction at the Willoughbys'?"

"Merely that I am willing to hazard that the Trelyn party has gone on there."

"With your luck at wagers, I take it as a certainty, then."

"Knowledge, not luck. Which is why I generally win. At this time of year there are few entertainments that Lord Trelyn would think worthy of his presence. They have either gone to Lady Willoughby's or home. My money is on the Willoughbys'."

"How much?" asked Andover with a faint spark of interest.

They had reached the entrance hall, and servants brought their cloaks. "My dear Andover," said Bryght, "do you really wish to part with more of your wealth?"

"I wish to part you from some of yours. I say they are not at the Willoughbys'."

Bryght sighed. "A hundred only. I am feeling compassionate."

As they passed out of the double doors and into the night air, Andover said, "Care to hazard a pony, then, that you can speak to Nerissa without her husband by her side?"

Bryght laughed. "The secret of my success is never betting against a certainty. The man would have to be dead to permit it. I am his *bête noire*. Heaven alone knows why."

"The fact that you have rutted with his wife?"

"My dear, so has half London before he grew suspicious. I could almost pity him." They summoned a waiting link boy and headed a few streets away to the Willoughbys' house.

"Not Nerissa, then," said Andover. "Jenny Findlayson? You seemed rather cool toward her."

"I begin to think we would not suit."

"Thank the lord for that. Who then is your current amorous interest?" When Bryght did not answer, Andover mused, "Anyway, I thought you were chasing after Upcott's sister."

"Chase? Is that in my nature?"

"It is not in your nature to attend these events, or to buy virgins."

Bryght met his friend's eyes ruefully. Andover had made no previous remark about the strange event. "Touché."

"So, do I get an explanation?"

"Novel wagers amuse me."

"It is not a matter for discussion?" Andover hazarded.

"How perspicacious you are."

"Don't bite my head off. If you must become the talk of the clubs, it's not my fault. The general opinion gives you the accolade for finesse."

"Could it be otherwise?"

After a few moments, Andover said, "So? What has become of the fair Amazon of Dresden Street?"

"Her brother has left London and she is safe in the bosom of her family."

"Speedy work, even for you."

"I had little to do with it."

They turned the corner into the street where the Willoughbys had their house. "So," Andover mused, "we are now interested in Nerissa's cousin, Miss St. Claire. She seems unlikely to create scandals, but I see no wager in it. What is to prevent you from speaking with her?"

"My conscience. You heard her. I am not to intrude upon her in any way unless I can prove I did not lie."

Andover laughed. "I had forgotten that. She seems to have taken you in dislike."

"She labors under misapprehensions."

"Does she? And can you not prove you spoke the truth?"

"Of a certainty, but it amuses me to choose when and where to claim my forfeit."

Andover glanced at Bryght. "What's the attraction there? She seems rather strait-laced. She is too forthright to be pleasing, and is rather lacking in curves."

"Do you think so?" said Bryght with faint amusement. "Strait-laces can be loosened, and I find forthright quite attractive. For example, I have a fatal weakness for women who try to shoot me."

Andover burst out laughing. "Fatal indeed! When did that happen, and why the devil would she do such a thing?"

"She told me to stop, and I had no mind to."

"So you've already had her, have you? And her not your slave?"

"My dear Andover, you are developing a low turn of mind. Let us enter Lady Willoughby's and see if it can be improved by screeching sopranos and fervent harpists."

Fifteen

The soirée was much more to Portia's taste than the rout, though it too was crowded. But there were seats, and in two rooms there was excellent music.

Portia would have been happy just to listen to the music, but Nerissa wanted to talk. "I do wish you would tell me what is between you and Lord Bryght. I am dying of curiosity."

"There is nothing to tell, Nerissa. If the man has any honor at all, he will never approach me again."

"But there, see, there must be something, or you would not say such a thing."

Portia met the avid brown eyes. "I dislike him, that is all. Because he encouraged my brother to play."

"If you dislike him so, you should want your revenge."

That again. Portia wished she knew what was really in Nerissa's mind, for she did not trust her. "I assure you, I want nothing that involves spending time with Bryght Malloren."

Nerissa fluttered her fan. "Lud, you are fierce upon the subject. But it shall be as you wish. I think."

At the change in Nerissa's voice, Portia followed her cousin's gaze and caught her breath. He was here!

"How strange," murmured Nerissa. "It is rare enough to see Bryght at a rout, but at a soirée such as this. . . ."

Portia deliberately turned away from the doorway. So he

was following her. Stalking her like a predator. Well, he would find she was no field mouse.

She prayed he would keep his distance, but within moments he crossed to speak to them. "Lady Trelyn, Miss St. Claire. What a charming surprise. And Lord Trelyn."

Portia realized Lord Trelyn must have come almost at a run as soon as he saw Bryght approaching his wife. Perhaps they *were* lovers.

"I didn't know you had a taste for music, Malloren," said Lord Trelyn frostily.

"I have a taste for all things excellent. Tell me, Trelyn, what do you think of Amazons?"

Portia almost leapt out of her seat with alarm.

"Amazons?" repeated Lord Trelyn blankly. "Why nothing. What have they to do with anything?"

"Do you not find the idea of female warriors intriguing? Perhaps we should mount a battalion of them."

"The idea is absurd."

"It would surely dismay the enemy. What do you think, ladies?"

Nerissa laughed uneasily. "Why would we want to go to war, my lord? We have enough work here at home."

"How true. And you, Miss St. Claire? Do you agree?"

She had to look at him. "I would not want to fight, my lord."

His lips twitched. "Really? You surprise me."

Portia felt her cheeks heat. "Unless the enemy was wicked," she added with meaning. "Then I would fight to the death."

His eyes turned serious. "Ah, but wickedness is so hard to detect, don't you think?"

"No, I don't think that at all. Gaming is wicked, as are brothels and fornication."

"Cousin Portia!" exclaimed Lord Trelyn. "You speak too boldly."

Portia controlled her unfortunate temper. "I beg your pardon, my lord." She deliberately looked up at Bryght and dared him to protest his virtue.

He bowed instead. "My dear Trelyn, perhaps you should have waited and wed the cousin. You seem to be in agreement on all matters."

With that he was gone, leaving a seething atmosphere behind him. After an eloquent silence, Lord Trelyn extended his arm to his wife. "I think you would like to listen to Madame Honorette play on the harp, my dear."

It was after they left the crimson saloon where the harpist had entertained them for a half hour, that the party was divided.

Lord Trelyn received a note on a silver salver. He read it in frowning silence. "Something has arisen at St. James, my dear. I must attend to it. I will be gone less than an hour."

"Oh, poor Tea-cup," said Nerissa, laying a hand on his sleeve, and causing Lord Trelyn to cast a rather embarrassed look at Portia. "Surely it can wait until tomorrow."

"Now, now, Sugar Plum," he murmured, "you know my duty must always come first."

"But what are we to do?"

"You will be quite safe here and there is excellent music to enjoy. I will take the carriage and be back in no time."

After a few more playful protests, Nerissa let her husband leave. "Do not marry a political man, Portia," she said with a plaintive sigh that almost convinced Portia she was bereft. "Come, let us stroll about."

The next few minutes reminded Portia of their time at the Debenhams' rout, with Nerissa steering skillfully through the rooms as if afraid she might miss something. Portia greeted people absentmindedly and kept a weather eye open for Mallorens ahead.

But it was not a Malloren they encountered. It was Lord Heatherington. He bowed. "Lady Trelyn, and the lovely Miss St. Claire. How delightful. May I escort you to the choral recital?"

He held out a hand to each and they began to move with the flow of people toward the ballroom where the recital was to take place.

But then Nerissa stopped. "Oh dear. I'm afraid I cannot bear the thought of more singing. Portia, do you wish to go?"

"Not particularly. Do you have a headache, Cousin? Perhaps Lord Heatherington could find you something to drink."

"Or perhaps I can escort you both to the refreshments, ladies."

This was agreed on, and they went toward the back of the house, moving against the flow of people.

"The choral recital is very popular," Portia remarked.

Lord Heatherington looked down at her. "The choir of Westminster Abbey, Miss St. Claire. Are you sure you would not wish to hear them? I promise to take excellent care of Lady Trelyn."

"No, thank you, my lord. I think I have a little of the headache, too."

In fact, Portia would have liked to hear the famous choir, but she was afraid to be alone. She was sure Bryght would somehow discover that fact and harass her.

They reached the refreshment room at last, but Nerissa

halted in the doorway. "Oh dear. Fish! The smell of fish quite turns my stomach these days. Perhaps if I could just sit in a quiet room . . ."

"But of course," said Heatherington, all concern. "I'm sure there must be one down here."

Within moments they were in a small room further down the corridor and away from the soirée. Portia helped Nerissa to a chaise. "Lord Heatherington, perhaps you could find some water."

"Oh, no," Nerissa protested. "I just need a moment's rest away from the smell of fish."

The atmosphere in the room suddenly reminded Portia of her discomfort with these two earlier in the day. Her suspicions must be absurd, but even so, she resolved not to leave them alone.

Lord Heatherington took a pinch of snuff and dusted his fingers. "You have an unfortunate brother, Miss St. Claire."

Portia knew the remark was more than idle conversation. "He is unlucky," she admitted watchfully.

Nerissa suddenly spoke to the viscount. "Bryght Malloren came up to us and was speaking of Amazons. Did you not say that was the key, Heather?"

Portia looked between them sharply, alarm sounding.

Lord Heatherington smiled. "Hippolyta. I thought so."

Portia's knees went weak, and she collapsed in a chair.

"Don't worry," said Lord Heatherington quite kindly. "We mean you no harm. It merely suits us to have you on our side."

"Your side?" But she knew.

"To not have you tattling to Trelyn every time we meet."

Portia looked at Nerissa. "What have you done to get rid of your husband, Cousin? Sent him a false note?"

It was Lord Heatherington who answered. "Not at all.

We are opportunists, Miss St. Claire, and Lord Trelyn is a very busy man. Matters will doubtless be even easier now you are our supporter."

"I am no supporter of adultery, my lord."

"Then you are Hippolyta, virgin queen of the brothel, bought by Bryght Malloren in a business that is the talk of the clubs."

Portia was terrified, but tried not to show it. "What purpose would there be in revealing that?"

"None," he said. "But it is our weapon."

Before Portia could respond to this, Nerissa said, "We're wasting time! Portia, you have no choice but to dance to our tune. If you will just wait in the next room . . ."

"Nerissa, you *can't*—"

"Or," said Lord Heatherington, "the world will learn all."

Portia leapt to her feet. "This is *wicked!*"

"Save your moralizing," snapped Nerissa, and rose to her feet with remarkable energy. She walked over and opened the adjoining door. "How appropriate. It's the library. You can study your Bible. Stay here, and give warning if anyone should come."

Portia wanted to be a holy martyr, but she knew it would do no good. This pair would destroy her reputation, then find some other way of meeting. She walked into the library and Nerissa closed the door behind her with a firm click.

Portia turned to look at it, and was deeply grateful that it was solid. She wanted to know nothing of what went on in there. She turned back to the library which was hardly worthy of the name. There was only one wall of glass-doored bookcases. A large library table held two lecterns, but there was little evidence of study here. A sofa and two easy chairs were probably better used than the books.

The room was lit only by a low fire and one candle, but

the dimness suited Portia's despondent thoughts. London did have pleasures to offer—music and fascinating people—but she wanted no more of its danger and wickedness. If only Oliver had taken her back to Dorset.

She heard the click of the door, and spun around. If it was Lord Trelyn would she give the alarm or let him catch his wife?

It was Bryght. He glanced around the room. "I thought you were with Nerissa. You shouldn't be wandering alone—"

"It is none of your business, my lord. Please leave me in peace!"

Instead, he closed the door. "What's happened?"

"Nothing!"

"Just haunting the library, are we? Checking different Bibles?"

It took Portia a moment to follow his train of thought. That silly wager. "My lord, desist. You sought to fool me and you failed. If you had the honor of a newt, you would leave me be!"

He laughed. "Toads, snakes, and now *newts?* What pray do you know of the honor of newts? They may have a strong code of ethics."

"Then what, pray, would *you* know of newts?"

He sighed. "You are a rash woman."

Portia desperately wanted to flee him, but coward that she was, she did not dare leave her post. If Lord Trelyn came and discovered his wife and her lover, she had no doubt that her own shame would be all over London tomorrow.

She waited, therefore, senses twitching, for Bryght's next move. He did not come near her. Instead, he lit the candles on the table.

"What are you doing?" she demanded nervously.

He said nothing, but took down a book. With a trickle of unease, Portia saw it was a Bible. He laid it open on one of the lecterns and flipped through the pages until he came to a place. Then he stood back and gestured. "Come, Miss St. Claire, and prepare to admit your fault."

Portia would have dearly liked to refuse, but pride and honor would not permit it. She walked forward.

The Song Of Songs. What on earth was that?

And there were the words he had quoted. And more like them!

Suspiciously, she checked the title of the book, the other sections, and even peered to see if these pages could have been inserted. Then, with a sinking feeling, she turned to face him. "My Bible does not have this."

"I think you will find that the pages have been neatly cut out. I have heard of such barbarous practices."

"Those words do seem unsuited to a Holy Book."

His smile was suspiciously innocent. "It is all an allegory of the soul and God."

She glanced at the lectern. "It does not seem so to me."

"Nor to me. It is a lovely representation of God's gift to humanity." In a soft, gentle voice he asked, "Do you admit your fault, Portia?"

He had never used her name before, and instead of undiluted outrage, Portia felt a shock of intimacy. She closed her eyes. Her head told her he was a wicked gamester and philanderer, but he could still weave a spell about her heart.

A hand touched her cheek. Her eyes sprang open and she flinched away.

He caught her in his arms, "You do not learn easily, Hippolyta. Again you tempted Dame Fortune and lost. It is time to pay your forfeit." He smiled at her. "You really can't scream here, you know. Nor would it be fair."

He was right. Not only would the fuss and commotion cast her reputation into doubt, but it could expose Nerissa. That would lead to her own ruin.

"Please don't," she whispered.

His hand curved softly around her neck, causing a shiver to pass down her spine. "You look as if I'm about to torture you. Was our previous encounter so terrible?"

Portia summoned ice for her voice. "You would do better not to mention that at all, my lord."

Magical fingers played at her nape. "I admit there were some shortcomings, but I was laboring under a considerable handicap. Would you not care to try again in more favorable circumstances?"

Portia fought, then, but he was too strong and willing to use his strength. She stopped at the first touch of pain.

"You're hurting me!"

"You're fighting."

"I have the right to fight."

"Not this time. You lost and must pay."

"You're vile!"

She saw his jaw tighten. "Do you deny that you made a wager and lost?"

Portia met his eyes. "You cheated."

He shook his head. "You really are going to have to learn caution. First I am a liar. When proved truthful, I am a cheat. How do you arrive at that conclusion, oh wise one?"

"You *knew* it was true!" she protested. "There's no honesty in laying bets when you know you will win."

He laughed. "What a strange notion of gaming you have. No wonder your brother loses all the time." He swept her into his arms and carried her squirming to the sofa, where he sat with her in his lap.

When she tried to slide off he used his strength again

and she had to stop. "This is so unfair!" she hissed. "You know I do not have the strength to break free."

"If I have an ace, I play it. If you were wise, you would learn not to bet against a certainty."

"I was certain I knew my Bible!"

Portia was in despair, not because of her fate here but because her resistance was melting like candle wax. His closeness was sweeter than a fine wine, and in a moment he was even going to make her laugh. That would signal total defeat.

"If you seek to be a successful gamester," he advised, settling back comfortably as if at ease with the world, "study the players as well as the cards. You need a strong hand indeed to bet against me."

"I have no desire to be a gamester, successful or otherwise." She tested his grip again, and found it unbreakable. "My lord, release me. This is intolerable."

"I find it highly tolerable, and you have the soul of a gamester."

"No!"

"Then why do you leap into wagers with such enthusiasm? I've been making enquiries. Your father was a gamester in his time, and then turned to industrial speculation."

"And ruined himself. I learn by that."

"He was unlucky. Or perhaps just rash, like you." He compelled her to rest against his chest. "Or are you?" he whispered. "It depends what you want to win. . . ."

This was unbearable. He was too intimate, too disturbing, and too close to the truth. "Just kiss me, my lord, if that is your price, and let us have done with it."

"But I never specified the terms of the wager. You really should watch that kind of thing, you know."

She twisted to glare into his eyes. "I will not pay an outlandish price, my lord." She saw that he understood her.

"I would hardly expect that here, my dear. You will pay with a kiss?"

Portia distrusted his tone, but she wanted this settled before she became even more foolish. "Yes."

"Your word on it?"

"Yes."

He let her go. "Then kiss me."

Portia stared at him, then leaned forward to give him a peck on the lips. She was snared before she could escape. "Not fair payment," he whispered. "A proper kiss. A lover's kiss."

"You didn't specify."

His eyes glinted with infuriating amusement. "But I'm setting the terms."

"I *loathe* you. I want you to know that."

"We'll see," he said with infuriating calm. "Are you going to kiss me? If not, I will have to think of some other forfeit. . . ."

She longed to call his bluff, but knew she was mastered here. "You promise? One kiss and it will be over?"

"I promise."

"You will leave me alone? Cease stalking me?"

His eyes widened. "Stalking? Is that what I'm doing? But yes, if that is your wish I will leave you alone after a proper kiss, a lover's kiss."

Portia sensed that this was another wager. He was betting that after a kiss she wouldn't want to be left alone, but would continue into his bed. She was betting that she could resist. It seemed horribly like their wager the night before, one she had lost resoundingly.

But this was different. There was no nakedness, and it was just a kiss.

She swallowed nervously. "I know little of lovers' kisses, my lord. You must excuse me if my effort is feeble."

"If your effort is feeble, I will tutor you until you get it right."

Portia's heart began to pound, and she licked suddenly dry lips. "This is not fair," she whispered.

"Yes it is. Just apply your lips to mine, dear gamester, and follow your instincts. . . ."

She leaned forward tentatively, but he leaned away, sliding sideways until he was against the arm of the chaise and she was along him rather than in his lap. "My lord!"

"Much more comfortable. You are on top. You are in control. I am not even holding you. Just your lips to mine, Portia, but remember we are lovers. . . ."

He made it not a fantasy, but a statement of fact. Her body hummed with agreement, already remembering another time and another place.

"Oh dear."

He smiled into her eyes. "Can you say with truth that you do not want to kiss me, fair one?"

Portia not only wanted to kiss him, she wanted to do—in a small way—what he had done to her. She remembered Nerissa's revenge. Could she kiss Bryght and summon his desire, then send him on his way forbidden to seek her out in future?

"A kiss and you will leave me alone?" she asked again.

"If you still want to be left alone."

So Portia leaned forward, but found she could not balance without resting her arms on his shoulders. His coat was velvet and beautifully soft against her palms.

She eased down closer and his smell reached her—a touch of perfume, and another smell, his smell. . . .

When their lips touched, his moved in greeting but they made no assault. She pressed a little closer and he parted his lips so a moist, intimate heat tickled her. She moved back then, but his hands came around to hold her there.

"You aren't finished yet, I hope."

"I don't know what to do! Truly I don't."

"Try this." He tilted his head slightly so their lips fit together better. His hand slid into her hair and played gently on her scalp. "Your own hair is so much more beautiful," he whispered. "So silky, so alive . . ."

Her scalp was a place he hadn't been able to explore the night before, and now his touch there was so sweet she gasped.

"That's right," he murmured against her open lips. "A lovers' kiss is intimate, Portia, a lowering of all barriers, a tasting of the heart. We have never had a true lovers' kiss. Relax now and kiss me. . . ."

One hand roamed her back and she could hardly help but relax, but she did not know what he meant about a tasting of the heart until she tasted him.

Last night he had tasted of that perfumed oil. It had been erotic, but not sweet. Now the flavor was all his own, and delicious. Her body recognized it and moved as it had learned to move, pressing closer despite hoops and stays, stirring a muted, sensuous rustle of silk.

She was vaguely aware of him continuing to touch her—her scalp, her nape, her spine. Drawing her close against him . . .

"You said no hands," she protested.

He immediately stopped.

That was better. He was affected, she knew it, and she

had always been told that men's passions were stronger and wilder than women's. Just a little longer, then, and he would be desperate for her.

As she kissed him again, Portia let her hands explore his skin by feel alone. He was cleaner shaven tonight, and almost smooth. His hair was less silky because of the powder. The muscles of his neck were firm and she felt his blood beating there, fast and strong. Her memory showed her his bare neck, his magnificent naked torso. . . .

Dear lord! Almost too late, she recognized her danger, recognized that she was affected as much as he. She drew back, but immediately he snared her and rolled so she was under him.

She struggled then, and silk ripped.

"Hell," he muttered, ceasing his assault and moving off her a little to inspect the damage to her gown.

Portia was shocked that he could control his passion so swiftly. For a moment there he had been wild for her, she knew he had. She pulled his head down and kissed him again.

After a startled moment, he laughed and kissed her back. Soon he was kissing her as she wanted to be kissed, as he had kissed her last night, with all his body. She started to laugh too, laughing into his mouth even as they kissed.

Then they rolled again and fell off the narrow sofa, landing in a tangle of silk and velvet with him on top. Wild laughter won, and their mouths roamed, tasting, nipping. . . .

This was madness, and Portia knew it, but it was the sweetest madness the world had ever known. His hand was under her skirt now and she didn't care!

At least, she did care, but only that it complete its anticipated journey. Last night he hadn't touched her bare thigh. Tonight he was going to touch higher—

"Cousin Portia!" It was the horrified voice of Lord Trelyn. Bryght's hand froze.

Portia looked up to see his eyes turn suddenly cool and watchful. Then he smiled at her in reassurance. With remarkable efficiency, he got them to their feet in good order to face Lord Trelyn.

Then, only then, did Portia come to her senses and realize what she had done. She didn't understand how it had happened, but she had finally proved her mother correct. She had tempted fortune, she had thought herself cleverer than others, and now she had lost all.

For it was not only Lord Trelyn who had seen them. Stately Lady Willoughby was with him, and from behind peered a footman and a wide-eyed maid. The story would be all over Town in hours.

Dear God, now she understood Oliver, who had always thought he would win the next time.

Portia turned to hide her face against the nearest convenient object—Bryght's chest—then pushed away with revulsion.

"Come come, Cousin Portia," said Lord Trelyn. "After such a disgusting exhibition, you cannot persuade us Lord Bryght was forcing himself upon you."

Portia realized one side of her bodice was ripped, and there was real danger that her breast could be exposed. She clutched it closed. "I am not trying to persuade you of anything," she said shortly. She tried to work her pearl brooch free one-handed so she could use it to mend the gown.

Bryght came to help her but she turned angrily away. It was his fault. He had started all this.

"We will talk later," said Lord Trelyn coldly. "Where is my wife?"

Portia turned at that, the whole sorry situation flooding

back. What should she do now? Perhaps it no longer mattered, for she was surely ruined anyway.

But the adjoining door opened and Nerissa came out, perfectly in order and mildly curious. "What is all this commotion? What is going on?"

Lord Trelyn went to his wife, but managed a quick glance into the small anteroom as well. "What have you been doing, my dear?" His tone was moderate but suspicious.

Nerissa leaned into his arms. "I felt a little unwell, Trelyn. The smell of the food turned my stomach, so Portia kindly escorted me here." She turned to her hostess. "I am sorry for invading your private rooms, Lady Willoughby, but I needed a few moments of peace. My condition, you know . . ." Then she turned to Portia in wide-eyed innocence. "Why, whatever has been going on?"

"I came seeking you," said Lord Trelyn, "and found your cousin and Lord Bryght in a most improper situation."

Nerissa's eyes widened. "Cousin Portia!" she exclaimed. "I am astonished. There is nothing for it, though, but marriage."

Portia abandoned her attempt to loosen the brooch. "Certainly not!"

"But it is essential," said Nerissa earnestly, "or you will have no scrap of reputation left, not even if you fight . . . *like an Amazon.*"

Portia gasped and looked to Bryght. Surely he could find a way out of this tangle, for he could want it no more than she.

But he took a slow, elegant pinch of snuff. "I am, of course, completely happy to marry Miss St. Claire. Our passion proves to be both overwhelming and delightful, so once it is sanctified, we can all be a great deal more comfortable."

Lady Willoughby muttered, "Well, really!"

"I am glad all will be so properly managed," said Lord Trelyn with unexpected enthusiasm. "We will arrange it, and within the week."

Portia felt as if she were being tangled in a web. "I will *not* marry him!"

At a pointed look from Nerissa, however, she fell silent. She was not truly accepting defeat, just postponing discussion. There could be no reason for Nerissa to be forcing this match, and once they had a moment's conversation it could be sorted out.

"We will leave privately," said Lord Trelyn. "Lady Willoughby, if you could arrange for our cloaks." He turned to Bryght. "Since Miss St. Claire is cousin to my wife, I have some responsibility. I will see you tomorrow to discuss settlements?"

Bryght bowed. "I am at your service, Trelyn." He turned to Portia and undid the brooch. When she tried to resist, he murmured, "Show some wisdom, *mignon.*" His face was completely unreadable, but he did not look angry or alarmed. He must already see the way out of this.

So Portia relaxed as he pinned her gown together, but she tried not to show how the light touches of his fingers sent shivers along her over-sensitized nerves.

When he'd finished, he touched his lips to hers. "We will talk later," he said softly. "Good night, sweet wanton."

With an ironic bow to the Trelyns he left the room.

Portia inhaled deeply, relieved to have Bryght gone. She couldn't think straight with him in the room. Now her brain was clearing and she saw she had nothing to fear. In the calm of the morning, the unfortunate events could be explained away.

"A Malloren," snapped Lord Trelyn. "I am most disappointed in you, Cousin Portia. For a lady under my protection to behave in such a way . . ."

He went on at length, and Portia decided it was wisest just to hang her head and accept the lecture. She deserved it for allowing wanton lust to overcome restraint and good sense. And for wagering. As Bryght said, it must be in her blood. She was fortunate that the consequences would not be a great deal worse.

The lecture continued in the coach all the way back to Trelyn House, but as Portia's shock began to fade she realized some disquieting things. She suspected that Lord Trelyn was acting as he thought he should rather than speaking out of deep feeling. There was no real anger in him, and a glance caught an expression in his eyes that could have been glee.

And though Nerissa contributed a few exclamations of shock and horror, the same glance showed that she looked as content as a cream-filled cat. That could just be satisfaction with her lover, but Portia didn't think so. The way Nerissa was looking at her was most disquieting.

But why would Portia's disgrace so please these two? She had done nothing to hurt them. On the other hand, Nerissa had certainly felt spiteful toward Bryght Malloren.

Once back at Trelyn House, Portia was sent to her bed rather like a naughty child, but she was pleased enough to escape.

As she prepared for bed, she berated herself for foolishness. She had thought she could control her wanton nature, but she knew that only Lord Trelyn's arrival had saved her from true ruin. She would never be so foolish again.

She had to accept that her normally sensible body turned mad in the arms of Bryght Malloren. Even now, a small part of her was hoping the dreadful marriage would come to pass so she could taste the full cup of passion.

She suddenly imagined Bryght Malloren, naked, here in her bed, awaiting her. . . .

Oh, this was ridiculous!

She settled into the warm empty bed, assuring herself that she wanted nothing whatever to do with Bryght Malloren, notorious rake and gamester.

Then you should have stopped kissing him when you'd paid your debt, shouldn't you?

Portia turned and beat her pillow into shape, wishing she could beat her conscience into the form that suited her.

And you never would have fallen into this predicament if you hadn't allowed yourself to be lured into a wager.

And that was true. Bryght had trapped her like the hawk he was, leading her to believe that she was sure to win, and thus tempting her to wager far more than she should.

"I will never wager again," she said out loud. "Never."

With that settled she had to face the consequences of her folly. For this brief moment, she was betrothed to Bryght Malloren! She squashed a spurt of excitement and reminded herself that the one thing she required in a husband was that he be trustworthy, and certainly not a gamester.

Not even a handsome gamester who could drive her mad with a touch.

No one could force her into marriage. There was no pressure that would make her go willingly, and Lord Hardwick's Act of ten years past had outlawed force. These days, marriages had to be properly solemnized in a sanctioned place, and all parties had to be clearly willing.

As her nerves steadied, Portia laughed a little at her folly. What did she fear? Bryght Malloren drugging her and dragging her to the altar? He must be as dismayed as she at their situation. It was just possible that he wanted a brief affair with her, but he could have no desire to be legally tied to a plain and penniless spinster.

Portia was a little concerned about the Trelyns' gloating. She knew that neither of them wished Bryght well, but was that the sum of it, that it pleased them to see him embarrassed? Would they try to force the marriage in order to complete the embarrassment?

Well, what if they did?

Portia reminded herself again that she lived in modern times when forced marriages were no longer possible.

Sixteen

When a maid brought her chocolate the next morning Portia was not well rested. Sleep had been hard to find and disturbed by dreams of rapture, grinning Trelyns, and rapacious hawks. Underlying it all had been the unnerving awareness of the power Bryght Malloren had over her.

Portia was too honest by nature to deny it, and anyway, she believed a peril faced was preferable to one ignored.

So in the sanity of daylight, she sipped the chocolate, reminding herself that it was her life at stake here not a few nights of pleasure. It would be madness to bind herself to such a man for mere pleasures of the flesh.

Wouldn't it?

But, oh, what pleasures . . .

Her hand tilted and chocolate splashed onto the pristine white coverlet.

With a grimace, Portia placed the cup on a bedside stand and tried to mop the mark away with her handkerchief. It was hopeless. She feared the silk was ruined. She hoped it wasn't a sign.

In fact, it probably was. If she weakened, her life would be ruined. All that was required was that when Bryght came to discuss marriage, she be resolute in refusing. Portia dressed plainly and awaited her summons.

After a fretful hour, she began to suspect that matters

might be going ahead without her and went in search of Nerissa. To her surprise, she found her cousin not in her boudoir, but in the white drawing room in close conversation with Lord Trelyn.

"Ah, Cousin Portia," said the earl, even producing a smile. "Come in. We are planning your wedding. You need not fear that it will be a sparse affair—"

Portia's nerves jumped. "There will be no wedding."

"We will have it here—"

"There will be no wedding!"

He looked at her in mild surprise. "There must be a wedding. You have no choice."

"Of course I have a choice! I can refuse to take the vows."

"I would not recommend that." Nerissa's sly smile was intended to remind Portia of the hold she had over her.

Portia stared at her cousin, projecting an equal threat. *"My* reputation is not at risk," she declared.

"My dear, do not be foolish. Your reputation is in shreds. But it can be pieced together very well by a speedy wedding. Why all the heat? Your groom is a handsome man of high estate."

"And clearly one you find pleasing," added Lord Trelyn.

Portia raised her hands to her burning cheeks. "I admit I allowed . . . physical attraction to guide me astray. But nothing truly bad happened. I do not want to marry the man."

"Why ever not?" asked Nerissa, in seemingly genuine curiosity.

"He's a gamester."

"All the world is," said Trelyn.

"Are you, my lord?"

"No." He looked at her with a touch of compassion.

"Cousin Portia, if you feel that way it is a pity you allowed your passions to exceed your good sense, but what is done is done. I do not allow scandal to touch my house. You must marry."

Portia saw that he was completely serious. She looked to her cousin, and put a threat in it. "Nerissa?"

Nerissa appeared entirely at ease. "You must marry him, Portia. If you make your bet and lose, you must pay."

At this echo of Bryght's words, Portia wanted to kill somebody, preferable herself. Why on earth had she let herself be tricked into wagering?

Twice!

Nerissa was a gamester, too, and was coolly calling Portia's bluff. Portia found she could not betray her cousin. She was not sure it would improve her own case, nor was she sure she would be believed. If he chose to, Lord Trelyn could see the story as mere spite.

Portia took a new tack. "Lord Trelyn, I am very sorry to have brought embarrassment to your house. I will, of course, leave immediately."

The earl's lips thinned. "I cannot possibly allow you to wander London penniless, Cousin."

"You are too kind, my lord, but I am not penniless."

He raised his thin brows. "You refer perhaps to some money you had in a pouch in your drawer? It is a little foolish to keep such a sum where it is temptation to the servants. I have put it in my safe."

A flutter of panic started in Portia's chest. "Then I must ask you to return it, my lord."

"I think it would be wiser to give it into your husband's charge in a few days time."

"That is *thievery!*"

Color touched his cheeks "You are intemperate! It is my duty to take care of such matters for you."

"You have *no* duty to me, my lord! I will return to my rooms in Dresden Street. We have paid for heat and food, so I can survive there until my brother returns. *He* is the head of my family and will speak to you on this matter."

"Portia, you are being most ungrateful!" chided Nerissa. "Trelyn is only arranging matters for your advantage, and in return you are upbraiding him. If you leave here, people will say we threw you out because of your scandalous behavior."

"I will tell them otherwise," Portia protested.

Lord Trelyn said, "I fear you do not move in circles where your words would carry weight, Cousin Portia. I cannot allow such foolishness. Until your brother returns, you must stay under my protection. I will send a message to your landlady asking that she inform us as soon as Sir Oliver returns to London, and to ensure that she does not encourage you in this madness."

Portia could have protested further—she could have threatened them with the law—but she sensed the noose of power and influence tightening around her.

Dry mouthed, she stated, "You are keeping me prisoner."

"Cousin!" exclaimed Lord Trelyn angrily. "How can you think such a thing? It is my duty to ensure your safety, that is all. You have not been in London long enough to realize that it is full of hazards."

Considering her few days in London, Portia thought that hilarious.

"Persist in this," he added sharply, "and I will begin to think that the shock of your situation has turned your wits."

Any temptation to find this funny fled. He was threatening her with the madhouse.

"Come, come," he said more moderately. "A little

thought will show you that it is not so bad. You will have as pretty a wedding as we can arrange in short-order—Lady Trelyn assures me that a beautiful gown will be ready in time—and you will soon be part of one of our greatest families. In the meantime, no more talk of imprisonment, please. You may leave the house whenever you wish. I only insist that you do so properly accompanied for your safety."

Portia looked between her two persecutors, then turned on her heel and left. In the hall she stopped and sucked in a deep breath, fighting panic. She must keep her wits clear.

They could not force her into marriage, not in this day and age. They could not!

Seeing a footman eying her curiously, she hurried up to the sanctuary of her room. Just in case, she checked her drawers, but Lord Trelyn had been telling the truth. Her money was gone.

So, she could not return to Dresden Street, and she could not pay for a coach seat to Dorset. She would not panic. Oliver would be back soon, and if necessary she could escape and flee to Fort. He would put a stop to this.

She began to calm and settled to trying to understand the motives of the Trelyns. Lord Trelyn was so able to appear noble and virtuous that she could almost believe he had her best interests in mind. She could not believe that of Nerissa. Was she just humoring her husband, or had she more underhanded motives?

With the briefest tap, Nerissa came in smiling. "How clever of you to trap Bryght, my dear."

Portia turned at bay. "I did not trap Bryght. I do not *want* Bryght."

Nerissa chuckled coyly. "Your fiery protests prove the point! Portia, *everyone* wants Bryght Malloren."

"Including you?" Portia shot back. "If he's your ideal lover, Nerissa, then take him instead of Lord Heatherington."

The attack bounced off Nerissa. "Oh, at one time I hoped to have both," she admitted, "but Heather suits me very well. The wedding will be on Wednesday at—"

"I will not be there."

Nerissa's smile became less pleasant. "I think you will."

Portia's belief that they could not force her to the altar was weakening. "Why? Why are you and Lord Trelyn so adamant about a match that will suit neither party?"

Nerissa subsided onto a sofa in a cloud of perfumed silk.

That perfume.

Lord Heatherington.

Portia realized that Nerissa *had* been the author of that disgusting letter, and that Lord Heatherington was probably Hercules. It hardly seemed to matter any more except that it confirmed her cousin's villainy.

And because Bryght had cared. He had loved Nerissa . . .

"Why?" Nerissa mused. "Do you really want to know?"

"Yes."

Nerissa shrugged. "It will not help you. Trelyn is motivated by a passionate desire to see Bryght busy with some woman other than myself. He believes in that smokescreen quite firmly."

Portia, too, sat down, finding some relief in the fact that they appeared to be at the point of honesty. "Is that all Bryght is to you, a smokescreen?"

"If you have no interest in the man," asked Nerissa, "why are you jealous?"

"I am not jealous!"

Nerissa leaned back languorously. "Then you will not mind that he wanted to marry me . . ."

"But you chose a richer man!"

" . . . and that he and I have been lovers."

Portia looked away from those perceptive catlike eyes, aware of a pain near her heart. She didn't know which was worse—that he had wanted to marry Nerissa, or that he might have rubbed perfumed oil into her feet. Had he told her of her beauty, and teased her skin with tongue and teeth . . . ?

She summoned a casual tone to say, "If Bryght and I are forced to marry, won't that blow away your smokescreen?"

"Alas, yes, but the rewards will compensate."

Portia turned back sharply, "What rewards?"

"He won't be able to marry Jenny Findlayson."

Portia's pain intensified. "You think he loves her?"

Nerissa burst out laughing. *"Loves* her! Oh, you dear ninny. You are so amusing. Bryght loves her money. He needs her money. I have made it my business to learn about Bryght Malloren's affairs, and he is virtually penniless these days. Heaven knows where the money has gone for he had a modest fortune when he wooed me—I would not have considered him otherwise. His luck at the tables must have abandoned him, though I hear rumors he has sunk money in Bridgewater's crazy venture."

"So, you want me to marry a broken gamester? Is that it?"

"Broken? Somehow, I do not see Bryght as broken. And he is a Malloren still, which is worth a great deal. But only the second son of the Mallorens and thus dependent on Rothgar's bounty. You can guess how that galls. Having lost what little fortune he had, his only door to freedom is by marrying money. A lot of money. Marriage to you will trap him as Rothgar's pensioner forever."

She was to be his *prison?* "Why do you hate him so?" Portia whispered.

Nerissa's face became almost pinched. "I have my reasons, which brings me to my other motive. He has a letter of mine."

"I know of it, and you should be ashamed."

For once she had dumbfounded Nerissa. "You *know?* And I thought you such an innocent!"

"If you mean I am virtuous, of course I am."

"How then, are you so familiar with a letter Bryght keeps by his bedside?"

Portia colored. "I know nothing of his bedchamber. I learned of it elsewhere. What has this letter to do with my marriage?"

"Who better to find a letter kept in a bedchamber than a wife?"

Portia stared. "You will trap me into a vile marriage just so I can steal a letter?"

"But of course. And to call marriage with Bryght vile is to be ridiculous."

"Then I am ridiculous! You cannot make me marry him, Nerissa. I will walk to Dorset if necessary."

For the first time Nerissa looked less than complacent. "If you refuse, the world will learn about Hippolyta."

Portia shuddered but hoped she concealed it. "So be it. I am headed for a life of obscurity where it will not matter."

"You overestimate provincial tolerance." Nerissa looked less certain of herself, however. "And what of your brother?"

"What of him?"

"If the whole world talks of your shame, Sir Oliver will have to defend your honor."

Portia struggled against this new loop of the noose. "He will challenge Bryght? For buying me in a brothel? Hardly."

"It would be novel, wouldn't it? No, I think we would conceal your wilder adventures. He would hear slander about your behavior at the Willoughbys', learn of it in such a way that he would have no choice but to challenge the slanderer. Of course we would ensure that his opponent has far greater skill with a sword." Nerissa leaned forward, eyes hard and cold. "You are going to marry Bryght Malloren and retrieve my letter, Portia, because if you refuse, you will condemn your brother to death."

Portia started to tremble. "You can't do this!"

"I assure you, I can. There are always hired swords." Sensing victory, Nerissa lounged back, once more the contented predator. "And Bryght could be forced into duels as well. You do not like him, but do you want his life on your conscience?"

"If I get the letter in some other way," Portia asked desperately, "will you give up this plan?"

"Oh, no," said Nerissa. "It is too complete a revenge." She rose and shook out her skirts, creating a wave of Otto of Roses that made Portia feel physically sick. "You will marry Bryght on Wednesday, Hippolyta. I will give you no time to escape. Now I must go. There is so much to do if such a hasty wedding is to be worthy of us all."

The door clicked behind her and Portia sat frozen like a stone statue. It was too much. She could endure almost anything herself, but she could not condemn Oliver and Bryght to death. The noose had finally tightened beyond all hope of escape.

Bryght ate his breakfast unsure whether matters were working out well or badly. He had decided he wanted to win the heart and hand of Portia St. Claire and now it appeared they would have to marry.

That was not, however, the same thing.

He was not at all sure that such a marriage would gain

him her heart for she had appeared thoroughly alarmed at the prospect. If she'd had a pistol, she doubtless would have shot him, and before witnesses, too.

He refilled his coffee cup, smiling at the thought of his intemperate Amazon. Last night had reaffirmed that she was as fiery in love as she was in anger, and he couldn't wait to let her burn him to a cinder.

Rothgar came in and Boudicca went to join Zeno by the fire. "You are amused by the coffeepot?"

Bryght tried to straighten his face. "I am amused by fate. You may congratulate me, Bey. I am to be married."

Rothgar was serving himself from chafing dishes, for they let no servants hover over this meal. His hand froze in the act of reaching for a spoon. "I may not, as well. To whom?"

Bryght was surprised that his brother would reveal such overt opposition. "I doubt you know her. Miss Portia St. Claire of Overstead, Dorset."

Rothgar's dark eyes studied him for a moment then he continued to fill a plate. "Nerissa Trelyn's cousin."

"How the devil do you know that?"

"I was introduced to her last night. Short, slender, red haired. Not in your usual style." He came to sit at the table.

"That should please you. You haven't regarded the other contenders with approval."

"It would depend on your reasons. I have become a convert to love in marriage."

Bryght laughed. "Am I to wish you happy?"

"A philosophical convert only. Why are you marrying her?"

"That's none of your business," said Bryght amiably.

It seemed for a moment that Rothgar would insist, but then he said, "True. *When* are you marrying her? I might have a practical interest in that."

"I'm not sure, but soon."

"Ah." There was a wealth of meaning in the word and the raised eyebrow that accompanied it.

Bryght felt damnably like a guilty schoolboy. "I haven't taken her virtue, Bey. Or not much of it."

"But enough, I gather. So be it. Honor above all. I suppose Elf should come to lend the girl credit."

"The 'girl' is twenty-five years old."

Rothgar's brows rose. "Is she indeed? She looks younger. She will still be in need of credit and support, and I doubt the Trelyns are an unfailing bulwark. Do you not want your sister at your wedding?"

Bryght was finding Rothgar's acceptance rather more abrasive than his opposition. "I would be delighted, of course. Why not the whole clan? Brand, Cyn and Chastity, Hilda and Steen and their family?"

"Cyn and Chastity are still newlyweds," said Rothgar blandly, "and it is too far for Hilda and her brood. Brand, Elf, and myself along with a few distant connections who are in town should form an adequate family presence. An aura of respectability."

"A massing of Mallorens is hardly likely to convey respectability."

"It will, at least, silence any troublesome tongues. What of Candleford?"

"No, thank you." Bryght could feel his jaw tighten.

"You will need a home." Rothgar's dark eyes were searching, which meant Bryght could not look away.

"We will not be welcome here and at the Abbey?"

"Of course you will."

"Then that is where we will live until I can afford to buy a place of my own."

"How very bourgeois," drawled Rothgar.

Bryght rose and stalked out of the room, Zeno hurrying to catch up.

Bryght regretted within moments letting Rothgar catch him on the raw. It was unreasonable not to allow his brother to buy the property and give him the use of it. He received no special reward for his work, which had increased the family fortune immensely, just the normal portion allocated to all the younger Malloren men.

By rights nearly all the Malloren property was Rothgar's alone. Their father had left dowries for the girls, and the marriage portion of the second marchioness went to her three sons—Bryght, Brand, and Cyn. Her early death had meant it was sufficient to provide a start for them in whatever profession they chose to follow. It was not enough, however, to support them in idleness for the rest of their lives.

The bulk of the property had gone, of course, to the new Marquess of Rothgar.

Rothgar, however, had chosen not to use it solely for his own purposes. He had decided that the business of the marquisate would provide employment for all the Malloren men, and all would receive a handsome income from it.

Rothgar had devised matters according to their talents. Bryght had been introduced to the delights of finance and investment. Brand, whose tastes were more practical, was in charge of the twenty or more estates that made up the marquisate. Cyn, the youngest, had been destined for the law.

Cyn, however, had rejected the plan and joined the army. Rothgar's one failure, and it had taught him something about people, thank God—that they could not always be shaped to his will.

Cyn had taken his portion from his mother but refused all further financial help. Even so, his part of the family profits was put aside for him. If he never touched it, it would go one day to his children.

Hilda and Elf also received small incomes.

Bryght found the arrangement agreeable on the whole, but he did not like to feel that he was Rothgar's pensioner. It was his own damn fault that he did not have the ready funds to buy Candleford and he would have to live with it. He could hardly expect all his dreams to come true. To have Portia as his wife would be enough.

Bryght went up to his room to change for his appointment with Trelyn. He might as well do the thing with full honors. As his valet powdered him, he pondered an additional problem presented by the current situation.

As Portia's representative, Trelyn might feel entitled to enquire about Bryght's financial standing. Since it was a marriage of compulsion, Bryght decided, Trelyn wouldn't be able to insist. Bryght could agree to a respectable settlement for Portia, and that would have to satisfy everyone.

When Bryght presented himself at Trelyn House in full elegance of silk and powder it went much as he had expected. Once Trelyn realized he would not be allowed to pore over Bryght's circumstances, they settled the matter quickly enough.

When all was arranged, Trelyn offered claret and Bryght felt obliged to take it. He had nothing against Nerissa's husband except the man's patent antipathy to himself.

The earl raised his glass. "You have my congratulations, Malloren. Miss St. Claire is in most respects an admirable and sensible woman."

Bryght reflected that a sensible woman would not get herself into such predicaments, but merely said, "I think so."

Trelyn cleared his throat. "I . . . er . . . I do hope you intend well by her."

Bryght raised a brow. The dull stick was genuinely concerned. He was devilish anxious to see this match made—and Bryght could guess why, the poor fool—but his conscience was pricking him. "Why would I not?" asked Bryght blandly.

"Well, there is an . . . er . . . element of compulsion. . . ."

"But I am delighted to marry Miss St. Claire."

Trelyn stared at him with a slight frown, clearly not believing a word of it.

"Or do you mean Miss St. Claire is under some compulsion?"

The touch of color in Trelyn's cheeks was answer enough.

Bryght said, "I must be assured that the lady is willing."

"Willing? Of course she is willing. She showed her partiality by her behavior, and why would a simple country miss not be delighted to marry so high?"

"Why indeed? The simplest way to ease my concern is for me to speak with Miss St. Claire."

They looked at one another for long moments, Bryght pleasantly implacable, Trelyn angry, but then the earl rose. "I will see to it."

Bryght looked thoughtfully at the door which the earl had closed behind himself. The fact that he had not simply summoned a footman was very revealing. What the devil was going on?

He was tempted to follow, to search the house until he found Portia and could be sure she was safe, but he assumed Trelyn would have to produce her. Then they'd have truth.

He sipped the excellent claret and reflected upon the fact that his beloved was probably not the least willing to marry him. Never mind. He did not dare let her escape this net.

Once they were wed he would prove to her that he was not such a bad bargain.

And soon she would be able to judge by his actions.

A word with Heatherington had diminished the danger from that quarter, though Heather was not easily controlled. He would not make trouble, however, unless Portia exposed his relationship with Nerissa.

As for money, after a couple of nights at the tables, Bryght hoped to be able to assure Portia that her home was safe. Quite apart from covering Upcott's debt, he had a strong desire to pluck Prestonly to the skin.

He would get rid of Cuthbertson.

The door clicked open and Bryght turned, heart speeding a little. It was not Portia, however, but Lord Trelyn. "Miss St. Claire awaits you in the Laocoon Room, Lord Arcenbryght."

Bryght rose and followed across the classical hall to a small chamber—an alcove really—in which Portia awaited, with Nerissa nearby. Lord Trelyn left, and Bryght considered the situation.

Had this location been chosen with forethought? The room was small, but graced with three long windows. It had clearly been designed to display a magnificent set of Grecian marbles all addressing the theme of Laocoon, the Trojan priest killed, along with his sons, by a sea serpent. The sight of so many people writhing in monstrous toils was not merely symbolic, it was almost laughably heavy-handed.

He detected Nerissa's touch.

Bryght glanced at Portia, hoping to share amusement, but she was not even looking at him. She was pale and almost haggard.

Damnation.

Bryght turned to Nerissa, who appeared positively stuffed

with contentment. "I hardly think we need a duenna, my lady."

"Do you not? But you both seem so governed by your passions. Lord Trelyn feels it best that you be accompanied. He is such a stickler for the proprieties."

"Indeed he is." He put a touch of threat behind it and saw Nerissa register it with a slight frown. She made no move to leave, however, and he decided the letter was a weapon best held for a more serious battle than this.

He went over and sat beside Portia on a cold marble bench. "I'm afraid you must have had a restless night, Miss St. Claire, but all is in order. You must not distress yourself."

She looked up at him then, but blankly. There were shadows as deep as bruises beneath her eyes. "I am not distressed, my lord."

"Are you not? You have stronger nerves than I, then. I am not at all distressed to be marrying you, my dear, but I cannot like the manner of it."

"You are very kind, my lord."

Bryght desperately wanted his Amazon back, not this limp doll. "I am not at all kind," he said bracingly. "I am intolerably selfish." When she did not react, he knew he could not force Portia to go through with this.

He took her chilly hand. "Miss St. Claire, I am not such a monster that I will pursue this marriage against your wishes. No serious harm was done, and if there is any scandal at all it will soon die down. If you do not wish to marry me, you must tell me so. I will ensure that there is no more said on the matter."

Out of the corner of his eye, he saw Nerissa stir as if she would object. He could understand Trelyn's desire for the match—the man had a genuine obsession with correct behavior, and also would like to see Bryght married. He wasn't sure why Nerissa would want to see her cousin married to him.

Yet again, Portia surprised him. "I am completely willing to marry you, my lord." It was said in a flat, unconvincing voice, but it was said.

What the devil?

He made appropriate remarks of delight and satisfaction, wondering all the while what was going on in her head. There was no point in lingering, however, for Nerissa clearly had no intention of giving them privacy. He took out the ring he had brought with him and slid it onto her chilly finger.

When he left, she was staring at it with a slight frown.

Portia considered the beautiful ring—a yellow stone surrounded by diamonds—and wished it symbolized more than a trap. She wondered where it had come from so quickly.

There was just a faint trace of a familiar perfume left in the air to tease at Portia's senses. Against her will, her hand slid over the bench to find the place still warm from him. . . .

"There," said Nerissa complacently. "That was not too hard, was it? And really, I could almost envy you. He is quite deliciously handsome, and I can attest to his bed-skills. But then, so can you. Are you not eager to complete your education—"

"Oh, shut up!" Portia erupted to her feet and fled to her room.

The worst of it was that Nerissa was right. Her body had learned its first lessons and longed for more. Portia was tormented by the thought that perhaps there was escape, and she was blind to it.

That she was governed by her lust for Bryght Malloren.

Seventeen

Bryght was thoughtful as he walked back to Marlborough Square.

It had all been a shock, he was sure, but that did not explain Portia's state. He had given her the opportunity to escape and she had refused to take it. He had looked into her eyes and seen that she meant the words she said, but was deeply distressed.

He didn't understand it, but could not marry any woman so against her will.

When he arrived at Malloren House he went to the offices, hoping to drown concern in hard work. He could not concentrate, however. After listening to a clerk's explanation of wine imports and prices, and realizing that he hadn't taken in more than a tenth of it, he gave up the effort.

When he entered the hall, he encountered Rothgar in full Court magnificence, including his Orders.

"And how are our beloved monarchs?" Bryght asked.

"Dull as always," said Rothgar. "I intend to be dissipated and drink strong coffee. Do you care to join me?"

Bryght was tempted to find a hole to hide in but refused to succumb.

They went to the library, Rothgar's favorite haven, an oak-paneled room lined with a disorderly collection of well-read books. As they waited for the coffeepot, Bryght said,

"Do you think the Song Of Songs is allegorical or simply a love story?"

"Cannot it be both?" Rothgar took a seat close to the fire, flipping back the encrusted brocade skirts of his coat and adjusting his rapier to settle comfortably by his side. Like Bryght he was powdered, but for Court he had clearly intended to impress. His buttons were rubies, his sword-hilt was set with diamonds, and he wore three heavy rings on his elegant, pale hands.

"I feel positively underdressed," said Bryght, taking the opposite chair. "Are we asking for something?"

"Quite the opposite. When petitioning, one appears gentlemanly but unostentatious. I am merely making an impression against the time it becomes necessary. There are some people still looking to the old order, and paying their greatest attention to the king's mother and Lord Bute. I look to the future."

"Will the king ever break free of his mother and Bute?"

"Undoubtedly. Especially with my help."

" 'Struth! Are you turning king-maker?"

Rothgar smiled. "Hardly that. But he is somewhat in awe of me, and I am one of the few around him not constantly asking for favors. A little heart-to-heart we had at the Abbey after Cyn's wedding didn't hurt either."

Bryght couldn't help but grin. "About politics?"

"Devil a bit. About the marriage bed. He and the queen are most grateful, though she, of course, does not know from whence the blessings came."

Bryght dissolved into laughter. "Gads, Bey. I don't know how you do it!"

Rothgar looked slightly hurt. "It is merely that I have everyone's best interests at heart. Now, as to *your* love-life . . ."

The arrival of the coffee was fortuitous. By the time the footman had poured the drink, handed the cups, and been dismissed, Bryght had composed himself.

"My lovelife goes ahead smoothly without your aid. The wedding is to be on Wednesday."

"Then I had best send for Elf and Brand immediately. Perhaps your bride would like to dine here tonight. With the Trelyns, of course."

"I'm not sure."

"If that is not convenient, I must call upon her." When Bryght remained silent, he added, "To do less would be discourteous."

"Yes, I suppose it would."

"Bryght, if there is about to be a disaster in the family, I would like to know."

Bryght put down his empty cup. He had always guarded his personal affairs from Rothgar, but his brother was right. This could go beyond the personal. "Make no mistake of it," he said, "I want to marry Portia St. Claire. It is not a particularly prudent marriage, but I want it."

"I would be positively alarmed if my family were to start being prudent."

Bryght laughed at that. "Your composure is safe, I assure you. I was caught kissing Portia at Lady Willoughby's soirée last night. Kissing her with considerable enthusiasm."

"Was she kissing you back?"

"With equal enthusiasm."

"Where, then, is the fly in this ointment?"

"I'm not sure. Trelyn is preaching propriety and insisting on marriage. I think he's three parts honest. The other part is a desire to see me married and thus less likely to rut with his wife."

"What an optimistic view of marriage, to be sure."

That made Bryght laugh again. "I think his optimistic view of marriage is a little dented, but he doesn't yet realize the full truth. It's not my business to enlighten him."

"Assuredly not. So, he is insisting on marriage. You wish to marry. The lady is enthusiastic. Where is the problem?"

"The lady is not enthusiastic. She was not exactly enthusiastic last night, and now she is as keen as someone invited to sleep the night in a plague house."

Rothgar leaned back. "Bryght, I will not assist you to capture an unwilling bride."

"I would hope not. I offered her escape and she refused it. I don't know what the hell's going on." He rose to pace the room. "I tricked her into that kiss last night, Bey, but nothing will persuade me she didn't enjoy it."

"Perhaps you should tell me all about your bride-to-be."

There was nothing Bryght wanted less, other than to hurt Portia. He sat down and complied, but left out everything about the brothel.

"So," said Rothgar at the end, "her brother is ruined, and has possibly fled abroad, and she doubtless holds you to blame."

"Me? Why?"

Rothgar shook his head. "You let him win. That was remarkably foolish. You should have fleeced him thoroughly, let him sweat for a few days, then torn up his notes."

Bryght rolled his head back. "Damnation, so I should. I didn't know then how deep in he was."

"And of course, after two such unfortunate experiences of gaming—both father and brother—Miss St. Claire cannot feel easy about linking her life to an inveterate gamester."

"Me? I am no such thing."

"To her, you doubtless are. My suggestion is that you

explain the truth—that you are not a slave to Chance, and are willing to give up the tables forever."

"I'm sure her brother promised that too," said Bryght, but he was hedging.

"A little of your recent history might convince her. I doubt you'd played more than a sociable game of whist in years until you involved yourself in Bridgewater's affairs."

But Bryght couldn't give up the tables just yet—not if he was to keep Bridgewater afloat and cover Upcott's debt. He had no intention of telling Rothgar that, however, for then his brother would offer funds from his own fortune. "I doubt she'd be so easily convinced," he said. "She is not rational on the subject. No, I think I should withdraw my offer. If the Trelyns are forcing her, that will block them. If she can be convinced I am of the angels, we can achieve a new agreement over time."

"It will look peculiar."

"To the devil with how it looks. Even at the worst interpretation, there is no need of such a hasty wedding, and Lady Willoughby can attest to that. If the Trelyns make trouble, I have the means to deal with them. I do not want to watch Portia walk down the aisle toward me with that dread on her face."

Rothgar studied Bryght thoughtfully as the clock ticked and a coal tumbled in the grate. Then he rose and went to his desk. He took a small stack of letters from a drawer and handed them to Bryght.

Bryght looked at them in surprise. They were all addressed to him, the papers were of many shades, and a distressing ferment of perfumes wafted from them. "What the devil . . . ?"

"Your post. If Miss St. Claire does not find you to her taste, it does not seem to be the common opinion."

Bryght ripped open a nasty-looking purple missive drenched with oil of lavender. It was a frankly lewd invitation to disport himself with a lady calling herself Sybella, and naming the time and place.

He threw it, and the rest of them unopened, on the fire then faced his brother. "What do you know?"

"It is all over the clubs that you have dedicated yourself to public education."

"So few men have panache in these matters."

"How true. But to pay six hundred guineas for the honor of demonstrating the art seems quixotic at the least."

Bryght tapped a finger on the arm of his chair. "It was a wager and I won."

Rothgar merely looked at him.

Bryght sighed. "The tender virgin was Portia."

"Ah. I suspected as much. A rash gamester for a brother does rather point the way."

"Hopefully not too clearly."

"Certainly no one speaks of it. No one questions Hippolyta's extreme youth, and Cuthbertson's prey are usually of the petty classes. The wager was a clever twist, too. Who would question a wager?"

"Quite. And I was able to set the terms."

"I'm pleased your acuity has not entirely deserted you. It was also very clever to connect her with the Trelyns. Virtually untouchable. I congratulate you."

Bryght laughed. "Call me rather a Prince of Serendip. That was not planned."

"And the scandal at the Willoughbys' is yet more luck? I was feeling positively overwhelmed by your genius! If anyone thinks to wonder why you are marrying rather lower than you might, they will have a reason. You were caught at the game and decided to act honorably."

"And there you have some truth in it," Bryght admitted. "I wanted to bind her."

"But in view of all this," asked Rothgar, "can you in honor retract your offer of marriage?"

"Can I in honor enforce it? She's still a virgin, Bey."

Rothgar's brows rose. "So I gather, but as the story has already entered the realm of the fabulous I could not be sure."

Bryght suddenly laughed. "Hence the letters. I am now a lover of mythic proportions and can expect to be hotly pursued by lustful ladies. I had best marry, and soon!"

"Don't forget the lustful swains," remarked Rothgar. "I overheard Ramage compose an ode to your torso. I hinted that I would treat such matters as if they were offenses against one of my sisters. He was chastened but confused."

Bryght collapsed in helpless laughter. "I wish I could see you out to defend my honor! 'Struth, but I had a simple life before a certain Amazon decided to shoot me."

"Perhaps *she* will defend your honor," said Rothgar. "If she's of that mettle, you must certainly marry. It seems marriages that open with pistols work out very well."

Bryght stood, still smiling. "I intend to marry her, but not on Wednesday under duress. I had best arrange matters."

Rothgar waved a negligent hand. "I will take this news to Trelyn House."

"There is no need—"

"It will go better. You still have Nerissa's letter?"

"Yes."

"Do you have the means to communicate with her secretly?"

"I know how. I hardly make a practice of it."

"I should hope not. Very well. Send a message telling her to support her cousin's liberation. I will deal with Trelyn. He would like my support in some matters to do with the Cinque Ports. What Miss St. Claire does will perhaps be interesting."

He rose languorously and studied himself in a gilded pier glass. "Should I mute my glory? The orders, perhaps." He removed a sash and a couple of showy jewels, and handed them to Bryght. "Do you have a message for Miss St. Claire if I should see her?"

Bryght considered the glittering baubles in his hands. "Just that I wish her well."

Rothgar left, and Bryght felt strangely bereft. It was the only thing to do and yet it left him uncertain of the future.

He did not deceive himself that it would be easy to woo Portia back to hand after setting her free. She would not again be tricked, or ruled by her passions. She would have solid defenses in place, and be determined to have nothing to do with a rakish gamester. She would doubtless leave immediately for the country, and he could hardly go to Dorset to pine at her gates.

As he went to lock the jewels in the safe, Bryght pondered the fact that he had never considered how his foolish kindness to her brother might have appeared. No wonder she had bristled with hostility on every occasion.

It was further evidence that the woman had the unique ability to tangle his mind.

Perhaps it would be wiser and kinder for both of them just to let her go.

As he locked the safe, however, he knew it was a kindness beyond him. He wanted Portia. He wanted to guard her from her own folly, and cherish her as she deserved. He wanted his fiery Amazon in his bed, and he wanted to see her run in the sun, chasing after a happy child.

A child of his.

He went to remove his courting finery. When he emerged it was to the news that Rothgar had returned home. Bryght went in search of his brother and found him in his suite of rooms, in the dressing room, being divested of his glory by two valets. When he was in plain breeches and shirt, he waved away the minions.

"You are now dis-engaged," he said, passing over the topaz and diamond ring. "I don't know if felicitations are in order or not."

Bryght fingered the ring. "Did you speak with Portia?"

"Assuredly. She gave me that, even though Nerissa protested that she should keep it. But she was devilish hard to read. She seemed both relieved and alarmed."

Bryght put the ring in his pocket and went to look out the window. "I'm afraid she's being pressured, but I'm not sure how. No one should know of the brothel affair. What else could be used to manipulate her?"

"We can only hope you will have the opportunity to ask her one day. "What will you do now?"

"The first thing is to find out who holds Upcott's debt and purchase it."

"An excellent plan. Once that pressure is eased, presumably the lady will be able to think more clearly about other matters."

Thinking clearly seemed like an excellent idea for all concerned, especially as Bryght had to gain some money if he were to pay that debt.

He left Rothgar's room to go pigeon hunting, for hells and clubs did not wait for darkness.

Bryght was particularly hoping to find the revolting Mr. Prestonly, but some other of the same sort would do. It was impossible these days for Bryght to take more than a handful of guineas from the common run of gamester—even from ones like Upcott who seemed hell-bent on losing their all to someone. No, he needed victims who deserved their fate, and preferably ones who were also worthy opponents.

Mr. Prestonly would fit the bill exactly but Bryght did not come across him. Bryght joined a game of Macao at White's but as it was a friendly game for moderate stakes, he rose an hour later with only a hundred or so. He went on to the Cocoa Tree, and found a lot of money moving there. There was no one he felt able to fleece, however, and so he merely watched for a while and then moved on.

Down the scale.

At Harker's he gathered nearly five hundred without being obvious about it. He would have done better had it not been for one desperate man. Norton was clearly dipped far deeper than he could afford and trying to recoup. Bryght wished he could help but as Andover said, trying to help every drowning soul in London was impossible.

Bryght played a couple of hands, trying to ignore the man but failing. Well, if he were to do something, the wisest thing would be to follow Rothgar's prescription and fleece him well then tear up the notes later. But Norton was an older man who might not accept that kind of charity.

Bryght gave in to foolishness and let him win fifty guineas then took his leave, praying it didn't lead to deeper play.

At the next hell—Mrs. Marlowe's—Bryght had a most enjoyable encounter with a Frenchman. He appeared to be a veritable popinjay, positively awash with ribbons, flowers, and perfume and with no brain to speak of. He played cards as if he scarcely understood the suits.

He was clearly a professional hawk.

Bryght enjoyed fencing with him for he was extremely skillful, but after a while with the money still even the Frenchman looked up and grinned. "Ah so, *monsieur.*"

"Ah so, indeed. You are new in London?"

"*Vraiment.* You are well-known here?"

"I am known for my luck. Lord Arcenbryght Malloren."

The Frenchman quirked a painted eyebrow. *"Enchanté,* milord. But it is a little more than luck, *hein?"*

Bryght straightened the pack and stood. "Perhaps. *Bon chance, monsieur."*

Bryght left Mrs. Marlowe's discreet establishment to find the light beginning to go, and his limited enthusiasm for the enterprise fading too. He headed back toward Marlborough Square, knowing there was one more likely hell en route. Inclination drove him straight home. Duty took him into Dante's.

The owner claimed that Dante was his real name, but Bryght doubted it. He was sure he enjoyed the fact that his establishment was nicknamed "The Inferno." It was a place for high play and no quailing at the odds.

Hygiene was not a priority with Signor Dante, and the place stank of mold, rot, and stale urine. The blinds were drawn and the candles were inadequate—all the better for the card sharps and other cheats. Really, Bryght had to wonder why anyone, even a lustful gamester, would choose to play in such a hellhole. It was fashionable, however, with a certain kind of blade.

It was a hawk's roost, and Bryght was seeking one particular hawk. He spotted him and wove through the crowded room nodding coolly to some acquaintances. He pulled a chair up to a small round table. "Good day to you, Cuthbertson."

The swarthy man looked up in idle surprise. "Lord Arcenbryght? I'm honored."

It had slipped Bryght's mind that Cuthbertson knew nothing of his connection to Portia, and therefore was unaware of how deeply he was loathed. "I have heard of your skill at cards, sir. I hope to test it."

The man's eyes narrowed, but at Dante's one did not refuse to play. "I am at your service, my lord."

"Piquet?" Bryght deliberately chose a game of considerable skill. He did not want to leave this to chance.

Cuthbertson gnawed his lip nervously, but agreed. A few idlers had gathered so he could afford no sign of weakness. Like a pack of rats, these creatures would turn on the vulnerable.

Signor Dante himself brought the fresh pack of cards, and stayed to watch.

Bryght had encountered Cuthbertson here and there, but had never played against him. Bryght was definitely not the sort of prey this hawk searched for. For the first few hands he tested the man, assessing his skills.

He decided he was a cheat.

Oh, Cuthbertson wasn't trying to cheat now—that would be foolhardy indeed—but he didn't have the degree of skill to win consistently by brain alone.

Bryght began to take his money. Playing the hawk at his own game, he allowed small wins to encourage him, and to prevent him from calling a halt. If Cuthbertson tried to stop when he had just won, it would look bad.

Soon Bryght had gathered the three hundred guineas Cuthbertson had taken from Portia and her brother. He won another hundred before the sweating hawk stopped the play.

"My lord, I confess, my luck is out and yours is in. I will have to concede."

"Already? I am willing to take your vowels, sir."

Cuthbertson rose. "Alas, I am engaged for dinner, my lord."

Bryght rose too, and favored his opponent with an ironic bow. "I am desolate. This has been most enjoyable."

"Indeed it has, my lord." But clearly the hawk wanted only to escape with a few feathers left.

As he left the house, however, Bryght went with him. "Perhaps we are walking the same way, Cuthbertson."

The gamester turned, his face ugly. "That might not be wise, my lord."

"It would not be wise," said Bryght softly, "to presume to threaten me."

Despite the fact that his henchman had appeared at his shoulder, Cuthbertson blanched. "I meant no such thing. . . ."

"Good. You took money from a connection of mine—Sir Oliver Upcott. I am displeased."

The man stepped back. "I did not know, my lord."

"Assuredly. I have corrected your error. I am sure that pleases you."

"I'm quivering with delight," Cuthbertson snarled.

"I thought you would be. I met a delightful young man at Mrs. Marlowe's. . . ."

"So?"

"A Frenchman. He spoke so warmly of the delights of the Paris clubs that I am tempted to try them myself."

"Why don't you then?"

"Alas, I have commitments at the moment. You, however, are free to travel."

Cuthbertson's eyes narrowed. "I have no desire to travel."

"I think if you consider the advantages and alternatives, you will find it a most enticing prospect."

With that, Bryght turned and walked away, wondering if he would hear rushing feet and have to turn and fight for his life. The street was not entirely deserted, however, and no attack occurred.

He headed back for Malloren House, thinking that sponging off Rothgar—his course of last resort—was beginning to look damned attractive.

Portia sat in her bedroom in Trelyn House, contemplating the shapes and shadows in the leaping fire. The past twenty-four hours had been enough to turn anyone's wits, but she was beginning to feel almost calm.

The marquess's announcement that his brother was withdrawing his offer of marriage had been like an explosion. Lord Trelyn had been livid with rage. Nerissa had pretended to faint with horror, but was clearly furious.

Portia had not been able to suppress glee at these reactions, but mainly she was worried to death about the consequences.

"It is my brother's considered opinion," said the marquess calmly despite the outrage, "and it is an opinion I share, that his behavior was not extreme enough to make a hasty marriage necessary. Such a marriage might cast some shadow on the reputation of Miss St. Claire. He hopes to woo her in a more normal fashion."

"He will never darken my door again!" declared Lord Trelyn, almost quivering with fury.

"As I am sure Miss St. Claire will wish to rejoin her family in Dorset, you will not be put to that inconvenience, Lord Trelyn."

"We will not pay to send her there," snapped Nerissa.

"You have my money!" Portia declared.

The marquess looked at the Trelyns with such amazement that they both reddened with guilt.

"It is in safekeeping, you silly creature," snapped Lord Trelyn. "Are you accusing me of being a thief?"

Portia smiled sweetly. "No, Cousin, of course not. I am just pointing out that I have the means to return home tomorrow."

"Then go," snapped Nerissa. "We arrange a most advantageous marriage for you, and you treat us as villains! I hope you are miserable in muddy, boring Dorset."

"Lady Trelyn," said her husband sharply, "you are forgetting Christian charity. And you are forgetting where the blame lies. In my opinion, Lord Arcenbryght has behaved in a most deplorable manner, and I will not forget it. In the meantime, Cousin Portia must need your loving care not your cruelty."

Cousin Portia wanted no such thing, but she allowed herself to be taken off by a superficially chastened Nerissa. She expected more attacks as soon as they were out of Lord Trelyn's earshot, but once in Nerissa's rooms her dresser handed her a note. "From the mantua maker, milady."

Nerissa almost jumped. She read the note warily, her lips tightening. "Another delay. Such people are so tiresome these days." She tossed it on the fire and Portia watched it burn. Why would a mantua-maker's note bring new flags of anger to Nerissa's cheeks?

But Nerissa turned to her with a smile. "Dearest, forgive me? I was so furious about the way that wretch treated you!"

Portia guessed that Nerissa's fury was because she would not now get her letter back, but she played along. "It is what one would expect of a Malloren."

"Indeed it is! The wretch! The lizard! Word must get out so that he may be shunned as he deserves!"

"No! Please, Nerissa. You will ruin me in the process!"

Nerissa sat with an angry flounce. "But he must be made to suffer."

"I prefer to forget it and return home."

"You are a poor little mouse, aren't you? I will put my mind to avenging you. . . ."

"No, please!"

Nerissa ignored her. "Word must get out. . . ."

Portia had escaped, just hoping that Nerissa's plans would come to naught. Now she sat in her room fighting a foolish urge to go to Bryght Malloren and warn him that Nerissa continued to plot. By heaven but she wished she had never met him!

If only Oliver had not come to London, had not started gaming, how happy they would be. Now he would end up in the army and probably die far away in a foreign land. Overstead would struggle under a burden of debt. And Portia would struggle under the burden of a broken heart.

She was not a person given to denying the truth. The simple truth was that Bryght Malloren had wormed his way into her heart and started a rot there that was likely to consume her even if they never met again.

Eighteen

That evening Bryght went hunting again, and this time he found the right quarry. Sir William and Prestonly were in White's and delighted to play. Prestonly sealed his fate by gloating over his past winnings and making a few filthy remarks about Hippolyta.

Andover was there, and quickly understood Bryght's mood and motives. They settled to play bézique—Andover against Sir William, and Bryght against Prestonly—and this time Bryght found he had an opponent who understood the subtleties of the game. He was glad of it for it soothed his conscience.

Having settled to his purpose, he was careful and gave the sugar-planter no reason to realize he was out-classed. The man was not stupid. If Bryght wanted to take a large chunk of money from him—say four thousand—he would have to reel him slowly and with great skill.

Because Prestonly was a shrewd player, it was easy for Bryght to keep the game even. After three hours of play, he had won only a few hundred.

Prestonly called for more wine. "This is dull stuff, my lord!" he declared. "A guinea here, a guinea there! Raise the stakes, I say." They were playing for guinea points, a hundred the match, and the split on the points had never been more than two hundred.

"By all means," drawled Bryght, as if he had no interest in the matter at all. "Ten guineas the point, and a thousand the match?"

Prestonly's hand paused in the process of raising his glass to his lips. "A man could sink deep at that."

Bryght thought he had misjudged, but Sir William had strolled over, and now intervened. "Lord Bryght is joking, Prestonly. He's a damned fine player. . . ."

"Ten and a thousand it is," snapped Prestonly and drained his glass. "I hope you're good for it, my lord."

Several men were watching and at this breach of good manners there was a mutter of disgust.

This suited Bryght for he wanted no sympathy for his prey. Now it was just a matter of winning, of hoping that his skill and luck held out. Skill alone would hold off total disaster, but as with most things in life, only the addition of luck would bring full success.

He suppressed a smile, wondering what Prestonly would think if he knew he was part of a noble knight's battle for his lady's hand and heart. He won the cut for deal, then turned up the knave of diamonds for trumps, and a chance at a bézique.

Luck did appear to be with him. He could only hope that was not an ill omen for his affairs of the heart.

Two hours later Bryght played out the last cards of a hand and achieved the score of one thousand a little ahead of his opponent. "Eight hundred and twenty guineas in points and a thousand for the match, sir. I make it a little over four thousand. Perhaps it is time to stop."

Bryght was ready. He had lost the taste for plucking feathers even from a man like Prestonly, and he had achieved his aim. Once he knew who held the note on Upcott's estate, he could redeem it.

"The night's still young, my lord," Prestonly snarled, mopping his red face. "You've had the cards and it's time they turned. I demand a chance to get my revenge."

Sir William, who was now a spectator, intervened. "Prestonly, I'm sure Lord Bryght will play you another night. . . ."

"I say we play now. It's only one o'clock."

Bryght had a strange impulse to caution, to hold what he had won and not risk it. It was so unnatural to him that he ignored it and humored the sugar-planter. "By all means."

Anger had turned Prestonly rash, however, and he'd also taken to drinking deep. Without really trying, by three in the morning Bryght had won over twelve thousand guineas—enough to cover Portia's debt, and to cover most of the cost of an estate of his own.

An estate like Candleford if it was still on the market.

He was hardpressed not to grin like a delighted schoolboy. He pretended a yawn. "I really must decline another hand, Mr. Prestonly, enjoyable though this has been. I am for my bed."

"Someone waiting for you?" sneered the man, but he looked shaken.

Bryght ignored that and rose to his feet. Prestonly gripped his arm. "You can't leave now, my lord!"

Bryght looked down at the fat hand creasing the silk of his sleeve until the man removed it. "Mr. Prestonly, I enjoy play, but I do not ruin people. Your luck is clearly out."

"Ruin?" Prestonly laughed. "Twelve thousand? Hardly notice it."

Bryght inclined his head. "I will sleep the sleep of the just, therefore. Alone, of course." He then left before the revolting specimen spat out some of the insults that were clearly churning in his brain. It would be farce to challenge such a man, but he could tolerate little more.

He was lighthearted, however. With luck he would not need to involve himself in serious gaming again.

He and Andover were just emerging from the club, and Bryght was enjoying a deep breath of clean crisp air, when they encountered Lord Walgrave and a couple of friends.

"Ah, Lord Arcenbryght," said Fort, a distinct curl to his lip. "I have been looking for you."

Bryght's instincts signaled the alarm. "Yes?"

"Name your seconds."

Shock froze Bryght for a moment. "Barclay and Andover," he said levelly. "But I would be interested to know why I am going to kill you."

Fort smiled coldly. "It will not be so easy, I assure you. The cause? Let us say I do not care for your management of your Brazilian affairs."

Amazonian affairs, in other words. Hippolyta. What the devil . . . ? "I was unaware that you had such a passionate interest in that part of the world, Walgrave."

"I have interest in fair play, Malloren. I hear you have made commitments there and failed to honor them. Where and when?"

"My lord," Andover protested. "It is the duty of the seconds to attempt a reconciliation. How can we do that if we do not know the cause?"

"But we do," said Bryght flatly. "Lord Walgrave wants to ravage South America himself."

Fort's hands formed fists and he took a step forward, but one of his friends grabbed his arm and pulled him away. "Lord Andover," the man said hurriedly, "may we meet in your rooms in the morning?"

"Aye."

Andover and Bryght watched as Fort's friends persuaded him into the club.

"He always was a hothead," said Andover. "It must be some mistake. . . ."

"Certainly it must, since I am pure as the driven snow."

"Bryght . . . ?"

Bryght snapped out of his trancelike state. "Andover, would you oblige me by lingering a little? Try to find out what the devil's going on. I'm for home to tell Rothgar that there's likely to be a death in the family."

"You can best him. . . ."

"You forget. He's my brother-in-law." With that, Fort strode off into the dark.

Rothgar, however, was not at home. Boudicca and Zeno were uninformative and Bryght would not descend to questioning the staff. It was highly unlikely that they would have anything to tell him anyway.

Bryght could guess. It was possible that Rothgar was at some entertainment, but there were few enough events at this time of year, and even fewer enthralling enough to hold the marquess into the dead hours of the morning.

He could be with friends.

He was probably with Sappho.

To call Sappho Rothgar's mistress was like calling Bryght Rothgar's employee. They appeared to have an intimate sexual friendship that was, paradoxically, largely intellectual.

Sappho—who never went by any other name—was of such mixed blood that no one could ever specify her race. Her mother, she said, had been a pale-skinned Tunisian, and her father a Russian sailor with Mongol blood. She was six foot tall with coffee-colored skin, wide cheekbones, fine features, slanted eyes, and heavy straight black hair that fell to her knees.

She was a poet of considerable skill in three languages, and she made no secret of the fact that she was a lover of women. Rothgar was the only man she was known to be intimate with, if intimate they were.

Bryght occasionally whiled away idle moments wondering about that relationship. Rothgar had various sexual arrangements, but Sappho was the only woman with whom he ever spent the night.

This was not, however, an idle moment.

This was a damnable hour.

Bryght went up to his suite attended by both Zeno and Boudicca, and stripped off without wakening his valet. He prowled the room naked, wondering what the devil had happened. Clearly Fort had learned he had withdrawn his offer to Portia. After having goaded Bryght into vowing to marry her, he was annoyed.

But it was unlike even Fort to go off half-cocked like this. He must know there was danger of harming Portia's reputation, and even of drawing attention to the brothel and Hippolyta.

Bryght detected Nerissa's spiteful hand, and fingered the book of sermons which contained that letter. If he died in this affair, he'd damned well make sure that letter was sent to Trelyn.

The main question was, why was Fort in such a rage? The affair at Lady Willoughby's had not been nearly the scandal they had all pretended. An embarrassment, yes, but it had been collusion between Bryght and the Trelyns that had painted it a desperate situation.

To trap Portia.

Had *Portia* complained to Fort that she'd been jilted?

The idea was ridiculous.

Bryght sensed a plot, and needed a rational talk with

TEMPTING FORTUNE   301

Fort. When the earl became hot-headed, however, it took him time to cool, and time they might not have.

Bryght flung himself down on his bed to seek sleep. He'd need his wits tomorrow.

Rothgar did not appear for breakfast the next morning, but Andover did. When the footman who had let him in disappeared, he said, "You're not going to like it."

"You surprise me," said Bryght who was breakfasting on coffee alone.

"Walgrave is maintaining that it is a personal matter to do with South American trade. No one believes it any more than they'd believe it if he'd taken your hat and stamped on it, saying it offended him."

"So what do people believe?"

Andover toyed with a bread roll. "That you raped, or as good as raped, Portia St. Claire at Lady Willoughby's."

"What?"

Andover grimaced. "It's all whispers and innuendo—to preserve the lady's reputation, they say—but the message is clear. You tried to prove your skill on another virgin, but this one wanted no part of it. You insisted. You were interrupted by Lady Willoughby and Lord and Lady Trelyn, all seeking Miss St. Claire. The lady was disheveled, distressed, and her gown was half ripped off her."

" 'Struth."

"Lady Trelyn is denying the whole thing, with enough fervor to convince the doubting that every word is true. It is known that a wedding was planned, but that the groom has since declined to be present. The lady is prostrate with shock and shame, or possibly recovering from her injuries.

Walgrave is apparently a close neighbor of Miss St. Claire's and as good as a brother to her. . . ."

"Dare I show my face out of doors?"

"It's not as bad as that, Bryght. It's all rumor, and no one knows the truth. If Miss St. Claire were to appear, composed and uninjured, most of it would die. The Trelyns claim she is suffering from a mild head cold, but again, the manner of their protests. . . . Fort calling you out does rather add color to it."

"Damn fool. Then I suppose the only thing is for *me* to appear composed and uninjured."

"Speaking of injury, Barclay and I met with Walgrave's men. . . ."

"Has he come to his senses?"

"Perhaps." Andover frowned. "It's damned strange, Bryght. He admits privately that the cause is Miss St. Claire, and says he will retract his challenge if you marry her. Perhaps he believes the stories."

Bryght looked at his friend. "It sounds as if you are beginning to believe them."

Andover colored slightly. "Of course not. But why would Walgrave be so serious about pushing the marriage?"

"He obviously regards the lady as a galling cross for me to bear." Bryght poured himself more coffee.

"So?" Andover prompted. "If he is willing to drop the matter if the marriage goes ahead, why not appease him? Do you not wish to marry her?"

"Yes, but not against her will."

"Damnation, Bryght, this could be serious. You can pleasure any wench out of her sulks!"

A look from Bryght had Andover blanching, but the man said, "I can't understand her. You're a rare catch for such a woman."

"She values herself higher than that."

"Do you *want* to fight Walgrave? He'll do his damndest to kill you and I hear rumors he's been training hard with Angeli. Even had him down in the country to coach him."

"Good, then he'll offer some sort of challenge. Let us go face the lions."

Andover tried further reasoning, but then abandoned it as useless. He did not abandon Bryght, however, but stayed by him as they strolled around the more fashionable parts of London.

It was not pleasant, but it was not disastrous. No one attempted to cut Bryght, though he was the focus of curious, suggestive looks. There were a few innuendoes at which he could have taken offense, but one duel a week was sufficient, even for a Malloren.

It did still appear, however, that Bryght was going to have to fight Fort.

It only slowly dawned on Portia that she was a prisoner.

After Bryght withdrew his offer, she had demanded her money, and been put off.

Next, she sent a message to Fort. When there was no response, she began to suspect that it had gone no further than the nearest fireplace.

The next morning, she asked Lord Trelyn to arrange for the purchase of a coach ticket to Shaftesbury. He protested that no lady of his family ever traveled on the common stage, and promised to arrange her journey in his own traveling coach, and with suitable escort.

"I wish to leave today, Lord Trelyn!"

"That would be unwise, Cousin Portia. After all, Lord

Arcenbryght may come to his senses and agree to the wedding. It would be unfortunate if you were not here."

Trying a subtle move, Portia decided to take Lord Trelyn up on his promise that she could leave the house with a suitable escort. The suitable escort proved unavailable.

After battling this strange lack of servants, Portia put on her cloak and attempted to leave the house alone. Two footmen forced her back into her room and locked the door.

She pounded on it and shouted, but no one came to her aid. How could she expect them to? She stopped from weariness, and because she feared Lord Trelyn might seriously try to put her into an insane asylum.

Now she was trying to make sense of all this.

The plan to make her Bryght Malloren's ball and chain had fallen through. It was possible that Nerissa might carry through her spiteful revenge and try to kill Oliver, but Portia staying or going had little to do with that.

Portia paced her luxurious prison knowing there was something afoot, and that she was being kept in ignorance.

Had Oliver returned? Yes, that could be it!

If so, she must escape and warn him of his danger.

She assessed her prison.

The door between the two rooms was not locked, but the doors to the corridor were. The keys were not in the locks, so any plan dependent upon them was hopeless. She supposed someone would come—either a servant with food, or the Trelyns to gloat—but Portia was not of a build to overcome them by strength alone.

She turned her attention to the windows.

The windows in both rooms were large and opened smoothly. They looked out onto the back garden so that an escape would not be easily witnessed, but they were nearly twenty feet off the ground. How could she escape this way?

Knotted sheets?

Portia had been a tomboy in her youth, and thought she could make the climb given a rope. She was dubious, however, about anyone creating a sturdy rope out of sheets and silk coverlets.

Her thoughts were interrupted by the turning of the lock, and she hastily closed the window.

Nerissa came in, gently reproachful. "Portia, my dear cousin, the servants say you are behaving most strangely."

"It is not strange to want to leave the house."

"But where would you wish to go, alone?"

"Nerissa, enough of this. If I am free to leave, let me leave now!"

"We are merely seeking to keep you safe—"

"Spare me. Tell me the real reason for this imprisonment."

Nerissa cocked her head then sat. Portia's nerves tightened. Her cousin looked so very pleased with herself.

"You cannot leave just yet, Portia, because you are prostrate with shock and injuries."

"What?"

"After the vicious way Bryght Malloren treated you, the way he almost raped you . . . or perhaps he did. The stories are *so* confused. . . ."

"Nerissa! You *cannot*—"

Her cousin's eyes shone with satisfaction. "Oh, but I can! The whole town is abuzz with it. And, of course, now that he has refused to marry you the matter looks even worse."

Portia shook her head. "No, you cannot. This is wicked! He will be ruined!"

Nerissa laughed. "Ruined? A Malloren ruined by the ravishing of a creature like you? Lud! No, with any luck, he will be dead."

Portia's breath caught. "What?"

"I sought merely to sully his name, but it works out better than I'd thought. Your neighbor, Lord Walgrave, has challenged him. They meet tomorrow."

"They must not!"

"Ah, but they must."

"But what if *Fort* dies? He is entirely innocent!"

"Fort Ware? He hasn't been innocent since the day he was breeched. If he dies, it will still serve. Bryght's name will be tarnished for ever. Don't you wish you could witness the event? See the blood flow, watch the dying grimace . . . ?"

"Nerissa, you are truly wicked. I will tell the world everything!"

"Will you? Including that you were Hippolyta?"

"Yes."

"What good would it do, when Bryght is dead?"

"Revenge," said Portia coldly.

Nerissa just smiled. "Ah, at last you see. Revenge is sweet. And at last I see. You poor fool. You don't hate him. You love him." She rose to her feet. "In that case, it is rather pleasant to make you the means of his destruction. Heather tells me Lord Walgrave has been working hard with his sword, learning clever ways to kill and maim."

With that she left and Portia stared at the door with loathing.

Never. She would never give Nerissa the victory in this. She flung open the window again and eyed the sheets. Then she saw the silver cords that held back the curtains and were draped and knotted all over the bed-hangings. They were not very thick but there was plenty of them.

Portia took her scissors out of her needlework case and began to unpick the stitches that held the cord in its ornamental position. Soon she had a substantial pile of it on the carpet. But was it strong enough to support even such a light creature as herself?

She pulled at it, and it seemed sturdy.

With a shrug, she knotted one end securely around the leg of an armoire near one window. Then she pulled on it with all her might. The armoire did not move and the rope gave no appearance of weakening.

Her heart was pounding with nervousness, and her hands were dangerously slippery, but she would go through with this. She would put an end to being a victim, a thing to be moved to everyone else's pleasure, and she would never be part of Nerissa's evil revenge. To help with the climb, she tied a half dozen knots in the cord, hoping her feet could find purchase on the silky stuff.

She looked out of the window again. The garden was deserted, and indeed, who would be out there for pleasure on such a chilly day?

What else need be done?

She was wearing light hoops under her dress and they would have to go. Having done that, her skirts hung rather long. She pinned them up so that her calves were free like a working woman's. Not proper, but propriety was the furthest thing from her mind.

Portia found her spirits lightening. Matters were still difficult, but it was being powerless and a prisoner that had worn her down.

On with it.

She threw out her cloak, shoes, and muff, then sent the free end of the rope after. It fell to within feet of the ground.

So far, so good. She took a towel and wrapped it around the cord where it might rub against the sill. Then she climbed on the sill and dropped her legs over while grasping the rope. She slid her feet down until she felt the first knot. Gripping tight, she let the rope take her weight.

It swayed and stretched alarmingly, but then seemed to settle. She could imagine all too clearly, however, a weak place where the silk was already shredding. . . .

Heart thundering, Portia began to work her way down as quickly as possible. The silk was hard to grip and she had made the knots a bit too far apart. She slithered at one point and felt her hands burn. She was sure the rope was stretching more and more. . . .

How high did one have to be for a fall to kill or maim . . . ?

She scrambled and slid down the last few yards.

As soon as her feet touched solid ground, Portia collapsed against the wall to let her heart settle. She was too old for this sort of thing!

She looked up, amazed at how high the window appeared.

But she'd done it!

At last she had done *something* to change fate.

Quickly, unsteadily, she slipped on her shoes, gathered her cloak and muff, and darted through the garden toward the back gate. Near there, behind some bushes, she let down her skirt, put on her cloak and muff, and pulled the hood up over her head.

Then she unlatched the gate and slipped out into the mews lane.

Into freedom.

Perhaps into danger.

But it was afternoon and still daylight—though a daylight dimmed by sullen clouds—so she did not feel much afraid except of pursuit. She hurried to mingle with the passersby.

There was a street market nearby and among those crowds she soon felt very safe. Her mind steadied and she set about her purpose. She must get to Fort and stop the duel.

She no longer had her map, but she could remember some of the principal streets. She made only a few mistakes before arriving in Abingdon Street at Ware House.

Yet again she was turning up disheveled and unescorted. She prayed that the door would not be answered by the same footman.

It was. He looked at her in outrage and began to close the door.

"Don't you dare!" said Portia with such force that he stopped, mouth agape.

"I wish to see the earl, and the earl will wish to see me. Let me in!"

"There's no point in letting you in because he's not here."

"I'll wait—"

But the door closed with a firm click. Portia could have screamed, and was very tempted to sneak round and try to enter the house anyway. But she suspected that the servant had told the truth and Fort was not in the house. He might not return all night. She had no idea what rituals men went through on the night before they were going to try and kill someone.

On this short day of the year, dark was settling fast. Servants at nearby houses were lighting the flambeaux by the doors—to welcome their masters home, and to provide a little security on the dark streets. A chill wind was rising and there was even a hint of icy rain in the air.

Portia shivered and clutched her cloak around her more tightly.

She thought of going to Dresden Street, but it was a considerable distance, and she had no real reason to believe that Oliver was there. It was too soon to expect his return from Dorset.

Also, it was one of the first places the Trelyns would look. This was another. She hastily left the street, hood well pulled up.

There really was only one place in London she could go for help, and even there she had been refused admittance last time she had approached.

She turned and hurried toward Marlborough Square.

There were flambeaux beside the door here, too, and the night porter was in his niche. Portia hesitated in some shadows nearby. She suspected that going into Malloren House would be like crossing the Rubicon. But she must. She could not let men kill and be killed in such a wicked plot without lifting a finger to stop it.

Her experience at Ware House had made her cautious, however. The main thing here was to get inside. Presumably Bryght or his brother would either be home or come home at some point, and she could not stay on the streets all night.

Holding her dark cloak around her, Portia slipped through the shadows and down the gap between Malloren House and its neighbor. It was wide, wide enough for a cart to pass, and she suspected it might be used for deliveries.

There was a gate, a pretty ornamental wrought iron gate, but a barrier for all that, and about ten feet high. Beyond, she could make out the lane which appeared to go all the way back to the mews and the road that served it. In the wall of the house she saw shadows that must surely be doors.

She tried the gate, but it was locked. It was also very sturdy, though, and gave no rattle.

Portia shrugged. She'd climbed down; now she would

climb up. She took off her cloak and slung it over the top of the gate. She hitched her skirts up as best she could without pins, tucking them into the waist and bodice and leaving only her knee-length shift to guard her modesty. Then, giving thanks for a misspent youth of climbing trees, gates, and walls, she clambered up and over the gate.

The ornate iron made it quite an easy climb, but the muscles for this sort of thing had grown weak over her years as a proper lady. She was panting by the time she straddled the top.

She paused for a moment, sitting there half naked, her hair beginning to escape down her back, and wondered what on earth her mother would think to see her now.

Pray heaven Hannah never learned the details of her daughter's London exploits! Portia pushed down her cloak, hooked her leg over and made short work of climbing down the other side. She was inside the Malloren enclave.

She was therefore relatively safe, and could huddle here until she knew Bryght was home.

But for all she knew, he was home now, and the night was promising to be a bitter one. She rejected a cowardly impulse to delay, pulled on her cloak and went to investigate the first door. She gingerly lowered the latch and pushed. Nothing. She pushed harder, but had to accept that this door was locked.

She went on to the next door. It, too, was firmly locked.

Why had she thought it would be otherwise? That gate was mainly ornamental as she had proved, and a nobleman's house was not open for anyone who cared to enter.

There was only one more door before the corner. Portia tried it without much hope, and almost fell in when the door opened. Thank heavens it was well-maintained and made no noise.

The shadowy outside light showed her nothing, but the blast of cold air might give her away. Portia hastily closed the door and stood in the dark, trying to sense where she was.

There were general smells from kitchens and stores, but nothing in particular. She put out her hand and touched a wall to her right. A few steps to the left found another one. She suspected she was in a corridor, possibly one with storerooms opening off it.

This was of no interest to her, however, and she groped her way forward, seeking a way to the rest of the house. She bumped into a barrier, and her fingers told her it was a door.

It might open straight into the servant's hall or kitchen.

She pressed her ear to it, and did hear sounds, but distant ones.

She took a deep breath for courage, and opened the door. Light.

Not bright, for it spilled from a nearby doorway, but blessed after the darkness. And the door opened into another corridor.

There were voices in the nearby room, chattering of friends and flirtation. Delicious smells of cooking meat and spices crept out to make Portia's stomach rumble. She had eaten little today and despite her small size, she did have a healthy appetite.

Well, once she contacted a member of the family, perhaps they would feed her.

To her left, Portia saw stairs going up, and she slipped silently toward them.

It occurred to her that the penalty for invasion of private property was probably hanging or transportation. It would not come to that, of course, but if a servant caught her she might be hauled off to jail before the Mallorens knew anything of it. Presumably they would correct matters as soon as they heard, but to end up in Newgate would be the final, degrading limit to her London adventures.

The stairs were wide enough, but being servants' stairs, the treads were plain wood. Her shoes were noisy on them, so she slipped them off.

She paused at the first door, but it must surely open into the main floor where there would be public rooms and such facilities as the dining room and library. The chances were high that servants would be busy there, perhaps even stationed there. She carried on up to the next floor.

At the next door she paused, surprisingly reluctant to go through it, for there was nothing about the plain wood to tell her what was on the other side. If she went through this door, she might walk straight into a servant or a Malloren.

The latter, she reminded herself, was exactly what she wanted, and yet she felt so guilty at this housebreaking that she hardly had the nerve.

Housebreaking!

Portia sagged for a moment against the wall. Her life kept turning in circles. This had all started with housebreaking. What would the next spiral bring?

Enough of this. She turned the knob and opened the door.

She stepped into luxury.

She should have expected it, but coming from the dark plain stairway it was startling to walk into warm light, gleaming oak paneling, and fine furniture and art. Beneath her feet was a luxurious carpet runner from Persia, and figured red velvet draped a nearby window.

It was as fine as Lord Trelyn's house, but a great deal warmer in tone.

What now?

Portia listened, but could hear nothing but the tick of clocks. The corridor had doors opening off one side and turned into other corridors at either end. Should she just enter the first room and wait there?

For what?

She berated herself for arrant cowardice.

Should she check each room?

But the chance of encountering a servant was great and she did not want to do that without finding a Malloren first.

On the other hand, if someone walked around one of the corners there was nowhere for her to hide. . . .

Portia put aside her useless fears and walked forward, listening at each door.

Silence.

It was as if the house were deserted. What was she going to do if the Mallorens were out all night, too?

She halted at the corner. The end wall here had four magnificent windows for it was the head of the stairway. A peep showed her wide stairs coiling down toward the hall, where a footman crossed.

Where was he going? To answer a summons from a Malloren? She wasn't sure enough of that to go down and announce her presence. She turned back to avoid crossing the open space at the top of the stairs, and checked each door in the other corridor.

She was halfway down, ear pressed to a panel trying to decide if the noises she heard were made by a person, and if so whom, when a voice said, "May I perhaps help you?"

Portia spun around.

She was face-to-face with the Marquess of Rothgar in quiet dark blue magnificence. His brows rose. "Miss St. Claire. What a delightful surprise."

Nineteen

Portia could feel her face turn red. It was such an extraordinary situation in which to find herself. "I . . . I need to speak to Bryght, my lord."

"Do you? Did he refuse to see you?"

Portia went redder. "No. I . . . I didn't try the front door."

He smiled. "How enterprising! I am charmed." He reached past her to open the door she had been checking. "Please, come in where we can be more comfortable."

He ushered her in before she could collect her wits, but Portia froze when she saw she was in his bedroom.

He looked at her rather quizzically. "I have no designs on your virtue. My private rooms are downstairs. Up here I have only this room and my dressing room."

Portia stayed where she was, close to the door. "I came to see Lord Bryght."

"Why? And, why in this manner? Forgive me for mentioning it, but your involvement with my brother has caused him some difficulty."

"*My* involvement with *him!*" gasped Portia. "He has turned my life upside down!"

"Has he indeed? Then perhaps you are well rid of him. So what is your purpose here?"

Portia realized with a shiver that despite his courteous

manner, the marquess was not best pleased with her. It was
hardly surprising when she was the cause of a duel. "It
isn't my fault," she said. "I only just found out about the
duel and—"

"What duel?"

Portia took a step backward. "The one between Lord
Bryght and the Earl of Walgrave. It is all a mistake though,
or rather—"

"It most certainly is," he said icily. "What is the cause?"

Portia swallowed. Logic told her this man would not really harm her, but her nerves were carrying another message. "Me," she whispered.

He raised a brow. "The earl has an interest in you, too?
What a remarkable woman you appear to be."

Portia was red again, but this time with mortification. "I
know I am no beauty, my lord. The earl regards me as a
sister."

"And he feels his sister has need of defense? What have
you been telling him?"

"Nothing! I have not been able to speak to him. The
Trelyns have kept me prisoner and spread the most malicious lies!"

"Ah," he said softly. "Do I detect the touch of the beau-
teous Nerissa?"

"She seems to hate Bryght. She wants him dead."

"Then she should have chosen an opponent other than
Walgrave."

"I don't think she chose him," Portia admitted. "I think
Fort chose himself. He's somewhat hot-headed."

"My dear Miss St. Claire, you appear to be two of a
kind." But the icy disdain had thawed. "Come, tell me what
tales have been racing around Town. I have been engaged."

Portia relaxed enough to move a little closer to the fire.

She flinched, however, when a pale shape there stirred. Then she saw it was a dog.

"That is Boudicca." The dog waved a lazy tail. "Well, Miss St. Claire? The whole tale, please. I will not have this kind of débacle in my family."

"Dueling is not so uncommon, I gather," she said, trying to match his tone.

"It is within the family. Are you not aware that Lord Walgrave is our brother-in-law?"

Portia shook her head. "I had forgotten. He does not seem to feel warmly about you."

"That has nothing to do with it. The cause of the duel, Miss St. Claire. The brothel?"

It was snapped at her like an accusation, and Portia's gaze flew to his. "How did you know . . . ?"

"Bryght told me. Miss St. Claire, may we get to the issue?"

"Yes. . . . No, not the brothel . . ." Portia gathered herself. "Someone has spread stories about the Willoughbys'. False stories, but close enough, I gather, that even Lady Willoughby is not denying them. . . ."

"And the stories say?"

Portia swallowed, for though she was not at fault in this, he might not believe it. "That Bryght attempted to seduce me," she whispered, "and when I refused, he tried to rape me."

She looked up at him, and what she saw there made her shiver.

"I see. Presumably you were discovered not just disheveled from your fun, but distressed, half-clothed, bruised . . . ?"

Portia nodded. "I wanted to go out so that everyone could see that I was well, but they locked me in."

He was standing by a chair and a finger tapped on the

back. "It appears to me that you should be at Walgrave's House with this story."

"I tried! They would not let me in. That's why I broke in here. And because I was afraid to be out in the dark. . . ."

"How did you get in? As the householder, I am curious."

Portia wondered how he would take her unladylike exploits. "I climbed the gate into the lane, and found an unlocked door."

He suddenly smiled. "I delight in resourceful women. You are correct. You should discuss this with Bryght." He went to open the door.

Portia wanted to hold him back. "You cannot deal with this, my lord?"

"Of course I can, but if I do not take you to my brother, I fear we would have another duel in the family. Come. Of what are you afraid?"

Bryght. Herself. That she would end up tying a man in a marriage he did not want.

Surely not a fate worse than death, however.

She let the marquess guide her back to the part of the house she had first explored. After a brief tap, he opened a door to reveal Bryght in shirtsleeves at a desk piled with papers.

"Is that your last will and testament?" Rothgar asked caustically.

Bryght rose and stared at Portia. Then he looked at his brother. "You have been unavailable."

"True. You cannot duel with Fort."

"Tell him that."

"I intend to. There is apparently no cause, but I think you and Miss St. Claire have matters to discuss."

Portia was aware of Bryght staring at her, though she had her eyes fixed on the fire.

"Miss St. Claire!"

At the marquess's sharp tone, she looked up at him. "Yes, my lord?"

"Your gowns are presumably at the Trelyns."

"Yes, my lord."

He looked at Bryght. "I'll take Zeno."

At a word from Bryght the dog rose and went to the marquess's side.

"Talk to each other," Rothgar said, and then left.

At a click Portia whirled to the door.

"He's locked it," Bryght confirmed. "He's not best pleased with us, I fear. We had better do as we are told and talk to each other."

Portia turned. He was coming toward her, smiling. "Don't!" she exclaimed, backing away.

He stopped. "What's the matter?"

"Don't touch me!" She meant it as much as a warning as a protest, for she knew she was vulnerable to his slightest touch and she did not want to entangle them any more than they already were. She saw him take it as outright rejection.

With distant courtesy, he asked, "Do you have any objection to sitting by the fire where it is warm? May I pour you some wine? I'm afraid I have no food here."

Portia stared at him. "Of course I don't want wine. The marquess has locked us in, time is flying, and in the morning there will be a duel. We must do something!"

"I doubt there will be a duel, Portia. Relax a little and talk to me. Do you realize how little we have actually talked?"

Portia was fixed against the door as if glued there. "Of course I do. That's why this whole thing is so absurd. No one marries a person they have met only a handful of times!"

"But such very interesting meetings." He poured the wine and came over to offer her a glass.

After a moment, Portia took it and drank, hoping to steady her nerves. She was trapped here with Bryght, but at least it was a study not a bedroom. The only furniture was two upholstered chairs by the fire, some small tables, a desk, and many bookshelves. The shelves were not filled with elegant leatherbound philosophers, however, but with ledgers, bundles of papers, and almanacs.

It seemed businesslike and that was a safe thing to focus on rather than his casual attire, his smile, and his over-whelming presence. How could her wretched body be shivering with excitement just to be in a room with this man?

Seeking a commonplace topic of conversation, she walked over to the desk. "What were you doing here?"

"Putting my affairs in order."

Her hand flinched in the act of touching a paper. "This doesn't look like a will."

"No. It's actually details of some investigations to do with guano." At her questioning look, he said, "Bird droppings."

Portia turned away sharply. "There's no need to make fun of me, my lord. I apologize for my vulgar curiosity."

"I am not making fun." He was behind her then, taking her cloak. She turned, but it was gone and in truth it had been too hot for this room.

"Portia," he said gently, "we do need to talk. Come sit by the fire. I promise, I have no evil intentions."

She allowed herself to be placed in a chair by the fire and sipped the wine. The lightest touch of his hand on her arm had been like fire, but she must remember that he did not want to marry her. He had withdrawn his offer, even at danger to his life.

"Perhaps I should apologize," she said. "Your brother implied that I am the cause of your troubles, my lord, and he is right." She looked up seriously. "That's why I had to do something. Neither you nor Fort are to blame for this. It would not be fair for you to fight."

He had taken the opposite chair and lounged there, far too beautiful in the firelight for her composure. "You are not blameless. But your brother takes the greater share. And if Fort and I fight, it will be little to do with you. The quarrel goes deeper than that."

"What quarrel?"

"Our families have been at odds for years. The old earl hated Rothgar. Of course, Rothgar is the sort of man the old earl despised—despite everything he was a genuine prude—but they clashed on other matters. Rothgar was one of the few willing to take on Walgrave, the Incorruptible."

Portia sipped her wine, the commonplace nature of this conversation soothing her. "But Fort is not like his father. He's hardly a prude and I doubt he even shared his politics. Why would the feud continue?"

"Perhaps there's a tendency to offer reverence for the dead in continuing their causes. . . ." After a moment, he added, "The trouble was exacerbated by matters to do with my youngest brother and his bride, Lady Chastity Ware. You must know Chastity."

"Yes, a little. But the earl's daughters were guarded and not permitted to mingle much with lesser mortals. Did Fort not want your brother to marry his sister?"

"Not particularly, but you must have heard of the scandal that surrounded Chastity. That she was caught with a man in her bed?"

"Yes, but it was all a mistake, I understand."

"Indeed it was, but it took a great deal of maneuvering to establish that. Particularly as her father had spread the lie to begin with."

"The earl! Why would he do that?"

"It is complex, but unraveling it caused his death. Fort blames us for that."

Portia had a sudden insight. "And unraveling it involved that letter, didn't it? That's why you were in the earl's house in Maidenhead."

He nodded. "Exactly. Fort would be happy to do any Malloren an ill turn, though I doubt he actually wants to kill me. He's more subtle than that. He wants, I believe, to have us married."

Portia looked down at her glass. "An ill turn," she echoed, trying not to show how much that hurt. "The Trelyns also wish to punish you with me."

"How very obtuse of them."

Portia looked up to see that he was watching her, watching her like a hawk. That reminded her of what he was besides wonderful, and she leaped to her feet to put the room between them. "There is no need to be polite, my lord. Having had time to think, I believe I understand the situation very well." Portia stared at a fine picture of a foreign land, a sun-washed land of spice. "It was gallantry that drove you to purchase me at Mirabelle's. I see now that no one would wish to do such a thing. I was disguised, but you were known. I'm sorry for accusing you of selfish desires."

"You are forgiven."

He sounded almost amused, but she did not dare look at him. "And I'm sure you never did intend to make improper advances to me in the square that day. It was entirely my ridiculous assumption. . . ."

"True enough."

She bit her unsteady lips. "And I should never have suggested you were lying to me about that quotation."

"I am amazed," he remarked. "I had no idea I was so

entirely innocent. Can you whitewash my behavior at Lady Willoughby's, too?"

She turned, warily. "You jest, my lord, but it's true. It is my folly and my brother's that has caused the problems. It would be the grossest injustice for you to suffer for it."

"Undoubtedly. So, Lady Willoughby's? Come, at least attempt it."

She could not understand him. "It appears to me that you do not take this seriously enough, my lord. It is your life we speak of."

"I realize that, but I'm still curious as to the interpretation you can put on the Affair Willoughby."

She frowned at his levity. "Well, I do think you were a little to blame. You shouldn't have trapped me into a wager, and you shouldn't have made the forfeit such an intimate one."

That recalled another intimate wager and Portia blushed, praying he would not refer to it. Here, in a civilized room, with a gentleman fairly decently dressed, it was possible to try to forget that other occasion. Possible, but not easy once the memory was stirred.

His lids were lowered in a way that concealed his thoughts and made him deeply mysterious. "What other price could you have met, Hippolyta?"

"Don't call me that!"

"But I like it. Don't fear, I won't call you that in public. In bed, now . . ."

Alarm shivered through her. "There is no question of bed between us, my lord!"

"No, there probably isn't. Or not in the near future. So," he said calmly, "what would you rather have paid at the Willoughbys'?"

"I don't know! Sixpence. A pair of embroidered slippers. An apple pie . . ."

He raised a brow. "What wondrous things you carry in the pockets of your evening gown."

She glared at him. "You know what I mean."

"Yes, but I have no need of money, or pies, or embroidered slippers, and I wanted you to kiss me. As much as you wanted to kiss me. As much as you want to kiss me now."

Portia stiffened. "No, I don't."

"Ladies shouldn't lie either, you know."

"Are you saying you want to kiss me now?"

"Oh yes. Absolutely."

At the tone of his voice, Portia shivered. "Why?" she demanded faintly.

"Still so innocent? In the natural desire that it will go as it did the other night, and that Rothgar will not return for an hour or so. Why else?"

She raised a hand to her heaving chest. "You are still trying to ruin me?"

His eyes snapped open, sparking anger. "It appears you are still trying to insult me." Then his tone softened. "I have every expectation of marrying you, Portia, and I have no objection to anticipating the ceremony."

"But you don't have to marry me!" she protested, feeling as if she were trying to explain matters to a simpleton. "You say there will be no duel, and I realize now that what happened at Lady Willoughby's was not so terrible. Even if my reputation is tarnished, I'm headed for a life of obscurity where no one will care a fig."

He stood and came toward her. "I, however, am not. I must continue to move in Society. I have no intention of being dogged by rumors that I raped a woman and abandoned her to a life of dismal shame in the provinces."

She backed away. "I will tell the world it is not true."

"From Dorset? And half the world will not believe you, no matter what you say."

He was only feet away now. She was reminded of Maidenhead where his size and purpose had defeated her opposition.

"Are you saying I must marry you to save *your* reputation?" she asked faintly.

His eyes twinkled. "Precisely. And our subsequent delight and happiness will kill any shreds of doubt." He pulled her into his arms.

She braced her hands against his chest. "There must be another way!"

"Can you see it?"

Her arms lost strength and she was against him. "No."

His fingers moved into her hair.

"What . . . ?"

"I am completing the disintegration of your hair arrangement. I have had a driving desire to see it long and loose since our first meeting."

The pins were gone and his hands threaded gently through her hair and spread it. "It is fire in the firelight. . . ."

"My lord," said Portia faintly, "this is madness. . . ."

"Then let us be mad." And he kissed her.

The power of it almost buckled her knees, but she struggled for sanity and wrenched her mouth away. "My lord, this is wrong!"

He captured her hair and looked into her eyes. "We will marry on Wednesday. Do not deny me now."

Something she saw there—a need, a wanting—almost

melted Portia's resistance, but she tried one more time. "We need not marry. We need not. There must be a way."

"There is not. You are my wife. Surrender to me."

Desire—a raw need created in her by this man—hovered, ready to strike, but still Portia resisted. "It would bind us. . . ."

"We are already bound." He swept her into his arms and carried her toward the fire to lay her on the carpet there. She felt sudden heat along her body, but she was no hotter there than inside, where wild passion flickered.

She was a wanton. Decent, proper Portia St. Claire had fallen away like a shell to reveal the creature beneath, a creature of desires, a lover of sensation, a woman who lusted after this man and the pleasure he could bring.

He stripped off his shirt and tugged the ribbon from his hair so he looked just as he had at Mirabelle's. Portia just lay there, hair loose, skirts disordered, drinking in the sight of him.

He knelt by her and cradled her cheek. "Firelight becomes you. You are a creature of flame, Hippolyta, and very beautiful."

And Portia, in the mirror of his eyes, was beautiful. "I am wicked," she murmured, a lingering protest of her other self.

"I love your wickedness. May I see more of you?"

When she made no protest, he eased her up and unfastened the back of her dress. She knew she should stop him, but she did not, though the last tatters of her modesty had her clutching her dress to her breasts at the front.

His hand spread hot against her back where it was exposed above her stays. As he put his lips there and kissed her she stared helpless at the wall, but then the flickering heat of it had her arching back toward him. His arm came around to support her, to press against her already sensitive breasts.

"I touch you and you sing like a harp," he said against her nape. "Let us make music. . . ."

She clutched his arm against her. "Bryght, truly we should not. This is wrong. This is foolish. . . ."

"We are as good as married." He lifted her, casually dislodging her grip on her bodice so her dress fell away. When he set her on her feet, she was standing in her shift and stays and tried to conceal herself.

He pulled her hands down. "Let me see you, love."

In the passionate heat of his gaze the last crystals of her resistance melted. She blushed and laughed shakily. "If I'd known, I'd have worn my best underwear."

He traced the simple cotton-over-bone of her stays. "I will give you exquisite garments of silk and lace and love you in and out of them, but at this moment, these are perfect."

He deftly unknotted the laces and pulled the strings loose so her stays, too, fell to the carpet. Portia's frantic conscience tried to remind her that his very dexterity proved he was not a decent man, but it was drowned out by the clamor of her senses.

She wanted him. She wanted him so badly that it was a physical ache.

His hands cherished her liberated torso over the plain cotton of her shift, making the ache worse. "Now you look a little like my Hippolyta, but much prettier."

"I am not pretty," she protested, grasping his wrists. "Truly I'm not!"

"Am I bewitched, then? It doesn't matter, for I am happy with it." He twisted free, captured her right hand and pressed it to the front of his breeches. "See."

She tried to pull away, but he held her there.

"Men are lustful creatures," she said weakly. "Easily stirred."

"Some of us are more discriminating than others. My friend there doesn't dance for just anyone, you know."

Yes, my beautiful one. Dance for me, show me that you want the gift of Venus. . . .

She felt him move beneath her hand and colored. But sinful woman that she was, she loved it. He moved her hand up and down the hardness. "See what you do to me. Since this will soon be your friend, too, perhaps you should christen it."

Portia jerked her hand away. *"Christen* it?"

"How else are we to talk of it in public?"

Portia stepped back. "Why ever would we want to talk of such a thing in public?"

"To prepare for what we intend to do as soon as we get home?" he suggested with a grin. "Or perhaps for what we are going to do in some quiet corner of our host's house." He captured her and pulled her hard against him. "I am inviting you to live a very wicked life, my Amazon. Do you accept?"

"You will be disappointed!" she protested. "I'm not wicked. Oh, Bryght, stop and think!"

"You are wicked enough, and rash enough for me, too." He released her, but only to undo his buttons so his flap fell. He captured her hand again and pressed it to him, but to hot flesh now. "Name it," he whispered, and she felt the shudder that rippled through him.

It conquered her. This was not artifice. Perhaps he lied, perhaps he danced for anyone, but at this moment he danced for her.

"The Thames," she whispered.

He looked at her with bemusement. "I hope you don't think its flow can equal England's greatest river."

"No." She couldn't believe she was saying this. "I think it goes through Maidenhead."

He laughed and picked her up to swing her around and around until she was dizzy, then collapsed them both on the carpet to pleasure her.

It was like at Mirabelle's and yet unlike, for this time Portia was willing. More than willing, she was eager.

She made no protest when he pulled off her shift, her last barrier to him. He ran his hand over her in gentle exploration. "Delicate bones, skin like finest silk that shows the veins beneath . . . I am afraid of hurting you."

And indeed, his hand trembled. "You are so small," he said. "I know you are not fragile, but you are small. Did I bruise you last time?"

"No, of course not." But he insisted on inspecting every inch of her with laughter and kisses.

Portia discovered that to be naked with Bryght seemed natural, the most natural thing in the world. And she wanted him naked too. With more teasing games they stripped him and she admired his splendor.

"Strong bones," she said, sliding an exploratory hand up his thigh, over his hip. "Skin like velvet over steel. You could model for David."

He shook his head. "Heaven forbid! But if I please you, I'm pleased. And I love your touch, Portia. Touch me where I please you. . . ."

Blushing, Portia continued her exploration, running her hand over his chest, his shoulders, down over his muscular abdomen. She halted there, however, embarrassed to go further even though she wanted to, wanted to feel the heat and hardness of him again. . . .

His hands wandered her at the same time—almost without conscious thought, it seemed, but summoning desire. "Your touch has such power over me, I am afraid. I want to be gentle, Portia, but I'm not sure I can be. Tell me if I hurt you."

She kissed his chest. "I expect it to hurt."

He tilted her chin and kissed her lips. "Perhaps we can exceed your expectations. . . ."

Portia hesitated then, however. Talk of the breaching of her virginity forced her to face the fact that if she surrendered there would be no going back. . . .

He seized her hair and kissed her, kissed her as if he sensed her doubts and wished to drive them out. Under the heat of his hands, his mouth, his body she could not think. She could only desire. Portia nipped and stroked, kissed and nibbled at every piece of his mobile body that became available, always wanting more and more.

When his sinuous movements brought the ultimate temptation in her way, she took it and put her lips over the head of the River Thames. He went rigid and twisted his head to look at her.

Portia came to her senses a little then. What in heaven's name had come over her? Something in his expression, however, filled her with a sense of gleeful power. Watching him carefully, she rubbed her tongue against him.

He shuddered and muttered, "Hades," like a dying man.

Portia stroked him with her tongue and saw him flush. She sucked a little and he gasped. He collapsed down on the carpet. "Go on, then, oh precocious one. Have your wicked way with me."

There was a sheen of sweat on his face and Portia didn't think it was from the fire. She felt extremely hot herself. Her rash impulsiveness had landed her in another situation completely beyond her competence, but she sensed that this one held only delight.

She settled to licking and sucking the novel item, enjoying the new sensation and a sweet musky taste she found there. To be so hard, the River Thames would have to be solid ice, but this one was hot and almost fluid in the way it danced to her touch.

She slid one hand over his rigid torso, and curled the other around him, then flared it downward to explore the smooth pouches beneath. How strange, how wonderful, how very interesting a man was. . . .

From this angle she couldn't see his face, but she could see his hand on his thigh, his left hand with the large emerald signet. Suddenly it formed a fist, and she covered it with her own paler one, soothing it even as she tormented him. He grasped her hand almost to bruising point and she could hear each breath he took.

What now?

She was trapped in a spiral of heat and power. It was entrancing, but she felt as if something were about to explode. . . .

Suddenly he moved. He freed the river from captivity, hauling her up to face him. "If you dice with the devil, Hippolyta, you must burn."

He was not gentle. He drove her like a chariot into passion and entered her suddenly, violently, then froze, holding her there, knees looped high over his arms.

Portia stared into his dark eyes, drowning in intense sensation, shocked by their position, but immensely satisfied to be filled by him at last. He saw it and released her legs, swooping down to kiss her. Portia met the kiss fiercely, locking her legs around him as he drove her onward to destruction.

Portia tried to keep her eyes open, to see him in his passion, but the power became too strong. It denied all sensations except the one, the new one, the one she could hardly believe was part of the body she had inhabited for twenty-five years.

Twenty

Portia came back to reality lying in his arms, sweaty and sticky, nerves still humming and twitching from his onslaught. She ached in places, burned a little between her legs, and suddenly her whole body shuddered with an after-tremor of that passion.

He threaded his hand into her hair and turned her to face him. "Too much for you?" His expression reminded her of the first time—when he had tackled her to the floor in Maidenhead and seemed so concerned. She realized that all along, even at their worst times, that concern had formed a reassurance in her mind.

She shook her head. "But I didn't expect . . ."

He smiled ruefully, "I'd have been a little more restrained if you'd not tried to drain the River Thames."

She felt herself flame. "I don't know what came over me."

"I do and I don't mind," he said, stroking her gently. "I liked it. But it broke my control. If you play with fire you will be burned. Or at least, get singed. As long as you understand that."

Portia snuggled against him, needing him in so many ways that it bewildered her. And now they would have to marry. All escape was gone. At least she could soothe her conscience with the knowledge that it was his doing, and she had tried to save him from himself.

She couldn't help it. She smiled with delight.

Those who dice with the devil must indeed burn. They were not supposed to find the flames so pleasant, though. Portia snuggled closer to his sweat-damp body and played with fire. He captured her hand. "You do like living dangerously, don't you?"

"Alas," she murmured into his chest, "I fear I do."

He chuckled. "I look forward to the future with great anticipation but for now, love, I'm going to protect you from yourself." He disentangled them and helped her to her feet. "Assess your hurts and be cautious."

Portia did so and winced. "Rather more in some muscles than from the attack on Maidenhead." She glanced at him mischievously. "Well, my lord, was it worth six hundred guineas?"

He immediately swung her up, sat in the chair, and laid her across his knees for spanking. Shocked, Portia writhed madly. "Don't you *dare!*"

His hand rested on her buttocks. "Then stop calling me my lord."

She twisted to glare at him. He raised his brows and hand. The wretch would do it, too. "Well, Bryght," she bit out, "was it worth six hundred guineas?"

"Every penny," he said and turned her to sit on his lap.

Portia glared at him. "If you ever spank me, I'll tie you down and flog you!"

"That sounds like fun," he said with a grin.

She gasped and pulled away from him.

"I said we would be wicked," he reminded her.

"I will not be beaten!" she protested.

He shook his head. "Hush, love, I'm teasing. If we ever

do that sort of thing it will be for fun, and you will be able to stop whenever you want."

"For fun!"

He waggled his brows. "Confess. Before today, would you ever have thought to have such fun playing with the River Thames?"

And Portia hid her flaming face against his chest.

He laughed but separated them again. "It's quite possible that Rothgar will be back soon, perhaps even with Fort in tow. I don't insist on it, but I think perhaps we should have some clothes on."

Portia leaped from his arms and began to scramble into her garments, half an eye on the door. He watched her, grinning, but at her entreaties began to dress himself.

Portia was struggling with the fastenings at the back of her dress when she detected footsteps. "Someone's coming!" she hissed.

He laughed again and came to close the last two hooks.

"Your shirt!" Portia grabbed for him and was fastening the buttons at his neck as the lock turned. He detached her fingers so they were facing the door when it opened.

Rothgar came in and closed the door behind him. He glanced around. Portia saw her stockings and garters strewn across the floor and could have died. She looked despairingly at Bryght and he put his arm around her and held her close.

The marquess merely said, "I suspected it would be better to leave Walgrave downstairs. He merely wishes to know that the wedding will go forward as planned. I assume that is the case."

Bryght said, "Of course, though it doesn't please me to marry under the Trelyns' auspices."

"It will silence gossip, however."

"But people will still believe those horrible lies!" said Portia. "It isn't fair."

"Life is rarely fair," said Rothgar, "but sometimes it can be adjusted. After tonight, most voices will be silenced."

Portia wondered how their passionate love-making could silence gossip.

The marquess must be able to read her like a book. "I was thinking more of your *public* adventures, Miss St. Claire. We are going to dine in twenty minutes, then we are going to the Willoughbys', where the lady is having yet another of her delightful entertainments. . . ."

"But—"

He ignored her. "Bryght will be by your side. Walgrave and the Trelyns will also accompany us. Lady Willoughby will gush over you. The whole world will see it has been the victim of at least an error."

It sounded like an evening of torture. Portia grasped at an excuse. "I have nothing suitable to wear."

"Lady Trelyn has sent one of your gowns. I believe my sister's rooms should provide anything else you need and it would be quite in order for you to wear some of the lesser family jewels."

Portia looked between Bryght and his brother. It seemed indecent to go from such passion to a public appearance, and she hated the thought of being the focus of speculation.

Bryght kissed her. "When Rothgar takes the reins there is nothing for it but to go where he directs. Nothing and no one will harm you. I'll take you to Elf's suite."

He led her through the house to another corridor. The cool of the house brought cool to Portia's head. She realized with dismay that she really had burned her bridges. She was going to have to marry Bryght and though he was wonderful in many ways, he was still a gamester.

Bryght took her into a bedroom hung with pale green silk. Portia saw her second-best dress, a cream silk with a quilted petticoat, lying on the bed.

Would the passion in bed compensate for the constant worry and inevitable crises? Portia began to try to build bridges for retreat. "Surely if everyone is willing to retract their stories, I don't have to be there."

"Of course you do. They'll need proof that you are in one piece. More or less," he added with a wink that had her flaming.

He was investigating the various drawers and cupboards, which all seemed to be fuller than one would expect when the owner was not in residence. "Elf should stop buying every item that catches her fancy," he commented pulling out a black stomacher trimmed with red and gold. He shook his head and replaced it.

"Oh, we should not be going through her things!" Portia protested.

"Elf won't mind." He tossed a lace fichu on the bed. "She's your age, by the way. She'll welcome you into the family."

Portia picked up the neckerchief and found that it was of gossamer silk trimmed with the most beautiful silk lace she had ever seen. The lace contained a spider-web of fine gold threads that made it glimmer magically in the candle-light.

"This is too precious," she protested.

"Nonsense." He riffled through a small chest that seemed to be full of stockings. "Elfled," he said, as if the bemused Portia had asked. "We're all named after Anglo-Saxon rulers and heroes. Ah."

He pulled out a pair of stockings that seemed to be made

entirely of lace, and a pair of ornately frilled garters. He frowned at them. "We really must find Elf a husband."

"Why?"

He laid the stockings and garters by her dress. "No woman buys such things unless she hopes a man will see them."

Portia suspected he was right. "Then perhaps she would not want you to know she has them."

He nodded. "Wise Portia." He carefully replaced the items in the depth of the chest and took out a plain but pretty pair of stockings clocked with roses, and plain garters to hold them up. He put them on the bed and came to kiss her. "You see, we need you. Elf will like a sister and you can matchmake for her."

"I know no one suitable to marry the daughter of a marquess!"

"You soon will. You will be Lady Bryght, a leading light of Society. . . ."

"I can't—"

He kissed her again. "You can do anything. You'll be good for Elf. She's as spirited as you inside—lord, you should have seen some of the things she and Cyn got up to as children. Practically turned us gray. But she's too kind to take risks now she's a woman for fear of what Rothgar might do. Like most rakes he's not reasonable when it comes to men and his sisters."

Portia found this rush into family life alarming. "Bryght, I'm not sure—"

He sealed her lips with his fingers. "There's no going back now."

It was the gleam of triumph in his eyes that chilled her. "You seduced me deliberately!"

He colored slightly. "You didn't protest much, Hippolyta."

"Yes I did, and you over-rode me!"

"Are you going to accuse me of rape in truth?"

Portia whirled away, hands to cheeks. "No, but you kissed me out of my senses." She turned back to confront him. "You wanted this marriage and I didn't, so you made sure I would have to agree."

"I don't think you have much to complain about."

At his complacency, his *smugness,* Portia felt the fury rising in her like a pillar of flame. "Oh, don't you? Well, I tell you this, Bryght Malloren. Your scheme has failed. I will *never* marry you."

"Not even if you're with child?"

Icy shock doused the flames. "I can't be! Not after just one . . ."

"It's perfectly possible."

"Then I'll raise it a bastard!"

"No, you damn well won't!"

"You can't stop me! It's no longer possible to drag a bride to the altar bound and gagged!"

He was as dark and dangerous as at their first meeting reminding her of the many reasons she shouldn't bind her life to his. "You will marry me, Portia. You have no choice."

She grabbed the water jug and hurled the contents at him. He dodged most of it, capturing the jug before she could throw that too. He tossed it on the bed, so she seized the porcelain basin, intending to smash it over his head. He tackled her onto the bed and captured it from her.

"Admit it, Portia. You wanted that love-making, and you want me."

She fought him with all her strength. "I want *choice* and you stole it from me!"

He confined her easily. "I fight for what I want, and I want you."

"You just want to end this scandal!" she snapped.

Before he could respond, there was a tap at the door. He hesitated a moment, then slid off her and went to open it.

A blank-faced middle-aged maid came in and curtsied.

Bryght said to her, "My future bride needs to prepare for the evening. But she is not to leave this room without one of the family as escort."

She was a prisoner again. Portia closed her eyes and tried to control a wash of rage and misery. How could she go so quickly from that scintillating love to this bleak despair?

Then she realized that she was lying in disorder on a bed in a highly disordered room. She scrambled to her feet, wondering what the maid could be thinking.

The woman just said, "I'll ring for more water, ma'am."

A footman appeared and was sent on the errand while the maid efficiently cleared away the remains of battle.

Portia stood there wondering frantically what the likelihood was of her already carrying a child. She quelled panic. Such things became clear. The main thing was to play for time, and not to marry on Wednesday.

They couldn't force her into it. They couldn't.

She would go through with this evening, however, for she owed Bryght that. It would not be fair to leave him with such a scar on his reputation.

The footman returned with fresh water and the maid assisted Portia out of her crumpled clothing. What adventures she'd had since she dressed this morning.

Portia washed, then she dressed in the underwear Bryght had picked out for her, feeling each item like his hand against her skin. *I will give you exquisite garments of silk and lace, and love you in and out of them. . . .*

The memory rippled over Portia's nerves like a skillful touch, both longed-for and hated. She had given him her virginity, and in honor she should marry him. But she reminded herself fiercely that he certainly hadn't married the first woman he'd made love with.

When she was in her gown, made elegant by the beautiful fichu, there was another knock on the door.

Portia started, thinking it must be Bryght. But it was the marquess in magnificent ruby satin. A quiet servant followed, carrying a box. Lord Rothgar studied Portia dispassionately, and she blushed and raised her chin. "I make no pretense to be more than I am, my lord."

"It would be foolish to do so," he replied, making her feel stupid for using such a trite phrase.

"I mean that I am no beauty, my lord, and no grand society lady. I have no desire to pretend to be."

"You have charms enough to ensnare my brother, and you are about to become a Malloren. There are few higher." He raised a finger and the servant stepped forward to place the box on a table. The man unlocked it and slid open some drawers. It was a jewel chest, each drawer glittering with precious stones.

Portia couldn't help but gape.

"Come here," the marquess said.

"No. I need no such jewels!"

"That was not a request." Lord Rothgar's eyes were cool and she remembered his earlier anger before he had locked her in with Bryght. "You have come close to causing disaster in this family, Portia. Tonight we will put it right and set the stage for a harmonious future. You will play your part."

Portia glanced frantically between the two servants, but they might as well be statues. "I am willing, but I do not need jewels."

"You will play your part."

And Portia found herself going forward to accept the ornaments. She told herself it was just a small concession, and did not mean she was agreeing to everything. But her heart beat fast with panic as he fixed a necklace about her throat, and drops in her ears. A headdress of some sort was settled in her curls.

When his fingers touched her bodice she jerked in alarm, but saw he was only pinning an ornate brooch at the join of the fichu. It consisted of scintillating yellow stones bordered by small, brilliant diamonds. Trailing strings of the stones fell to sway down her bodice toward her waist.

These jewels matched the engagement ring she had returned to Bryght. She supposed she would get it back, and wished she could avoid it.

Rothgar turned her to a mirror. The design of the jewels gave the impression of twining golden ribbons edged with light, and they shimmered all over her—in her bodice, her ears, and around her neck. The item in her hair was a delicate tiara that seemed to blend with the color of her hair, enhancing both.

In some way the lacy fichu and the exquisite jewels made of Portia St. Claire something entirely different, something more beautiful, more special. It would be foolish to deny it, but just as foolish to take credit for it.

"They are very beautiful," she said flatly.

"I think so. They are not part of the estate, however, so you need not feel at all uneasy about wearing them. Are you ready?" He held out an elegant white hand.

Portia reminded herself that she was obeying only in order to clear Bryght's name. She was agreeing to nothing more. She placed her hand in Lord Rothgar's and allowed him to lead her into the corridor and toward the stairs.

At the head of the stairs he halted and directed her attention to a portrait between the long windows there. "My father and his second wife, Bryght's mother. Their wedding portrait."

Portia saw a charming couple seated on a bench beneath a tree while a pair of spaniels played at their feet. The gentleman was dark, but the lady's hair was a russet-gold almost as red as Portia's. Both were smiling, but she gained the impression that the lady was more accustomed to smiles than the gentleman.

Nerissa had said that Rothgar's mother had turned mad and murdered her second child. In the portrait, Portia detected the shadows of that event in the husband's eyes. She thought that his new bride might be able to wipe away shadows, however. It was a beautiful face, but also a good one.

"I wish I had known her. She looks charming."

"She was, and very kind-hearted. She was also high-spirited and seems to have passed that trait on to most of her offspring. They give me endless trouble."

Then Portia saw the jewels. Except for the tiara, the marchioness was wearing the jewels the marquess had put on her. Her hand went to the necklace. "They are the same. . . ."

"They were her bridal gift from my father."

She looked at him in shock. "Then I mustn't wear them!"

"They were always intended for Bryght's bride."

Portia suddenly felt trapped by the ornaments, as if they were chains not jewels. She looked at the smiling woman who had taken on a family under a dark cloud and brought love. "She would want better than this artificial marriage for her firstborn son."

Rothgar guided her to the stairs. "She wanted the best, as any parent would. The important thing is that those jewels were Gabrielle's favorite pieces, and well known. Your wearing them will be understood by all."

So it had been a practical gesture, not a sentimental one. That suited Portia's mood entirely.

Rothgar led her to a gilded room where she found the Trelyn's present. Both of them looked coldly at Portia before applying practiced, polite smiles. "Why, how pretty you look!" declared Nerissa with a degree of astonishment that was insulting.

Portia replied with a wary curtsy.

Fort was present, too. "How are you?" he asked, and his gray eyes searched her for damage.

"I am in perfect health, Fort," Portia said firmly, but before she could say anything else, Rothgar moved her on to meet the two strangers present. She realized these were more Mallorens.

"My sister, Lady Elfled, generally called Elf," the marquess said. Lady Elf was not a beauty, and her hair was browner than her mother's, but Portia thought she might have much of her mother's warmth and charm.

Portia curtsied, and Elf embraced her. "How wonderful! Not many weeks since Cyn married and I am to have another new sister! And since Cyn and Chastity will travel to Canada in the spring, it is delightful to have a sister who will keep me company from time to time."

Portia was dizzied by this apparently genuine warmth.

"And mother's jewels!" Elf exclaimed. "How lovely they look on you. They need brilliant hair such as yours. How clever you are, Bryght!"

Portia spun to see that Bryght had entered the room. There had not been time for him to be powdered, but he was otherwise in full magnificence of green-bronze watered silk, heavily braided in gold. His earring was a golden stone to match Portia's jewels, and he smiled at his brother. "Thank you."

"They were always intended for your wife," said Rothgar. "Portia, can you take your eyes off my showy brother long enough to greet another Malloren? Brand."

Blushing, Portia hastily turned back. Brand Malloren was powdered, but he had the same unalarming degree of good looks as his sister. He smiled in a surprisingly normal manner for a Malloren and kissed her hand and cheek. "Welcome to the family. I gather we are to venture forward *en masse* and conquer the world."

"To conquer the Willoughbys will be sufficient." Rothgar drew Brand and Elf away, leaving Portia and Bryght together.

"You look very beautiful," he said softly.

"I don't like this, Bryght. I don't like any of it."

He captured her hand and led her to a far corner of the room where a plinth surmounted by a huge urn even provided a little privacy. "What don't you like, love?"

She snatched her hand free. "For one thing, I don't like deception. I am *not* your love!"

"You're upset," he said patiently. "I understand. I'd rather we were being left alone to explore our feelings. I do love you, though."

Portia turned away. "I don't want to be alone with you. I want to be free."

Patiently, he asked, "What upsets you about the thought of us marrying?"

Portia opened and closed her fan. "That we have nothing in common. That we don't really want to."

"We have a great deal in common, and I want to."

She turned her head to meet his eyes. "Why? Other than to preserve your fragile reputation?"

"Damned if I know," he said lightly, "and that's the most persuasive argument of all. If you were a raving beauty whom all men would envy me—like Nerissa, or if you were rich—like Jenny Findlayson, then it would be easy to explain, wouldn't it? I just want you, Portia."

"Passion will fade."

He shook his head. "Don't debase what we have. I want your companionship. I want your spirit. I want your children."

It was dangerously sweet. "Why?" she demanded.

"Where did you get the notion that love is logical? Why do you love me?"

Phrased that way, it was tempting to give him reasons, for she knew she did have warm feelings for him underneath the fear and bitterness. But Portia knew that she must not weaken. "I don't."

She saw it surprise him, and perhaps hurt as well. "Ah. I'm sorry, then, that I haven't worked harder to avoid this." Almost wistfully, he added, "I can be quite a pleasant companion, given the chance. What do you want in this marriage?"

"Respect."

"I respect you."

"I mean," she said, looking straight at him, "I want to respect my husband."

He sucked in a breath. "In what way do I not deserve respect?"

"You're a gamester." Before he could speak she carried on, "Don't deny it! You're as bad as Oliver, just luckier, and luck never lasts. I'll never be sure my house won't be wagered away."

"Portia," he said patiently, "I would never do that."

"That's what gamesters always say!"

"I'm not a gamester."

"Ha!"

He looked as if he would retort sharply, but then he frowned. "Amazon tears again . . ."

Portia turned away, brushing at tears she had not been aware of spilling.

"From this day forward," he said quietly, "I will not play games of chance for more than minor stakes."

She turned back. "What?"

"You heard. I do not lie, and I keep my word. Trust me."

"But . . . ?"

He captured her again and kissed her. "Hush. You will never lose your home through me."

She stared up at him, trying to believe, wanting to trust. "But how will we survive if you give up the tables?"

He grinned. "Oh, bird droppings and such." Before she could protest, he explained. "Investments. My income comes mostly from dealing in imports, exports, mining, and manufactories."

Portia was confused but not reassured. "My father ruined himself at that, and put a pistol ball in his head."

He would have responded, but the meal was announced.

He sighed. "I can prove what I say, Portia, but there is no time now. You will have to take me on trust." He took a ring out of his pocket and slid it onto her finger.

It was the square golden stone bordered by tiny diamonds that matched the others that she wore. "This should mean love," she said sadly.

"It means commitment. That will have to do for now. The meal is ready. Come."

It was a meal of elegant competence, with witty and erudite talk flowing around the table. No one would guess that there were bitter enemies present. No one would guess that Portia was a sacrificial victim.

Had Bryght been honest when he'd said he loved her? It should mean so much, but it foundered on the fact that he was a gambler in every aspect of his life. Portia's father had truly loved her mother—he would not have married so much beneath him otherwise. It had not staved off disaster in the end.

Portia was determined to evade the Laocoon tails that tangled her. She looked around the table and assessed her enemies.

The marquess merely wanted his brother's safety.

Nerissa wanted the marriage, but she mainly wanted that letter. Perhaps Portia could get it in some other way.

Fort was the biggest problem because he wanted the marriage itself, wanted it because he knew it would be disastrous for Bryght. How could her friend so ill-wish her?

She would find an opportunity to talk to him and make him see that he would be hurting her as well as Bryght. Looking at him, however, seeing how cold and cynical he had become since his father's death, she had doubts.

Eventually there were toasts and then Elf led Portia and Nerissa away to take tea in her boudoir.

"The men will not be long," Elf said, "for we are to be at Lady Willoughby's soon. At least, I hope they will not be long. The last thing we need is for them to be in their cups."

"I can't imagine the marquess in his cups," said Portia, sipping tea, wondering if she could recruit Elf to her cause.

"Oh, it happens," said Elf with a chuckle. "Sometimes at the Abbey, they all relax and become very silly."

"And do you become drunk, too?" asked Nerissa.

"Why no."

"You should. It is delightful. Is it not, Portia?"

"I have never been drunk either, Nerissa. It is not lady-like."

Nerissa laughed. "What a dull stick you are. Poor Bryght. He'll probably shoot himself of boredom!"

"Lady Trelyn!" protested Elf.

Nerissa laughed, but then the tone changed and she dissolved into tears.

"Oh dear." Elf hurried to her side.

Portia had never seen Nerissa in such a state. "She's increasing. . . ."

"That may explain it. Perhaps we should let her lie down next door."

So they supported the distraught Nerissa into the green bedchamber and laid her on the bed. "I'm so sorry!" Nerissa gasped. "I don't know how I could. . . . Oh dear, Trelyn will be so displeased!"

"We won't say anything," said Elf soothingly. "It is just your condition. It disorders some women. Would you like your tea here?"

Nerissa shook her head. "Perhaps if I just lie quietly. I must be ready to play my part later." She looked at Portia. "I never meant you ill! I could not bear the thought of you languishing a spinster, and this will be a brilliant match. . . ."

Portia almost believed her until she added, "But, oh, poor Bryght!"

Elf pulled Portia out of the room and back to the tea. "She is the most complete cat. I was terrified for a while that Bryght would marry her. So was Rothgar. Well, not terrified. But disturbed."

"I assume that if the marquess did not want Bryght to marry Nerissa, they would not marry."

"Well, perhaps," said Elf dubiously. "Bryght is past being ruled by Rothgar, though, and he has money enough to snap his fingers at him if he wishes."

"He does?" From speculation, Portia. Remember that.

"Oh yes. We all have handsome allowances, though Bryght has made even more through his speculations. He is very clever at it."

"He must lose money sometimes, though."

"Rarely. There was something to do with a new kind of steel furnace which proved completely unsafe. And there's Bridgewater's canal, which most people think will be a disaster. I understand that the duke has signed an agreement that he will sell coal in Manchester and Liverpool for fourpence a ton for forty years. No one believes he can make a profit at that."

Portia really did not want to hear this. "I wish there was no necessity for such a hasty wedding," she hazarded, watching for Elf's response.

"But there is, isn't there?"

Portia turned red. Bryght's sister had a pleasant, comfortable face and a light manner that seemed almost silly at times. When she posed her question, however, there was a shrewdness in her eyes that reminded Portia of Bryght and Rothgar.

As much to escape the question as anything, Portia went to the adjoining door. "I had best check that Nerissa is all right."

She walked into an empty room. After a puzzled moment, she remembered Nerissa's disordered health at the Willoughbys'. "That woman is doubtless healthy as a peasant," she snapped to an astonished Elf, and headed for the corridor.

"Where are you going?" Elf gasped from behind her. "She may have gone downstairs."

"Why?" Portia demanded, and let instinct guide her. "Where are Bryght's rooms? I've forgotten."

"This way," said Elf, picking up her skirts to run around the corner into the next corridor. She opened a door and they burst in to see Nerissa watching a paper shrivel and burn. She turned with a glowing smile. "Too late! I am free of the Mallorens at last!"

"What was that?" Elf asked in confusion.

But Portia knew. It was that horrible letter from Maidenhead and she was glad to see it go, though she felt as if somehow she should have prevented the destruction.

Nerissa moved away from the fireplace. "Now I am free! I need never dance to a Malloren's tune again, and I'll do my best to ensure that Trelyn thwarts them at every turn."

"Then there is no reason to push for this marriage any more," said Portia, eager to see one toil cut free.

"Still reluctant?" asked Nerissa in surprise. "Alas, cousin dear, the damage is done. We can whitewash you at the Willoughbys', but the world will still believe you ruined. If you do not marry, it will be disastrous. If you stay in London, you will always be the focus of scandal. If you leave, it will be believed you have fled to escape it. Or perhaps even to bear a child. Is that not so, Lady Elfled?"

Elf looked at Portia with compassion. "It is, Portia. Truly."

"And Bryght would never live it down," added Nerissa. "Is that not true, Lady Elfled?"

"I fear so. To have a mistress is one thing. To ruin a lady is another."

"Then all is settled." Nerissa strolled to the bed, and ran a jeweled hand across the brown brocade cover. "I will enjoy thinking of you here, Cousin. I'm sure Bryght will be very

understanding of your awkwardness and ignorance. . . ."
With a throaty laugh she carried on her way.

"Ugh," shivered Elf. "Despite her beauty, Nerissa Trelyn makes me think of the slimy things one finds under stones. But what was she doing in here?"

Portia stirred herself to go look in the fire, but there was no longer even a scrap of ash as evidence. "Bryght had a letter of hers. A letter to her lover. He must have been using it to control her actions for she was desperate to get it back."

But her mind was on other things. Was it possible that marriage was the only way to clear Bryght's reputation?

Elf came to put an arm about Portia's waist and draw her out of the room. "Don't let her upset you, my dear. She throws darts purely for amusement. We must tell Bryght and Rothgar, though."

"They will be annoyed. If she chooses to, she could damage me."

"They will take care of it," Elf said with confidence. "Truly, having such formidable brothers can be tedious at times, but they are useful when problems need sorting out. Nothing is allowed to thwart them."

Such as a reluctant bride?

They found Nerissa composedly drinking tea, and they all went down to join the men who awaited in the hall. Elf had a quiet word with her brothers and Bryght came over to Portia. "Don't worry. The letter doesn't matter anymore."

"I should have remembered her trick that other time."

"You have enough on your mind. It's a shame Zeno was in Rothgar's rooms—he'd have set up the alarm. On the other hand, he might have bitten her and died of poisoning."

A laugh startled Portia, and she looked at him, wanting to surrender to the optimistic view of the future. But then she saw Fort watching them with grim satisfaction, and was reminded that for him and the Trelyns, she was a millstone to tie around Bryght's neck.

Marriage would be a prison cell for both of them, and surely the mighty Mallorens could avoid the minor scandal she had created.

"It will be all right," he assured her. "I suspect Nerissa will be content to see us married."

Having confirmed her bleak thoughts, he wrapped a cloak around her—not her own serviceable garment, but one of rich blue velvet lined with soft wool—and kissed her cheek before escorting her out.

The ladies traveled by sedan chair, the men walking alongside. Portia was grateful not to have to chatter, especially to Nerissa, and she needed some time of cool thought.

A child was a disastrous possibility, but it was only that. The main thing was to avoid being married on Wednesday.

That meant she must speak with Fort.

Twenty-one

The Willoughbys' house was exactly as it had been, but the haughty lady was almost avid as she greeted the new party of guests. Portia suspected that despite her cool dignity, Lady Willoughby was ecstatic to be the center of such a notorious affair.

She grasped both Portia's hands, her hooded eyes taking in the betrothal ring. "Miss St. Claire! How happy I am to see you in such fine state. You look amazingly well."

Portia kept her chin up and a slight smile on her lips. "I am completely well."

"And of course," added Bryght at her shoulder, "completely happy."

"I do not doubt it," Lady Willoughby said with a cynical edge which told Portia that she, too, thought the match unequal. "And dear Lady Rothgar's jewels. I remember her wearing them. They suit you almost as well, my dear."

She led them into her principal saloon and Portia was immediately the focus of inspection. She froze.

Bryght took her hand and stepped in front of her. "Talk to me and ignore everyone else."

"I don't like this," she said, but managed a smile. "I hate London."

"You will grow accustomed." He was smiling, too, but it didn't reach his eyes. "Tell me how much you love me."

She raised her hand, her fingers a scant inch apart. "That much."

He suddenly laughed, and the chill fled. "That is something to build upon. Come and talk to the Chivenhams. They are not given to low gossip."

Indeed, the older couple gave no indication of knowing any scandal at all, and Lady Chivenham commented favorably on the jewels. Other people were not so discreet. Some reassured Bryght that they had been sure it was all gossip, going on to complain of the wicked stories that flew around London like the wind.

Some even mentioned the case of Chastity Ware, which had all turned out to be malice and speculation.

"Gossips should be horse-whipped," one man said sternly. "Whipped at the cart then put in the stocks!"

Portia glanced over at Nerissa and silently agreed.

She soon gathered that the current story was that Lady Willoughby had interrupted a betrothal kiss, and that servants' gossip had made it out to be something more. The fact that the wedding was to take place in only two days time was explained by the ardor of the groom and the approach of Christmas. Most people would be leaving London soon for their estates.

Bryght stayed by Portia's side, frustrating her need to have a few moments alone with Fort. But then he did go to speak to an elderly gentleman and Portia caught Fort's eye and stepped aside.

He came to her side.

"Fort. You must drop this idea of challenging Bryght. As you can see, it was all an unfortunate misunderstanding."

"Mirabelle's wasn't."

Portia stared at him. "Bryght wasn't responsible for what happened there."

"But he was intimate enough with you to require marriage."

Portia felt a chill. "I don't want to marry him, Fort."

"Then you shouldn't have become so entangled." Before she could protest, he said, "Don't be missish, Portia. It's a brilliant match for you, and though I'm no admirer of Mallorens, Bryght's not vicious."

The block-headed wretch actually seemed to think he was doing her a favor! "Fort, I'm going to refuse to go through with this, and you are not to interfere."

His gray eyes turned cold and resolute. "If you aren't married within the week, Portia, Bryght and I will cross swords over it. I give you my word. And I will do my best to kill him."

"Fort, you can't!"

"I'm the mighty Earl of Walgrave. You'll be astonished at what I can do." With that, he bowed and moved away, leaving Portia in sick despair.

If she remained resolute, not only would she risk bearing a bastard, but she would condemn either Bryght or Fort to death.

The unbearable pain of that forced honesty upon her. She loved Fort like a brother, but if it came to the terrible choice she would see him dead rather than Bryght.

She loved Bryght with a depth and intensity that approached madness.

And, disastrous though it promised to be, she was going to marry him on Wednesday.

Then Lady Willoughby announced that there would be dancing before the recital. Somehow—and Portia thought she detected Lord Rothgar's hand—it was arranged that Bryght and Portia start the dancing with a minuet.

"I do not have much practice at this," she warned him.

"I do. Trust me."

And in this, at least, she did.

The music started and he executed a perfect bow. Portia curtsied and concentrated on remembering the delicate, swaying steps that wove them together.

He was a beautiful dancer, adapting his steps to hers with ease, touching her only gently on hand or waist, but managing to guide her if she faltered.

Soon Portia relaxed and had no difficulty in keeping her eyes on him as correct posture dictated. She was entranced by the slight smile on his lips and in his eyes, a smile that seemed created for her alone.

Though they danced with complete propriety, she began to remember another dance—the dance of love. Her skin longed for a naked touch, her mouth for the taste of him. It became hot in the room, and yet she felt shivery, as if with a fever. . . .

The music stopped. Portia came to herself with a jolt and looked around, wondering what she had revealed. But they no longer danced alone. Elf was partnered by Fort, Nerissa by her husband, and other couples had taken to the floor, too.

Bryght raised Portia's hand and kissed it, most improperly, in the palm. "I knew there would be occasions for ducking behind an arras. I don't suppose . . . ?"

She snatched her hand away as Elf came over with Fort close behind, hilarity sparkling in her eyes. "Lud, that was becoming so interesting I thought we had best provide distraction. I dragged poor Fort into the dance, even though he would have preferred to stand apart looking dark and mysterious."

Fort would have objected to this, but Portia exclaimed, "I was just acting a part!"

"Yes, but what part?" demanded the mischievous Elf.

"Elf," said Bryght, "behave yourself. We are here to cast decency and decorum over scandal and a hasty marriage."

"Phoo to that. We are here to cast a romantic glow over it."

"Then," said Fort coldly, "you should not contribute suggestive remarks, Lady Elfled."

"Lud," declared Elf, "you are beginning to sound just like your father!"

Then she moved away to greet a friend, leaving Portia and Bryght with a seething earl.

"She needs a firm hand," said Fort between his teeth.

"Try it," said Bryght, "and learn to live one-handed."

Fort took a precise pinch of snuff. "I would not dream of it. I am only interested in gentle, well-behaved young ladies."

Bryght's hand went to his dress-sword. "If you're suggesting my sister isn't—"

"Bryght!" Portia put her hand over his. "I'm sure Fort meant no such thing."

"Of course not," said Fort, dusting his fingers with a silk handkerchief. "I was referring more to age. A young bride has so many advantages."

Bryght's hand didn't leave his sword. "Are you insulting my bride now? She is of an age with my sister."

Fort reddened. "Devil take it! I've no desire to insult Portia. I'm talking about *my* preferences. Portia is fortunate to be making such a fine marriage at her age."

Portia would have liked to skewer him herself. "I regard a fine marriage as more than rank, Fort."

"So do I," Fort said cynically. "Rank *and* money. Which allows me to hope that you and Oliver will make life hell for the Mallorens."

With that he stalked off, and in minutes left the affair entirely. Portia could only be glad of it.

Other than that small contretemps, the evening progressed as planned. Portia danced with a number of men, then sat by Bryght to listen to excellent music, then sat with him and the Trelyns to eat supper. There could be no doubt in anyone's mind that she was well and happy, that all was harmony, and that the strange stories circulating had been malicious rumors.

At the end, however, she found she was to return to Trelyn House.

"No!" She turned instinctively to Bryght.

"There's no help for it," he said quietly. "They are sponsoring your wedding, and as far as the world is concerned you have never left their protection. Nerissa cannot harm you."

"She is vicious and spiteful."

"Only with words. Ignore her." Then he added with a smile, "I'll send over a pistol if you'd like."

Portia refused to smile at his teasing. "After all this effort, I don't want to end up a murderess."

He kissed her quickly on the lips. "Good. I'll sleep easier beside you."

The mere thought had Portia's face flaming.

Bryght escorted her down to her chair and she remembered something else. She turned to him. "I know we must marry, Bryght, but can we not delay matters? I would like my family at my wedding."

"Portia, truly, it would not be wise. After Nerissa's meddling and Fort's rashness any delay would start new speculation. We can travel to your home for our wedding trip."

"Perhaps if the fastest messenger were sent, Oliver might be able to be here in time."

"Do we know where he is?"

"I suppose he might be on the road, but if a messenger rode to Dorset and asked along the way . . ."

"You think he went to your home and is now returning?"

There was something strange in his tone that she could not interpret, but the chairs were ready and she had to go. "Please," she said. "I would like someone from my family at my wedding."

He settled her in the chair. "Then of course, I will send the messenger. Good night, my bride."

As Portia traveled to Trelyn House, she achieved a state of balanced resignation. She had burned her bridges when she surrendered to Bryght. She had lost her virtue, she could be carrying his child, but more importantly she had let down some barrier in her mind and soul.

She could no more put him out of her mind and life than she could Oliver or Fort, but her feelings towards him were not those of a sister.

Her battle now must be to make their marriage work despite the gap between their ranks, and his mad taste for speculation.

The next morning, having committed Portia to marriage, Bryght found himself able to attend efficiently to business at last. As he read through the reports and documents, his conscience occasionally pricked him for trapping Portia but he suppressed it. He could make her happy, but left to herself she would probably have run off into more danger to escape him.

He understood her misgivings, however.

He paused in the middle of a complicated letter about currency transfers to wonder how he could persuade his bride that his business dealings were not the road to ruin. Since her father had ruined himself through investments, it would not be easy. It would help if his affairs were in the relatively healthy state they had been before he'd plunged deep into Bridgewater's affairs. Now, details could support her fears that he was headed for bankruptcy.

Perhaps if he took her north to see the work . . .

He turned back to business. He'd concentrate now on getting her to the altar. In time, she'd see that he could be trusted.

Reports arrived from the servants who were watching over Portia's affairs. Cuthbertson had apparently fled the country. Moreover, the hawk had left a number of creditors behind, some the type who would be as cruel as he if they got their hands on him. That revenge would have to suffice for now.

He frowned over one report from Dorset, for it told him that Portia's mother and sister had left to visit Manchester, and Sir Oliver had only paused at his home for an hour or so before riding on. As a result, Bryght's man had lost track of him.

Bryght cursed. He definitely didn't want Oliver Upcott on the loose and gaming again. He hoped his man had tracked him down by now.

To keep his word to Portia, he had sent off a new messenger last night, ordered to head for Overstead Manor at all speed with a wedding invitation. Even if Upcott were there he'd never get to London on time, but he had kept his word. As it was, Bryght suspected that Portia's brother had fled the country, leaving her to cope alone.

Well, if true, it made paying Upcott's debt less hazardous, and redeeming the estate should warm Portia's heart a little. He sat back to contemplate her resistance. At times he was convinced that she felt as passionately as he. At others, such as when she had claimed not to love him, he had doubts.

Was it possible to love a woman desperately and not be able to win her? He need only look at the Trelyns to see that miserable situation.

At least Portia was no Nerissa. If she disliked him, she'd tell him so. Hell, if she took lovers, she'd doubtless tell him that, too!

Grinning at the thought, he went out to visit his thorny beloved to find out who her brother's debt-holder was. This time they were permitted privacy.

She did not look quite as haggard as at her worst, but she was clearly not a glowing bride. He noted ruefully how warily she regarded him and discarded any notions of kissing her.

"I wondered if you knew the name of the man who won Overstead," he asked her.

"Why yes. It was a Major Barclay."

"Barclay . . . ?" Bryght felt he had fallen into a theatrical performance. After all this, the debt was held by his friend?

Her eyes turned sharp. "A familiar of yours?"

Bryght was for once unsure what to do and say. He did not like to be dishonest, but he couldn't give Portia cause to flee now. "I think I may know the man," he said as calmly as possible, then deflected discussion toward some minor matters of their wedding.

He took his leave as soon as possible before he gave himself away. Hell and the devil, what would happen when Portia discovered Barclay was one of his closest friends?

As Bryght was leaving Trelyn House he was found by one of his running footmen with an urgent message. When he read it, he cursed under his breath, ready to tear his hair out.

He headed for Barclay's rooms and demanded, "Why the devil didn't you tell me you were the one who won Upcott's estate?"

"Why should I?" asked his startled friend. "Deuce take it, Bryght, I'm not the sort of man to boast of such foolishness."

Bryght took a deep breath. "Upcott is my future wife's half-brother."

"Good lord, I had no idea. Is he here for the wedding?"

"No. I just received word that my plague-ridden people have exceeded their orders. They've kidnapped him and carried him off a prisoner to the Abbey!"

"Heavens above! Why?"

"The devil only knows. They seem to have decided he was trying to flee the country to avoid paying a debt to me."

Barclay suddenly chuckled. "You're looking decidedly ragged, my friend."

"I feel it. Not unreasonably, Upcott resisted. He's somewhat battered and is walking with a limp. Even were I to restore him to his sister's loving arms, she'd hardly be pleased with me. Look, sign me over that debt."

Barclay's pleasant face fell. "Bryght, I wish I could. Walgrave purchased the note off me yesterday."

"Fort? Damnation. She must have asked him for help."

"It can't matter, can it?"

Bryght contemplated a very ugly vase. "I don't like it, but at least he's as determined on this marriage as I am." He turned back to his friend. "Don't speak of this, please."

"Of course not. It was a lesson to me not to game with pigeons even when they insist. Damned embarrassing to have a man stake his estate, but what could I do? Refuse to play with him?"

"No, of course not. But I'll be happy enough not to take part in such matters again."

"Not to game again?" echoed Barclay in astonishment.

"Part of my wedding vows." Bryght picked up his wine-glass. "Come, toast my happiness."

"With pleasure," said Barclay, "but—forgive me for mentioning it—isn't keeping your brother-in-law under lock and key likely to cast a shadow on your future?"

"If Portia finds out, it'll be more than a shadow. The worst of it is I still don't know what to do to solve the problem. I can't have him constantly gaming away his property.

"Put him on a ship?"

"Out of sight, out of mind? I don't think Portia has such a convenient memory. *She* wants him at her wedding."

Barclay chuckled. "I don't think I've ever seen you in such a tangle. What will you do?"

Bryght drained his glass. "Get married first. The rest is for later. But if you care to oblige me . . ."

"Yes?"

"You could go down to the Abbey and keep an eye on things. The family are all away, either here or down at Steen's place. My men had their orders, but they appear to be getting carried away. I don't care to think they might have locked Upcott in the cellars. You could make sure they're tending his wounds with loving care. On the other hand, you could prevent him imitating his sister and climbing out of windows."

Barclay chuckled. "Remarkable woman, your future wife."

"I think so. Can you leave now?"

"I'll miss your nuptials."

"That's the idea," said Bryght with a wry smile. "The last thing I need is for Portia to be introduced to Major Barclay, close friend of her husband's. At least, not before the knot is tied."

The next day—and far too soon—Portia found herself preparing for her wedding.

At least she had hardly seen Nerissa. Once assured the wedding would go ahead, her cousin had thrown herself into the arrangements with enthusiasm, and appeared to be enjoying herself mightily. It appeared that Nerissa's love of entertainment and display had overwhelmed her bitterness. Or perhaps it was just the destruction of that letter that had her so merry.

On the other hand, Nerissa was cunning. Her enthusiasm for this wedding was convincing Lord Trelyn that she had absolutely no interest in Bryght Malloren. He was once more the proud, indulgent spouse.

Portia had moments when she positively longed to go to the earl and tell him all she knew about his wife. She wasn't sure she would be believed, however, and it would be an act of pure spite.

Portia had just finished her bath and was drying herself when Nerissa came into the room preceding a maid carrying a large cloth bundle. "See!" Nerissa declared, and unraveled the linen herself to reveal the dress made out of the embroidered silk.

Portia was clutching her towel for modesty, but she stared at the lovely gown.

"It is perfect for your wedding!" Nerissa declared.

"It is too fine. It is an evening gown."

"Nothing is too fine for a wedding. I wore silk embroidered with silver and pearls. Chastity Ware wore the most ridiculous confection of white lace. When one thinks . . . but no more of that. You must wear this gown. The king is to be present, you know."

"What?" Portia clutched the towel more tightly.

"Oh yes. You are to be married in the Chapel Royal. Rothgar's work. He is determined to cover you with respectability. Oh, and there was another package. From Bryght." She dispatched the maid to find it then turned to Portia with a smirk. "Judging from the seamstress who sent it, however, I am not at all sure it is proper."

"Then I will not wear it."

"No? You are going to vow obedience, Cousin. Shouldn't you perhaps anticipate the wedding?"

Portia fought it, but at the words "anticipate the wedding" color rose in her face. She turned away to dry herself further.

"I wonder if you are still a virgin," Nerissa mused behind her. "Rumor says that Bryght did not deflower little Hippolyta at Mirabelle's. But what happened when you went running to him two days ago?"

Portia ignored her and sat at the dressing table, still swathed in the towel. She would not take it off in front of Nerissa. She unpinned her hair.

"As the matron present, perhaps I should prepare you for the dreadful shock of the marriage bed." Nerissa came up behind so that Portia could see her beautiful, wicked face in the mirror, and smell her cloying perfume—a perfume that took her back to Maidenhead and a diabolic intruder.

How could she ever have imagined that her rashness that day would lead to this?

Nerissa smiled. "Does your silence mean you prefer ignorance? Or that you are no longer ignorant?"

Portia made herself meet the avid eyes. "It means that I need no assistance of yours in my marriage."

"You have experienced his bed?"

"No, I have not," Portia said, strengthened by the fact that it was true. "Until I chased you, I had never entered Bryght's bedchamber."

Nerissa's brows rose. "But what wonders are to be revealed! It will go better, though, if you are well prepared." She leaned forward, so her face was next to Portia's, and even slid her hand onto Portia's bare shoulder. "Ignorance is not bliss. I have some most instructive books concealed from Trelyn."

Portia shrugged the hand off. "Why conceal them? Perhaps your husband would find them instructive and you would not then need a lover."

Nerissa flinched back as if hit. "Very well," she snapped, standing straight. "Linger in ignorance and suffer for it. I merely sought to help. Your bible-reading ways will not serve in bed with Bryght Malloren."

The maid returned then with a box and opened it. Without asking permission, Nerissa pawed through it then laughed. "Jupiter, but I wish I could be a fly on the wall!" She blew Portia a malicious kiss and left.

Under the intrigued eyes of the maid, Portia went to see what was in the box, though she could guess. Suggestive, wicked undergarments.

She was wrong.

The delicate items were not risqué at all. The shift was finest silk edged with precious lace, but decently opaque; the stays were prettily embroidered with flowers, but ladylike. The stockings made her smile a little, for they were identical to the ones they had found in Elf's chest, silk lace and very fancy garters.

With Bryght Malloren, nothing was ever as she expected.

There was another knock, and Portia turned, expecting Nerissa back to taunt.

It was Elf, however, in magnificent amber silk and fairly bubbling with excitement. "I love weddings." She saw the dress and gasped. "Portia! That is the most beautiful fabric! Oh, I am consumed with jealousy. Come. Let us see you in it."

Portia was caught up in a whirlwind. First, she was helped into the beautiful, discreet underwear. She noticed Elf hesitate at the sight of the stockings and garters, but nothing was said.

The maid tied the wide but light cane hoops around Portia's waist and added a petticoat. Then the dress was eased over her head. It was an exquisite fabric, light but heavily textured. The cream silk was the perfect background for the jewel-like birds in blue, yellow, and green. As the mantua-maker had said, with such rich fabric there was no point in ornament. The design was simple—full skirted, low bodiced, and with elbow-length sleeves. The lovely lace of the shift flowed out there to almost cover Portia's forearms.

She wished her bosom was as well covered.

The stays were designed to push up her breasts and make the most of their modest dimensions. Now the bodice of the dress ended a fraction lower so that the narrow lace frill of the stays showed.

Along with a great deal else! She hardly felt it was decent for church, but Elf's bodice was as low.

Portia had given the jewels to Lord Trelyn to take care of and now his valet brought them to her. Portia thought them too grand for day wear, even if royalty were to be present and only put on the earrings. She gave the rest into Elf's care.

All the activity had distracted Portia from the occasion, but when it was time to go downstairs to enter the coach, panic hit her. She started to tremble.

"What's the matter?" asked Elf, dismissing the maid. "Portia, what is it? You really cannot back out now. You can't."

"I suppose not." But Portia was tempted. Rip off the cords, through the window, and away.

"Bryght will make you a good husband."

"But I hardly know him! I'm not like you. I've been raised to see marriage as a holy vow."

"So have I," protested Elf.

Portia pressed her hands to her cheeks. "Oh, I'm sorry. I mean that the nobility marry for money, for land, for titles. I have always intended to marry for . . ."

"For love?"

Portia shook her head. "Not even that. For a deep regard. For absolute trust in my partner's integrity. I have rejected offers because I was not sure of that and now I am going to marry a rakish gamester!"

"He's not quite that bad," Elf protested.

"Whatever he is, I hardly know him!"

But, Portia reminded herself, in the biblical sense she knew him all too well. "I'm sorry, Elf. Just bridal nerves."

With that, she raised her chin and headed off to her wedding.

Twenty-two

Bryght was genuinely nervous that Portia would not turn up for her wedding. That would certainly create a stir for Rothgar had arranged for it to be in the Chapel Royal with the king and queen in attendance.

When she appeared, small and shining in a remarkable dress, he let out a slow sigh of relief. He had her, and what he had, he held.

When she arrived by his side, Bryght took her hand, searching her face for a hint of her feelings. She was too calm, but she didn't appear terrorized or in despair.

It would be all right.

When it came time to say her vows, she said them clearly and firmly, as did Bryght. When it was over, he turned her and kissed her lightly—a kiss, he hoped, of peace. "You will be as happy as I can make you, Portia. I promise."

She frowned up at him as if puzzled, but then she did smile back.

They signed the register as was the new custom, so that all marriages should be properly recorded, then traveled back to the reception at Trelyn House in a coach accompanied by Elf and Brand. As usual, Elf could be relied on to cover awkward silences with chat.

Bryght was just aware of Portia and desire, and aware that it would be many weary hours before he could surrender to that desire. He would have liked to at least look at her, but as Elf had insisted that they sit side by side he would have to gaze sideways like a lovesick fool.

He was such a fool, of course, but he hoped he could conceal it.

Once in the house, they greeted the monarchs, who had arrived first, then Nerissa fussed them into position to receive their guests and their best wishes.

All went smoothly until Kinbolton, damn him, said to Bryght, "I assume Barclay's here. Need to have a word with him."

"No," said Bryght, knowing Portia must have heard. "He's out of Town."

"Pity."

Kinbolton went on into the rooms and Portia smiled and greeted the next person in line.

Bryght waited for the cannon to explode.

As soon as they had greeted the last guest Portia drew Bryght to one side. "This Barclay is a close friend of yours?" She was quiet as a naked blade is quiet.

"Very close," he said.

"A gamester?"

"Hardly that."

"But he plays?"

"Everyone plays."

Her eyes flashed. "Would this perhaps be the same Major Barclay who cheated Oliver out of his estate?"

"Hush," he said, for her voice had turned shrill. "Gentlemen don't cheat at cards, Portia."

"Hawks do," she spat.

Damnation, she couldn't do this here. "Portia, Barclay is not a hawk. Nor am I. Yes, he won your brother's estate, but he won it in fair play." When she started to argue that, he said sharply, "Later. We can discuss this later."

She pulled on a cloak of composure, but the expression in her eyes was seething. "I want to discuss it *now*."

"We are the focus of too many eyes."

"Then let us leave."

That showed how angry she was. "Don't be absurd. We can't leave before the king and queen. Come and talk to Aunt Caroline."

She sucked in a deep breath, but allowed herself to be led over to his elderly aunt.

There he left her, for he felt sure there was much less chance of disaster if they kept far apart.

Brand came over and grinned. "I do like variety in a family, don't you? A few weeks ago Cyn and Chastity were wandering through their reception like sleepwalkers, blushing and smiling every time their eyes met."

"Perhaps, being older, Portia and I have more control and discretion."

"Perhaps," said Brand. "But I tell you, when I choose a bride she'll be a quiet, comfortable woman."

Bryght looked at him. "You mean some people get a *choice?*"

He left his brother laughing and moved through the room, talking to one group then another, hoping he was giving a fair representation of a happy but mature bridegroom whose mind was too well-disciplined to be obsessed by the marriage bed.

He saw Portia catch Fort's eye and cross the room directly to him. They didn't blush and smile, thank God, but there was something between them. Even as Bryght took part in a desultory discussion about poor relief, he watched his wife.

Therefore he saw Fort give her a letter.

* * *

Portia had been trying to be polite to strangers at the same time as she tried to come to terms with the fact that the horrible Barclay was a friend of Bryght's. It was so wearing, that when Fort caught her eye she was glad to go to talk to him. At least with Fort she didn't have to pretend.

"I know that look," he said with a grin. "You'd like to spear someone. Remember you're the happy bride."

"Happy! You're partly responsible for this. If it hadn't been for that duel—"

"But I wanted this marriage. It'll serve very well, and you'll do all right out of it."

Portia gritted her teeth. "Bryght is a gamester. When he's not a gamester, he's indulging in rash monetary speculations. He'll end up in debtor's prison!"

"True enough," he said in excellent humor. "He's apparently deep in Bridgewater's scheme, and that is likely to come to a disastrous end because I'm about to take a hand."

"But what about me?" she demanded.

"The Mallorens will take care of you."

Before Portia could tell him her opinion of this and him, he sobered and said, "I wanted to speak with you about something else, even if it is under the glowering eye of your husband. . . ."

Portia looked over and saw that Bryght was watching them. He wasn't glowering, but she could not think he approved. She deliberately turned back to Fort with a smile. "Is something the matter?"

"Perhaps. You're not to worry, because I intend to look into it, but I have a letter here you should read."

"A letter?" Portia's first thought was of Nerissa's letter. That had surely burned, so what was this? A suggestive

perfumed missive from a lover to her husband? The paper
Fort passed to her, however, was plain and addressed to
him.

She concealed it in her hand. "What is it?"

"It's from my steward. Find a private place to read it
then tell me what you want to do."

With creeping unease, Portia went to the lady's withdrawing room. Finding it deserted, she unfolded the paper.

She skimmed over the salutations and general business,
seeking something that concerned her.

*I have to report some funny doings at Overstead, my
lord. The family have left, for a visit north so it is said, but
rumor reports that they are all rolled up. That young Sir
Oliver has lost all at gaming.*

Her mother and sister had gone to Manchester already?
Hannah must have given up hope, but what must she be
thinking about Portia's absence? And what was she going
to think when Portia turned up married?

This wouldn't have alarmed Fort, however.

Portia read on.

*A few days since, the young squire came back here, and
in a pother they say, though perhaps just to find his mother
and sister gone. He gathered a change of clothes, some
money, and his favorite horse then dashed off toward Salis-
bury. He hasn't been heard of since. But a hat that seemed
mighty like his was found on the road.*

*Round about that time, there were men here asking ques-
tions about him, and one of the pot-boys at the Bald Abbott
heard them mention Rothgar. Knowing as I do that your
father thought poorly of that man, I thought it wise to bring
this to your attention, my lord, for I haven't been able to
find word of Sir Oliver in these parts, and the marquess's*

men, if such they were, disappeared about the time the young squire did.

For all his foolishness, I would not like to see harm come to Sir Oliver, him being the old earl's godchild, and known to us all from birth.

Portia stared at the letter. Surely the marquess would not hurt Oliver. Surely Bryght would be no part of such a scheme.

But Bryght had said he would take care of her family's problems and make sure their home stayed safe. He might think disposing of Oliver was part of the solution.

She could be married to the man who had killed her brother!

She hurried back into the reception, which was now beginning to appear positively macabre, and found Fort standing alone. She slipped the letter back to him. "What should we do?"

"There's nothing you can do. I'm going to post down tomorrow and look into things. It might all be nonsense anyway."

She gripped her hands together, feeling the unfamiliar rings. "Oh, why did you not say something before the ceremony?"

"Because I knew you'd create a fuss."

Portia stared at him. "You *wanted* me married to him, even with this possibility?"

"Of course. Don't look so dismal. Perhaps Bryght will hang for it and you'll be free."

Portia was glad there was no lethal weapon within reach. "You kept this from me, then gave it me here hoping to destroy any chance of harmony in this match. How can you be so cruel?"

Color touched his cheeks but he met her eyes. "I do what I must."

She was appalled at the depth of his hatred. "Why, Fort?"

"I have my reasons. They are none of your concern."

"But they are ruining my life! Have you thought of that? What am I supposed to do tonight?"

He smiled then. "Are you going to refuse him? Gads, this is better than I thought. I wish I could witness it." With that he walked off, leaving Portia in despair.

She tried to persuade herself that it wasn't possible, that Bryght could not have been party to harming Oliver. Fort's malice to the Mallorens was so naked that she shouldn't believe a word he said.

And yet, she did not think he would go so far as to make up that letter.

And Bryght had thought it perfectly in order for a friend of his to win her home at cards.

And he had deliberately seduced her into this commitment, without thought for her wishes.

An image of their naked bodies twined willingly together slid into her head and she fought it off.

It was followed by a memory of Bryght saying, "I do love you, though."

Could he love her and murder her brother? She thought perhaps a Malloren could.

Portia knew she could not cower in this corner forever, but she lacked the courage to mingle as if nothing were wrong. She slipped away to the pale blue reception room—the one she had been shown to when she had first visited Nerissa. It was deserted, being too small and plain to be open to guests.

* * *

Bryght had watched the two encounters between Portia and the Earl of Walgrave. At least they did not seem to part on good terms, but nothing could persuade him the discussions were innocent.

What the devil could be going on, and what had been in that letter?

He was still struggling with his suspicions and desires—mainly a desire to wring Portia's neck and call Fort out—when Rothgar, damn him, told the king that Bryght knew about the tea trade. George insisted on discussing it, and one could not talk to a monarch with eyes wandering.

When Bryght finally escaped, Portia was nowhere to be seen. He scanned the room swiftly and was relieved to see Fort talking to some men. But where was Portia? Damnation, the woman was quite capable of setting off on some wild adventure, even in her wedding finery.

He was headed for the entrance to query the servants when he was halted by Rothgar. "There's no need to start a hue and cry. She is in that room over there. Alone."

Bryght walked in on her without knocking, but found Portia sitting innocently in a chair by the fireplace. She leapt to her feet almost guiltily, and yet he could see nothing wrong here except her lack of happiness.

He decided to attack their problem head-on. "I had no idea until recently that Barclay was your brother's debt-holder."

"Even though you are such close friends?"

"Men don't talk of everything. He had no desire to spread word of Oliver's ruin. He hoped, in fact, that your brother could find the money and redeem the place."

"But he wanted the money."

He held onto his thinning patience. "He won the money, Portia. Play and pay. To refuse to play would be an insult."

That sparked anger in her at least. "Better to insult than to ruin!"

"Perhaps. Since I'm not going to play anymore, it hardly matters, does it?"

"If I can trust your word."

"Portia," he said, "be careful how far you push me."

"Why?" She began to pace the room with an angry swish of silk. "Are you threatening to beat me if I cross you?"

"Damnation, Portia, what the devil is the matter with you? If you will but consider, none of this is my fault. Your brother gamed away his estate. Barclay won it. Your brother lost you to Cuthbertson—"

She stopped to point at him. "And you teased me into that kiss in the library that led to this!"

"And in the whole list that counts the highest?"

She turned away. "It is what has trapped me for life!"

"And me," he said. "Don't forget we are in this trap together."

"I don't." After a moment, she turned back to him, superficially calm. "Where is Oliver?"

The question caught him unawares. "Why do you ask me?"

Her eyes were cool but keen. "Because two days ago you promised to find him for me, to see if he could come to our wedding."

Bryght had honestly forgotten, having since found out exactly where her brother was. He tried to put together some sort of truth. "I did send a man to Dorset, but as your brother is not here, he cannot have been found in time."

"Oh well," she said with ominous sweetness. "Since we are to go to Overstead on our wedding trip, I will doubtless see him then."

Oh no. Bryght remembered speaking of traveling to Dorset, but he had no intention of dealing with the problem of Oliver Upcott until he had thoroughly won his bride.

"I do have some news from Dorset," he said. "Apparently your mother and sister have gone to visit relatives in Manchester. We had best go there for our wedding journey."

She looked so distressed at that news that he wanted to take her in his arms and comfort her. There were a number of dangerous weapons close to her hand, however, including a heavy statuette and a poker, so he desisted.

Then she raised her chin in the fighting gesture so typical of her. "We can send my mother a letter. I prefer to go to Overstead on the chance that Oliver is there."

"We can send *him* a letter," he countered.

She looked him in the eye. "I want to go to Overstead." Just as firmly, he said, "No."

When she drew in breath to object, he said, "Remember those vows to obey? We are going north, wife. And," he added, seeing rebellion flash in her eyes, "if you try to go alone, I will drag you back by the hair."

She hissed with rage and tried to sweep past him, but he caught her arm and when she struggled he tightened his grip. "We will send a message to Dorset. There is absolutely no reason for you to go there." He could feel dangerous anger licking at his control.

"Perhaps I just want to, and am used to doing as I want."

"The name for that, madam wife, is spoiled."

Her eyes flashed fire. "Then you, my lord, are spoiled beyond redemption!"

He dragged her into his arms. "Am I? Then perhaps I should take what I want. We've made love on the floor in front of a fire before, haven't we?"

She fought for a moment then went rigid. "I suppose you think you have the right now, regardless of my wishes."

It was like a shower of icy water and he took a steadying breath. He forced her chin up, but gently, so she had to look at him. "Why are we fighting, Portia? What do you want?"

He saw his own bewildered pain reflected in her eyes. "I want to go to Overstead."

Pain was swamped by furious incomprehension. He'd never seen any sign in her before of this sort of mulishness. He knew Portia was not always sensible in her rage, and was reminded he didn't know her very well.

She was high-spirited, rash, and brave. Was she also irrationally stubborn and demanding? He couldn't take her to Overstead where she might learn that her brother had been kidnapped by the Mallorens.

He couldn't let Oliver go until he'd decided what to do about the situation.

He made a conscious effort to relax and to soothe her. "Portia, your brother might be anywhere. It makes more sense to send a messenger to find him and for us to go north to see your mother. I also have business near Manchester with the Duke of Bridgewater."

She was not noticeably soothed. "But Fort has promised to save the estate. As soon as my mother and sister have the happy news, they will return home. If we go north, we could cross them on the way. And I'm sure your business can wait."

Damn. He wasn't surprised to hear what Fort had done, but he'd wanted to be the knight in shining armor. And her reasoning made altogether too much sense. "I'm afraid my business cannot wait. But we can go to Overstead immediately on our return south."

She pulled sharply against his hold and he had to hurt her or let her go. He let her go.

"I see you are determined," she said icily, "and you now have the right to order me as you will. We should return to our guests, my lord. They might begin to think we are up to no good."

She marched toward the door but waited for him to open it for her. He was tempted to keep her here and try to talk sense into her but, as she said, their absence might have been noted.

There would be time enough later. Time enough tonight, and during a long, leisurely journey to Lancashire to wear down her sense of ill-usage, teach her to trust, and make her completely his.

He opened the door, and as she swept through it to rejoin the reception he noted that she was wearing a serene smile. His courageous Amazon. There were times, however, when he'd rather she were a timid mouse.

He steered her toward some safe family members then passed by Rothgar. "Keep an eye on her, Bey. I'm not at all sure she won't try to bolt."

"If she has reason, I'm likely to abet her."

" 'Struth, I don't need you snarling at me, too." He quickly explained about Barclay and the debt. "I have Oliver Upcott held in secure comfort at the Abbey and Barclay's gone down there to make sure all is well. Portia is hell-bent on setting out for Dorset to find him. I can't permit that until I decide what to do about him, and I do need to go north to inform Bridgewater of the new circumstances. The fact that the rest of her family are there makes a convenient excuse."

"What do you intend to do with the brother?"

"If I knew, matters would be somewhat simpler."

"Murder is so messy," said Rothgar, "but few other methods cure an inveterate gamester."

"Somehow I don't think fratricide would enhance my marital bliss."

"Nor would refusing to pay his debts next time he sinks deep."

"Do you think I don't know that? I need to woo Portia before we confront that problem. Hence the leisurely journey north."

Rothgar looked over to where Portia stood conversing with a group of ladies. Despite the smile, she looked as stiff as an iron rod, and as cold. "I think your reputation as a mythic lover is about to be tested. Meanwhile, perhaps Brand should return to the Abbey. Having had the late Earl of Walgrave come to a messy end there not long ago, another death might raise questions."

"You are fixed in town?" Bryght asked.

"For a little while." Rothgar took a pinch of snuff. "I didn't want to add to your concerns, but Fort has wind of your involvement with Bridgewater—I smell an unholy collusion with Nerissa Trelyn there—and is supporting Brooke in the opposition to the canal bill. With such weight behind them, it becomes interesting."

"Christ! But he has no interest in the matter."

"He has an interest in all things Malloren. I will handle it. Don't worry."

"I didn't think you were much concerned about the canal."

"I let no one act with spite against my family. Which reminds me, I really should have a word with Lady Trelyn."

"You can't harm her," Bryght said with some alarm.

"I don't suppose I can at the moment. But I can warn her."

Bryght hoped Nerissa took the warning.

"This does mean," said Rothgar, "that you have no pressing need to seek out Bridgewater. I'll make sure he doesn't founder in the next few weeks."

"I still intend to go north. If Portia doesn't come around, we'll keep going up to the Highlands, perhaps even to the Arctic. It would suit the current state of our marriage." Then he saw that the king and queen were finally preparing to take their leave and muttered, "Thank God."

Bryght headed toward his icy bride. The sooner he had her out of here, the sooner he could start thawing her.

Despite everything, he felt a lightning of his spirit. The situation was not ideal, but he knew Portia and he were bound at the deepest levels, and he had her.

Possession, so they said, is eleven points in the law.

When he spoke her name and she turned, however, his optimism faded. She did not look hostile as much as despairing. In God's name, what had happened to distress her so?

Should he insist on knowing about that letter?

He almost laughed aloud. If Portia did not want him to know, he suspected he'd need a fully-equipped torture chamber to squeeze the information out of her.

He led her to say farewell to the monarchs and stood by while the plain-faced queen kissed her cheek and wished her all joy and happiness in her marriage.

Bryght wondered wryly if such royal wishes had any mystical effect. After all, the king's touch was supposed to heal the King's Evil.

Then they were in the coach and he wanted very much to gather her into his arms. She looked so brittle, though, he feared she'd break.

He'd swear she was afraid, but of what? He couldn't imagine that she was scared of the marriage bed, but if she was, didn't she know he'd never force her?

He sought a neutral topic. "Your family will be staying with relatives in Manchester?"

She was looking down at her rings. "Yes. An uncle."

"What kind of man is he?"

"A tradesman. A stocking-maker. Far below your touch."

He wished she'd look at him. "You'd be surprised. Is he involved with the new manufactories?"

"I don't know."

"You've never been there?"

"I've visited."

"Then you must know something of it," Bryght said, fighting an alarming desire to shake her.

"No. I had no interest in such things."

"Such manufactories are the way of the future."

She faced him then, but with hostility. "The strength of England will always be in the land."

At last he had a spirited reaction. "Or under the land." At her look, he said, "Coal."

"Nasty stuff!"

"But valuable," he countered. "So, if you believe in the land, what do you know of it?"

He expected her to have to admit ignorance, but being Portia she surprised him.

"I am a believer in the intensive use of manure on the land, and the rotation of crops. At Overstead we have used many of the improvements recommended by Mr. Tull and by Viscount Townsend, with excellent results."

"How excellent?"

"Our yield per acre has risen from twelve to eighteen bushels, and should continue to increase. Our breeding program increased our production of quality meat by twenty percent per carcass."

He almost laughed. He did admire a woman who knew

her subject. "It's as well I have bought us an estate then," he said.

She stared at him. "You've *bought* one?"

"Didn't you think I had the money? It's called Candleford Park. You can have a free hand in the managing of it. I know little of such things." Talk of money had reminded him of something. He dug in his pocket, brought out a pouch of guineas, and tossed it in her lap. "Trelyn gave that to me as your mighty lord and master."

She clutched it. "Thank you, but you are not my master."

He decided he would not leave her untouched tonight. Unless she fought and screamed he was going to seduce her, break through this icy shell, and find Hippolyta.

When they arrived at Malloren House, the whole staff was out to congratulate them and to welcome Lady Bryght. Bryght wished them at the devil but went through the motions. Portia, he noticed, even managed to smile and he loved her for it.

Then he could take her to his study, a room he hoped she remembered well and fondly.

He eased off her cloak then drew her into his arms. "Lady Bryght suits you. You shine like a candlelit window in a winter storm."

He felt her shiver, and prayed it was with desire. But when she looked up at him, he saw only bewildered pain. "Promise you will take me to Overstead," she whispered.

Abruptly he let her go. "For God's sake, Portia, is this some kind of test? Fetch me the horn of a unicorn? Tomorrow we go north," he said firmly. "Later we will visit Overstead."

Twenty-three

Portia wanted to argue, but what was the point? She went to the fire to warm her hands, and to put distance between them. She wish the heat could penetrate deeper, into the icy core of fear and pain.

She kept fighting, fighting against her terrible suspicions, but he kept reinforcing them.

He knew that her mother and sister had gone to Manchester. How did he know that unless he had agents down in Dorset? She had realized soon after her request that no messenger could get to Dorset and back in time for the wedding.

Now he was being unreasonably stubborn in his refusal to go to Overstead.

She was sure Bryght was never unreasonable, and she feared she knew what his reasons were.

She thought briefly of telling him everything in the hope that there was an innocent explanation, but if the worst was true he was capable of anything. She certainly doubted that he would give her the chance to flee, to run off alone and find out the truth.

And that was what she was going to have to do. She didn't know how she was going to escape, but she had to.

She didn't hear him approach, so she started when he

slid his hands over her exposed shoulders. "We can do better than this, Portia. Can we not at least try?"

Portia wanted nothing more, but had lost faith. She didn't resist, however, when he freed her hair from its pins and spread it around her shoulders, turning her to face him. "Your hair is like flame, and could warm my soul. Can you not tell me what stands between us?"

His fingers traced the swell of her breasts. She watched those long clever fingers, remembering other pleasures and trying to hold back any response.

"I know you better," he said, "than to think you mindlessly demanding . . ."

Portia made herself see his gentle words as a trick, a trap, designed to pry free her secrets.

He sighed and raised her chin. "Could you perhaps say something?"

At the blend of desire and anger in him, her heart began to race and her mouth went dry. She said the first neutral thing that occurred to her. "Where's Zeno?"

He laughed, bitterly. "Surprisingly to the point! Enjoying his mate, or thinking of it constantly. Boudicca has come into heat."

Portia knew she was red. "We humans have no need of heat."

"Some warmth is pleasant, however."

She flinched at the edge in his voice. "I'm sorry if you find me cold. But we are married. You do not need my consent."

"Do I not?" After a dangerous moment, he asked, "Are you by any chance thinking to withhold your warmth until I do as you wish and take you to your home?"

The thought hadn't occurred to her, but now she grasped it. "Yes!"

After a moment he let her go. He picked up her velvet cloak and the pouch of money. "Come." He was leading the way into the bedroom.

Portia almost refused, but what good would it do? She would not respond, she vowed, no matter what pressure or skills he brought to bear. She would not.

But he led her through his bedroom, through a small dressing room, and into another bedchamber where a fire glowed in the hearth, and a warming pan protruded from the big bed.

Portia looked at him in total bewilderment.

"Your bedchamber," he said. "As you see, the servants have followed the fiction that it will be used. Do you need help with your gown?"

"N—no."

"Then I will say good night."

"But . . ."

He turned in polite, distant query.

"But it's only seven in the evening."

"There are books. I have work to do." After a moment he added, "Portia, I will not beg you or rape you, so I see no alternative." With that, he went back through the door and closed it with a click.

Portia felt like a child sternly rebuked. But she was not a child, nor was she concerned with childish matters. She had to remember that.

There were, as he said, books—some poetry, some sermons, a book of travels, and Mr. Richardson's *Pamela*. Had the story of the maid who trapped the lord into marriage been left here deliberately?

She was burningly aware of Bryght, not many doors away, available for pleasure if she would but submit. She grimly chose a book of sermons and sat to read.

Her eyes tracked the words but her mind wandered, seeking an innocent explanation for his refusing to take her to Dorset. She found none except an arrogant insistence on his way that was almost as bad as her suspicions.

She let the book droop onto her knees and stared into the flames as she reviewed her recent past and the disaster of it. She could not even see clearly a point at which she could have stopped the wheel of fortune and escaped. . . .

It was hours later that she stirred, thinking she might as well go to bed, and abruptly realized she was a total fool.

Here she had been given the ideal opportunity to escape and make her way to Overstead alone and she had wasted it.

She looked out of the window at the dark. There was no clock here, but it must be late. It was too late to venture anywhere. But this might be her only chance.

She took a deep breath. If it had to be done, she would do it. But how?

She wondered if she ought to go first to Dresden Street to check if Oliver was there, but if he had arrived in Town she couldn't imagine him not coming to see her.

So, she needed transport to Dorset.

It was too late for a stage, and so she would have to wait for the morning. How was she to avoid capture until the morning, and then travel on the stage with the Mallorens on the hunt? Bryght would know exactly where she had gone.

Almost she gave up, but then she realized she had one possible course. Fort. It was he, after all, who had alerted her to the problem, and he had said he was going to Dorset in the morning to check on the matter.

He had also made it clear that he had forced her into this marriage out of deep hatred for the Mallorens.

She clasped her hands, going round and round the dreadful dilemma. She could not stay to be taken north and forced into lovemaking with Bryght. She could not hesitate in trying to discover what had happened to Oliver, and in rescuing him if he was still alive. But surely she could not run off on her wedding night with her husband's worst enemy!

She was hesitating now out of simple terror, but she made herself go forward. She had no choice.

She had the pouch of guineas. Did she have any clothes? When she opened the chests and armoires she found that all her belongings were neatly disposed there. Of course they were. This was now one of her homes along with Rothgar Abbey and a place called Candleford Park.

Refusing to think of such things, Portia took off her wedding gown and hoops, and changed into a plain dark brown traveling dress and sturdy shoes. She put on her warm cloak and slipped the pouch of guineas into her pocket.

At least she did not to have to attempt this penniless.

She sadly folded the beautiful lace stockings and put them away in a drawer. Perhaps one day there would be a chance to wear them for Bryght without shadows.

She paused in the act of closing the drawer. If that became true, it would have to mean that she was misjudging him. She couldn't imagine what his reaction would be to this flight then.

She couldn't forget that he'd promised to drag her back by the hair if she ran off. She was aware of anger in him, perhaps the more dangerous for the coolness he used to hide it. She remembered their first meeting when his anger had escaped his control, and shivered.

She would not let fear rule her.

She did, however, wish she had a pistol.

* * *

At least Portia knew a way out of Malloren House as long as that door was barred rather than locked. She slipped out into the corridor, ears alert for any sound. The solid house was peaceful, though.

She had to pass Bryght's rooms to get to the door to the servants' stairs. She hesitated for a moment, wondering if he really were calmly applying himself to whatever work he did. She hadn't discussed it with him, but it did appear he was not entirely idle.

She gave herself a shake and hurried on. Just as long as he did not check her room before morning.

The unobtrusive servants' door opened with efficient silence and she felt her way down the dark stairs to the bottom. There she paused for signs of people in the passageway, but most of the servants would now be in their beds.

She entered the corridor, found the door to the outer passageway, and was once more in darkness.

A few steps forward brought her to the outer door and her fingers found the bar across it. She let out a long relieved breath. The marquess had made sure it would be secure, but only against intruders.

Who, after all, would wish to escape this grand house?

She lifted the bar and set it aside, opened the door, and was outside in the chill dark. She hesitated a moment, aware that this might be the end of all chance of happiness.

But any chance had been lost hours ago, perhaps days ago when Bryght arranged for her brother's abduction.

There was an icy damp that threatened rain, and Portia pulled her hood up. This time she went away from the square toward the mews, made a circuitous route to a nearby street, and set off for Fort's house.

She was almost becoming accustomed to roaming London in the gloom, she thought wryly. In fact there would be some to relief in being set upon by thieves and put out of her misery.

She reached Abingdon Street without hazard, however, and had to consider her next problem—whether to try the front door again, or a back entrance. She shrugged and marched up to rap on the door.

It was the same footman, and his jaw dropped.

"Tell Lord Walgrave I am here." Would the servant know that Miss Portia St. Claire had married Bryght Malloren today? Was that why he looked so astonished?

No, he was just dumbstruck at her boldness, but when she stepped forward, he let her in. He wore a sneer that said he knew she'd be out on her ear in a moment, but he allowed her into the house and led her to a tiny, bleak reception room. It was definitely the place to put unwanted visitors of the lower orders, but she was in, which meant Fort was at home.

The footman left, but in moments was back, looking rather resentful, to lead her to another room.

This was a handsome study, and Fort was there.

As soon as the door closed, he said, "What in Hades are you doing here?" He was simply astonished.

"I want to go with you to Overstead."

He gaped. It was the only word for it. "But this is your wedding night!"

Portia's face was hot. "What is that to do with anything? Bryght refuses to take me there. He says we are to go north. He won't change his mind, so I am resolved to go alone."

"But . . . but what have you done to him?"

Portia frowned at him. "Done?"

"Have you drugged him? You haven't shot him, have you?"

At his alarmed tone, Portia bit her lip to stifle a giggle that would be part tears. "Of course not. I made it clear that I did not wish. . . . He is far too much of a gentleman . . ." Tears threatened, to become a reality. "I have retired for the night."

" 'Struth." Fort was looking at her as if she were a loaded weapon. "And you want me to take you to Dorset, a three-day journey?"

Portia eyed him with disgust. "Why do I have the feeling I'm lucky not to be bundled back to Malloren House on the instant?"

"Because you are," he snapped. "Damn lucky. We're not children anymore! What do you think Bryght's going to do if he discovers you've been here?"

Portia hadn't really thought of that. "He'd never think there was anything untoward. . . ." She wasn't sure what Bryght might think, but she held on to her resolve. "Fort, I need to get to Overstead. I must. But if I go on the stage, I'm afraid Bryght will overtake me before I get there."

"He'll overtake you sooner or later," he said grimly, "and there'll be hell to pay. By the sounds of it, you could go back now and he might never know."

"I'm not afraid of him," Portia lied, chin high. "I have to know the truth about Oliver."

Fort considered her a moment. "Well, if you have to know the truth, we had best go to Rothgar Abbey not Overstead."

"The Abbey?"

"That's where he's been taken if he's been taken anywhere."

Portia considered, and realized that was true. "And you'll accompany me there?"

"I wouldn't let you go alone." He suddenly smiled, and looked like the Fort of old. "I've always suspected my fate is to be killed by a Malloren, so why fight it? And I, too, want to know what they've done with Oliver. I have little sympathy for the fool, but outright murder I can't accept."

"Nor can I," she said quietly, thinking bleakly of the long years ahead without Bryght. "Well, if we're to do it, let's go."

"We can't leave now." Fort was looking out of the window. "It's started to rain, and there are clouds over the moon."

"What?" Portia went over to look for herself, but saw immediately that he was right. "I can't stay here all night!"

"You should have thought of that earlier. I always knew your crazy starts would lead to trouble. Of course," he said, "perhaps we can get you back into Malloren House . . ."

Portia actually considered it before saying, "No. But when will we be able to leave? We have to leave before morning!"

He let the curtain drop. "Even the high nobility can't control the elements, Portia. If the clouds clear, we can travel. If they don't we have to wait for dawn, but we should be able to make some kind of start then. You'd best stay in here. I'll tell the footman to keep his mouth shut."

Portia sat down on a chaise feeling chilled and weary. As long as she was active she could put off thoughts, but now they returned to torment her. If only she had been able to surrender to Bryght, surrender to her husband and the marriage bed. If only Oliver's disastrous affairs had not intervened.

But without Oliver's disastrous affairs, she doubted she would ever have even met a Malloren.

It was Oliver's debt that had taken them to Maidenhead. Doubtless that wild meeting had caused Bryght to approach her in the park. That and his gaming with Oliver.

What, she wondered, had caused him to game with Oliver? She knew him now and really could not believe him a hawk. Perhaps it was just as Bryght said, and one gentleman could not refuse to game with another.

It would have ended there, however, if not for Oliver and Cuthbertson. After the brothel, it was as if Bryght had been pursuing her.

Fort came back into the room and Portia looked up at him. "You bid for me at Mirabelle's."

"Yes." He looked away, making the excuse of checking the fire.

"What would you have done if you'd purchased me?"

He turned to face her. "Probably more than Bryght Malloren did." He shrugged. "I wouldn't have left you to Steenholt or D'Ebercall, but there was no getting out of there without a riot. I admit, I'd have probably just tried to make it quick for you. It would not have occurred to me to trump up a wager like that. You might consider," he added rather severely, "that you owe the man this wedding night."

Portia ignored that. "Trump up a wager? What do you mean?"

"I gather Bryght forced that wager on the sugar planter. The man's been heard to mutter that it was underhanded, but at least he doesn't suspect that you were not what you appeared."

The wager that saved her had been Bryght's inspiration?

"I gather it was a virtuoso performance," Fort said. "Are you sure you don't want to go back and enjoy even more of the same?" Portia sensed that he really wanted her to. Perhaps it was just to save his own skin, but perhaps it was to save hers.

"I cannot," she said, but she wondered just what Bryght would do when he caught her.

"Very well," he said with a sigh. "Why don't you lie on the chaise and rest. I'll call you as soon as it becomes possible to travel."

He left her alone, and despite her tangled thoughts Portia even managed to doze. Fort woke her to say they could set out. "The visibility's not perfect, but the moon is clear. We can go, if we go slowly, and I think we'd be better on our way."

Portia agreed, shivering at being woken in the chill morning hours. Shivering perhaps with fear. She was beginning to truly dread a meeting with her husband and as Fort said, it could not be put off forever.

Like death, it must be faced one day.

Her heart said Bryght would never hurt her. But if she thought him capable of killing Oliver, she had to think him capable of hurting her.

"What time is it?" she asked, wrapping her cloak around her.

"Nearly four. We're going to steal out to the mews like robbers." He flashed her an encouraging grin. "Lord, this reminds me of some of our youthful adventures."

She grinned back for him, but she feared it was a feeble effort. "How far is it?" she whispered as they crossed the hall. "How long will it take?"

"It's about thirty miles to the Abbey, so I'd say five to six hours if the roads are fair."

"So we might be there by nine? What will we do when we arrive?"

"Demand admittance. I am a connection, and an earl."

"But . . ."

"Shhhh."

They tiptoed through the kitchen, by the lowly kitchen servants sleeping on mats near the fire, then he eased open a door into the garden. It did remind Portia poignantly of some of their childhood escapades. How innocent they had been then.

Even though the moon was clear, the garden seemed bleak and dark. Portia shivered in the chill air. "I don't think humans are supposed to be about at this time of night," she whispered.

"If we were to drive by St. James, you'd find the place very much awake. Some people scarce see daylight at this time of year."

"Which is proof of the rottenness of London."

The coach was waiting. They climbed in and the coachman set the four horses into motion.

Fort looked at Portia with a puzzled frown. "I'm at a loss as to why Bryght Malloren was willing to marry you. He's just the sort to spend the night gaming, whereas you think that despicable. You have nothing in common."

"I know that," said Portia, hands gripped tight. "I suppose he felt obliged to."

"Devil a bit. That business at Mirabelle's made marriage less likely not more."

"Probably. I was thinking of Lady Willoughby's."

"Ah, yes. But there was nothing to that really until I decided to force his hand."

She looked at him. "Do you not regret that now?"

"No. It gets better and better."

Portia turned to look out of the window. She knew this journey was taking her straight to disaster, but she had never had any other choice.

Twenty-four

Like most coach journeys it was tedious and gave too much time to think. Portia sat looking out at the moon-silvered landscape wondering when Bryght would realize she was missing, and what he would do.

Any and all prospects terrified her.

The best possibility was that he might chase after her to Overstead, which would give them plenty of time to investigate matters at the Abbey. If everything turned out to be innocent, she would just await her fate.

If not, and if Oliver was still alive, she would have to rescue him and take him to safety. But where? Could she hide from Bryght if he chose to seek her?

And he would have to seek her. What would the world say if his possibly-mistreated bride disappeared within hours of the ceremony?

Perhaps the best hope was that he would never want to see her again. Then she could even return to Overstead and look after it for Oliver. If Bryght didn't tell the world their marriage was an empty shell, she wouldn't, and their living apart would not surprise the cynical world of the aristocracy.

Unless he wanted children.

Unless she was carrying his child.

She imagined bearing a child only to have it torn from

her and taken to be raised by its father. The law would
allow it, and perhaps Bryght would think it a just revenge.

If she were pregnant, perhaps she would flee the country . . .

"What's the matter?" Fort said. "It's too late for second
thoughts now."

"I know. It's other thoughts that torment me."

"Of Bryght Malloren? You're not as cool to him as you
try to pretend, are you?"

She turned to him. "Would you be willing to kiss me?"

In the shadowy coach she could not see his expression,
but she sensed wariness. "Why?"

"Perhaps I just need comfort."

"Then you should have stayed with your husband."

"Even if he has killed my brother?"

After a moment, he said, "You are not seeking comfort."

"No," she sighed, "not exactly. I need to know. . . .
Bryght is the only man who has really kissed me. I need
to know."

After a moment he laughed. "Well, I'm likely to get
skewered for what they think I've done, so why not?" He
took her hand, tugged her against him, cradled her head
and kissed her.

It was the same business of lips and hot breath, and it
was not unpleasant. It was Fort, and Portia liked Fort. But
there was something missing, the something that excited
her senses and drove her wild. She would not be carried
beyond wisdom by this.

When he tilted her further back and his hand traveled to
cover her breast, she broke free. "No, Fort."

His hand moved over her breast in gentle suggestion.
"Perhaps I could persuade you . . ."

"No," she said again, firmly but calmly, though her heart was speeding.

Still he didn't let her go. "It would quite please me to cuckold a Malloren. Especially if I were the first."

Portia shuddered and pushed at him. "Stop it, Fort. I won't be part of your feud."

"You already are. Has he had you yet?"

Portia realized she had leapt into a deeper pit than she'd imagined. "That's none of your business. Think what you're doing."

He jerked as if she'd hit him, but his hand still rested on her bodice. She was grateful it was high and modest, but still felt soiled.

"I'm causing problems for the Mallorens. My life's cause."

"Why?" she demanded.

"Because they killed my father."

Portia gently removed his hand from her bodice. "What happened?"

She thought he wouldn't speak, but then he said, "He wasn't entirely sane, you know. He was brilliant, but unbalanced. It was through the Mallorens that I discovered what was wrong. . . . When Cynric Malloren decided he wanted to marry Chastity, it became a cause for Rothgar, and nothing and no one was allowed to stand in his way."

"Bryght said that your father created that scandal over Chastity."

"That's true. But there was no need to destroy father. And," he added softly, "there was no need to make me their tool."

Portia took his hand and looked him in the eye. "What happened, Fort? I heard that your father died of a seizure."

"It was cleverly hushed up. He died of a pistol ball while

trying to kill the king's mother. I fired the pistol. . . ." He
closed his eyes and leaned his head back against the squabs.
"He was raving by then, driven mad by Rothgar, and by
the destruction of his plans. I couldn't let him kill Princess
Augusta. She was innocent, and it would have ruined the
family entirely. . . ."

Portia squeezed his hand. "You cannot entirely blame the
Mallorens."

He opened his eyes then. "I can blame them enough.
And I rather begrudge you to Bryght. I gather my kisses
do not have the potency of his."

"Bryght has never been intent on rape."

"I wonder. If you don't give in to him, he will force you
one day. How else is he to get children? And he needs
children. That way, since Rothgar will not marry, he con-
trols the marquisate from the grave."

Portia thought of children, children taken from her, and
wanted to weep for all of them. "Don't impose your own
twisted thinking upon Bryght. Don't hate so much. You will
hurt yourself more than you could possibly hurt them."

He turned away. "I have no choice. Don't worry, though,"
he added lightly. "Tempting though it is, I won't rape you
in the cause."

Portia huddled away and looked out the window again.
Bryght had warned her that the enmity between the Wares
and the Mallorens ran deep, but she had not realized the
truth of it.

That Fort could even contemplate raping her for venge-
ance terrified her.

She watched moon-touched fields and trees roll by and
prayed for safety, prayed too that Oliver was safe. Not only
would it ease her fears about Bryght, but it would not further fuel this inferno.

They did not stop, but they hit a patch of bad road where recent rains had created axle-deep mud. They had to wait for extra horses to be brought from a nearby farm before the coach could be freed. That added hours to their journey. Matters became worse when the moon clouded over again in the dim pre-dawn and they had to slow to a crawl. The wintry sun was high by the time they arrived at the drive up to the Abbey, and shone bright on the handsome white house on the rise.

The park was not gated, so there was no hindrance to their arrival at the doors. Fort helped Portia down and she shivered. It was partly tiredness, and partly the chill air, but it was largely fear as to what she would find here.

Bryght found it hard to concentrate on balance sheets and profit calculations, but he forced his mind to discipline. Portia had already turned his life upside down and shattered his ability to think. He would not let her rule him entirely.

As midnight struck he stretched wearily and decided he could cease work with honor. The problem now was being able to sleep. He tended the fire, extinguished the candles and went into his bedroom, where he had expected to enjoy Portia as his wife. He laughed bitterly. He should have known that with Portia nothing would go as expected.

He'd had very pleasant plans, however, plans of a relaxed, leisurely loving with no strains or guilt between them. Plans of introducing a very eager student to some of the finer points of sensual love.

The memory of her mouth hot upon him had him hard. He sucked in a deep breath. The damn witch was not going to rule him with his cock.

He prepared for bed burningly aware of the object of

his desire lying in a bed only two doors away. And his. By laws of God and man, his to take when and where he wished.

But he had no wish to *take* Portia. None at all. He'd had enough of fighting and was ready for peace. He wanted her to come to him in joyous wanting, without compulsion or wager.

Sly temptations crept upon him. Perhaps she was as eager as he, just not sure how to break this stalemate without losing face. If he went to her, would she smile with relief and drop her unreasonable demands?

He had his hand on the knob of her bedroom door before he found the control to stop. No, she must see that she could not rule him or he was a hopeless case.

He retreated to his bed to toss and turn until he got up to drink a few glasses of brandy. Not enough to lose all restraint, for God knows what he would do then, but enough to blunt awareness and eventually to bring him sleep.

He was woken by daylight and rang for his valet. He stretched, not feeling his best by any means, but proud of the fact he'd survived the night without groveling or violence. They had a lifetime. He could wait.

"We'll breakfast in my study," he told his man when he arrived. "Have word sent to milady."

The man bowed out and Bryght rose to look out the window. Misty, but it promised to be clear. Good traveling weather. Once they were on their way north Portia would have to see that he was adamant. That still left the problem of Upcott to be faced, but once she was his body and soul that would be easier.

"Milord . . ."

Bryght turned, detecting a strange note in his valet's voice.

"Yes?"

The man was red-faced and bewildered. "Milord, her ladyship is not in her bedchamber." The man's eyes flicked around as if seeking her here.

A chill went through Bryght. Damn it to Hades! "Has her bed been slept in?"

"Er . . . no, milord . . ."

He'd wring her beautiful neck! He made instant decisions. "Who knows? Just you and her maid?"

The man nodded.

"Then no one else is to. Is the maid tall or short?"

"Quite short, milord."

"Good. Have my coach ready in twenty minutes and tell the maid to put on a cloak like my wife's. She will enter the coach with me. I'll let her off nearby. As far as anyone is concerned, my wife and I have left on our journey north."

The valet's eyes were widening despite his training. "Yes, milord."

While the man arranged matters, Bryght dressed and ran through options. He feared he had seriously misjudged matters.

There had to be more to it than willfulness. Portia would never act this way in a simple fight as to whether they went north or west. He remembered now a desperation in her manner when she'd asked that they go to Overstead.

Why?

He traced back her behavior after the wedding.

She had not been radiant, but she had been resigned.

Then she'd found out about Barclay and been furious, but there'd been no talk of going to Overstead.

That had come . . . after she'd been talking to Fort.

Overstead was in his area, and it was possible news from there would travel.

Bryght got out of the house without a hitch—such as running into Rothgar—and dropped off the maid nearby with a reminder that she was to keep this matter to herself. Then he directed the coach to Ware House.

A footman opened the door, clearly ready to send away anyone who called at such an early hour. He was immediately quelled by rank. "I wish to see my brother-in-law," said Bryght crisply, walking into the house.

"He is not at home, milord."

Bryght stiffened. "At this hour?" Again he made a swift analysis. "Gads," he said lightly, "has he left already?"

The man's eyes flickered revealingly.

"Were there three women with him—or four?"

The footman's eyes almost popped. "But one, milord!"

Bryght hid his triumph. "How moderate, though on a long journey into Dorset, a full coach would be inconvenient." He gave the man a knowing wink and a coin.

The footman almost sniggered as he pocketed the coin. "Not Dorset, milord," he said quickly. "Surrey."

Bryght flicked him another coin and left.

The Abbey! And Portia alone in a coach for hours with Fort Ware, the man she seemed to prefer. Fort clearly was not devoted to Portia, but it might suit him to seduce a Malloren bride.

"I'll kill him," Bryght muttered as the coach sped out of town. "Family connection or no."

This wasn't fast enough. On the edge of London, Bryght got rid of the coach and its servants, telling them to stay in a quiet inn for a few days. He hired a fast riding horse and set off for the Abbey at a gallop.

* * *

Portia stared at the imposing entrance of Rothgar Abbey with dismay. "I suppose we should have tried to slip in quietly rather than announcing our arrival."

Fort's look of astonishment reminded her of his stiff-rumped father. "Be damned to that." His groom was already rapping on the door and Fort led Portia to it.

It opened almost exactly as they arrived there, making Portia wonder if there was a skill to it—both servants and lord trained with military precision.

Clearly a night of anxiety and no sleep was not good for her sanity.

They were soon inside the handsome house, and Portia began to fret about what excuse they should make.

But Fort merely said, "We are here to see Sir Oliver Upcott."

The footman was well-trained and did not so much as blink before directing them to a reception room and saying, "I will enquire, milord."

An admirably noncommittal answer. Portia thought that his very woodenness had been revealing, however.

"He knows something," she said as soon as they were alone.

"Or he was just astonished to be asked about a perfect stranger. Come to the fire, Portia."

She went over and tried to warm herself, but the chill went deeper. "What do we do if they deny all knowledge? After all, if the Mallorens have done away with Oliver, they would scarcely let their servants know."

"With the Mallorens all things are possible," Fort said dryly, explaining, "it's one of their favorite sayings. I have to admit, they have the best-trained servants I've ever come across. They favor old family retainers, of course, but they manage to hold their loyalty. It's hard to even get them to gossip, as I have discovered."

"I think it disgusting for you to be prying into other people's affairs."

He was about to make an angry retort, but the door opened. It was Brand Malloren. He stared at them with blank astonishment then shut the door. "What the devil's going on?"

Portia decided on attack. "I've come to see my brother."

"Where's *my* brother?"

"Following," she said, knowing that in one way or another it was true.

Brand lacked his brother's dark, dramatic beauty, but his expression was all Malloren. "Forgive me for mentioning it, Lady Bryght, but it does rather leap to mind that last night was your wedding night, and that you appear to have spent it with Lord Walgrave."

Portia remained resolute. "I want to see my brother."

"All you'll get, if you want it, is breakfast."

Portia looked to Fort for help, but he appeared to have chosen a passive role. He took a measured pinch of snuff.

Portia actually stamped her foot. "I demand to see my brother. Now!"

Brand opened the door. "The breakfast parlor is across the hall. You will find an adequate selection, I believe, though there may not be eggs to your liking. . . ."

Portia swept through and headed straight for the stairs.

Brand seized her by the arm. "No."

Portia tested his grip, but he tightened it unhesitatingly. "Fort!" she protested.

"You were the one who thought it disgusting to be prying into other people's affairs," said her untrustworthy accomplice. "You wouldn't actually want to search someone's house, would you? They will have to take us to Oliver eventually."

But Bryght could be here by then, Portia thought wildly. She was growing terrified of meeting her husband. "Anything could be happening," she protested. "I can't just sit and eat breakfast!"

Brand towed her toward the breakfast room. "Yes you can. Terribly bad form to interrupt a torture session, you know." He relieved her of her cloak and pushed her into a chair at the well-laden table.

Portia landed with a thump and stared at him. She'd swear that comment about torture was a joke, but could one be sure of anything with a Malloren? Especially an angry Malloren?

Her dazed eyes settled on a stranger at the table, a pleasantly ordinary brown-haired man who, she noticed, lacked a hand.

He smiled, "Major Cranton Barclay, at your service, ma'am."

"She's not 'ma'am,' " Brand said shortly. "She's Lady Bryght Malloren. Sit down, Walgrave. As far as I know we have no standing orders to poison brothers-in-law."

"I'm relieved to hear it." Fort settled at the table and helped himself to ham.

Major Barclay was looking uncomfortable and confused, but all Portia's wary attention was on Brand. It was almost impossible to believe that he was party to murder, but he was clearly furious at her adventure.

And he wasn't her husband.

He passed her a plate of bread rolls. "We don't have servants at the breakfast table unless there are a number of guests. If there's anything you require, I will ring for it."

Portia took a roll with unsteady fingers and made a botch of buttering it.

"We only have coffee and small beer," he said. "Would you like anything else, Portia?"

Just to be difficult, Portia said, "Chocolate, please."

He rang a bell and ordered it.

Silence settled, with Portia and Brand radiating animosity, Barclay looking bewildered, and Fort almost appearing amused. Portia knew now that involving Fort in this had been like throwing oil on a fire, but what else could she have done? Then something clicked in her weary brain.

"Barclay!" she exclaimed staring at the man across the table, a man innocently taking a bite of toast. "You're the wretch who stole our estate!"

He flushed. "Certainly not. I won it fair and square, Miss St. Claire."

"Lady Arcenbryght Malloren," corrected Brand with emphasis.

Portia ignored him. "How can it be fair to throw a family out onto the streets?"

"How can it be fair for a man to stake his family's welfare?" the major retorted.

He was right. "But still," Portia protested, "if no one gamed, no one would stake anything."

The major raised his brows. "As well say, if no one waged war, no one would have to fight. Unlikely, and demmed dull."

The servant returned with the chocolate pot, poured a cup for Portia, and then left.

"There are many people," she said, "who enjoy such a dull existence, enjoy the simple pleasures of peace and security, of family life and honest labor."

"How *did* you come to marry Bryght?" murmured Fort maliciously. "Perhaps it's not too late for an annulment."

Vicious antagonism sparked between Brand and Fort and Portia leapt to her feet. "I must—"

"Sit down," said Brand coldly. "I'll bind and gag you if I have to. You're doing nothing until Bryght gets here."

"No!"

"Don't worry. I won't let him kill you. Rothgar don't care for murder in the house."

At that, Fort snarled something, and Portia feared he would lunge across the table and throttle the Malloren. He assumed control again, however, and contented himself with silent animosity.

Portia looked wildly to Major Barclay, who might be the only sane man here. He did look uncomfortable, but she could not believe the villain in her life might help her.

So she would have to help herself. She turned to Brand. "I need to relieve myself."

A flicker of amusement showed in his eyes, but he said, "Of course," and rose to open the door for her. He led her through and up the wide staircase to the next floor. There he stopped to open a door. "An unused bedchamber, but I think you will find a close stool. There is no other door, so don't think to start wandering."

His smile said that he had seen through all her tricks.

Portia walked through and slammed the door in his face.

She did need to use it, so she found the pot. Then she checked the window just in case. With astonishment, she found the wall on this side was covered by heavy ivy. She was a good thirty feet off the ground but still, it was this or captivity, and she was well-practiced at the art. She eased up the window and checked. The vine was firm against the wall and as sturdy as a ladder!

"Ha, Brand Malloren," she muttered as she shed her hoops. "Now we'll see."

Lacking pins, she knotted her skirts then climbed out of the window, not allowing herself to think of how high she was. If the ivy was safe, the height didn't matter.

She worked her way down, expecting a shout from above at any moment. But she reached the ground without incident and looked up at the window with a grim smile of triumph.

It was a temporary victory, she knew, but at least she wouldn't be sitting meekly at the breakfast table when Bryght turned up to strangle her. And it was possible that in the meantime she might find Oliver and solve the mystery once and for all.

She unknotted her skirts and ran round the corner, looking for another way into the house. How long would it be before Brand intruded to find out what was keeping her? The silly man clearly thought a guarded door meant that she was quite secure. With any luck he'd give her time, thinking she'd be sulking.

She came across a side door and tried it. Unlocked! That wasn't surprising in the country, but it made her feel the fates were on her side. She found herself in a passageway, and walked quickly down it by the kitchen and scullery. There were servants there, but none saw her.

Now, where would the Mallorens keep Oliver?

She wondered if this house had a cellar, but a quick exploration showed no sign of one. She had to slip into a corner at the bottom of some stairs to avoid one undermaid carrying a bucket, but otherwise she met no one.

Attics?

She went up the stairs, climbing them all the way to the top. She heard a door open and close lower down, but no sound of anyone near by, and no sound of pursuit.

When she reached the limit of the stairs, she went through a door into a plain corridor. Long past caution, she opened a door and found, as she'd expected, a servants' bedroom. She checked each room and found them all the same. There was no sign of Oliver.

What now?

She would have to search the family part of the house. She didn't want to, but she must.

Portia came to a second set of stairs and went down them, trying to be quiet. By now Brand must have realized she'd given him the slip. She shrugged. Cowering would do her no good, and no amount of caution would avoid the eventual confrontation with Bryght. She opened a door and entered a carpeted corridor, pausing to listen.

She thought perhaps she did hear distant voices, but was somewhat surprised not to find a hullabaloo. Since no one seemed to be nearby, she began again methodically checking rooms, opening each door. The corridors in this old house wandered, and it wasn't easy for her to be sure she had checked everywhere.

There were suites of rooms, and she thought that perhaps each member of the family had such a set of rooms, always in readiness. In one bedroom—possibly Major Barclay's for it seemed more recently used and yet less settled than others—she found a pistol case. She calmly loaded one of the weapons and took it with her.

Then she looked into a bedroom with a wide open window. This seemed so strange in December that she went over and peered out, thinking perhaps Oliver might have been here and escaped.

She heard a *click* behind her.

She spun around to see Bryght pocketing the key.

Twenty-five

Portia's heart leaped into her throat and she raised her hand to cover the area, only then remembering the pistol. She pointed it at him, but with a trembling hand.

"This is where we came in, I think," he said, walking toward her. "Put that down."

"No! Where is Oliver?"

"Your wretched brother is perfectly safe. Put down the pistol." He was muddy, disheveled, and very angry.

"Take me to him. I don't trust—"

He kicked the pistol from her hand. It fired deafeningly even as he grabbed her by the gown and hauled her to him. "You don't trust me? That's obvious. You'd rather trust Fort Ware!"

Her hands were stinging but she was almost dizzy with fear. "I don't trust anyone anymore!"

"Why? What did he do?" The rage in him was positively terrifying, reminding her brutally of their first meeting.

"Nothing," she whispered. "He brought me here."

"He didn't touch you?"

She shook her head.

"Kiss you?"

Her guilt must have shown for the fury burned brighter. "I asked him to!" she cried. "Don't fight him!"

He threw her aside so she stumbled.

"I should have let him buy you," he said coldly, anger banked, but still glowing. "Perhaps guilt would have changed his mind about marrying you. Or perhaps he'd have been entranced by your charms. Either way, you'd have preferred it, wouldn't you?"

"Fort would never—"

"Fort would have raped you on the slim chance that I might care. I wonder why he didn't."

Portia turned away from his bitterness and covered her mouth with a trembling hand. "Because he thinks I'll be a greater cross for you to bear as it is."

"Surprisingly astute of him. You've caused me nothing but grief from the moment we met." She heard him unlock the door and turned.

He opened it. "Come."

"Where?"

"Do you have the right to ask?"

"Yes, but there's probably no purpose to it." Portia raised her chin and walked through into the corridor.

Bryght did not touch her in any way, but led her across to the part of this floor she had not yet checked. He unlocked a door. Inside was Oliver in his shirtsleeves, sitting despondently in front of the fire.

He looked up suspiciously, then a blend of confusion and anger crossed his face. "Portia? Malloren! Why in the name of heaven have you kept me prisoner here?" By then he was standing belligerently.

Portia saw with horror that he had a virulent black eye, and was limping. "Oliver!" She ran to him. "What have they done to you? But, oh, thank heavens. I was so afraid. . . ."

He caught her in his arms. "Afraid? Of what?" He pushed her away a little and looked into her eyes. "What have they done to *you?*"

"Nothing!" she said quickly, brushing his loose hair back from a swollen temple, then the absurdity of that statement struck her and control fell away. "Oh God!" And she started to cry.

She felt other hands upon her shoulders, and heard Bryght say, "If you don't give her to me, I'm like to kill you."

"Why the devil should I?" Oliver demanded, holding her tight.

Portia tried to choke out an explanation but tears swamped her voice.

"Because she's my wife," said Bryght.

Oliver's grasp loosened, probably through shock. Portia was turned into Bryght's arms. "Portia, stop," he said, holding her tight. "You'll break my heart, crying like this."

She tried to control herself, gulping in deep breaths, but tears started again. She tried to speak, but nothing coherent came out. He rocked her and murmured comfort, and in a while it began to help.

"I'm sorry," she choked and found her handkerchief.

He relaxed his hold. "You have reason enough for tears, *petite,* but we need to talk."

Portia pulled herself out of his arms and blew her nose. "I don't cry," she said truculently.

"So I see." His tone was dry but his expression was much milder than before.

"I don't!" she protested. "Oliver, when did I last cry?" But then she remembered that time at Mirabelle's which Oliver knew nothing about.

"She doesn't," Oliver said. "When I was in the nursery, my father would berate me for crying more than a girl."

"I was four years older than you," Portia said. "That wasn't fair!"

"But girls cry at any age. Everyone knows that. Look at Pru. She gushes forth at the sight of a pretty sunset!"

"That's because she knows she cries prettily. . . ."

Bryght cleared his throat and Portia suddenly recollected the disastrous state of her life. She looked at him warily, but though somber he did not seem to be in an ungovernable rage.

"Sir Oliver," he said, "it was not precisely part of my orders that you be brought here and confined, but I did send men to find you and watch over you. I accept responsibility for their over-enthusiasm and apologize."

"But why did you do such a thing?"

"I intended to marry your sister, but had no mind to cover even more of your debts."

Oliver flushed. "I am done with gaming forever."

"I'm delighted to hear it," said Bryght dryly. "Can we believe you?"

"I don't see that you have much choice."

"Don't you?"

Portia stepped between them. "You will not harm him," she stated fiercely. "I will not permit it."

"I didn't think you would." She couldn't read him at all. "What reason do you have to distrust his word, when you have made the same promise to me and expected to be believed?"

"I have never been a besotted gamester."

"You're known the length of the country for it!"

"But not for losing."

Portia could see his temper shortening, but would not back down. "Does that make it right?"

"It helps."

"Not for the people you steal from."

He hissed in a breath. "Portia—"

"My lord," said Oliver stepping forward and pushing Portia behind him, "you will have to trust me."

Bryght turned his cold eyes on him, and Portia could only be glad of it. She was brutally reminded that there was a reckoning still to come.

"In case I prove frail," Oliver said with dignity, "other measures have been taken. I am to join the army. In fact, I had an appointment with the colonel of the 5th, which your men made me miss."

"My apologies. But it is possible to game in the army, you know."

"But he won't," said Portia quickly. "Oliver has always wanted the army. It is boredom that has led to gaming. I don't want to see him in a war, but . . ."

". . . but it is better," completed Bryght. "Since I am apparently not permitted to wring his neck, I suppose it will have to do."

"There is more," said Oliver stiffly. "I would not have told you, my lord, were it not for the fact that you seem to be my brother-in-law. Which I still find peculiar. But, while Lord Walgrave has bought up the debt on Overstead, he is not returning the property to me just yet. It is a mortgage of sorts, but more stringent than most mortgages. My mother and sisters . . ." he cast a puzzled look at Portia, ". . . sister, will live at Overstead, but I cannot lose what I do not own. He has given me his word that he will not release the property to me to pay any kind of debt."

"Neat. Walgrave has more wit that I took him for." Bryght turned to Portia. "If you had told me this, you could have saved me and your brother a great deal of trouble."

She raised her chin. "I didn't know the details, but even if I had I would not have thought it any of your business!"

"I see. And it is none of my business, I suppose, why

you were exchanging *billets doux* with Walgrave, and ran off with him?"

"Because you wouldn't bring me!"

"Or what happened other than kisses during the journey."

"Nothing happened! You're going to have to trust me."

"Why, when you never trust me? Why didn't you tell me your real reasons for wanting to travel to Overstead?"

Because she hadn't trusted him. "You have given me no reason to trust you!" she protested, and her wild words created an icy wall between them.

"Have I not?" He turned toward the door.

"Wait!" she cried. "Where are you going?"

He turned back, distantly polite. "I am giving you and your brother an opportunity to talk in peace, after which I assume he will want to leave to speak to the colonel. You may go with him if you wish. If you wish to talk to me, a servant will doubtless find me."

The door closed behind him with a steely click.

Portia stared at it. *You may go with him if you wish.*

"Portia?" Oliver asked. "What the devil's going on?"

"Oh, Oliver, it has become such a coil."

"Then you had best tell me all about it. I know I'm only your younger brother, but perhaps I can help."

So Portia sat with a sigh and told him of all her adventures. She even included the events at Mirabelle's since they seemed part of the whole.

"Lord above," he muttered, running a hand down his face. "The risks you've run!"

"I did what I had to, and I've had few enough choices along the way."

"And now you're married to him."

"Yes."

He chewed his lip. "Perhaps we can get you out of it.

Duress or something. After all, you fled on your wedding night. . . ."

Portia blushed. "I'm not a virgin, Oliver. And I don't want to get out of it. I just wonder if he's disgusted by me."

"Plague take it," muttered Oliver, staring into the fire. "And it's all my fault. If I hadn't been so foolish . . ."

"If you hadn't been so foolish, I would have stayed contentedly at Overstead counting turnips, and never so much as set eyes on Bryght Malloren." It seemed to her impossible that she could have lived without ever knowing the man who was now the center of her world. She stood to roam the room restlessly. "I suppose I should leave with you. Perhaps an annulment is possible. You need me anyway to take care of Overstead. I can return home and . . . and count turnips for the rest of my . . . my life. . . ." She swallowed fiercely. She would *not* cry.

"I think you should go and talk to him," said Oliver with surprising understanding. "Judging from the way he looked when you were crying, I don't think he wants you to leave."

"He probably wants to wring my neck."

"If you really did run off with Fort on your wedding night, he probably does. You've never been a coward, though, Portia. Face your devils."

It was good advice and she turned to him. "You truly want to be in the army?"

"With all my heart."

She kissed his cheek. "Be happy then. And wish me luck. War is probably a safer course than the one I'm choosing."

Portia left the room and found the corridor empty. Where would Bryght be? She could start searching rooms again, but the prospect wearied her. Instead she descended the stairs to the hall, seeking a servant.

The hall appeared empty, but then she heard a blast from a horn. Within moments the space was teeming with staff. She froze with surprise, but then two footmen swung open the doors to reveal the Marquess of Rothgar mounting the steps, his sister on his arm. Another gentleman came behind and they were trailed by a small retinue of personal servants. Two coaches each drawn by six horses, stood in the drive.

Portia was rooted to the steps by shock. As servants bustled around divesting the arrivals of cloaks, hats, and muffs Lord Rothgar looked up and saw her.

He raised a cold brow.

He wasn't the devil she had intended to face but there was nothing for it. Portia descended the stairs, wishing Bryght would appear to support her.

"Bridgewater," said the marquess coolly to the pale, lanky young man by his side. "May I present Lady Arcenbryght Malloren?"

The duke took her hand and kissed it warmly. "Lady Bryght. I posted down to be sure he wasn't doing something foolish in my cause." He sounded pleased, but Portia wasn't sure how to take his words.

Elf stepped into the situation. "Oh, do let's go into the Tapestry Room where there will be a fire." She linked arms with Portia. "Came long. It was a lovely wedding, wasn't it . . . ?" She swept them all along on a ripple of light chatter until they were in the room and the door was shut.

"Where's Bryght?" asked Rothgar crisply.

Portia flinched. "I don't know. He's here somewhere."

"You left the house separately. How did you get here?"

Portia swallowed. Perhaps *Rothgar* would wring her neck. "Fort brought me," she whispered.

"You are a rash and dangerous woman."

Portia began to wonder if she would be tossed out of Rothgar Abbey on her ear but Brand and Fort walked in.

"She certainly is," Brand said, shaking his head at her. "Lord, Bey, I recall you taking a switch to the twins when they climbed the north wall."

Rothgar's brows rose as he looked at Portia. "A very rash woman."

"He locked me in!" But she had seen the flicker of amusement on the marquess's eyes. "It's an easy climb."

"True enough. But not to be encouraged for eight-year-olds. One assumes older people will have more sense. Is your brother well?"

"Yes."

"Oliver's safe?" asked Fort sharply.

"Yes," Portia told him, praying he'd make no further trouble. "It was all a mistake."

He smiled slightly. "What a shame. Does Bryght want to kill me?" He sounded mildly hopeful.

Portia could have killed him herself. "Fort, stop this! Go away and leave my life alone!"

"But you're a Malloren," he said. He strolled toward her and took her hand, raising it for a kiss. "Are you sure you wouldn't prefer to run away with me?"

Portia was burningly aware of a roomful of Mallorens and a total stranger. "Not in the slightest," she said icily, dragging her hand from his.

"How ungrateful you are," he lamented. He looked around the room then bowed. *"Au revoir. A la prochaine."*

Portia sadly watched him leave. Until the next, he said. But what next? Would he succeed in getting his revenge, or in finding death at the hands of a Malloren?

"Portia!"

The marquess's sharp tone brought her attention back to him.

"If you wish to leave with Lord Walgrave, I will not stop you." He sounded as if he might wave her on her way.

Portia licked her lips. "I don't."

"What are your feelings for Bryght?"

Portia looked around at the watchful faces, and Elf flashed her an encouraging smile.

"I love him," she admitted.

Rothgar's expression did not lighten. "Then you had best find him, don't you think?"

Portia wished he would offer a little support and guidance. "I don't know where to look."

"It rather depends on whether he wants to be found, doesn't it?" Then he smiled slightly. "His rooms would be an optimistic place to start. Elf, could you play guide to this architectural mass?"

"Of course." Elf took Portia's hand to lead her from the room.

"And Portia," said the marquess, halting them, "if necessary, scream very loudly. We have had our due allotment of violent deaths here for one year."

Portia was trembling as Elf led her to the stairs.

Elf paused to smile. "Don't worry. Bryght won't harm you."

"Can you be sure?" Portia asked. "I tried to shoot him. Again!" Her heart was racing and her knees were knocking, but it wasn't so much fear of violence—though that was possible—as fear of rejection.

Elf laughed. "That is probably part of your charm."

Portia wasn't sure she had any charm anymore. Bryght had said he loved her, but that was before she had betrayed him. Not betrayed him physically, but emotionally, in fearing the worst.

They were in a side corridor and Elf stopped by a door. "Here we are." She suddenly gathered Portia into her arms and hugged her. "It will be all right. Just be honest!"

With that, she turned and retraced her steps, not looking back to see what Portia would do.

Portia wiped a damp hand on her skirt. If there were any sensible choices she might have walked away from this door, but Bryght had to be faced. If he were here at all.

What if he did not want to be found?

She turned the knob and went in, to find only an empty room. Her heart turned to a painful lump in her chest.

It was a kind of study with a well-stocked library and desk, but with chairs by the fire and a sideboard bearing decanters and a bowl of fruit. It was a comfortable, well-used room which spoke to her senses of Bryght.

But he wasn't here.

He didn't want to be found.

Then she saw the half-open adjoining door to the bedroom. That room too looked empty, but she entered it anyway.

Bryght was leaning against the windowsill, stark naked.

Portia's mouth dropped open.

"Naked to your malice or your love," he said, and though his body concealed nothing, his feelings were cloaked.

Portia couldn't see her way, and it appeared he wasn't going to guide her. "I can't say I'm sorry," she whispered. "In the same situations, I would do the same things."

"I know. But I have to know you'll trust me in the future, that when you have doubts you'll tell me of them, not run off on some crazy start."

"Will you trust me?" she demanded. "You thought I was capable of committing adultery on my wedding night!"

His jaw twitched. "You've expressed a preference for Fort."

"I've known him since we were children."

"That hardly makes it better."

"He's like a brother." Portia clasped and unclasped her hands. "I asked him to kiss me in the coach because I had never been truly kissed by a man other than you. I wanted to know if the effect was from the kisses or the man."

"And?" he asked softly.

She shrugged uneasily and looked away. "He had little effect on me. . . . Of course, that isn't a very wide test. . . ."

"Portia," he warned.

She realized her hands were tight together now. "Bryght, I'm scared. Tell me you love me."

"Ah no. I've done that and had it thrown back at me. It's your turn."

She eyed him uncertainly, wondering if he wanted a chance to reject her love. Perhaps his nakedness was an insult.

"What is love?" she whispered.

"What do you feel?"

She turned away from the distracting sight of him. "I can't imagine life without you. I care about you. I want you to be happy. I . . . I want to bear your children. . . ." Still he said nothing. "I desire you."

His bare feet had made no sound, so she jumped when he touched her shoulders. He turned her and undid the clasp that held her gown together at the front.

"What . . . ?"

"If you want to bear my children, we had best work at it."

She gripped his hands. "Bryght!"

He stopped. "I'm sorry. That was unfortunate. I'm still a little angry with you." He raised his hands to cradle her face. "But I love you, Portia. I, too, cannot imagine life without you. I want your happiness, your children, and your desire. Always. And," he added with a smile, "the River Thames is rather insistently rising."

She looked down and saw it was true. She curled her hand around him. He felt as hot as her face. "I can't believe how bold I am with you. It's as if I'm not me at all."

"You are entrancingly you." He slipped her gown off her shoulders, then ran his hands restlessly over her pretty bridal stays and petticoats. "No hoops?"

"I climbed out of another window."

His hands paused. "The north wall. I know. 'Struth, Portia! Try to live a cautious life, for my sake."

"How can I, married to you?"

He laughed and they kissed then, first tenderly, then deeply, then endlessly, lovingly exploring each other fully for the first time.

Portia was dizzy when they finished, and weak with desire. "I am sorry!" she exclaimed. "Sorry for not trusting you."

"Now, now. Don't make me think I've married a weak, vacillating woman." Even with unsteady hands he was efficient. Her stays were gone, and her petticoat fell to the floor. He took out the pins and spread her hair.

Then he kissed her again until she was limp and expecting to be carried to the bed.

But he left her then and went to slip under the bed covers alone. "Come join me in our marriage bed, wife, if that is your will."

"It is my will," she whispered, and took off her shift so she too was naked. But then, under his intent gaze, she suffered an attack of insecurity and covered herself with her hands. "I'm sorry I don't have more curves."

"I'm not." He flipped back a corner of the covers. "Come. Come of your own will. I'm done with traps and seduction."

"That seems a shame," she said with a laugh.

He didn't laugh with her, just waited. She knew then how much she'd hurt him and her heart ached.

"I think I'm scared," she whispered.

Humor flickered in his darkened eyes. "Imagine I'm a wall to climb, love."

Portia laughed and dashed under the covers. He immediately pulled her crushingly close. "I love you. Deeply, irrevocably. Remember that." He looked into her eyes. "I meant my wedding vows. This is for all time."

She kissed him. "For all time, this life and after . . ."

As they kissed, he eased her on top of him, his hardness nestled between her thighs.

Portia pulled her mouth free so she could shower kisses all over his face, his neck, his shoulders. "I love you, too. I'll try not to be so rash."

His touch was gentle, cherishing skill. "Oh, some forms of rashness I like," he teased.

She grinned and twisted to delve beneath the covers and assault the River Thames, but he seized her. "No, not today. This is our marriage bed, Portia, and today is for simple love. No tricks, no cleverness, just you and me in blessed harmony."

Even in her inexperience, she could tell his touch was just that—an expression of love, not an attempt to dominate her senses. Portia allowed herself to do the same. She explored his body with no intent other than to satisfy her desire to know, her need to touch him—learn him—with mouth, hands, and every portion of her skin.

She pushed back the covers so that her eyes, too, could feast. "You are so beautiful."

"As are you." His lips played on her breast, and she stilled to take in the pleasure he could bring.

"That feels wonderful," she murmured.

"Mmmmmm."

She was laughing when he sucked, and the sweet pleasure became wild. Portia squeaked, then stopped the noise.

He grinned at her. "Just one squeak? Surely we can do better than that."

And he proved he could.

"What if someone hears?" Portia gasped.

"You'll just be supporting my reputation as a mythic lover."

"What?"

"Our demonstration at Mirabelle's was much admired. I had to marry to avoid a pack of salivating ladies."

Portia had other questions, but he was demonstrating that he could raise wild cries by touch as well as mouth. "This isn't fair," she gasped, her body dancing beneath to his tune. "I want to do this to you!"

He smiled into her eyes, his own dark, his cheeks touched with the color of desire. "You will. If you don't discover how by natural genius, I'll teach you. But let me pleasure you now, love. I have never done this before—lain with a beloved in innocent joy and trust." His hand slid firm between her thighs. "Rise up my beloved, and open to me. And that," he added with a smile, "is almost from the Bible, too."

So Portia did rise up and open to him, closing her eyes to savor his skillful touch, then the blessed relief when he slid in to ease her desire. He was slow this time, so slow she moved restlessly to meet him, to hasten their joining.

"Open your eyes, love," he whispered.

She did, and gazed breathlessly at him as he filled her with heat and power.

"To think I could have lived my life without this," he murmured and moved subtly in a way that made her gasp.

"Exactly what I was thinking," she said. "But with even greater fervor!"

They burst into laughter as he moved in her, and the laughter blended with their release, so they rolled together afterward, still chuckling as they kissed with joy.

Epilogue

"So, the canal will go through to the Mersey, Francis?" Bryght poured coffee for the duke, who had just arrived at Candleford Park, which lay some four miles west of Winchester.

"Aye," said Bridgewater with satisfaction. "But it's been a devil of a trial to get the bills passed and the money raised, particularly when Walgrave took a hand."

"My fault, that. He'd not have interfered if I hadn't been involved."

It balanced out, for it brought Rothgar in. I'm still not sure why he took such an interest, but I'm grateful."

"It became a family affair. But when do we see some profit for all our efforts?"

Bridgewater laughed. "Well, that's another matter. I'm so sunk it debt it's ceased to worry me! I'm glad you weren't tempted to sink your windfall into my business though. Candleford is a prime estate, and it suits you."

"Like a new coat?" Bryght queried.

"Perhaps. You certainly look comfortable enough in it. I can't wait to meet my godson. He must be beyond lying still and blowing bubbles by now."

"He is assuredly that. He is nearly two years old, Francis."

"Is it so long? Damme, in that time we should have made further progress with the canal!"

Bryght laughed and then heard other laughter. He went to the bay window that looked out over the mellow lawns of Candleford, lawns dotted with spreading trees, and scattered with small daisies. Francis followed him.

Zeno came to rise up by Bryght's side, and gave a plaintive *woof*.

"Yes," said Bryght, ruffling the dog's fur. "It is certainly our duty to go and make sure they are safe. Come along, Francis, and meet your godson and namesake."

For out on the lawns Portia ran laughing through the sun, hair escaping its pins, pursuing a merry, twinkle-legged lad with the same bright curls.

Author's Note

Tempting Fortune is about gambling—risk taking—with money, with property, and with lives. It is a suitable theme for the mid-eighteenth century when a seething love of risk consumed everyone. Its most obvious feature was the high-stakes gaming that absorbed so many people, but it also led to the decadent abuse of drugs, alcohol, and sex, and to the exhilarated exploration of new philosophies, technologies, and lands.

To the visionaries of this time nothing seemed impossible, and they had no doubt that the new would be wonderful. They had not learned as we have that progress inevitably brings costs. Or perhaps they simply did not care.

The Duke of Bridgewater was such a visionary.

It is hard to tell now what drove Bridgewater, though the fact that he had grown up a sickly youth called the Poor Duke may have spurred him on to success. Love certainly had something to do with it, however, for it was after his betrothed wife jilted him that he devoted all his energies to construction.

Elizabeth, Duchess of Hamilton, was one of the famous Gunning sisters who took London by storm in the 1750s. As with modern pop stars, people couldn't get enough of them. When they walked the streets of London, the king had to order out an escort of the Guards to keep back the adoring crowds.

Maria, the elder sister, married Lord Coventry but died young, poisoned by the lead in the makeup she wore to make her beautiful face fashionable pale. Apparently her poor husband, knowing the dangers, scrubbed the stuff off her whenever he saw it.

Elizabeth married the dissolute Duke of Hamilton but was soon left a rich widow. Bridgewater, just back from his Grand Tour and still a young man, fell deeply in love, proposed, and was accepted. Elizabeth, however, changed her mind and married a Colonel Campbell, who would one day be the Duke of Argyll.

Thus, Elizabeth Gunning married two dukes and jilted a third. In time she was the mother of four.

After this blow, Bridgewater turned his back on Society and matrimony and became entranced with canals.

Like many great events in history, the Bridgewater Canal came about almost by accident. The duke owned a coal mine in Lancashire, but it was in a poor location and transportation costs made the mine unprofitable. He came up with the idea of using the drainage channel from his mine to float the coal along part of its journey.

This worked so well that he decided to send the coal by water all the way to Manchester. Manchester was a new city, growing rapidly as the spinning and weaving of cotton became an industry. Development there was being held back only by the high price of coal. If the duke could get his coal there at reasonable cost, he'd make a killing.

Bridgewater's original plan was merely to link up with an established river-route which used the rivers Irwell and Mersey. The Mersey and Irwell Navigation Company, however, thought they had a monopoly and demanded an extortionate rate to use their system. That pushed Bridgewater into taking the bold leap and planning a canal all the way to Manchester. There was one obvious problem, however. The River Irwell was in his way.

So he decided to build an aqueduct to carry his canal over his competitors' river.

Nearly everyone thought him mad. No one had constructed a canal in England since Roman times; there had never been an aqueduct in England; and his engineers—Brindley and Gilbert—were largely self-taught. He could not find many investors. But Bridgewater at only twenty-four proved determined. When he could not raise money by other means, he sold or mortgaged just about everything he owned and went around soliciting small loans from anyone with money to spare.

Money, however, wasn't his only problem. Canal construction required acts of Parliament for each stage, and those proved hard to get. Many MPs regularly sold their vote to the highest bidder. Others believed canals would ruin the countryside. In addition, there were honest doubters who thought the plans, particularly that for the aqueduct, simply could not work. In order to persuade the committee of Parliament to approve the act permitting the aqueduct, Brindley had to build a working model in front of them.

And after all that, the real one began to fail as the first water ran through it. It was a minor flaw, fortunately, and the engineers fixed it, working without sophisticated plans, almost by string and sealing wax. Soon people were making special trips to see this modern marvel, to watch ships seem to sail through the air.

And beneath, the proprietors of the Mersey and Irwell

Navigation Company gnashed their teeth and feared the future.

Though there were many years of struggle still ahead for Bridgewater, it was the beginning of a new age, the new age Bryght foresees. By the end of the century, England was crisscrossed by canals facilitating rapid industrial expansion. England was poised for the Victorian age, when it would be the richest and most powerful nation on earth.

The result of all this was to make the Duke of Bridgewater an extremely wealthy man by the time he died, still unmarried, in 1803. The profit from his coal mines had risen from £406 per annum at the time of this book, to £48,000 at the time of his death. In addition, he had the income from fees for the use of his canals, and from many other ventures such as land purchased on the new dockland in Liverpool. I'm sure Bryght became just as rich in the process, but great wealth was never really his motivation. It was the fascination of new opportunities and ideas that stirred him.

You may have noticed that in this book I have used precise figures for many costs. Such things fascinate me. In a time when a workingman was pleased to get a shilling a day, a gamester could lose a hundred guineas and hardly notice it. A man like Prestonly could lose ten thousand and shrug it off.

The value of money is never simply a matter of how many shillings in a guinea. (Twenty-one, by the way.)

I hope you enjoyed *Tempting Fortune*. There will, of course, be other books about the Mallorens. (The first in the series was *My Lady Notorious*, published in 1993.) I think the next one will be about Elf who is, of course, destined to bring Fort back from the brink of hate and despair. Though neither of them would believe it if I told them that now! The twelfth and most recent book in the Malloren series, *A Scandalous Countess*, published in February 2012, and follows the story of Georgia, Countess of Maybury.

Also seek out the next Rogues book in the series, *Dangerous Joy* (Zebra Books). It is set in 1816 in Ireland and England. For those of you who read *Forbidden* (Zebra Books), it is the story of Miles and Felicity, surely the most ferociously antagonist lovers I have ever written about. To my surprise, this book turned out to have a thread of Irish magic and mystery running through it.

I have signed bookplates for *Tempting Fortune* and my other books available. To obtain these, send a SASE to the address on my website below, listing the books you own.

I am sorry many of you are having trouble finding copies of my older books. It's the one downside of success—my books have mostly sold out, and people hold on to them as "keepers." (Not that *that* is a downside. I love the fact that people enjoy my books too much to let them go.)

If you want to avoid future disappointment and keep up to date on new titles and reissues, however, subscribe to my digital newsletter via my website, www.jobev.com. Feel free to email me through the website to tell me what you think of the books.

And don't miss Jo's novella
in the upcoming holiday anthology
MISCHIEF AND MISTLETOE . . .

In this sparkling holiday collection,
eight acclaimed authors unwrap
the most daring of Regency delights . . .

Christmastime in England—a time for passionate secrets,
delicious whispers, and wicked-sweet gifts by the fire.
From a spirited lady who sets out to save her rakish best
friend from an unsuitable engagement, to a bold spy who
gets the unexpected chance to win the woman he's always
loved, to a vicar's daughter who pretends to be a saucy
wench, these holiday tales will make you curl up in front
of the fire for a memorable season of mischief and mistletoe . . .

Featuring stories from Jo Beverley, Mary Jo Putney, Patricia
Rice, Nicola Cornick, Joanna Bourne, Cara Elliott, Anne
Gracie, and Susan Fraser King!

In this irresistibly festive novel from #1 New York Times *bestselling author Victoria Alexander, a beautiful, self-sufficient woman has only one Christmas wish—to be a mistress . . .*

For three years, Lady Veronica Smithson has been perfectly happy as a widow—and thoroughly independent. Still, the right gentleman could provide the benefits of marriage without the tedious restrictions. And in Sir Sebastian Hadley-Attwater, renowned explorer and rogue, Veronica is sure she has found him.

Sebastian will come into his inheritance in a matter of weeks—*if* his family deems him responsible enough. There's no better way to prove his maturity than with a home and a wife. But though the lovely Veronica will share his bed, she steadfastly refuses to marry. However, Sebastian has a plan.

An intimate sojourn at his new country house will surely change Veronica's mind. For Sebastian never takes no for an answer. And even in the midst of mischief-making relatives and unexpected complications, he intends to persuade his Christmas mistress that they belong together—in this, and every season to come . . .

Please turn the page for an exciting sneak peek of Victoria Alexander's HIS MISTRESS BY CHRISTMAS, now on sale!

November 30, 1885

"He's the one," Veronica, Lady Smithson, said softly, more to herself than to the woman beside her. She smiled with satisfaction. She did so love it when all went according to plan.

"Shhh." Portia, Lady Redwell, hushed her and gazed with pride at the speaker behind the podium on the stage at the far end of the room.

". . . and admittedly, while it was somewhat more adventure than we had bargained for, in hindsight it was not merely exciting but quite remarkable." Sir Sebastian Hadley-Attwater paused in the polished manner of an expert speaker and gazed out at the audience seated before him in the Explorers Club lecture hall.

A knowing smile carved deep dimples in a face that would be altogether too handsome were it not a bit browner than was fashionable. An intriguing scar slanted across his forehead above his right brow. His blue eyes, under hair so dark a blond it was nearly brown, gleamed with humor and intelligence. He scanned the room slowly, and only a woman long in her grave would fail to wonder what it would be like to have those eyes gaze at her and her alone.

Veronica noted the moment he caught sight of his cousin,

sitting beside her toward the back of the hall. His eyes lit in recognition, and Portia beamed. Portia's parents had died when she was very young, and her aunt and uncle had taken her in. She'd grown up with Sebastian and six other cousins. He nodded slightly in acknowledgment of her presence, then continued his perusal of the audience. His gaze settled on Veronica briefly, although he was no doubt staring at her hat, one of her most impressive, then continued on.

"In conclusion, allow me to say there is only one thing in life that stirs the senses more than stepping foot upon an unknown land or seeing with your own eyes sights only a handful of your fellow men have ever seen."

His gaze returned to Veronica, this time meeting hers. She raised her chin slightly and cast him a slow smile. A smile of acknowledgment and encouragement, although from what she had heard of the famous adventurer, little encouragement was needed. His exploits with women were as extensive as his adventures in foreign lands, at least according to gossip and Portia.

"And that"—his smile widened and his dimples deepened, if possible—"is at last returning home."

The most delightful sense of anticipation shivered through her. Oh yes, he would do.

Applause erupted from the crowd that had gathered to spend the evening in the illustrious adventurer's presence and listen to his stories of uncivilized lands and unknown peoples. It had been an evening filled with the excitement of daring tales told by a master storyteller. Sir Sebastian had held the crowd in his hands.

Veronica leaned close to her friend and spoke low into her ear. "He's the one."

"I heard you the first time," Portia said absently, clapping with an unusual display of enthusiasm. A proud smile curved her lips. "The one what?"

"The one I want."

"The one you want for what?" Portia's attention remained on Sir Sebastian, who was now accepting the accolades of the crowd in a modest and unassuming manner. While Veronica suspected there was nothing modest and unassuming about the adventurer, his demeanor added to his appeal. He would do nicely.

"And now, as anyone who has heard me speak before will attest, I have been rather more efficient than usual tonight."

An amused chuckle washed through the crowd.

"Therefore we have time for a few questions." Again his gaze sought hers. A challenge sparked in his eyes, as if daring her to do more than meet his gaze. Veronica did indeed have a question, but not one she was prepared to ask. At least, not yet. Immediately a dozen hands shot up. Sir Sebastian pointed to a gentleman toward the front.

"Sir," the man began. "In your third book, you relate an encounter with a tribe during your expedition down the Amazon, and I was curious as to whether . . ."

"Oh, yes, he's perfect," Veronica murmured.

Portia snorted in a most unladylike manner. "Nonsense. I was raised with the man. I can tell you any number of ways in which he's not the least bit perfect. Why, I can recall . . ." Portia glanced at Veronica. "The one you want for what? What are you talking about?" Her eyes narrowed. "What are you planning?"

"Sir Sebastian." On Veronica's other side, her aunt Lotte rose to her feet. "I should like to know, given your renown as an explorer and adventurer and as I have been told you are most forward thinking . . ."

"Stop her." Portia clutched Veronica's arm.

"Would that I could." Veronica patted her friend's hand in a comforting manner and bit back a grin. She should have expected this. Miss Charlotte Bramhall had her own campaign to wage.

"Thank you, ma'am. I do try to be progressive." Sir Sebastian favored Aunt Lotte with his compelling smile. A smile that surely made every other gentleman in the hall wish to be him and every lady wish to be with him. Veronica wondered if the older woman was at all affected.

Apparently not. Aunt Lotte's expression remained firm.

"Excellent." Aunt Lotte nodded. "Then I should like to know your opinion as to the acceptance of women as members of the Explorers Club."

A groan passed through the crowd, and Portia's hand tightened.

Sir Sebastian's brows drew together. "I'm afraid I don't quite understand the question."

"It's very simple, young man. Do you or do you not support full membership for women?"

Sir Sebastian chose his words with obvious care. "It seems to me, as you are here tonight and the lectures of the society are open to all, there is no need to grant full membership to the fairer sex as it would only be a . . ." He thought for a moment. "An undue burden, as it were." Again he smiled an altogether pleasant smile, although Aunt Lotte might well interpret it as condescending. Poor man. He might have come face-to-face with uncivilized natives in the far jungles of the globe, but he had never done battle with Miss Charlotte Bramhall. Sir Sebastian continued with innocent disregard for his imminent danger. "It's my understanding that full members residing in London are required to participate fully in all matters regarding governing of the organization."

Veronica winced.

"And you think that a burden?" Aunt Lotte squared her

shoulders. "Rubbish. As progressive as you may be, Sir Sebastian, perhaps you are not aware of the significant advancements made in the last twenty years by women through independent travel and sheer determination. Women who can explore the reaches of the Nile can certainly handle the dubious burden of administration of a mere organization."

"I have no doubt of that." He chuckled. "But, my dear lady, there is also tradition to be considered. Progress cannot be allowed to simply sweep aside traditions that have been nourished through the years."

"Tradition, sir, is simply a male excuse—"

"Miss Bramhall!" Sir Hugo Tolliver, director of the Explorers Club, leaped to his feet, fairly pushed Sir Sebastian away from the podium, and glared at Lotte. "This is neither the time nor the place for a debate as to the merits of membership."

"Do tell me, then . . ." Lotte glared right back. "When would you suggest—"

"Now, ladies and gentlemen," Sir Hugo pointedly addressed the crowd. "Refreshments are being served in the foyer, and as is our *tradition*, Sir Sebastian will be joining us." With that, Sir Hugo escorted Sir Sebastian off the stage and toward the door.

People stood and headed toward the foyer, toward what was more than likely tepid lemonade and the chance to make the personal acquaintance of the adventurous Sir Sebastian.

Lotte stared after them. "What an annoying beast that man is."

Veronica rose to her feet. "I assume you are speaking of Sir Hugo. Sir Sebastian struck me as most cordial and quite charming."

Lotte scoffed. "Cut from the same cloth, no doubt."

"He is a man, dear." Veronica smiled. "We must make allowances."

"Ha." Lotte's brows drew together. "Women have allowed men to get away with this kind of nonsense for centuries. It's past time we took our proper place in society." She glanced at Portia, still seated and trying very hard to look as if she had never met Lotte, or Veronica, either, for that matter. "Are you coming?"

"Of course we are." Portia reluctantly got to her feet. "He is my cousin, after all."

"Then you should take him in hand."

"Go on, Aunt Lotte. We shall meet you there," Veronica said quickly.

"Very well." Lotte started off, determination in the set of her shoulders and the spring in her step.

"Whatever possessed you to bring her with us tonight?" Portia glared at her friend.

"I didn't bring her with us. It was simply a coincidence that she had already planned to attend. A *pleasant* coincidence."

"Not the word that immediately comes to my mind." Portia huffed. "I was afraid this sort of thing would happen."

"What sort of thing?"

"I knew she would make a spectacle of herself."

"Scarcely that, darling. She simply asked a question." Veronica took Portia's arm, and they started after the crowd streaming toward the exit.

"But what a question! Women as members of the Explorers Club indeed."

"She was entirely right and I quite agree with her, as you well know," Veronica said smoothly. "And if she hadn't asked, I very well might have."

Portia heaved a long-suffering sigh. "I don't know why the women of your family have to be so . . . so . . ."

"Independent in our thinking? Intelligent and not afraid to show it?"

"Yes," Portia snapped. "It's not at all becoming."

"Pity."

"You'll never find another husband if you don't learn to be more circumspect." A warning sounded in Portia's voice. "Men do not want women who are overly intelligent."

"And I do not want a man who would expect me to be someone I'm not," Veronica said in a lofty manner. "Besides, I have no intention of marrying again."

Portia stopped in mid-step and stared. "Good Lord, Veronica, don't be absurd. Of course you will. I know I will. Although I would prefer to choose a husband myself," Portia added under her breath. In recent months, her well-meaning family had begun a concerted, and not especially subtle, campaign to find Portia a new husband, placing one eligible bachelor after another in her path. "We're women. It's what's expected of us."

Veronica cast her a pleasant smile. "I prefer not to do what's expected of me."

"Yes, I know." Portia rolled her gaze heavenward.

"Furthermore, I don't see why women in our position should be expected to marry."

"And what position is that?"

"Marriage gives women financial security. Even in this day and age women have few ways to provide for themselves." Veronica shrugged. "You and I have independent wealth. Our financial futures are assured. Therefore there is no need to marry."

"No need to marry?" Portia's eyes widened at the blasphemy.

"None at all." She hooked her arm through Portia's and again herded her toward the door.

"But surely you don't intend to spend the rest of your life alone?"

"No, I don't." Veronica shook her head. "It's only been a

little more than three years since Charles died, and I am already tired of being alone. And I am not the type of woman to whom the idea of flitting from one man's bed to the next is especially appealing."

"Thank God." Relief sounded in Portia's voice.

Veronica smiled. She hadn't yet decided if she would tell Portia exactly what she planned. Still, she might need the other woman's assistance, even though Portia's proper nature might well be too shocked to permit her to render any true aid.

Veronica scanned the crowd in front of them. An indomitable Aunt Lotte was making her way toward the foyer. Through the open doors she could see Sir Sebastian, surrounded by admirers, most of them female. He spoke to everyone who approached him in what, even from this distance, struck Veronica as a charming and gracious manner. It was most admirable.

"Tell me more about your cousin."

"I don't know what more there is to tell." Portia thought for a moment. "You've read one of his books."

"Two, actually."

"Then you know of his foolish pursuit of adventure in the guise of expanding man's knowledge of the unknown. I can't bear to read them myself. They're rather heart-stopping, you know."

"But he does know how to tell a story," Veronica murmured. Indeed, she had found his prose to be evocative and even sensual.

"The family hoped he would go into business or study the law. Instead he has spent the last dozen or so years traveling to those places on this earth few civilized men have ventured. It's most distressing."

"Well, it's not law." Veronica bit back a grin.

"He always was something of a rebel as a child. Always

doing things he shouldn't. Never following anyone's rules but his own. Still . . ." Portia heaved a resigned sigh. "He has always been my favorite."

"Somewhere deep inside you, Portia, you long for adventure."

"My life is rather dull," Portia said under her breath, then realized what she'd said. "Not dull. How absurd. I don't know why I said that."

"Those least likely to bend . . ."

"Are most likely to snap. Yes, yes, you've said it before, but it's utter nonsense." Portia scoffed. "I have no intention of bending or snapping."

"Of course not," Veronica said. "You're quite content with your uneventful life."

Portia nodded. "Indeed I am."

Veronica knew better. It struck her on occasion as both odd and remarkable that she and Portia, along with Julia, Lady Winterset, knew one another as well as they did given they hadn't known each other at all until a few years ago. It was chance that they had happened to meet at Fenwick and Sons, Booksellers, but no doubt fate that they had become fast friends. They had each lost their husbands some three years ago to accident or illness or mishap and had met at a time when each needed a friend who was not tied to her loss. While not one given to overt displays of piety, Veronica often thanked God she had found these friends, in truth, these *sisters* she'd never had nor ever missed. Now she could not envision her life without them.

"Aside from Sebastian, we are quite a proper, well-behaved family," Portia said firmly, although Veronica did wonder how a proper, well-behaved family could produce a man who wandered the far reaches of the earth. Or perhaps it was only a proper, well-behaved family that could.

"He certainly doesn't look the least bit well behaved." In

truth, with his rugged good looks, Sir Sebastian looked like a hero from a novel. "He looks like a man who plunges headfirst into adventure."

"It's the scar." Portia studied her cousin. "It makes him look like, well, exactly what he is."

"No doubt a souvenir from one of his expeditions."

"I suspect he likes people to think that." Portia chuckled. "The truth is he fell out of a tree when he was a boy." The closer they got to Sir Sebastian, the slower the crowd moved. They were scarcely walking at all now. Portia tapped her foot in impatience.

"I gather it's been some time since you've seen him."

"He's been back in England for several months, according to the rest of the family. But he's yet to make an appearance at any one of the gatherings they have subjected me to of late. Although with Christmas less than a month away, those gatherings will become even more frequent and Sebastian is certain to attend." Portia craned her neck to see around the crowd. "I understand he's purchased a house in the country."

"Oh?" A casual note sounded in Veronica's voice. "Do you think he intends to stay in one place for a while, then?"

"I have no idea what he intends, but I will certainly ask him if we ever get close enough. Why are you asking questions about Sebastian?" Her eyes narrowed. "And you never answered me. What did you mean by he's the one you want? The one you want for what?"

"I haven't decided yet."